84
K

By Claire North

The First Fifteen Lives of Harry August
Touch
The Sudden Appearance of Hope
The End of the Day
84K

The Gameshouse **(ebook only)**
The Serpent
The Thief
The Master

By Kate Griffin

Matthew Swift
A Madness of Angels
The Midnight Mayor
The Neon Court
The Minority Council

Magicals Anonymous
Stray Souls
The Glass God

CLAIRE NORTH

84K

orbit

www.orbitbooks.net

ORBIT

First published in Great Britain in 2017 by Orbit

1 3 5 7 9 10 8 6 4 2

Copyright © 2018 by Claire North

The moral right of the author has been asserted.

A CIP catalogue record for this book
is available from the British Library.

HB ISBN 978-0-356-50737-8
C format 978-0-356-50738-5

Typeset in Bembo by M Rules
Printed and bound in Great Britain by
Clays Ltd, St Ives plc

Papers used by Orbit are from well-managed forests
and other responsible sources.

Orbit
An imprint of
Little, Brown Book Group
Carmelite House
50 Victoria Embankment
London EC4Y 0DZ

An Hachette UK Company
www.hachette.co.uk

www.orbitbooks.net

Part I

Chapter 1

At the beginning and ending of all things . . .

She had not seen the man called Theo in the cards, nor did they prophesy the meaning of her actions. When she called the ambulance they said they would come soon, and half an hour later she was still waiting by the water.

And when she called again they had no record of her call, and gave her the number of the complaints department.

The sun was down and the street lights distant, their backs turned to the towpath. On the other side of the water: an industrial estate where once patty-line men had loaded lorries with bikinis and bras, pillows and sofa throws, percale fitted sheets, gold-plated anklets and next season's striped trend-setting onesies for the discerning customer. Once, the men who laboured there had worn tags around their ankles to ensure that they didn't walk too slow, or spend too much time taking a piss. If they did, there were worse places they could be sent. There was always somewhere worse.

Now there was black spew up the walls, and the smell of melted plastic lingering on the winter air.

A few white lamps on the loading concourse still shone, their glow slithering across the high barbed-wire fences down to the canal. The light made the frost on the bank sparkle like witches' eyes, before being swallowed whole by the blackness of the water.

Neila thought of calling out for help, to anyone in the night,

3

but didn't have the courage and didn't think anyone would answer. People had their own problems to deal with, things being as they were. Instead she wrapped the man up as best she could in old towels she wouldn't miss, hiding her nice, fluffy towels under the bed. She felt a bit guilty about that, and alleviated her doubts by making him hot tea, which he could barely sip. Not knowing what else to do, she sat beside the man on the thin, mud-sunk grass by the gate of the lock and dialled 999 again, and got someone new who said:

"Oh my oh yes now of course yes bleeding by the canal do you have an address for that – no an address – how about a post-code, no I'm not seeing you on my map do you have premium or standard service support for an extra £4.99 a month you can upgrade to instant recovery and full rehabilitative therapies for the – oh you're not insured . . . "

The call ended there. Maybe a timer cut them off. Maybe there wasn't much signal at the moment. A pair of ducks waddled uneasily over crêpe-thin ice, now slipping into the water below, now lurching back up onto the transparent surface above, now flapping at the sound of an eager seagull looking for a snack, now quiet again beneath the thickening blue-brown sky, paddling in listless circles.

at the end and the beginning Neila spins in circles too

The man mumbled, through lips turned blue, "You've been very kind very kind I'm fine I'm sure I'll be fine it's just I'm fine . . . "

He'd tried saying this before, and fainted, only for a few seconds, then woke and picked up where he'd left off, and she hadn't had the heart to tell him that he'd passed out while trying to be so stoical, so she let him talk until he stopped, and they stayed there, waiting, and no one came.

She decided to leave him.

At the precise moment she reached that decision, like a truck driving into a concrete wall she knew that she wouldn't. The universe crumpled and blew apart, and at the centre of it she

4

exclaimed, "This is fucking ridiculous." She creaked to her feet, pulling him by a limp limb. "Get your backside inside the fucking boat."

She had to help him walk, and he nearly hit his head on the low door at the stern of the narrowboat as she guided him in, and was unconscious, bleeding out on her white faux-leather couch, before she had got her boots off.

Chapter 2

Time goes a little peculiar
                    when you're not feeling so
so sometimes you wake and you remember that you will be an
old, old man and that the one you love will die and you can't
work out
              if they die
                            or you first
              which would be more scary? Who will be
strongest without love, alone, loveless, devoid? What is worse –
for you to lose the one you love or for the one you love to be
destroyed by losing you?

The man on the couch is vaguely aware, when he's aware of
much of anything at all, that he's hit his head and that's making
things a little . . .

Neila wrung out blood-red water from her third-favourite tea
towel into the mop bucket at her feet, and the bleeding still
wouldn't stop, and there was silence on the canal, and silence on
the water.

In the early years when she had first started sailing, Neila
had thought she'd love the quiet, and for a week after buying
the *Hector* she hadn't slept, in terror at the roar of whispers over
still water. The creaking, the lapping of liquid, the insect-hiss
of thin ice popping before the bow of a passing boat, the roar
of a generator, the chug chug chug of the engine, the beating
of wings, birds not really built for flight hounding each other

half in sky, half on land for food, or sex, or maybe just something to do.

When exhaustion kicked in, she'd slept like a log, and now
she understood the silence of the canal wasn't silence at all. If
anything, it was a racket, annoying in its persistence.

Not tonight. Tonight the silence made her nervous, made
her think too much. She'd come to the canal to get away from
thinking. Alone, once you'd thought everything there was to
think, there was only being quiet left.

She turned on the radio, and listened to Pepsi Liverpool vs
CheapFlightsForU Manchester, even though she didn't really
like football.

Chapter 3

At the beginning of all things . . .

The man lies on the couch, and dreams and memories blur in a fitful crimson smear of paint.

Maybe it hadn't been the beginning, but in his dreams it seems that there must have been a point where it all started, where everything changed. Back when he had a job, back when "job" seemed like the most important thing ever, back in the Criminal Audit Office, before the winter and the snow and the blood, at the beginning there had been . . .

– it seemed ludicrously banal now, but it was perhaps the place where it all went to piss –

. . . a training weekend.

The weekend was voluntary.

If you did not attend you would be docked one week's pay and a note put on your file – "BBA". No one knew what BBA stood for, but the last woman to have these fated letters added had been given a job at a morgue, showing family members the corpses of their loved ones.

Besides, everyone knew that team players were happy volunteers.

The Teamwork Bonding Experience cost £172, payable at sign-up. On the first day he was told to put a cork in his mouth, stand in front of his colleagues and explain his Beliefs and Values.

"Come on, Mr Miller!" exclaimed the Management Strength Inspiration Course Leader. "Enunciate!"

The man called Theo Miller hesitated, hoping the burning in

his face could be mistaken for the effort of not spitting out the dry brown bung, bit a little deeper into the cork, then mumbled: "I belef fat ul pepl arg detherfin of jusfic an ..."

"Project! Pro-*ject*. Use your whole mouth, use your breath to lift you!"

At night they slept in dormitories on creaking metal beds, and were woken at 5 a.m. for a group run. He enjoyed that part. He stood on top of a hill and watched an eyelash of light peek above the horizon, growing hotter, bending the sky, liked the way the shadows of the trees broke out long and thin across the land, the visible light and visible darkness in the air as fog burned away. The walls of London were too high for him to see this sight, and the places in the country where sometimes he'd gone as a child had fallen to scroungers, and the trains didn't go there any more. For a moment he thought of the sea below the cliffs, and the memory filled his lungs with salty air – then someone told him to stop dawdling, Mr Miller!

So he ran on, and pretended to be out of breath and struggling at the back, where most of the senior staff were, even though he felt like he could have run for ever. It didn't do to stand out.

Management joined them at 10 a.m. Management were staying up the road at a golfing resort, but wanted to demonstrate leadership and muck in with the troops. Edward Witt, 37, fresh from Company central office – personal motto "I achieve for me" – roared across the waving long grass, "Come on! Put some welly into it!"

Theo Miller did not smile, did not blink, but concentrated harder on the painted picture of the wooden man before him, drew the axe back over his shoulder and threw it with all his might. He was aiming for the head, but by chance managed to hit it in the nuts.

"Keep going, guys!" barked Edward, bouncing impatiently on the edge of the field as the Fiscal Efficiency Team ran up and down, one statistician suspended by ankles and armpits between two others. "Don't let each other down!"

9

Theo wasn't sure what all of this had to do with his job. He didn't learn anything about the law, or finance, or governmental good practice. The only colleagues he felt any closer to were the ones he usually hung out with anyway, the hangdog dredges of the Criminal Audit Office who sometimes drank cheap wine on the seventh floor when the lights were out, and didn't go to the pub because they couldn't stand the noise.

If anything, the weekend only served to make office cliques tighter, as friends curled in for mutual support against the horror of the experience, shooting suspicious glances across the muddy field to ensure that everyone was suffering equally, losing all together. Edward Witt prowled up and down, encouraging competition, competition, get ahead, and one or two tried gamely, and Theo was always the third man eliminated in a contest, and penultimate man picked for a side.

It wasn't that he was inept, or even disliked. There wasn't enough personality in Theo Miller for people to love or hate. A psychic had once attempted to read his aura, and after a period of frowning so intense she started groaning with the effort of her grimace, announced that it was puce. Like everyone else from the mystic to the mundane, she too had failed to spot that his life was a lie, or that the real Theo Miller was fifteen years dead, buried in an unmarked grave. So much for the interconnected mysteries of the universe, Theo thought.

So much for all that.

At the end of the weekend they got into a coach.

The coach sat in traffic, covering twelve miles in an hour and twenty minutes, and Theo dozed. One time he saw a woman standing on the hard shoulder, waving frantically at the passing cars for help, but no one stopped, and tears rolled down her face. People didn't like to stop on this stretch of the M3. The security fence kept out most of the screamers, the scroungers and the children from the surrounding enclaves, but Company Police signs reminded all that YOUR SAFETY IS YOUR RESPONSIBILITY, and no one doubted it for a moment.

You heard rumours of tax dodgers breaking in through the fence and rushing down into the lanes when the traffic got too slow, to crack open boots and steal anything they could, until speed picked up again and they scuttled to safety or were mown down where they stood.

After four hours of snoozing to a soundtrack of inspirational speeches by Simon Fardell, Company ExO, the coach dropped them off at the office in Victoria. The pavements were too narrow for the tired, baggage-slung commuters waiting for their buses, leaves tumbling from the last of the shedding plane trees.

Though it was late, and they were tired and muddy and sore, Edward treated them to a sandwich dinner, held in the semi-sacred and barely used Large Media Suite, access usually limited to executive grade 2A and above. As they ate thin slices of cucumber between wet pieces of white bread, lights were dimmed, and Edward presented his PowerPoint of Vital Lessons Learned and Where We Go From Here, including a comic montage from the weekend of people falling into mud, dropping their axes and spraining their ankles to lighten the moment and boost team morale.

And when he was done the lights came up

and there were little pink pots of Angel Delight with a single half-strawberry on top and there

was Dani Cumali.

On the canal the man called Theo groans in his sleep and holds the blanket tight, and Neila sits with her head in her hands and wonders what the fuck she's even done

And in his dreams
            and in his memories
Dani is watching him, and that's where it all went wrong.

In the past
            These things are a little blurry but he thinks, yes, in the past, but not that past, the more recent past, the past had

already happened, the less important yet more urgent bit of the past that is

(Neila wonders if she should try and give him a blood transfusion, but where the fuck do you even start, times being what they are?)

Dani Cumali stood at the edge of the Large Media Suite in the Criminal Audit Office, and stared at Theo Miller, and that was where the world changed.

Her black hair was cut to a pudding bowl around her ears, her skin devoid of make-up, lines around her mouth, grey and thin, lines between her eyebrows, a cobweb face. Her nails were scrubbed down to thin ridges, she wore the navy blue one-piece of the catering company

and she looked at him

and he looked at her

and they knew each other immediately and without a word.

On the screen was a picture of that time during the weekend when he'd been punched in the face during the self-defence training session and his nose had bled everywhere and wasn't that hilarious our Theo Miller give him a hand

everyone clapped

and Dani saw and knew the truth.

And she knew that she could destroy him, bring down the house of lies, fraud and deceit that he had built around himself, around his name that was a lie, around teamwork bonding experiences and work reports and progress assessments and pension plans and rental deposits and

and the whole lie of his whole fucking life.

She could tear it down with a single word.

And in her eyes was the fire of the righteous and the sword.

In the beginning.

Chapter 4

The man whose name was sometimes Theo Miller had been twenty-two years old when they abolished human rights. The government insisted it was necessary to counter terrorism and bring stable leadership to the country. He'd voted for the opposition and felt very proud of himself, partially because he had a sense that this was the intangible *right* way of things, but mostly because it was the first time his new name had been tested at the polling station, and held up to scrutiny.

The opposition didn't have any funding, of course, and everyone knew that the Company was backing the winning team. But any fleeting disappointment he may have felt when they crumbled to a crushing defeat and the prime minister declared, "Too long our enemies have hidden behind human rights as if they were extended to all!" was lightened by the fact that his identity had held. He had voted as Theo Miller, and it hadn't made a difference, and no one had called his bluff.

He'd still somehow felt it would work out all right in the end.

When they shut down the newspapers for printing stories of corruption and dirty deals, he'd signed the petitions.

When they'd closed the universities for spreading warnings of impending social and economic calamity, he'd thought about attending the rallies, but then decided against it because work would probably frown on these things, and there were people there who took your photo and posted your face online – saboteurs and enemies of the people – and besides, it rained a lot that month and he just needed a morning off.

By then, of course, it was a little too late for petitions. Company men would run for parliament, Company newspapers would trumpet their excellence to the sky, Company TV stations would broadcast their election promises and say how wonderful they were. They would inevitably win, serve their seven years in office and then return to the banking or insurance branches happy to have completed their civic duty, and that was that. It was for the best, the adverts said. This was how democracy worked: corporate and public interests working together at last, for the greater good.

When it became legally compulsory to carry ID, £300 for the certified ID card, £500 fine if caught without it, he knew he was observing an injustice that sent thousands of innocent people to the patty line, too skint to buy, too skint to pay for being too skint to buy. When it became impossible to vote without the ID, he knew he lived in a tyranny, but by then he wasn't sure what there was left to do in protest. He'd be okay. If he kept his head down. He'd be fine.

He couldn't put his finger precisely on when parliament rebranded itself "The People's Engagement Forum", but he remembered thinking the logo was very well done.

Chapter 5

In the Criminal Audit Office, Dani Cumali clears away the remnants of a cucumber sandwich.

In the ancestral home of his family, Philip Arnslade stares at his mother's dribbling form and blurts, "Well so long as she's happy!"

On the canal, Neila is pleased to discover that she's not actually squeamish about head wounds at all.

By the sea, a man who may or may not be a father rages at the ocean.

In the past the man called Theo cycles home from a team bonding experience, and is terrified of the face he has just seen. He didn't try to talk to Dani. Didn't meet her eye again after that initial moment of shock. Fled without a word, chin down, expression fixed in stone. Half ran to his bicycle and pedalled away without bothering to tuck his trousers into his socks.

The queues at the Vauxhall Bridge toll weren't as bad as he'd feared, and the walls of Battersea Power Station were a brilliant cascade of colour bouncing back off the clouds promoting the latest reality TV escapade, huge painted faces pouting brilliant crimson lips into the dark.

He went the long way round, past the giant glass towers of the river, then south, towards houses growing lower and cracked,

15

overgrown front gardens, laundrettes with beige linoleum floors, churches in sloped-roof sheds proclaiming a new Jesus of fire and redemption, a criss-cross of silent railway lines and budget gyms above kebab shops for the men with vast shoulders encasing tiny pop-up heads.

He circled several times before pulling up at the stiff black gate in the crumbling red-brick wall. He couldn't remember what Mrs Italiaander, landlady folded in fuchsia, had said to him when he came through the door – she'd said something and he'd even replied, they'd maybe even had a whole conversation – but the memory of it slipped away in a moment.

He sat on the end of his bed and looked around the room, and saw as if for the first time the paucity of character it contained.

A wooden figurine of a woman dancing.

A painting of light across a misty sea.

A couple of 1950s films where everyone knew what to say and exactly how to say it.

A fern that refused to die.

With Dani Cumali's face overlaying his vision, these things suddenly seemed trivial, pathetic. The revelation jerked him almost to laughter, as the man somewhere beneath Theo Miller, who still faintly remembered the real name he'd been born with, and the hopes he'd had as a child, stared at the farcical illusion of Theo Miller he'd created and realised that in all his efforts to be anonymous he had in fact ceased to be a person whatsoever. The laughter rolled through him for half a minute, then stopped as abruptly as it had begun, and he stared again at nothing.

He sat in muddy clothes on the end of his bed, hands in his lap, and waited to be arrested. In the room next door, Marvin, Mrs Italiaander's teenage son, wannabe rock star, wannabe movie star, wannabe private detective wannabe martial artist wannabe somebody in a nobody world, played drum and bass far too loud and wondered if his mum had known all along that he'd stolen that fifty from her purse.

Downstairs, Nikesh, the other flatmate, who did something for the Company, something in insurance or actuarial or – he was never very good at explaining – cooked chicken so spicy it could burn the top off your mouth and listened to radio with the volume turned right down, too low to really hear, but it was the sound of the voices that Nikesh enjoyed, more than the words they spoke.

After a while – after the first twenty minutes of not being arrested – Theo lay back on his double bed, nearly always slept in by one, and stared at the ceiling. His room was five metres by six metres, luxurious by lodging standards. Theo had lived in it for nearly three years. He'd been renting in Streatham before, but his flatmate had got a job in something that paid more, been given a resident's permit to Zone 1 and moved in with his girlfriend. Theo's civil service salary didn't stretch to a mortgage, not with prices being what they were. Not with times being so . . .

. . . besides, he didn't have the papers to live in Kensington or Chiswick or anywhere like that, let alone the cash, so Tulse Hill it had been, two lodgers, a mother and a child pushed into a house built for three. Mrs Italiaander had never raised Theo's rent. She liked the way he cleaned the oven once a month and the new shower rail he'd installed. He was a nice, quiet tenant, and that was a rare thing indeed.

It struck Theo as likely that in three years' time he would probably be in this same bed, on these same sheets, staring at the same crack running to the ceiling rose. This made him feel . . . nothing.

He was masterful in feeling nothing. It was what he did best. He had cultivated the art over nearly fifteen years.

He checked his bank balance for the fifth time in the hope it was something better.

Wondered why the cops hadn't come for him yet.

Realised he had no idea what on earth he was doing with his life, or what the hell he was meant to do now.

Having no idea what to do with himself, he did as he always did and on Monday morning went to work.

*

The fact they let him through security was strange. He sat at his desk in the Criminal Audit Office, patiently expecting handcuffs. For nearly twenty minutes he slouched there, fingers hooked on the edge of the desk, staring straight ahead without seeing, and waited.

No one came.

After twenty-five minutes an automatic alert appeared warning him that his productivity levels appeared to be slipping and that he was ten minutes away from being put on notice.

He stared at the pop-up message in amazement. In nearly nine years of working at the Criminal Audit Office, he'd never seen such a thing. He took a paracetamol, obvious and slow for the benefit of the camera on top of his screen, and set to work.

The cops didn't come.

Men in black didn't burst through his window.

Dani Cumali didn't laugh like a banshee as they dragged him down, pointing and howling with mirth at the lie that only she could have broken.

Nothing changed, so Theo did his job.

This is the daily diet on which Theo Miller is fed:
    murder
    theft
    fraud
    burglary
    rape

Guidelines on rape vary depending on whether it is felt that the woman may have dressed in a provocative manner or appeared to be sexually enthusiastic prior to the act of penetration. A woman who does not dress modestly is more likely to be a victim of crime and as a consequence we recommend indemnity in the low-to-mid £30,000 as a starting point for assessing the . . .

    corporate espionage
    libel
    slander
    assault on a corporation

anti–corporate profit activity

> *By acting against corporate interests, individuals show a complete disregard for society and are harming all, not merely a few. Starting indemnities of £400,000 are a viable place to commence negotiation . . .*

riot

trespass

protest

Once he heard the minister for social responsibility explain: "Crime has huge financial cost on our communities. It is only right that we acknowledge its economic impact in a blue-skies thought-dynamic way that puts society back in the driving seat."

Theo remembered that phrase clearly – "put society back in the driving seat" – because he found it inherently confusing.

"It is time to hero the narrative of personal responsibility!"

The Criminal Audit Office had emerged some seven or so years before human rights were judged passé, from the outdated monolith of the Crown Prosecution Service. This was when the Company was still trading under many different names, a mess of loans and investments, debts and boards, but after they'd started investing in security. Prison was a deeply inefficient way of rehabilitating criminals, especially given how many were clearly irredeemable, and despite privatisation efficiencies overcrowding and reoffending were a perennial problem. Rehabilitation through work was an excellent and scientifically provable way of instilling good societal values. The first Commercial Reform Institute was opened when Theo was seven years old, and made meat patties for hamburgers.

> *Shall we go, shall we go to the patty line?*
> *I kissed my love, she swore she was mine,*
> *But they took me to the patty line.*

Theo hums a half-remembered tune from his childhood under his breath, doesn't notice, reads a report.

19

Semen was discovered but the victim was unwilling to pay £315 for the DNA test and thus we are unable to say whether the semen came from the accused. In light of this we would suggest a reduced charge of sexual harassment.

Theo checked the database. Sexual harassment had various subcategories, but the most he could levy was £780 for a first-time offence.

At first a lot of people had been excited by the indemnity system, until it emerged that the profits raised from prosecuting crimes were almost entirely eaten up by administrative costs from the various companies contracted to manage the cases.

Corporate Police, much more reliable than the tiny rump of Civic Police accessible by the uninsured or through NGO charity funding, had shareholders to consider when they invoiced for an investigation. The TV always showed the glamour, never the paperwork – forensics was expensive, best deployed only on really profitable cases.

Corporate rehabilitation centres had a similar problem. As corporations bought up local communities, transforming towns into Winchester by Visit the Soul or Bath Spa Deluxe Healthy Living, local judiciary fell under their purview and great savings were made all round and there was much rejoicing, except for the scroungers who were unable to pay their corporate community tax, clearly weren't contributing to society and thus couldn't ask society to support them.

Raising the price of manslaughter in line with inflation . . .

. . . a deduction in lieu of a promising corporate career . . .

Added fees: £480 for putting down victim's cat.

£48,912 for the first offence, reduced to £38,750 for prompt payment . . .

The victim transpired to be illegally resident on a student visa, and thus the indemnity must be reduced by £4500 to reflect that it was assault on an alien, rather than a UK citizen.

Impaled on a garden fork added hospital costs of . . .

Theo audited the cost of murder, mayhem and destruction, and when 5.15 p.m. came, he cycled home as the sun went down, made macaroni cheese, and ate it in his room and listened to Marvin's drum and bass through the wall, and waited for the men to come to take him away.

And no one came.

After the first three days, the failure of the powers-that-be to swoop down and arrest him left Theo slightly annoyed. The least you can ask when your life is about to be ripped apart is to get on with these things, rather than be left in suspense.

And no one came.

And a week became two.

And two weeks became three.

And for a moment Theo permitted himself to think that he'd imagined seeing Dani Cumali at all.

And at the end of the fourth week he was intellectually certain that it would be fine, absolutely fine because that was how these things were, and on the Tuesday of the fifth week, she found him.

"Hello."

"Hello, Dani."

They stood in the place behind the building where they chained the bicycles. Once he'd seen a rat scamper between the bins at the back. One early evening in summer he'd met a fox. The fox had sat and watched him, and he'd watched it, and neither had moved for a long time. Neither had been afraid. They had simply looked, to learn the nature of the other's gaze. And when the fox got bored, it stood up and walked briskly away, and there was nothing more to it.

She was waiting by his bicycle. He saw her too late to pretend he hadn't seen her, but didn't want to leave the bike, thought it would be stupid to just run away.

Going to the bicycle forced him to stand a little closer than he would have wanted, face angled away from the security camera, one hand resting on the seat protectively. She wore a faded blue raincoat, white cloth shoes, a tiny moonlight smile.

"So." This word seemed to take some thinking about, a gathering of the weight of the world, a slow orbit round the burning centre of the universe. "So," she repeated, trying out new ideas, studying his face. "It's Theo now?"

"Yes."

"Huh."

They stood a while, and Theo remembered the fox and felt almost relieved that all this would soon be over.

She shifted her weight from one foot to the other, and he huddled against a wall, and for nearly a minute they were silent. Then she said, "I saw you at that party. Or whatever it was."

"Team bonding experience."

"Right. Well. There."

They wavered, avoiding each other's gaze. Finally Theo mumbled, looking at some place a few hundred miles above and a little to the left of her forehead, "Are you ... "

"Catering."

"Right."

"The catering company bought my parole."

"You've been ... "

"I've got a shift starting at 9 p.m., near Sloane Square. It's a market. They're selling the paroles of the pretty girls to rich geezers. Maids. Cleaners, nannies. That sort of stuff. If you're rich enough, you get to pay less tax if you turn yourself into a company, and if you're a company you can buy a parole. It's all sex. I mean that's why they ... but I'm catering. I just clean the glasses."

"Right."

Her head bent down, then up, a curious cat not sure if the object before it is food or threat. The more he tried not to catch her eye, the harder she stared until finally his gaze met hers, and she held it with a frown. "We're gonna talk now," she explained, cold and flat. "That's what's happening. In case you're wondering. It's ... that's what happens now."

He tried to look away, couldn't, nodded once, mouth dry, and followed her.

Chapter 6

Later, on the canal.

Her name is Neila.

These are the cards that she drew when she did her reading that Friday morning:

Seven of staves, the Chariot, three of cups, nine of staves, king of swords, the Tower, eight of swords, the Fool, the Hanged Man (inverted).

She stared at the layout before her, and for a horrified moment realised she had spread the cards without focusing on a question. There had been something at the back of her mind but then . . .

On the couch behind her, the man rolled over a little, his head turned towards the wall, the grey light of day shining round the foil circles Blu-tacked to the portholes to keep the heat in, and today there was no fresh blood on the floor.

Neila folded the cards away, returned the pack to the walnut box beneath her bed, put some baked beans on the stove. As they warmed, she went outside and discovered that in the night something had smashed the pots of geraniums she grew on the front of the boat, thin magenta petals spilt across the water, black soil across the deck. She sighed and set to cleaning, and no one passed on the water or on the land.

Once she'd had a tomato plant uprooted and thrown into the canal. She'd found the sodden tendrils of broken leaves bumping against her hull in the morning, and she'd cried, howled almost, like her one true love was dead, and couldn't stop crying for the best part of a week.

Now she felt nothing. That too was why she'd come to the water, to get from that place to somewhere else.

She put some margarine into the baked beans and ate silently, sitting on a green foldable chair that in summer months she liked to have on the prow so she could read by the light of the fading day. She wondered if she should wake the man, and decided not to. She thought maybe she should give him some water, soak a sponge or something, try to dribble something into the corner of his drooping mouth, but thought he might choke.

She tried calling the local hospital, but the automated switchboard wouldn't let her proceed without inputting her eleven-digit insurance provider number, so she gave up.

At 3.30 p.m., as the sun slipped towards the horizon, she muttered, "Screw it," gunned the engine, retrieved her mooring hooks and steered the *Hector* north, towards Watford and the edge of the city, blue-grey fields to the left, shining black road to the right.

By 6 p.m. the canal was dark, her fingers cold and body stiff, so she went back inside. She had enough gas and water for a hot shower, but the idea of stripping naked with an unknown man in the cabin made her uneasy. Instead she made more tea and, as the man slept, she checked his hands again for truths and signs, and found there nothing she had not found before.

At 8.23 p.m. a cormorant, confused, lost, slams into the side of the canal boat, indignant that its journey has been disrupted by so solid a thing, and at its collision

the man called Theo jerks awake, and for a moment is terrified, and cannot remember his name, and does not know where he is, and wonders if this is what every awakening will be like for the rest of his days.

Clawing, pulling the blanket tight, then flinching, turning away from the pain, another moment of uncertainty as he tries to work out where it comes from – it would be unmanly to whimper at this point but screw it, he's only just woken and this was not how he planned on finding himself.

A cabin.

24

If he rolled out sideways his head could touch one wall, his feet the other, at a stretch. He might have to cheat and reach out a few fingertips, but that's fine. If he lies down lengthwise, the boat can probably fit six or seven of him end to end before it becomes a squeeze. A curtain above his head, purple, with a silver elephant on it, the moon, or possibly the sun, or maybe just a disc of light, rising or setting behind the ambling creature, a log curled in its trunk, lilies crushed beneath its feet. The curtain is suspended by a mesh of elastic rope, a parting in the middle. On the other side of the cabin, away from the sofa, a cubicle closed off from the rest of the boat by heavy plastic doors that fold like an accordion to create a little privacy, concealing a toilet. A tomb-sized cupboard next to that encloses a plastic shower.

Black iron stove, burning bright and loud, with two hobs set on top, one for a kettle, one for a pan. A gas oven too small to roast a chicken. Cupboards above made of laminated chipboard, the handles removed in an act of domestic whimsy, replaced with hand-painted ceramic baubles of blue and yellow. A small stainless-steel sink, a saucepan and cup drying beside it. On the walls of the cabin, little hand-sewn pieces of fabric adorned with blue-stitched cornflowers, red hearts, messages of love. "Believe in yourself." "Love thy neighbour." "Life is for living." And so on. One, circled by a weave of red roses and green thorns, framed and put between portholes, a little out of keeping with the others – "Deal with it, bitches" – in the same carefully embroidered hand. Round portholes covered with handmade foil circles, glued to cardboard and pressed against the glass. A clock on the wall counted away the hours. The numerals were embraced with happy, bounding rabbits. Here, a bunny balancing on the top of the 5, hugging the 8, pressed up against one o'clock in a pose which, once suggested as needlessly sexual, could be nothing else, all innocence gone.

A fold-down slatted wooden table for eating on. The couch he lay on, extending down towards the rear of the boat; more cupboards, installed a little crooked at first, then straightened up through careful addition of nails and wedges. A lampshade above his head on which ducks flew in an endless circle, eyes wide and terrified at the philosophical prison of their flight. Darkness outside, yellow light within, a few bulbs burning in the walls, candles lit on the kitchen counter, floating in white metal bowls.

The man called Theo clings to his blanket, to the back of the couch, to his side, to his head, and can't quite remember how he came to be here, and as sense returns, for a moment entertains the possibility that he is dead, and the Greeks were right, and the rivers of the damned flow through Hades after all.

Then Neila came through the curtains that separated the cabin from her bed, disturbed by the sound of movement, and saw him, and said, "Oh."

For a frozen moment they stared at each other and hadn't got a clue what they were meant to say next.

Then, in almost harmony, he blurted:

"I don't know if there . . ."

And she exclaimed, "You must be parched. Tea?"

Two people on a narrowboat, heading up the Grand Union Canal.

Neila makes tea.

She is six foot three, feeling less than her radiant self, wearing furry lion slippers, thick flannel pyjama trousers, a cyan-blue T-shirt, a fleece jumper given to her by someone who was hoping to also give her Jesus. Her hair is turning grey; she hasn't had a proper haircut for a while, and the cheap DIY dyes turn the long ends brittle. There's still a red sequin dress in her cupboard, knee-high boots so bright that they dazzle passing traffic. She hasn't worn either for a long time, and her bum and belly have got a little saggy. Sometimes she feels sad about that, and instantly tells herself to get over such stupid thoughts and appreciate her beauty for what it is. Her arms are strong, her shoulders broad, and she hides both from the gaze of men. Even though she's tall, she likes to wear a bit of a heel when she goes walking, to change the shape of her calves and the way her hips move. It helps; so does the lipstick.

Tonight she wears neither, and feels hot, exposed and foolish.

Fusses over making a cup of tea, puts in too much UHT milk, decides she'll drink that cup herself rather than throw it away, tries again, teabag, water, strange how hard these things become in the gaze of a stranger's eye, and as she works she says:

"You were by the canal. I called an ambulance. They didn't come. I don't know if I did the right thing, if there is family – do you have family?" The man didn't answer. "I moved the boat. I was by the lock, there are . . . "

She stopped talking as quickly as she had begun. Beat the teaspoon out on the side of the mug. The sound was painfully loud, irritating; once upon a time she'd found it relaxing, ping-ping-ping! Not tonight.

Silence from the couch. She passed him a mug, and maybe he said thank you, his lips moved and there was air in his throat, but the sound didn't quite come out whole. She cast around for something else to do, putting a saucepan away, poking at the fire in the stove, still burning strong but who cares, more wood, do excuse me I'm just going to . . .

more wood, taken from the pile under the tarp on top of the deck, her breath frozen in the air, the cold a sudden shock that lets her feel how fast her heart is pumping . . .

a moment to catch the chill, letting the cold through her skin, taking her time grasping the log, enjoying the feel of it beneath her fingers, broken bark and dry splinters

then back in.

More wood.

Well isn't that lovely it's just

it's just

Well.

She stood, silent, and found she had nothing more to say.

The man, dark hair, one side clumped with blood, stuck with dirt, a damn good wash and then whoosh, a static explosion around the head, she knows how hair like that behaves she used to cut the hair of a man called . . .

. . . a man called . . .

It was a long time ago.

27

Several weeks' growth of scraggy beard, eyes made smaller by the puffy lids that encase them. He was born with a harelip, which a doctor stitched together before he was six weeks old so that he could feed; you'd barely notice the scar, but there is a slight tugging to one side of his face, a slightly crooked smile when it appears, which hasn't been very often in recent years.

He was also born with the little finger and ring finger on his right hand fused together, but his parents never told him that, and it was an easy operation to separate them. His mother thought it was bad luck, an evil birth. His mother was not the kind of woman to be swayed once a thought was in her mind.

"My name is Neila."

The words were so obvious, so familiar on her lips, she was astonished she hadn't said them before.

Silence.

She turned, her whole body now, to look at the man on the couch. Still clutching the blanket. Staring up at her, eyes catching green-grey in the firelight. She put her head on one side, hands on her hips, waited.

"Theo," he mumbled at last. "My name is Theo."

Then hesitated, looked away, smiled, laughed, found laughing painful, curled away from the sound, looked back up, still smiling. "Actually," he said, "that's a complete and utter lie. Sorry. Habit. But . . . call me Theo."

Silence in the cabin.

Silence on the water.

Neila watches and feels a sudden heady rush of power. This man is the most vulnerable, pathetic creature she has ever seen. She is a saving angel. She is God-like in her authority. She holds another person's life in her hands. She's never done that before.

She thinks she might laugh, and it would be deeply inappropriate. Involuntarily puts one hand over her mouth, clapping the sound in.

Then she thinks she might cry, and that would be absolutely fucking ridiculous, what the fuck is she even thinking?

The man called Theo is contemplating his next words, staring

28

into his teacup, barely sipped, maybe he's a snob about these things, maybe he doesn't like . . .

"There's a code," she blurted to stop him before he could say something stupid, something that would destroy this knife-edged moment in which she is in charge, and all things hang in the balance. "On the canal. There's a code. You help people. That's what it is. Not many people stick with it now. You get a lot more rude people. People who don't know their boats. Triple-parking wankers, if you don't mind me saying. But I believe in the code. It's why I'm on the water, it's why . . ."

Stopped.

Worried she'd said too much. Tried to replay her words, thought perhaps they were okay.

"There's a code," she repeated into the silence. "That's the way of things."

The man nodded, taking it in, looked down, looked up, looked into her eyes. Said: "I'm going north to destroy a man. He killed my friends and took my daughter. He broke the country. He's why they're all dead." His face scrunched up for a moment, looking for something else, which he couldn't find. "That's all."

She thought about it.

Was surprisingly okay with just standing and being still and quiet and thinking about it.

Heard the clock ticking down towards a rabbity midnight.

Said: "Okay then. That's okay."

That was that.

Chapter 7

Theo walked through autumn streets with Dani, watching the cracks in the pavement, and had nothing to say for himself.

Dani strode, chin forward, glowering at all who dared look her way, fingers in fists at her side. The sun was setting, a sluggish grey-blue drifting to sodium-brown. The streets were padded in quiet autumn hush, traffic muffled and far away.

Frames of a film caught in office windows: women picking up their coats, two men playing ping-pong at the staff table above the reception area. The cleaners starting work, down from the top, buckets on wheels, sprays in a pouch, computer screens still live, the lights never going out. A queue for an ATM, a shop assistant pulling down the shutters on a wall of leather boots.

Laughter from the pubs.

A smile and a friendly nod from the man who guards the door of the strip club, hey mate, good to see you again, come in come in yes your favourite she's dancing tonight she's something else isn't she?

The buses do not stop to let people on. If you didn't prebook your place through the gold priority transport service, there's no chance tonight. Faces pressed to fortified glass, bodies standing right up front in that sacred place where only the driver should be, people up the stairwell, standing on the upper deck, unless someone gets off no one is getting on . . .

No one gets off.

Company Police move a beggar on. He has an abscess in his left leg that he proudly displays, destroyed bright pink flesh hollowed out almost to the bone, yellow fluid seeping slowly round the edges. When he just laughs in their faces, refuses to move, points and cackles, the security men carry him bodily to their truck, throw him in. He'll be for the suburbs, for the enclaves where the good people don't go, where they stopped the electricity after the scroungers couldn't pay, wouldn't pay, and where corporate councils don't see any need to invest.

Or maybe not. Maybe he's for somewhere else entirely. There's no one around who'll ask, fewer who'll care, not for a man like that. He makes people uncomfortable. He seems to like it. That's basically assault, that is. That's £125 for the initial crime plus £50 for malicious intent and . . .

Two men are on the verge of hitting each other over a taxi. The driver sits, meter running, unperturbed, as the men scream "I was here first I was here it was me I was—"

"He answered my flag it was me I waved him down didn't you see are you blind?"

Both men are heading towards Maida Vale. If they could just stop shouting for a minute, they could probably share the ride.

They went to a café. The café served coronation chicken, bacon and egg, egg mayo and cheese and pickle sandwiches. If you wanted anything else, the woman behind the counter tilted her mighty brow down and stared up from beneath its shadows, daring you to stick to your convictions. When you backed down, she tutted and exclaimed that you were being absurd and made it anyway, righteously going out of her way for the difficult customer despite their protestations that egg mayo was fine honest, and guessed at the price, which was usually £6.99. The woman used to be a teacher, but her students complained that she gave them too much homework, and one day she hit a boy who had punched staples into a girl's arm and couldn't afford to pay the indemnity, and here she is. Theo bought coffee. He used what cash he had, and as the woman fussed with the till, he slipped the battery from his phone and tried not to stare back over his shoulder as Dani settled at a beige Formica table carved with messages of love and abuse from strangers, scratched with the prongs of a fork.

He sat opposite.

Drank coffee.

Dani said, "So there was"

And the man called Theo replied, "It's been a really long"

She cut in: "I've been on the patty line."

They sipped coffee in silence. It was far too hot and better than he'd expected. In the silence Theo whispered sorry, I'm sorry to hear that, that sounds . . .

. . . but his mouth was smarter than his brain, and he looked down at his tea and said nothing at all.

"After you left . . . the town, there was – I mean, the factory closed. And there wasn't much of nothing else left and I got

it got bad.

I had to

I mean, yeah, you're not supposed to say that, you never *had* to. You chose to. You chose to steal, that's what they always said, but I couldn't see any other way to

Look. That's not what matters. I'm out now. I got in, and things got bad, and I'm clean now. I'm clean and

so.

So."

She ran the curve of the teaspoon over a bowl of sugar, flattening the surface to a smooth plateau, then heaping it up into a hill, then squashing the hill back down again. He watched, waited. In a moment of decision she drove the spoon down into the centre of the bowl, standing tail upright, and stared into his eyes.

"I've got this boss," she announced, tumour-factual, tombstone-hard. "Gatesman. He's my probation officer, but he also gets 5 per cent of whatever I make. It's how they motivate him to try real hard to get us girls jobs. Best jobs are sex, but I got the dirt on him. Embezzling. Not from us – we're fair game. But from his bosses, naughty. I got dirt, and now he's fucking scared of me. He's scared and I can ask for any job I want, and I said – I want into the Ministry. Get me into the Ministry, or

I'll . . . but he did. He got me inside. I've got this thing I need to do, and it's hard but it is . . .

And then I saw you. You and your stupid pudding face.

And I thought . . .

So. Your name is Theo now. And you work for the Ministry."

In the half-light of the candles burning on the kitchen counter of the narrowboat called *Hector*, the woman whose name now is Neila squats down before the man called Theo as you might hunker down to seem less frightening to a tiny, cowering cat, and hands out, fingers open, murmurs, "I read somewhere that you shouldn't change the dressing, just put more stuff on top until it stops bleeding."

Drinking coffee from a dirty cup on a dirty table, the man called Theo looked up and met Dani's eye for almost the first time in fifteen years, and knew that his world was probably going to end. "What do you want?"

"You have access to stuff. With your job, with computers, you can find things out."

"I don't just . . ."

"There's someone you gotta find for me."

"Why?"

She smiled, tiny teeth flashing between pale lips. "Cos I'm your oldest, bestest friend, and I'm asking."

"You can't ask me to look at secure documents."

"Why not?"

He didn't answer. She turned the spoon, once, a hard twist through sugar, picked it up, dug it back in, deeper. "Theo Miller," she mused. "Who the hell even is Theo Miller?"

"I am."

"Right."

"I buried it all, Dani. There's nothing. You won't find a piece of anything to prove . . ."

"So what? Who the fuck needs proof, these days?"

Theo half-closed his eyes, pinched his index fingers together at the bridge of his nose. The smile twitched at the edges of Dani's lips. She waited.

"Who are you trying to find?" he grunted.

"Lucy Rainbow Princess."

"What's that?"

"It's her name."

"That's a name?"

"She was franchised to a party company when she was four. Ads. Princess costumes, unicorns, blonde hair and plastic crowns – that sort of thing. They changed her name."

"Why do you need to break into the Ministry to find her?"

"Cos I'm a patty-line whore who isn't worth shit to the guys who do the paperwork, and cos she's in juvvy. You think women like me get to ask questions like this?"

"And if I can't find ... Rainbow Princess?"

"Her birth name was Lucy Cumali. She's fifteen years old, born March 11th in Shawford by Budgetfood."

Silence a while.

In the street outside, a garbage truck creaked to a halt by overflowing black bins. Two men climbed out the back, orange parole tabards across their chests, parole company logo stamped on their hands, their trousers, their lives.

Overhead a helicopter rushed towards a landing pad, while the passengers texted, eyes averted from the city below, *OMG u wont believ wat i jus heard . . .*

Behind the counter of the café, hot steam blasted into a tannin-stained mug, and bread burned in the toaster.

Theo stared down into the depths of his coffee cup and could only see the past, not the future, in its blackness. For a moment he considered refusing. The fantasy stretched out for a few seconds towards prophecy, before dissolving into disaster.

"Okay," he said. "Okay."

Chapter 8

In the beginning of all things
   fifteen years before hot coffee and blood on the canal
   fifteen years before time became a little . . .
            . . . and it seemed to the man called Theo that past
and future were not that different really and that all things came
back to a point where . . .
   In the beginning.

The boy who will become Theo lay on the beach with Dani
Cumali at the centre of the universe, and listened to the stones
being dragged into the ocean, and was fundamentally deeply
uncomfortable and really rather cold, as is the nature of most
beaches that face the North Sea. He was a flabby skinny boy.
There were no muscles on his body; he hated sports, hadn't even
looked at the footie pitch since the day his dad was . . .
   . . . but he didn't eat very much either, and it's a diet of microwave meals rejected by the factory, macaroni cheese mostly, so
his childish frame was moulded with a layer of squishy white skin
which could be pinched and shaped like putty, before sinking
painlessly, bloodless, back down into bone.
   His hair was thick and dark, his eyes were grey, he will never
be handsome, but one day he might have a girlfriend who thinks
he's sorta cute and know that he's grateful to be with her, and
maybe for a little while they'll be happy until he realises that he's
just playing this game and she's neither his mother nor is he cute at
all and in fact pretending to be cute is so fucking stupid it's just . . .

Theo and Dani lay on the shingle, at the start of all things, and it is extraordinarily uncomfortable and probably deeply romantic. At their feet, the ocean reflected orange-black from a stained sky, and the wind carried in the smell of rotten eggs and cow dung. Behind them, the chimneys of Shawford by Budgetfood's processing plant pumped smoke and steam into the sky, and the lorries growled and grumbled up the highway built by the company when they became community sponsor, though they'd had to knock down half the town to get it through. On the promenade before the pastel-painted houses, slanting grey roofs and tiny pink bullet-flowers in the garden, broad windows dive-bombed with seagull shit, four kids smoked pot and an old woman walked her dog between the shadows of the flickering street lights. Green algae had colonised long beards of colour beneath salt-scarred windows, a cross of St George tangled itself around the pole outside a porch, and the seagulls hung in the air, tipped wings steady as they tried to fly forwards, were blown backwards, and remained going nowhere at all, resigned to their fate.

The sea rolled in, and Theo lay on the shingle, and Dani lay in his arms.

Dani Cumali, hair cut short because she hated the blue hairnet they had to wear in the factory, nails clipped down to an impossible white thread on translucent pink, skin pushed even closer to ivory white by the light spotting of dark, dark moles and ebony-black freckles that pop across her body, tiny as a needle beneath her eyes, round as a penny coin across her back.

They lie together, children again, and watch the starless sky in silence.

Dani doesn't think she's beautiful, and doesn't think Theo is cute.

She thinks he's low-pressure and she is going through certain experiences. It's not so much the sex, which she's already starting to suspect may be overrated. What she really wants, what she actually *really* needs is this thing which is sort of like that thing where . . .

She's not sure if it's like anything, really, maybe one day she'll have the words for what it is, like some sort of love, but now it's
friendship, perhaps
or just a needed quiet thing.
A quiet moment by the sea. That's enough, for now.

Theo knows that Dani is beautiful, an opinion helped by the fact that she is a woman and he's also going through a certain set of experiences, biological imperatives that haven't been properly explained to him.

"We should go to the beach together. Like we used to when we were"

"Is 10 p.m. okay is that"

"You bring blankets, I'll bring booze, like when we used to run away – just . . . you and me, tonight."

Theo lay on the beach and at his back the theme tune of the town declared the hour, played through the speakers of Shawford. The speakers had been put in the day before the parade where the CEO of Budgetfood came to open the factory. His speech had been played to every corner of the town, from the little chapel with the large cemetery to the old ladies' home by the leafless white trees, where they grumbled through their broken teeth about the disturbance. Since then the speakers hadn't ever fallen silent, except once when a senior executive died, and once when someone had managed to find the main power inlet and set it on fire.

Proud to make the best low-salt meals at reasonable price!
Affordable consumption for the discerning client!
Today's special: chicken jalfrezi, now with improved rice formula!

Theo closed his eyes as the music drifted, slow and distorted, towards the sea, the sound deep, stretched as if slowed by opposition from the rumbling wind. The tune had been written by the executive mayor's youngest son, who did it for GCSE Music coursework. The boy was very talented. This had been made clear, and the school wisely waived all tuition fees in recognition of his ability. The music was played on the synth, and a chorus was sung at noon, 5 p.m., 9 p.m. and midnight by a choir of children. For the longest time the boy who would be called Theo thought the words went:

Together we march, together we sing, happy in our community. The children play, there are igloos on the green, happy happy happy, the aliens make noodles.

As a child, he never questioned this interpretation. Why couldn't there be igloos on the green? Why wouldn't aliens make noodles? Noodles were great.

Later, the suspicion grew that he might have been wrong all along, but no matter how hard he listened, he couldn't quite make out the actual words through the infantile chirruping of ageing speakers as they slithered down the hour to midnight. There were worse community sponsors than Budgetfood. At least you got cheap food on Fridays, and they still let the school do breakfast maths club on a Wednesday.

She said, "I didn't think you'd be back."

"Of course I would, I mean, it's not like I"

"Off to your fancy university your fancy friends . . ."

"I heard you and Andy, I mean that"

"Piss off!"

"So it's not a . . ."

"It's over."

"Really?"

"Really, are you kidding me, yes, it's over, he's a jerk, it's all just been . . ."

Time comes a little unstuck, they sit on the blanket spread across the shingle and it's . . .

"My bum is going to sleep."

"Hold on, if you . . . is that any"

"Ow!"

"Sorry, I was just . . ."

And in his dreams

and in his memories

This is where it begins of course, but now he can't remember if the moon was full or if they lay in starlight, and sometimes he remembers both, and both are true, and then he forgets for a little while, and it is almost certain that details, maybe more than details, were fantasy but still it's all he's got, all that's left.

And Dani is in his arms, or possibly he is in hers, the difference at this point is academic, and somewhere, he hears himself say:

"There's this thing at university, my mate, and I thought that maybe . . . but I was wrong and I did . . . I did this thing and . . ."

And she replies, or maybe she didn't, maybe this was in town the morning before or perhaps the morning after, no – not the morning after, "They sacked me. It's not called that. They didn't extend my contract. No point. They've got other kids coming up through the programme now, give the job to some sixteen-year-old, not like they need much training, let them work until they're twenty-one then give them the shove before they have to pay full wage and you just keep thinking, don't you, you keep thinking . . ."

And in his dreams, or possibly his memories, Theo is crying. "I fucked it up. Dani? I fucked up. I fucked up everything. I'm sorry. I didn't mean to . . ."

If he cried in reality too, she didn't hear it, couldn't see the tears on his face in the night, maybe tasted the salt with her tongue and thought it was spray blown in off the sea, the smear of seaweed on his skin, stone beneath his fingers, blood on his hands, and she whispered, "You're never coming back, are you? You're never coming back. I saw the look in your face, you hate this place now, you hate it just like I do. But I've got nowhere to go you're never coming back so where's the harm just once just tonight where's the . . ."

Later, he swore they'd used a condom.

"My foot's gone to sleep can you just . . ."

"Ow! You just head-butted me with your chin!"

"Sorry it was . . ."

Later, thinking about it, he couldn't work out why he would have brought a condom down to the beach, since the idea of having sex in the wind and on the shingle seemed so fundamentally absurd.

"Dani? Are you okay? Dani?"

39

"Could you just hold me a while?"
"Um yeah I suppose if it's . . ."
"And not talk. You can do that, right?"
"Uh-hum."
"Good. Thanks."

In his dreams
          in his past
              in the present
the man called Theo sleeps a rare, clawless sleep.

Chapter 9

Two days after Dani Cumali and the man called Theo had coffee in a teacher's café, Theo cycled to work with a plan in his mind and a twist in his stomach that made him wonder if he was actually physically ill.

He went via Battersea Bridge, because the queues for the tolls were usually faster there. He would never have the credit rating to enter Pimlico by LondonArts as anything other than a tourist of course, but his Criminal Audit Office ID got him waved through with a merry "Have a good day, sir!" and being on a bicycle he was even allowed to cut through some of the quieter streets where the Company men lived, so long as he didn't ding his bell.

The Criminal Audit Office was based in Victoria. Once they'd had an office in Whitehall, but it had been redeveloped for corporate headquarters, so they'd been pushed out to Canary Wharf. Then Canary Wharf had become too expensive, so they'd been dragged to Willesden and for a while Theo had thought about quitting his job rather than the hour-and-forty-minute commute on the train, head down and body swaying in carriages where once there had been seats before the train company judged them inefficient.

Thankfully the minister of civic responsibility had grown annoyed at having to go to Willesden for meetings, and they handled enough high-value white-collar crime for the managers and directors and their well-paid lawyers to grumble and mope about the commute, so back to Victoria they went, to an office abandoned when foreign aid was shut down.

Now they were on the fifth floor of an oil spill of a building. Black plastic windows reflected odd smears of green and pink against the sun. Dark grey walls turned darker with the diesel fumes of the coaches that queued up outside. An embarrassed sign printed on a browning piece of A4 paper and sellotaped to the door declared CRIMINAL AUDIT OFFICE. PLEASE SHOW ID.

A wooden board by the security gate stated that the security situation was Black 2. Theo had never known what Black 2 meant, and it had never been anything else, except for once, on a Wednesday, when it was Blue, and the security man had tonsillitis.

The lift, as it climbed to the fifth floor, rattled and bumped against the shaft. Sometimes you heard bits falling: a bolt or a piece of chain, vanishing down into an unknown abyss below, but whatever the component was it clearly wasn't that important. Theo took the stairs.

The fifth-floor walls were faded grey, with a tideline of black dirt above the radiators from those lost times when they'd worked. Here and there new plaques of laminated plastic offered inspirational advice for the employees who laboured within.

REIMBURSE SOCIETY!
JUSTICE AT REASONABLE COST!
TEAMWORK IS THE BEST WORK!

Theo wasn't sure who'd come up with these statements. For a little while, after they'd first been put up, they'd made him angry, especially as the coffee machine had been broken for four months and hadn't been fixed for budgetary reasons. But as the years went by, anger had faded. Most things faded, given time.

The office was technically open-plan, but hackers had once got into the webcams and filmed the lurid details of negotiations between the CAO and a stockbroker-turned-TV-personality to reduce his indemnity for sexual assault and battery down from £2.2 million to a mere £71,000. Since then all webcams in key offices had been covered with Blu Tack, and tacit acceptance given for pale-blue dividing boards to go up between the desks.

Theo's lair was in the furthest, darkest corner. He'd had a window and everything for a while, but then someone who was making good numbers on murder cases managed to convince Edward that he had seasonal affective disorder and needed Theo's seat. When it emerged that Theo had moved without even a quibble, another officer had stepped forward and suggested that she'd work so much better away from the high-frequency hum of the printers, and when again Theo had moved without complaint, it became open season. Six months and five desk moves later, he was between the toilets and the photocopier, cultivating a small bloom of orange mushrooms behind his waste-paper bin, and content to be ignored.

His file stated that his career progression was "steady". His performance was "consistent", closure rate "satisfactory" and average negotiated indemnity "a positive reflection of current guidelines". Once he'd been rated "very good" and lived in fear for nearly six months that this might lead to people paying attention to him. Thankfully, no one did, and he managed to return his performance to a more genteel average before his next review came round.

He hung his jacket over the back of his chair, put his satchel down by his left foot, turned on the computer, waited with hands in his lap for it to boot up, and at 9 a.m. precisely started working.

Chapter 10

A sexual harassment suit. "For fuck's sake I just said she was hot I mean what has the world come to when you say someone's hot and that gets you in with the courts it's just political correctness gone ..." £750, plus £35 photocopying fees.

A seventeen-year-old girl tried to change the cheques her grandmother was sending her, adding zeroes to the end – she didn't even bother to use the correct kind of biro, her corrections were in black against her grandmother's blue it was just so ...

£6421, dropping to £5100 if her grandmother was willing to lower the charges. To Theo's surprise, the grandmother was not, and the girl went to the patty line.

A group of drug dealers. The police had found most of it but not enough, not nearly enough. They were going to pay the indemnity and have cash in hand, but what were you to do?

£52,190, and the lawyer laughed when Theo told him, as if he'd just heard an old joke his dirty uncle used to tell at Christmas, and the money was in the Audit Office's clearing account within twenty minutes, transferred from a bank somewhere in the Maldives.

Corporate manslaughter. Ninety-three people dead after carbon monoxide leaks from faulty boilers. The safety test on the boilers had been rushed through, signed off without proper inspection, a hint of bribery perhaps, cutting corners, it was ...

In many ways, exactly what Theo needed.

*

At 4.55 p.m. Theo Miller leaves his desk, rushes to Edward Witt's office with a USB stick, so sorry to bother you, it's this corporate manslaughter case, I've finished doing the audit on it but if you look you'll see the accused is a Company subsidiary and I know we've got a policy on not necessarily . . .

"How much did you find them liable for?"

"Twenty-two point three million."

An explosion. You idiot! You bumbling buffoon! This is the Company we're talking about do you really think you can get twenty-two million out of them do you really think that you're that man that you can take on the corporate lawyers and win you're such a I don't even know what kind of give me the file!

But Mr Witt . . .

Give me the goddamn file you absolute . . .

Theo gave Edward Witt the file, and ran away, heart pounding.

Two days later, he slunk back into the office.

"Mr Witt? I'm sorry to intrude but . . ."

"What is it?"

"I left a USB stick with you a few days ago and I realise now that it still has some documents on it which are . . ."

"Bloody hell, Miller!"

They found the USB stick in an empty dagger case that Edward kept in his middle desk drawer. It hadn't held a dagger for years but the plush velvet interior had always appealed to the manager, and he liked to throw things inside that offended him.

"Thank you, Mr Witt, thank you . . ."

"Get out, Miller!"

That night, on an open Wi-Fi network in a café in Battersea, Theo puts the USB stick into his laptop, dials the office through a VPN, and uses the keystroke recording program buried within the antiviral software to retrieve Edward Witt's username and password.

He instinctively audits the cost of this crime in his mind – approximately £12,000 so far, rising with every minute he spends contemplating the data that he's illegally gathering – and feels not insignificantly pleased with himself.

Search: Lucy Rainbow Princess/Cumali.
Born on
mother arrested on
taken into
caught shoplifting on
alcohol abuse
arrested by
sent to
imprisoned at

They met in a different café, down in Limehouse. Dani read in silence, turning through the stolen pages. Theo had printed them on used paper, didn't notice until too late that behind Lucy's life story is advice on how to prevent damage from hyper-mobile knees and relaxation techniques for the busy office worker.

Lucy Cumali barely existed any more. Only Rainbow Princess, part-property of Princess Parties Gold, remained in the system.

Three years old, the care home where she'd been placed got sponsorship from a kids' party company. Lucy Rainbow Princess had been judged suitably cute, and the first fashion shoot had her dressed up in a rainbow tutu with a plastic crown in her hair, posing with the rest of the most winsome kids with the tagline "Make Your Child a Princess for the Day!"

It was cheaper to use kids from the home. Parents could be so pushy these days.

For the next few years, the kids were hired out for photo shoots, as extras in adverts needing a background of cute tots, and for bespoke party events in mansion houses that needed more children, preferably with semi-celebrity marketing kudos, to help make up the numbers. The money they brought in meant the home could afford two meals a day and a Victoria sponge cake at Christmas. The rest went towards management fees. You had to be careful to keep talented people happy.

When she was seven, Lucy Rainbow Princess was diagnosed with malnutrition. The cost of feeding her up to minimum standard required extra appearances at parties and ads to make up the budgetary shortfall, but as she began to put on weight, fewer advertisers wanted her. When she was eight, Lucy burst all the balloons at a party; three weeks later she stabbed a stuffed unicorn with a cake knife, leaving tattered shreds of polyester on the floor and the younger guests in tears. The care home withdrew her from the sponsorship scheme, put her on the third floor on the basic care package and didn't spot when she dropped out of school four years later.

The cops, when they arrested her aged twelve and a half for drunk and disorderly behaviour, had to give her a lift back to the home when no one came to collect her. On her thirteenth birthday she was picked up, stoned, booze on her breath, standing in the middle of the street not knowing where she was. One of the girls had taken her to the house of some friends of hers, older, all men, who'd put something in her drink and told her to smoke more, more, they had more mates coming come on it'd be great it'd be ...

But Lucy Rainbow Princess had a decent head on her shoulders, even when her face had gone walking elsewhere, and told the men to go fuck their mothers and stormed out of the flat and later

in the hospital

couldn't press charges because she didn't know where the flat had been or what the men were called.

And by the time her older friend came forward to tell the cops everything, the world had lost interest.

On her fourteenth birthday Lucy Cumali punched a cop in the nuts for trying to take her beer away while drinking in the square. The indemnity was set at £546 – a very low rate, given her crime – but no one was willing to pay it. She was sent to juvenile detention, where she worked copying and pasting five-star online reviews for sports products.

CAME IN PERFECT CONDITION REALLY HAPPY WITH
MY PRODUCT

FAST RELIABLE SERVICE IT WAS EXACTLY WHAT
I WANTED

OMG ITS JUST PERFECT I'M GOING TO USE THIS IN
ALL MY WORKOUTS

And so on.

The day before she was meant to receive parole, she set fire
to the unused gymnasium, and her sentence was extended. This
seemed to cause Lucy a great deal of satisfaction.

Chapter 11

Dani cried, and it wasn't pretty crying. It was gasping, sort of asthmatic crying, all puffy-cheeked, dribbling transparent snot and little half-whistles of indrawn breath as she tried and failed to calm down. People were staring at them and Theo felt really, really awkward and got her some more paper napkins in the hope that was sort of helpful.

Somewhere between the snot and the tears she gasped: help me.

Theo said: how?

I need to get Lucy back I need to get her out of there she needs to be

I can't help you

She needs to be I can if I can get her out of there then

There's nothing I can do

But you're part of it you're part of the system you work for

I can't do

I NEED TO GET HER BACK I NEED TO

I'm going now

SHE'S THE ONLY THING THAT MATTERS NOW SHE'S WHY I'M HERE SHE'S WHY I'M OUT WHY I'M CLEAN SHE'S

Don't contact me again.

FUCK YOU YOU'RE A FUCKING COWARD YOU'RE

Goodbye.

COWARD YOU PIG FILTH YOU MOTHER FUCKING

*

He left her mid-flow. She ran after him, crying, begging, and he got on his bicycle and pedalled away as she screamed abuse, and lay on his back on his bed in Tulse Hill and wondered what the fuck he was doing with this fucking stupid excuse for his fucking life.

Chapter 12

In the time before

> before the patties, before the wild things and the beautiful things and the things that need more things always and for ever

When the boy who was not yet called Theo Miller was sixteen years old, the police came to arrest his dad. They came at three o'clock in the morning, which was ridiculous, cos his dad had been in since 6.40 and they'd been watching the house for weeks. There wasn't any reason to break down the front door, smash the glass in the garden porch, wave their guns and shout "Move!" or "Down!" or sometimes "Don't move!" or a combination of all three in a confusing cacophony.

There wasn't any reason to put a gun against the boy's head as his mum screamed and screamed and cried because her son had a fucking gun against his fucking head are you fucking

His dad, as they took him away, was the quietest, stillest thing about the entire affair. He didn't panic, didn't look the boy in the eyes, and later Theo decided that was probably how he knew he was guilty.

Reluctantly, Theo and his mum tried to visit his dad, but Company Police said:

"We do not have that suspect currently within our files it is probable that he has been transferred for the expectation of his trial you must fill out form 189 for further information and there will be . . . "

They filled out the form.

"This form needs witnessing by an authorised signatory of the Company until you have an authorised signatory you will be . . . "

Eventually Mum got a signature, Theo didn't know how, and the cops told them it was £65 a visit, and Mum said they didn't have the cash. There was a company – this was before the company became the Company and these things were just taken for granted – but there was a company which owned a company who owned the company that Theo's dad was alleged to have robbed, and the company that owned the company also owned a company that was invested in Budgetfood, and the rest of Budgetfood anyway was owned by this conglomerate of investors and so all things considered . . .

"The Corporate Community Council is not sure that we can renew your benefits," declared the mayor, unable to meet his mum's eyes. "Things . . . being what they are."

The mayor wasn't a bad man. But he had his pension to consider, and Budgetfood had been putting pressure on him to cut social spending anyway. It didn't contribute to overall productivity, and his daughter had this condition that needed a lot of care; if he lost his place, if they sacked him then she'd go without the medicines and he just had to make these choices, these hard choices, these realistic . . .

It was £25 an hour to get an appointment with the chief investigative officer, and Theo wasn't making much from his off-book work cleaning down the pub, and by the time he had £65 saved up the case was already being heard and the fee had gone up to £180 as his dad was considered a flight risk.

Four weeks after his dad was taken away, the boy who would be Theo went with Dani Cumali to get their GCSE results.

They had been in six of the same GCSE classes, including food distribution and logistics, business studies and graphics for marketing. There was only one school in Shawford by Budgetfood. Once a year the mayor came to judge sports day, and they'd get special guest speakers from the factory to talk about Retail Branding for Social Media or Fish Waste Product Use.

As children, Dani and the boy called Theo hated each other.

Dani couldn't remember because it wasn't important to her, but when she was eight she told Theo that his father was a done-out crook who was going to the patty line, and Theo had run away and concocted ten thousand schemes for revenge, and carried out a grand total of none, and Dani hadn't realised that he was the last person in town to know his dad was a thief, or how close she'd come to having her hair set on fire.

And when he was eleven, Theo had muttered to Dani that maybe the reason she never had a proper school lunch was because her mother had left her when she was two and there wasn't anyone at home to make a lunchbox for her, and Dani had told him that he was the stupidest, weirdest kid in class and no one liked him and he'd never be anything other than a screamer or a fader or a zero and anyway she was . . .

By the time they were thirteen, the injuries had begun to fade behind new outrages of puberty, and slowly, suspiciously, they'd forged a cordial neutrality.

And when they were fourteen, they had to choose what GCSEs to do, and the company sponsor had come down to the classroom to talk to all the pupils, and explain the compulsory curriculum subjects, the core recommended subjects, and the extra-curricular activities that Budgetfood would not fund should you chose to pursue them further.

Both Dani and Theo wanted to do art, but it wasn't a sponsored subject, so they did graphics for marketing instead, and he finished with 131/160 and she had 132/160 and they both agreed that was the best possible way it could be.

Overall, she did better in every subject except maths.

"Dani Cumali!" exclaimed Mrs Lee, deputy head of the school, pastoral care officer, domestic science teacher, head of stationery, head of junior factory recruitment, sponsorship liaison committee, chair of . . .

"Dani Cumali! Fancy you doing so well! Such a turnaround such a – you should apply for A levels! You should apply and I'm sure you'd get sponsorship I'm confident that . . . "

Dani applied for A-level funding to the Sponsorship Committee. They replied:

It is with deep regret that we have to reject your application as this committee does not feel that the subjects you wish to study are conforming to the overall academic model of this institution; nor have you clearly defined your ten-year business objectives for study as required in article 729b of the standard educational practice document (2).

Theo also applied for A levels, having no idea what else he was meant to do. For his core subjects he chose maths, food science and agricultural studies.

Three weeks later he received the rejection letter, and no one was surprised.

That Sunday a woman knocked on the door and said, "Hello. I'm from Dover County Court. My son plays football down your husband's club. He always seemed like such a nice man. Sometimes – the paperwork you know how it is – and it's a corporate case so these things get – but the trial starts tomorrow. I do hope it goes well for you. Such a lovely fellow." She giggled and waved goodbye, hand stationary and little digits flying, and scampered away like a naughty mouse. Later Theo realised that she was probably terrified, and had done something very, very brave.

They went to Dover to watch the trial, but the first five hours were spent arguing over what evidence could be admitted, and the judge got bored and the whole thing was adjourned.

They went back the next day and there was Dad, dressed in blue, sat in the prisoner's cage as the judge exclaimed:

"This attack on our values, on society, on the property of people who thought that their investment was safe . . . "

It was the first time Theo had seen his father for nearly three months.

The father stared at the son, and Theo didn't know what was in his gaze, and imagined every possibility, and looked away and couldn't look back, because men didn't cry.

Chapter 13

The Grand Union Canal was finished just in time for the railways to be invented.

Neila lies awake and listens to the sounds of nightmares from the cabin next to hers, and is too tired to check on her guest.

At some point in the night Theo snores.

She stifles a laugh.

He stops snoring.

She does not sleep and then

wakes late, even though she did not close the curtains, not that they make much difference against the light off the water and

the stove is nearly out, the fire down to a few embers, but she puts kindling on it, the smashed-up remains of a wooden pallet someone discarded by the towpath, broken down to splinters, which catch and curl orange so she

gets more wood a field to the left, a field to the right, a low hill rising in the distance, a train track where the trains do not come, a couple of thick sheep blasting frozen breath out of nostrils, scampering to the places beneath the overgrown hedgerows to find the last vestiges of grass, a Zeppelin flying overhead, she has no idea why, it is advertising a brand of shaving cream but there's no one here no one to see maybe it got loose from its rope and ah yes, look up, see it go beneath the scudding clouds and

she is making tea.

Theo sleeps.

Neila dresses five layers deep, two pairs of gloves over her hands, goes to the back of the boat, out through the engine room, frees the ropes, guides the *Hector* away from its moorings, heading north.

Chapter 14

Three weeks after Theo ran away from Dani Cumali, from her
daughter and her despair and her fucked-up fucking life and
    and the past and the moment on the beach and a bit of maths
that he wasn't daring to do and
    after he ran away because that was the only thing he was ever
any good at doing
    Dani called again.

When you see a person you do not want to see
                    are caught picking your nose
                            scratching your backside
                                    kissing someone who should really
have known better than to be kissed

"Dani," he said, "You can't call me I'm not . . ."
    "It's important listen, I've found something important, some-
thing big."
    "I'm going to hang up now and . . ."
    "They've killed people – so many people – and his own
mother, they're . . . I'll fucking tell them who you are I'll tell
them and . . ."
    "Goodbye."
    "Lucy's in trouble she's in real trouble – I'll tell them you're a
fraud, that you're not Theo Miller I'll tell them that you're . . ."
    He hung up.
    For a moment he thought he'd felt . . . something. Perhaps

fear? Fear would have been an acceptable reaction and certainly, when he'd first seen Dani's face, he'd experienced a thing that was definitely . . .

But fear had faded, and in its place had come a resignation which had been only deepened by breaking into his boss's computer, compounding the legion offences at his back and now . . .

he sat on the end of his bed

in a life that meant nothing

and spent his days condemning people to slavery while murder purchased its way to freedom, tax-free.

And nothing was the only thing safe to feel.

Dani tried calling back, and he didn't answer, turned the world off and slept surprisingly easily.

The next morning, there were nearly a dozen text messages.

Names. Figures. Philip Arnslade. Simon Fardell. Seriously, this is big, this is so big this is

He deleted the messages and barred her number.

Two days later, she was waiting outside his office. He saw her before she saw him, and doubled back the way he'd come, and rode the bus home, even though it took forty minutes longer and someone spilt cider on his trousers.

Chapter 15

The day after his dad was sentenced, the boy who would be Theo sat on the steps of Dover County Court. The cuisine of Dover was fried chicken. The town was sponsored by the ferry companies but also did sterling business in internment camps. Salt had eaten the walls of the houses. Hardy shrubs grew between the cracks in the walls. The tourists went looking for the Roman ruins, but they were hidden behind the car park, and the signs sent you round in circles.

Mum was inside, trying to get one final meeting with Dad before they took him away, but they were on a deadline luv, they had three more drop-offs to make and didn't get paid overtime.

The boy ate fried chicken, listened to the arcade across the street, the fruit machines, the whack-a-mole, the speed racers and the shoot-em-ups, the kung-fu button crunchers and the tingalingalingaling of digital gold pouring from the speakers.

Wondered what he was going to do with his life.

He couldn't imagine any future in which he wasn't sat here for ever, eating fried chicken until he died. He couldn't imagine that there was any way, or any place, that wasn't a fucking naïve stupid fucking dream. The secret, he decided, was not to care. Care about dreams and of course you'll be disappointed; that was the point of living.

He licked his fingers, and the grease didn't shift, and sat and waited for the seagulls to get close enough to kick.

A car pulled up.

A man with dark hair growing thin on the top got out, looked at the boy, turned, murmured to his driver, a man in jeans and black leather jacket. Get us some chips, yeah – no salt, his missus had him on one of these blood pressure diet things, but vinegar and extra vinegar because there was always the bit at the bottom which the vinegar didn't get to. Commands given, he walked over to the boy who would be Theo, towered over him, the curve of his belly pulling the eye upwards in a concave motorway of flesh, and proclaimed:

"Mike's boy, right?"

"No."

The man raised both eyebrows, though perhaps he was trying to raise only one, because the expression was crooked, awkward, practised without success. Five foot five, thin hair down to his shoulders, usually in a ponytail, fingers covered in rings – a skull, a blue eye, a silver London bus, a pair of crossed gold knives and a flat band with a pinhole at the top – he was proud of his appearance, and had to remind people of this whenever they forgot to be impressed, which was most of the time.

"I've got no time for your boy-shit, boy."

"I don't have a dad."

"Mike said you might say that. Made it out like it didn't bother him, lying cunt."

"Who are you?"

"Name's Jacob. I'm a friend of your dad's. Him and me go back a long way. Said I'd keep an eye on you said I'd make sure you were okay, not fucking things up, keeping a straight head. Godfather, me, that's what I am, or like one of those uncles you only see at Christmas, the good kind, the kind that gives you sweets but doesn't take any nonsense not like others might, not that kind of uncle a proper uncle – I'm like that. That's what I'm like."

"Excuse me I'm . . . "

A hand caught the boy's wrist as he tried to stand. That hand is the hand that threw a perfect 180 at the Folkestone Champions' League Semi-Final back last year, the crowd went wild, his whole family had bought these sponge hands with fingers pointing up to the sky, which they waved triumphantly, his son had his face painted special like a dartboard and his missus got a tattoo of the winning triple twenty inscribed on her . . .

. . . well, never mind where it was inscribed, point was it was a mighty hand indeed that now grasped the boy.

"I heard you went and applied to do A levels. That's good. Nice. You should get educated. That's all your dad ever asked for you and I promised I'd see it was done right. Me, I never got educated, and sure, I made a go of things but that takes a special kind of backbone which I see you lack. It's something I'd wish for my own kids. Universities . . . any take your fancy?"

"They won't let me on the course. I'll never get to university."

"Of course they will, they just don't know you yet, that sort of negative attitude isn't healthy, now I can tell you, my missus she says that there's this psychosomatic link between the mind and the old ticker, between—"

"I can't get sponsorship. The factory won't sponsor a kid whose dad laundered money through the football club."

These words, calm, composed, are possibly the first adult things that the boy who will be Theo has ever said, and having spoken them out loud, he realises with a sudden jerk that shimmers through his whole body that he will never be a child again. A flicker of grief, a flash of mourning for a thing lost without a sound, and then he hardens his gaze, and looks into the eyes of Jacob Pritchard, and sees them smiling back.

"Sponsorship," the older man breathes. "Yeah, sponsorship. I heard about that. Two years get paid through A levels and it's what, like six years after that working for some bank? Good rate of return that, decent interest on time spent, I respect that, I understand that, not my language but it's my song. You should go to university. Your dad would like that. It'd make him proud, all warm and fuzzy inside. I see something in you. I feel this great soppy affection for your pasty gormless face, I could kiss you on the lips I could, hold you like my own son, you, me, Christmas turkey and bits of bacon round the sausage, yes I could, yes I can, and so you shall. You shall, boy. So you bloody shall."

This done, the man let the boy go, and his driver came back with chips – no salt, spare vinegar, malt not onion obviously – and Jacob Pritchard, king of the coast, bathed in petrol, blood and cheap French wine, got back into his car and drove away.

Four days later, a letter came from the school announcing that after due consideration the Sponsorship Committee was altering its decision, and the boy who would be Theo was very welcome to participate in its sponsored A-level scheme, and that he needed to provide ×4 pens (black), ×4 pens (blue), ×5 reams of ×250 sheets of lined white paper, ×6 large ring binders, ×3 small ring binders, ×100 paper plates and napkins and ×16 rolls of toilet paper for the sixth-form learning hub.

The day he started A levels, Dani Cumali began her student apprenticeship at Budgetfood's local fish-processing plant, where she maintained the fish-gut nets where the flies bred in order to produce maggots for the medicinal trade.

Very good at cleaning wounds your average maggot. They only actually eat dead flesh and that's why we value this by-product as a vital part of our environment consumer promise return strategy, bringing the company forward for the future.

Chapter 16

Time is

Theo isn't sure he knows what time is there is blood in his clothes in his hair in his fingers sometimes he sleeps and he dreams of

macaroni cheese

Helen in the snow in the ice in the

Dani Cumali, sat by the side of the couch

"Blessed are her hands blessed is the water beneath her fingers blessed are the stones at the bottom of the lake blessed are the roots that dig blessed is the moon that shines upon the ..."

The patty's prayer, the chant of those condemned to the prison work line, vanishes into the slop slop slop of water against the side of the boat and Theo

dreams.

Today's cards: nine of swords, five of swords, queen of cups, the Priestess, three of coins, knave of staves, the Moon (inverted), the Fool, the Hanged Man (inverted).

If only she knew the right question to ask, Neila felt sure that there would be a satisfactory answer in all of this.

The water pump at Cassiobridge Lock isn't working, and no one mans the gate.

Theo is awake, and walks to the prow of the boat as Neila begins cranking, the cold on the metal handle of the winch tearing through the double layers of wool and cotton on her hands, biting to the bone as she hauls open the sluice. He opens his mouth as if he might offer to help, then realises this is a silly idea and simply watches, waiting as the water rises, carrying the narrowboat up to the next level of the canal.

Neila's back curls into a circle, legs stiff castle buttresses as she heaves the gates shut behind them, ready for another passer-by. Theo watches and waits, hands buried inside his sleeves, shivering, as she comes back on board. She enters at the stern, past the engine, and he shuffles inside at the prow, closing the door behind him.

They eat lunch and it is
  very nice
  thank you it's very
  I don't have much you see but it's . . .
You were hurt. On the canal. There is a code on the canal you see but actually it's my principles that's more important to me, my sense of . . .
  I didn't do anything
Neila puts her spoon down in the bowl of chemical tomato soup, leans back in her folding chair, crosses her legs, says, "I read fortunes. Hands. Cards. I've got clients in Leighton Buzzard, and a pub in Tring has a psychic night and they said they'd have me. Nine years ago I was arrested for antisocial behaviour and criminal damage. I'd been protesting at the closing of a library. When I was a child we used to sing "the wheels on the bus" in the kids' section, but most people liked it for the DVDs. The police said we smashed a car. We had cardboard placards made from fruit-juice boxes. They gave me an indemnity of £17,000 or four years on the patty line. I paid the indemnity, and that took everything I had. Now I live on the canal. I thought it would be romantic. Sometimes it is. I spend most of my days thinking about fuel and drinking water. When I tell you to wait outside, you wait outside. Do you understand?"

Perhaps he did. He nodded, once, watching her.

"Some things are easier with two. Carrying coal, water, wood;

64

making repairs. The toilet has a tank which we'll need to pump out. Sometimes the pump freezes, then you have to do it by hand. The engine goes. Usually the coolant filter. Am I making myself clear here, I don't know if I'm making myself . . .

Before I read fortunes, I was a hairdresser. There's a woman in Water Eaton who swears she won't let anyone else touch her head. She has stories. I like her stories; she was a mayoress for a time, someone once buried a cow upside down in her front garden in protest at a planning permission, I hope the cow was dead first but imagine the effort. Getting the cow, getting the truck, getting the shovel, digging – the whole laying-the-corpse and they put the grass back too those hooves sticking in the air – are we good?" He nodded, but she repeated, firmer, one hand resting on the tabletop. "Are we good?"

Licked his lips, nodded again, harder. "Yes. We're good."

"Good. You should finish eating and rest. When you're feeling ready, I'll take you through the basics of the boat."

Chapter 17

Ring ring ring ring!

      Ring ring destiny is calling!
    ring ring ring ring

In Tulse Hill, lying on his belly, Theo struggles to wake, and only answered because he didn't recognise her number.

Dani said, "Theo?"

        He didn't speak, phone frozen, breath caught, mouth closing behind it.

"Are you there? I know you can hear me. Listen. Listen. I've fucked up. I've fucked up and now they're going to … I've fucked up."

This wasn't sadness or self-pity. Fact upon fact, truth that was necessary to be spoken. "Are you there?"

"I'm here," he replied, groggy.

"They're going to come and get me. I need you to … "

"I can't talk to you."

"Lucy is your daughter."

The words settled between them.

Theo looked round his room and remembered again how small and stupid and soulless it was, wondered why he bothered folding his pants. Did that make him mad? Pants could just be shoved into the drawer, there was room after all.

"Lucy is your daughter," repeated Dani. "She's your daughter."

Silence on the line.

A collision of probabilities – a coin thrown one hundred

times lands on heads one hundred times, and yet that does not mean that it must land on tails. Mean, median, middle, count backwards from the date of birth and maybe, the thinnest of maybes, and then what equation do you use for this moment, how do you equate her need, her lies, the truth, how do you even begin to . . .

"I . . . don't believe you," mumbled Theo. "I don't believe you."

"I didn't rat you out. Lucy's your daughter – I'd never snitch, whatever you've done, I'd never snitch, I thought that maybe . . . she's your daughter. Lucy is your daughter. She's yours. I went looking for some way to bring her back, and you wouldn't help me so I did it myself. Listen. I don't have much time. There's this woman, her name is Helen, she's seen the pits, she's got the . . .

Lucy is your daughter. I love her. I haven't seen her for fourteen years and I still love her, how fucked up is that? They've been watching me. I don't care what happens to me, but you've gotta use this shit, you hear me? You've gotta get her out before it's too late."

"Dani, it's not—"

"I can prove it. I can prove that they broke it. They broke everything. They broke the world. Can you hear me? I know you can hear me. I know you're there. I know you know it's true. You knew the moment you heard her birthday you knew you just didn't . . .

Lucy is your daughter. She's yours now. Don't fuck it up."

He closed his eyes.

"Where are you?"

He cycled from Tulse Hill to Sidcup. The trains stopped at 23.45, and the taxi ride was more than he could pay.

He had to swing wide to avoid the New Cross Gate enclave, the marks of the tribes painted white in dark streets, the smell of gasoline, the cracks in the road. Some places just couldn't get the corporate sponsorship, so people gave up, if they won't, can't, won't, whatever – what do you expect from the scroungers, the whiners, the mums who shouldn't have got pregnant, the dads who can't be redeemed, the druggies who just need to get over themselves seriously, like, just stop taking the fucking drugs it's not so hard it's not so . . .

Everyone avoided the enclaves. Sometimes the odd journalist would go inside, or stand by the gates with armed security out of shot, and the desperate ones – the children with no family left to call their own, the old biddies who liked to dine on flash-fried cat, the sewer-crawlers and the ones who picked their way through the landfills – before those were sold off to the parole companies and patties brought in from the patty line to go through the waste – they would shuffle and lurch and glare at the camera, and by their cracked faces and their brutal ugliness it was very clear that they were not human any more, and only knew how to resent and hate the intrusion of beautiful people into their scurrying lives.

"You! Off the bike on the ground now!! Get down get down you . . . "

The men at Blackheath had come so hard and fast out of the reinforced steel gate, Tasers up and ready to fire, that Theo nearly fell off his bike as he swung to avoid them, skidding and dropping hard onto one leg, ankle buckling against the tarmac.

"I'm lost I'm just lost I'm not I'm just lost!"

"Identification!"

"I don't have any I left it at home I'm going to see a friend my friend she's going into labour she can't afford the hospital she's going into labour I got turned round please the child is mine the child is . . . "

Why did he use that excuse? He wasn't sure, but clearly he sounded convincing enough because the men walked him back to the end of the street, pointed him at Sidcup and, quieter, wished him good luck and told him to be careful not to pedal too close to the gated communities, rare bubbles of wealth clinging to the railway lines, lest security take it personally.

Walls around the enclaves to keep the wild things in; walls around the sanctuaries, deluxe lifestyle housing estates and gated villages to keep the wild things out. These decisions had never been government policy. It had just worked out that way.

The lights of London stretched out behind, the brightness where the electricity flowed, the circles of darkness where the council didn't pay its bills, the zones where the insurance companies wouldn't go, rationed down to their mandatory six hours a day of illumination.

Flashes of light on the side of the road.

A Chinese takeaway, a golden cat in the window perpetually fascist-saluting a marching parade.

The off-licence, never closed, two boys outside trying to muster the courage to pinch a bag of crisps.

Bin-crawlers, tearing through the tips and overflowing plastic bins in search of things to burn, sell, melt or make.

A man ran out into the middle of the street as he pedalled down the final stretch towards the M20 approach, threw himself towards the bicycle – for a moment Theo thought he was in pain, needed help, he skidded to avoid hitting him and only then saw the other two men coming towards him, one on a low stunt bicycle that bounced and hugged the road, the other on foot, running to grab the handlebars, and with a snarl of unexpected fury he pushed harder on the pedals and kicked the man who'd lunged squarely in the chest as he pedalled by, outpacing his pursuers in a few streets of wind-blasted night.

There was no wall around the enclave where Dani lived, but three women guarded the entrance, hunkered down on a cracked bench by the main road, a barrier of rusted chain slung between two lamp posts, torches in their hands. As he approached one rose, shone a light in his eyes, grunted, "Who're you?"

"My name is Theo. I'm here for Dani Cumali."

"This is the women's place. The men don't come in here."

"I'm a friend of Dani's."

"This is the women's place!" she repeated, higher, angry. "This is our place!"

"She called me. She said it was urgent." Then, feeling almost ashamed: "She has a daughter."

A flicker, a scowl. "Wait here."

The women communed, heads together like the closed petals of a thorny flower, opened, returned to Theo, barked, "You got a phone?"

"Yes."

"Gimme the phone, wallet. We'll look after the bike. You get 'em back when you're done."

"She called me, she . . . "

"You deaf? We guard them."

Theo hesitated, then dismounted, let the woman take the bike by the handlebars, handed over his mobile phone and wallet. The woman pointed up a flagstone alley towards a low run of grey concrete buildings. "Cumali. She's in there, with the faders and the ones who bite. Try not to make a ruckus, yeah?"

Theo nodded and followed the line of her finger.

At his back, he thought he heard her whisper, murmurs to the faint white stain against the clouds where the moon huddled. Blessed is the moonlight through the cage blessed are those who weave and those who break blessed is the mother as she walks upon the mountain stone blessed is . . .

There was a concrete patio in front of the long, low concrete building with a metal roof where Dani lived. A few cracked plastic pots contained the remnants of grey shrubs and the occasional burst of yellow-petalled marigolds. Someone had made the effort of sweeping the leaves from the nearby trees into a corner, but hadn't had anything else to do with them, so slowly they blew back in tidelines. A privet hedge ran between the frosted-glass front doors of each apartment block. Very few lights burned. A generator grumbled somewhere behind low walls, scenting the air with diesel.

Theo found Dani's door by the light cast from the tower block opposite it. A long glass window was dark on the ground floor; a flag hung across showed a faded image of a giraffe in yellow and orange, walking away from a setting sun, head turned towards the earth.

One light shone dull on the first floor, glowing from a cracked-open window, the head of the lamp tilted back into the illuminated room. An arm moved across the light, casting a tentacle shadow over a wall, before flickering back down to darkness. Theo knocked on the front door, inaudibly. He knocked a little louder, and instantly felt afraid, looked around, wondering who'd been woken by the sound. Nothing moved, no shadows stirred. He reached out to try again, and a flicker of light caught his eye. The light vanished. A moment later it appeared again, a square of blue-white within the biting grip of the privet hedge. A mobile phone, confused by its present condition, pressing against the net of twigs that supported it, slipping steadily downwards. The motion of its slow descent through the hedge was setting off a sensor, waking and sleeping the screen. He could see the hollow it had already carved, torn leaves and snapped wood. It looked like it had landed in the hedge with some force. It looked like it hadn't been there for very long. He hesitated, then reached in. The screen was locked, the greasy journey a dirty thumb took across it clearly visible. He turned it over, glanced up and round and wondered if this was a test, couldn't fathom what kind, put the phone in his pocket and, moving now a little faster, feeling his heart tap-dance a head-spinning rush, pushed on the front door, testing it.

It opened on the latch, only a little pressure needed. He stepped inside, a smell of sticky dry beer, damp laundry and cigarette smoke on the air. Once the place had held a family, two parents, two kids, three at a squeeze. Now every room had been subdivided, padlocks put across the doors, nine people to a toilet. People liked to claim it was where the scroungers went, the traitors who couldn't get a job and had lived off the charity of the state, before the Company had moved in and sorted things out, businesslike, making sure people who didn't try couldn't get.

No one admitted that the enclaves held the bin men, cleaners, waiters, janitors, porters, shelf-stackers, carers who wiped the old women's bums, bus drivers and health assistants too skint to afford anywhere else. Everyone has to make a choice, the Company said. You have to choose success.

71

From the back of the building a lilt of guitar, played by a woman singing to herself, a glow of candlelight from beneath her door. From a door to the left the low grey buzz of a TV, playing through the night to the sleeping couple tangled in each other's limbs across the rustled mattress. Theo felt his way up the stairs, carpet giving way to lino, squeaking like an arthritic rat beneath his feet. A light beneath the door on the first floor, from which a woman's voice, hushed, spoke on a phone. He approached slowly, knocked once, barely brushing the painted chipboard with his knuckles. No answer, but the door was not locked or bolted, and the woman's voice continued, so he pushed it open.

The woman inside was tall, unusually so, with short yellow hair cut to a soft fall one side of her face. She wore a black T-shirt, black jeans and a pair of red wellington boots. Her arms were gently toned from light exercise, her neck was long and unadorned, her eyes were grey, her lips were pale, she held a mobile phone pressed against her ear and a 9mm pistol in her other hand, a silencer on the end. A light freckling of blood stained her face and bare skin, and probably her clothes, though Theo wasn't sure. A larger stain of blood and brain matter covered the wall behind the loosely made single bed in the centre of the room, still warm, still seeping down. A pair of feet stuck out from behind the bed, on the side away from the door. They were bare. They could have belonged to anyone. They belonged to Dani.

He couldn't see her face.

He couldn't imagine there was much of her face to see.

A little mass of matter, grey brain, shards of white bone, brilliant crimson blood, no bigger than a pinball, went *schloop* and detached itself by its own weight from where it had stuck to the wall, splatted onto the bedside table. The wardrobe, its door hanging by one hinge, was open. There was a bloody handprint on the handle. Clothes had been torn from their hangers and lay across the floor. A syringe, empty, sat on the sheets, small with a tiny needle point. A laptop stood open, the screen bright blue and welcoming.

The woman with the gun smiled at Theo in the door, a flicker of recognition not of familiarity, but of an awkward situation in need of a little resolution

tilted the gun a little, not threatening

requesting a moment of patience while she finished her conversation on the phone, so sorry, terribly rude, if you don't mind just holding on a moment . . . ?

She said, "Uh-huh. Uh-huh. Yes. That's right." She spelled out a postcode one letter at a time, "Sierra, echo . . . yes, echo . . . "

Theo stood in the door, the light from a single bedside lamp skimming across his feet and knees before fading into shadow behind him.

"Homicide. Yes, that's right. Yes, I am the killer. No, you're my first call. Yes, I can wait. What do you estimate as being your response time? That's fine. Thank you. Of course I can hold. Thanks."

This done, she turned the phone to one side, pressed it so the mouthpiece was buried in her shoulder, tilted her head the other way and, smiling at Theo, added, "So sorry – the police are on their way. Now if you just make like a heron, I can be with you in a mo."

Theo stands in the door, and wonders what a heron would make like. One leg high, one leg in the water, frozen in the act of catching a fish.

The woman went back to the phone. "Uh-huh. Uh-huh. Yes, two to the head, two to the chest. No witnesses but someone has just . . . Oh . . . "

Theo walked away.

Three women wait by the entrance to the estate
    one holds his bike, his mobile phone, wallet
    "That was quick," she says.
    "Dani is dead," he replied, taking his bike.
    "You kill her?" A flicker of anger, but it's deep, beneath the resignation, expectation. This was what happened.
    "No. The killer is still in there. She's just called the police."
    "Fuck. Mum's gonna kill me if the cops wake her tonight."

73

"Thank you for looking after my bike."
"The cops, for real?"
"Yes."
"And Dani's dead? Oh this is just the total fucking . . ."
Theo on his bike, pedalling into the night.

There are the streets
          this is the city
                    these are the darknesses that seemed to
threaten but turned out to be merely void, a place where
                              this is what brain sounds like as
a bit of it peels away from the wall, *schlooop*, and drops, *splat*,
onto a carpeted floor. If the floor was not carpeted it might have
sounded different and if anyone bothers to clean it then they'll
probably use a vacuum cleaner, something specially designed to
get at the dried bits basically it's like cleaning meat but really you
need a new carpet and
                    this is the man called Theo, riding away,
at the centre of the universe
     these are the times when the night is
               these are the words that
                         bang! Who'd have thought that the
gun wasn't loaded with blanks after all and splat down he goes
breathing breathing not breathing any more it's not your fault
you know that it's not your fault that
     this is the day Dani realised that dreams were for children
                    the news when the government announced
that corporations ran things so much better than civil servants
and it'd be better for everyone if the MPs focused on important
things like
     like
               well, whatever was left when the teachers, doctors
and judges were gone
     this is the dream where Theo still dreams of his father dying,
though he wasn't there, he never saw all he has is imagination of
the prison and the end

This is Theo, at three o'clock in the morning, cycling home from a murder scene, wondering why he doesn't cry.

This is Theo, at three o'clock in the morning, lying awake on a canal boat pointing north, and behind the curtain that keeps him separate from his host, a stranger who has made him tea and asked no questions, and now he puts his hands over his face to hide his eyes, and in silence cries like the summer rain.

Chapter 18

When the boy who would be Theo was six months away from finishing A levels his agricultural studies teacher said:

"You know you could really make something of yourself you could indeed you could you could do accountancy for Budgetfood! Or work in the logistics division or the management department you could be a real player, a real player in the world of microwave meal distribution you could even run for corporate councillor if you worked hard, kept your nose to the grindstone like this you could have a lovely house with three bedrooms and two bathrooms, two bathrooms now that's something to look forward to that's something!"

And three days later his maths teacher said:

"Get out. Get out while you can. You are young. You still have a chance to live. You can still be free. I know your dad was . . . but that's not who you are, you don't have to be . . . you have a talent you could get out just get out and be . . . "

Sitting on the beach with Dani Cumali, staring at the water as it dragged at the shingle, a bit of stained dark sand visible beneath, a sound like the clattering of crab's claws across a skull as the ocean rolled, he said:

"I was thinking of applying for university."

And Dani looked at him, and blurted, "That's the most fucking stupid thing I've ever heard. Do you seriously think they'd have you? I mean look at you, where are you gonna get the cash? Where are you gonna get the references – what the fuck do you

76

think you'd do with yourself, you can't get out there isn't any way out there isn't . . . "

And then she stopped, and looked at the sea, and knew that no amount of washing could flush away the stench of fish intestine, stomach, heart, eye, head, skin and scale from her skin, and that the maggots as they dropped into the collection bags beneath the nets would go to eat the wounds of rich men in places far, far away, and that her contract would not be renewed and that dreams were for children and she was a grown-up now. Grown-ups just dealt with things. They carried on – that's what being grown-up meant. She wrapped her arms around the boy who would be Theo and said:

"You should do it. I think it sounds great. I wish I was coming with you."

And he held her tight, and they watched the sea.

He wasn't surprised to find the man sitting in his mum's favourite chair. Mum always hated Jacob Pritchard, said he was a bad influence, a bad, bad influence it was his fault that . . .

But her benefits had been stopped because she was fit for work (though no one would hire her) and if no one would hire her in Shawford she just had to look elsewhere (there was nowhere to go) but somehow they'd kept going, paid the gas, paid the electric and will you look . . .

. . . there's Jacob Prichard now, rolling his mum's favourite glass bauble between his ringed fingers, a swan with cloudy blue pigment in its base. They say that once a Dutchman bringing petrol over the Channel tried to double-cross him, and his feet washed up in Lowestoft.

"So," he mused, as Theo put his school bag down and sat silent in the chair opposite him. "I hear you wanna go make something better of yourself. Mate of mine said Oxford was the business, but if you wanna go somewhere with fewer wankers I won't stop you. Your choice, boy. Your choice."

The day after the boy's eighteenth birthday, there was a bank deposit in his favour.

His dad had always kept his mouth shut about the job that landed him in the nick, and though Jacob Pritchard wasn't involved in that sort of thing, not theft, especially not those little blue pills for the

well, you know

he respected a man who knew not to grass.

Respect was important to men. One day, when Mike's boy was all grown up, he'd understand that too.

Dani saw him onto the train to London, a transfer for Oxford in his pocket.

She didn't stay on the platform once he boarded; there was this new guy she was going to watch TV with, but she felt it was important to be there, to say goodbye, tell him his face was stupid, absolutely refuse to cry.

He emailed, of course, in the first few weeks.

Told her about college, classes, some of the people he'd met. The boy in the room next to his was called Theo Miller, and was unbelievably posh, but also kinda nice, like, a nice kid just a bit . . . you know . . .

Dani replied sometimes. She'd met this guy, he was good, it was good. Her apprenticeship was ending; she was hoping to be bumped up on to a full-time contract or at least a fixed-term or maybe even just a six-month contract, out of the fish department into something better like packaging.

After a while his emails became less regular as the work piled up.

She stopped replying.

She was not offered a contract in packaging.

three-month fixed-term contract fourteen hours a week as a cleaning colleague 5 p.m.–7 p.m.

She supplemented her income working the local café 8 a.m.– 4 p.m., and that sort of saw her through a bit. And this one time she went to this class down the local church hall where they were making jewellery from recycled stuff from the beach like these pebbles but also washed-up glass and bits of plastic and metal and things and she thought she'd like to do that, as a hobby maybe. But finding the time was really tough because they met at 7.30 p.m. and sometimes she didn't finish work until 7.10 and then they did these spot-check searches on employees leaving the building and that could take twenty minutes and so by the time she got to the hall it was all finishing anyway and . . .

If Theo noticed that she was no longer replying to his emails, when they came

rarely when they came

he didn't say anything.

He told her that he was thinking of joining the rowing club, but that actually maybe he wasn't right for it after all. The guys who did that sort of thing, they'd done it a lot before and he hadn't – though he could handle a boat all right, but they didn't seem to think that would be enough; he didn't have the attitude.

The attitude, you see the attitude was . . .

and Theo

the real Theo Miller, the boy in the room next door, laughed and said:

"Fuck them! Fuck them. Come on, you know I'm right! Fuck them all. Let's have gin."

And maybe he'd underestimated his neighbour after all, and he was all right deep down.

Chapter 19

On the canal Neila said, "Oh, so you've done some sailing before."

Theo replied, "I grew up by the sea. I mean we didn't do much, my dad ran this local youth club, mostly football but also sailing sometimes, although mostly it was money laundering. Mostly . . . that. I think he liked the kids, though. He coached the under-11s. They did well and . . ."

For a while they sat on the back of the barge, Neila watching as Theo guided it round the lazy bends towards Marsworth Locks. After much consideration, they had removed the blood-soaked padding that pressed across his side, and for the first time Theo had seen the stitching she'd done and stared a long while before finally murmuring, a little green around the cheeks,

"Is that . . . cornflower blue?"

Her eyes flickered from the thread that held his side together to the embroidery on the wall, and she swallowed. "Yes. Well, it's what you have to hand, isn't it?"

At Marsworth they moored for the night opposite the water pump, and Neila turned the handle but no water came, just the chunk chunk chunk of air and ice deep within the iron, and she declared, "No showers, I think. Not for a little while."

They ate sliced bread with jam and margarine, and Theo sat at the back of the boat wearing his oversized stranger's woollen coat over his grey bloodstained jumper, and two pairs of socks and long johns beneath his tracksuit bottoms. He stank, but so did she, and after a while you just got used to these things.

And when the sun rose they began to climb through the

locks, heading east where the canal branched, and she opened and closed the gates and he sat with one hand on the rudder on a little wooden stool and waited for her command and it was . . .

. . . all things considered . . .

easier with two than it was with one, and she couldn't remember the last time she had cleared Marsworth so quickly.

The *Hector* sailed for Northampton.

Time on the water is

Neila would argue that it is the purest time which obeys only the laws of nature.

Dawn dusk

Winter summer

It is the time that must be taken to do the thing that needs to be done. It is not a time for

meetings conference calls texting email commuting running late jogging committing failing counting seconds until

Until whatever it is that seemed so important at the time, has ended.

At Bletchley Neila rambled: "The Company runs things – I mean they always have what are you going to do about it it's just how . . ."

And saw Theo's face, and stopped talking, and felt strangely embarrassed.

Half a mile later three men and a woman came the other way on a wide barge covered in tarps, and as they passed the woman slowed and called out across the water, "Are you going to Milton Keynes? There's nothing there. They closed the ski slope and they don't play hockey any more. The cows were taken up from the roundabouts and sold to a man who owns things. There's only patties, children and screamers there now, apart from the sanctuaries, and they shoot strangers. You don't want to go to Milton Keynes. If you go, if you see my daughter, tell her that

I didn't mean the things I said. I didn't mean them, it's just the meds. She'll understand."

Neila smiled and didn't answer, and Theo went inside and checked the bandages where he was bleeding again, and couldn't be bothered to change them, and didn't want to make a fuss.

Chapter 20

These are the rituals of Theo's life:

Up, run, 10km on a Saturday, trailing along at the back of a park jogging group who all sort of know each other vaguely enough to smile but not well enough to ask anyone their name.

Bicycle to work

murder rape arson abuse neglect negligence conspiracy fraud . . .

In the evenings he'd stop off at the supermarket in Balham. He didn't go there often, but there were ingredients he couldn't find elsewhere, and he'd overload his basket and struggle back to Mrs Italiaander's in second gear, huffing and puffing through the clogged-up traffic to get home and make

fish grilled with red peppers

lemon mushroom risotto

roast feta and black olive salad

aubergine and tomato baked with balsamic vinegar

When he first moved in, Theo worried that he was hogging the kitchen, had tried to keep every meal fast, take up no space on the long black counter. After a while he'd realised that he was almost the only resident who liked cooking at all. Marvin lived on microwave meals and takeaways – some of Budgetfood's products no less. Theo had tried to tell him about where it came from, about Shawford and the sea, but Marvin didn't pretend to care.

Mrs Italiaander lived on the same meal every day, which consisted of two slices of wholegrain, seed-studded bread, toasted without butter; an onion cut in half and microwaved, a couple of slices of smoked salmon, half a pot of yoghurt, some celery sticks, with hummus on Tuesdays and Fridays only, and a half-bottle of rosé wine.

Nikesh made curries with paste from a jar, to which he added whole chillies and a tablespoon of salt.

Every six or seven weeks Theo made food for everyone, though no one ate at the same time, and his contract was always peacefully renewed, and Mrs Italiaander whispered that he was almost like a son to her and not to tell her boy she felt that way.

Sometimes, when it was raining or there was something he really wanted to see, Theo went to the cinema. A local art-house place had installed screens in the basement where you could watch documentaries from its archive for no more than the price of an expensive cup of coffee. Once he'd got locked in when the cleaner hadn't spotted him, hunkered down in his alcove, watching a film about the hunting birds of Patagonia.

On the first Sunday of every month he helped the local community gardening group with their planting boxes down by the rookery, and one April he shared shovels with a woman called Celeste who had been funny and clever and beautiful and

Theo didn't have many friends

. . . but she'd checked her horoscope the morning after, and it warned that Saturn was entering an unwelcome aspect, and he was a Taurus and she didn't want to argue with the stars. Who did really?

They met again at the monthly gardening group and smiled at each other, but now the whimsy and the merriment that he had found enchanting before seemed frankly infantile and very, very annoying.

The morning after the night before . . .

Theo must have slept because he wakes and he is screaming, his head is screaming. He read once upon a time about a thing, exploding-head syndrome so your head doesn't actually explode but you feel like it's going bang boom a bomb going off in his skull

SHE'S YOUR DAUGHTER!

And then he sleeps again, and wakes, ashamed that he slept at all, and wasn't kept awake by the image of Dani's face/brains/blood by the guilt of . . .

         . . . of things he probably should be feeling guilty about he wasn't sure he had hoped for a certain clarity at least but even that was

He slept in his clothes, face down, a little wet pool of dribble on his pillow where he fell. Twelve hours ago Dani Cumali lived; now she is dead, and Theo's thighs ache from cycling, and he lies on his bed wide awake exactly two minutes before his alarm is due to go off, and his head is . . .

The pain already fading, with the rising light of dawn.

A grey sweep of a grey day across a world unchanged.

He looks out of the window.

Mrs Italiaander's front garden is almost entirely rose bush, which does not flower, and castor oil plant. If she ever loses patience with her family, she threatens to turn it into ricin for that truly cataclysmic Christmas dinner party. She read about it online. It's not that hard really . . .

Beyond, the world carries on.

Children are hurried out of bed

milk into cereal bowls

showers

steam

heat on tired muscles sigh of relief

tying shoelaces

checking the phone

rattling the rubbish cart down the street

smell of the bus

hiss of pneumatic door

Dani Cumali is dead and the world

continues.

And Theo Miller also.

Chapter 21

Theo took the train to work, and immediately remembered why he never did and how much he hated it.

He arrived five minutes late. Usually arriving late earned a place on the Efficiency Wall, where photos of shamed members of staff who were not holding up departmental standards were displayed. However, Theo was never late, never, and rather than the ritual chiding, he received an automatically generated email informing him that he had been docked one hour's pay, and a concerned knock on the door from Edward's secretary, El, asking him if he was okay.

"I'm fine. Think I'm coming down with something."

"Ah, yes . . ." she muttered, and beat a hasty retreat to the antibacterial gel she kept in the bottom drawer of her desk.

Words on a screen.

beaten to death with a clothes iron

run over then run over again three times he drove the car until she was

dropped the child out of the window

claims he didn't realise how hard he was hitting until it was too late

a kitchen knife, the relationship had been deteriorating for

When Theo's calendar beeped, reminding him of the weekly team performance meeting, he nearly laughed.

Sat at the back.

Did his best not to fall asleep.

Returned to his desk.

Forgot to eat lunch.

set on fire after school because she called her fat

strangled after refusing to consider marriage with the man in

trapped between the cot and the wall suffocated to death

police investigation fee: £7891.56 (ex. VAT)

societal responsibility levy: £81,000

victim assessment fee: £128,918

no. of pets left behind by deceased: 3

value of pets: £5680

cost of rehousing pets: £675

But hey! The cats have already been spayed otherwise that'd be another £240 on the indemnity for the killer to pay, can't have non-spayed cats running around it'd be . . .

Dependent children remaining to deceased: 1.

Age of child: 7.

Added value of dependent minor: £18,900, plus a further £2715 because the child witnessed her mother die and will thus require mandatory counselling with a recommended sponsor who will charge . . .

will charge . . .

a fee equivalent to . . .

on an hourly basis of . . .

Theo realised he'd been staring at nothing, and started hard enough to knock his empty coffee cup off the desk.

It tumbled to the floor, the handle cracking off the side, the rest of the ceramic surviving in one piece. He picked the handle up gingerly, wrapped it in tissue paper, put it in his bag. Maybe he'd be able to stick it back on. Superglue or tile grout or . . . something. Gripfill, perhaps.

Email.

A defendant had settled his indemnity, selling off a two-bedroom flat in Putney to cover the cost. Because he'd done so without taking the matter to court, he achieved a 10 per cent discount on the murder of his mother-in-law, thus taking the total profit to the department to a mere ...

But the woman on her third shoplifting charge had already sold her mother's wedding ring and the indemnity was overdue so her case was to be referred to the prison service for labour rehabilitation, making something useful for society, like circuit boards for mobile phones, or those glasses that don't have any lenses in to make you look cool, or face serum guaranteed to keep you both firm and soft all at once.

Theo looked away, marked the email as unread, went to the toilet, sat in the locked cubicle with his pants around his ankles, realised he had no idea what he was doing, sat a while longer, felt ridiculous, went back to work.

At 4.55 the new case arrived.

It hadn't gone to him initially. But Charlotte Burgess, who specialised in well-paying homicides, had taken one look and done some quick maths – cause of death, manner of arrest, value of deceased – and concluded that the matter was fairly open-and-shut and couldn't bring in more than £60,000, which wouldn't count for much on her performance review so ...

she sent it on.

Which was silly really, because if she'd looked closely she would have seen the discretion clause that any wise auditor could squeeze for at least another £90,000 if they played it right.

Hey, Theo. This arrived, but I'm snowed under. Can you take a look at it? Thanks! xx

All of Charlotte's emails ended with two kisses. She'd once signed off to a high court judge with *snuggles and lols!* and the judge hadn't known what these words meant, and assumed it was just a youth thing.

Theo opened the case file.

Homicide, suspect arrested and full confession given. Status: pending assessment.

Dani Cumali.

It occurred to him that he'd only seen her feet.

And her brain of course but actually the brain on the wall, her bare feet pointing upwards these weren't much to go by and he'd sort of assumed, he'd just thought well there it is, here we are but thinking about it he'd only really . . .

He opened the file.

The front of her face was remarkably intact, given the two bullets that had entered it. The back of her skull had taken most of the damage when the bullets exited, bursting open like an overheated pudding.

The bruising across the rest of her body was almost black, the blood congealing between broken arteries post-mortem.

A photo was attached of the killer.

Her name was Seph Atkins, and the cops suspected this was an alias.

Seph Atkins had called the police almost the second Dani's body hit the floor. A transcript was attached.

"Yes, I'd like to report a homicide . . . I'm sorry do you need to . . . yes, homicide, that's right. No, I did it. Yes. Yes. The address is . . . as in sierra, echo . . . yes, echo . . . what do you estimate as being your response time? Yes, that's fine. Thank you. Of course I can hold. Thanks."

And then in the distance, the sound of faint words, as if the killer was holding her phone against her shoulder, muffling her words, addressing someone else. The transcriber couldn't decipher what was said, but Theo knew the words, heard the truth of it.

"Now if you just make like a heron . . ."

He closed the file, copied it to a USB stick, put the stick in his pocket and went home twenty minutes early. Such action might have caused something of a stir, but it being Theo, no one really noticed.

Chapter 22

Nearly fifteen years before Dani died, the boy who would be Theo took the train to Oxford. He had imagined that Oxford was always bathed in autumn sunlight, but when he arrived it was raining, and despite his best efforts he couldn't seem to get invitations to any of those dinner clubs where they served whole roast pig and performed sexual acts with . . .

. . . well, he didn't know if he believed the rumours, but everyone said it was the best thing to do if you wanted to get ahead in life.

He imagined he'd live on a quadrangle overlooking immaculate lawns, in rooms with high walls and medieval locks. His hall of residence was certainly near an immaculate lawn, but had been tacked on in the 1980s as a discreet extension, and featured disappointingly modern electromagnetic key fobs.

He kept to himself. Sent Dani the odd email. Answered the phone when his mum called, and when they'd gone too long without talking would call her and they'd chat for an average of forty-three seconds.

"Hi, Mum."

"Oh, you called. How nice. Yes. Very nice of you to call, yes, good that you remembered well I'm all right. I'm all right and I'm doing well it was good of you to call."

"I wanted to see if you were . . . "

"Good of you to call, you are a good boy. Well, that's lovely. Goodbye!"

Mum didn't like to intrude in his life.

*

One day – at the beginning of all things, a new spring and a new season – when the rain had stopped and the sun was wet through the leaves

He stepped outside his room to find his neighbour also in the corridor, a skinny boy with the same dark hair and drooping shoulders as himself, and the boy said:

"Hello."

"Hello."

"We must be neighbours."

"Yes."

"It's all a little surreal, isn't it? Us, here, this place. Fount of learning and all that, passing the port to the left, snuff after dinner."

"Yeah."

"Are you doing law?"

"No, maths."

"Oh, maths! I can't understand maths at all, can't get my head around it, just like, hello no! Very impressive, maths, although I suppose at your level it's less about numbers and more about . . . ideas, yes?"

"I don't know yet."

"No, early days I imagine, early days and . . . my name's Theo. Theo Miller."

"Hello, Theo Miller," said the boy who would be Theo.

"Are you . . . have you met anyone yet?"

"No. I don't know anyone."

"Me neither! It's going to be a disaster. Say, shall we be disastrous together?"

Later, a little drunk, which was the obligatory thing to be between the hours of 7 p.m. and midnight:

"Family's a catastrophe. My family – Christ! So my dad's one of the biggest rubbish collectors in northern Europe. Don't laugh, he is, it's how he made his fortune, but he was also a survivor of the Scottish troubles, said he saw things during the campaigns that were . . . so he collects art. All these pictures of broken faces and wounded eyes, all these sculptures, bones and flesh in porcelain, things coming out of other things, I grew up with that can you imagine I grew up with—"

"Theo . . ."

"You don't even notice these things until someone points them out and then you're like yes, fuck me, yes, that is a bit fucking off actually, isn't it? And Mother, well, he never really loved her, I think. I mean, at the beginning, she was something young and beautiful after his first marriage – and then after the divorce he remarried and she was younger but also a good woman, amazing woman just the most – and I love my mother too but other Mum always did her best. I was mostly raised by Aunty – that was what we called my nanny – Aunty – she was the one who was there for me while Mum and Dad went sailing because I wasn't allowed to go sailing, I got in the way but anyway—"

"Theo, what is claret?"

"Something French. So there they are, sailing around the world and me I'm in boarding school, and with the schemes of course I ended up here and you know they forget my birthday but Aunty remembers, Aunty has always been—"

"I'm not sure I like claret."

"You won't last long in Oxford if you can't drink port or claret, believe me, more that's just what you need some more of it there you go and anyway what about your family what about—"

"Can I tell you a secret?"

"Of course! I'm a drunken ex-boarding-school lawyer-in-the-making! Your secrets are my sacred practice. Or duty. Whatever."

"My father was the driver for a mob, my mum is kinda mad, and the only reason I'm here is because the biggest petrol smuggler in Kent threatened to kill the dean's dog unless they let me in. As a favour, you see, for my dad, who's in prison, cos of the pharmaceutical job."

"Really?"

"Yeah."

"Well that does put Eton rather into perspective."

*

The boy who would one day be Theo sat next to the real Theo, the one born to the name, and ate strawberries on the grass and worried about stains on his gown and watched the sparrows fly between the pale brown spires of the college and thought that there was probably something he was missing, something very important which he'd forgotten and if only . . .

And the real Theo

the one who died, said:

"Oxford is beautiful – of course it's beautiful! I mean it's not real, but in a way it's so *real* because it's the old place, the place of facts – it's shaped the world but all the people dressed as wizards that's a bit . . . "

Somewhere out towards the suburbs, a fence is being put up to keep the riff-raff out. It's not that they're selling PhDs these days, not at all, candidates for the fast-track PhD programme have to hand in a 2000-word essay and complete an interview before making payment for their certificate. If you pay an extra £40,000 they'll even hire a couple of MA students to write a full-length dissertation for you. That's just how things are. They've always been that way, money was always what mattered, but the beauty of this system is that we're honest about it. It's just good business.

"Dad's selling the business to the Company, of course. It's not like they want it or need it, it's just that it's making a profit and they're making a profit so they may as well invest in something which makes more of a profit. He's going to stay on as a non-exec and I mean that's the castle in Scotland sorted, surprisingly cheap castles in Scotland if you buy them run-down then a few mil to refurbish that's what he says and the Company is very interested in . . . "

It occurs to Theo, later, that this was around the time people started to talk about the Company. Not a company, which owned a company which owned . . . but *the* Company. The one that owned it all. It had always been there. It was never a secret. Only now it owns so many things that it might as well own it all.

In a few months' time the real Theo Miller will be dead, BANG, and the boy who steals his name will slink back to Shawford and there will be a night with Dani Cumali on the beach

"Off to your fancy university your fancy friends . . ."

"I heard you and Andy, I mean that . . ."

After.

Dani and the boy who would be Theo lay together on shingle and it was deeply uncomfortable and rather cold but no one wanted to break the spell – not him, not her, so they lay tangled and it was . . .

The morning after, as Theo walked towards Dani's flat in the morning, bag on his back, head full of dreams of redemption and hope and the future, he saw Dani coming the other way, Andy slung across her shoulders, his arm across her back, owning her, pushing her down with his weight, pulling her along with his walk, and his eyes met Dani's and he saw . . .

All the truth written in them.

She pretended not to know him, as she and her boyfriend swaggered past, and he pretended not to know them either, and got on the first replacement bus service back to Dover Priory and when the train juddered to a halt in Ashford and sat for twenty minutes creaking and broken on the tracks, the boy who would be Theo threw his phone out of the window and never looked back.

Later he realised he was an idiot and that was a perfectly good handset he'd destroyed, he should have just jettisoned the SIM card, but at the time it felt like a gesture that mattered.

Chapter 23

The day after Dani Cumali died

 the man called Theo took a USB stick with the details of her murder home with him

  put it on the small plywood desk

  took out a mobile phone.

 The phone was a hefty brick, grey in colour. He'd found it in a privet hedge, thrown from a window.

  It still held its charge.

  He turned it off.

  Turned it on.

  Turned it off again.

 He sat on the end of his bed while in the room next door Marvin played bad music far too loud.

  He went downstairs and made pasta.

  Sat back on the end of his bed.

  Fell asleep in his clothes.

In the morning the phone was still there, and Dani was still dead, and he still had to audit the value of her life and death.

 Theo cycled to work, looked at the route as if for the first time, seeing now the phone repair shops, the laundrettes offering patch jobs on torn trousers, the chippy with a sign in the window explaining how fish was so much better than pizza

  children, going to school

  lunchboxes

  brushed hair

uniforms
texting
shuffling
running
he
nearly cycled into the back of a bus, slammed on the brakes, heard someone shout from an open window, "You're a vegetable!"

Laugh.

Cycled a little more carefully to work.

And work was . . .

She killed her because she was looking at her. She knew just knew that if she didn't move now it was going to be . . .

He said I did it. Sure I did it I did it. Because it needed to be done.

Look it's not even theft, the system let me get away with it so I did.

I dunno. I dunno. It was just. There was just this. I just got so mad.

Edward Witt said, "Why do you want to do pathology on the Cumali woman? No one will pay for it; she was a patty living in an enclave, we'll be lucky if we can squeeze seventy grand out of it, and time-wasting stuff like autopsies are the kind of thing a good defence lawyer will laugh out of court . . . "

In the too-hot or too-cold or too-wet or too-dry never enough of anything that was ever good enough walls of the Criminal Audit Office, Edward pushed one pink finger down point first in the middle of his desk, driving hard enough to tilt the tip almost to ninety degrees against the knuckle, and declared:

"Justice is doing the right thing for society. This Cumali case – now I know this sounds harsh – but seventy thousand is a fair sum for her life, the woman was a leech! A patty who was never going to contribute anything meaningful to society, she didn't even have a pension I mean she was just going to be . . . and it's very sad that she died but compared to someone useful, I mean someone who mattered, I think seventy is a good figure to aim for. So get over to Seph Atkins' lawyer and get this settled so we can move on to cases with greater profit margins."

Theo nodded and said not a word, and left the office and walked back to his corner where the orange mushrooms grew, and sat at his desk, and realised that he hadn't raised his voice at work for nearly twelve years, and had not fought or kicked or raged or wept or experienced anything of much at all to suggest that he was unhappy in his life. Nor could he remember the last time he smiled.

Chapter 24

On the canal Theo sat at the back of the boat, steering the *Hector* towards Cosgrove.

Neila drew the cards.

Four of cups, the Magician, the Lovers (inverted), ace of staves, two of swords, four of swords, the Sun (inverted), knave of cups, the Hanged Man (inverted).

Theo wound the engine down, stuck his head inside, careful to keep the door barely open lest the heat from the stove escape. "We're nearing the lock. Do you want to stop?"

There was another boat moored a hundred yards away.

Neila went to say hi. It was the right thing to do, especially in winter. She liked the simplicity of such things. They had a cup of tea.

In the night someone started a fire in the distance, the smell of smoke as it blew across the water strong enough to wake Neila, heart racing, fumbling for the light, terror, terror, the worst thing in the world but . . .

. . . the flames were elsewhere, a fist punching the clouds, a blistering smear that made the sky a bowl instead of a roof.

For a while she watched it from the back of the boat, and Theo came out too, shrouded in a coat, and they stood and watched the blaze, and the sirens did not sing, and no one came.

*

In the morning the fire was still burning, lower, and the magnif-icence of the night was faded to a black scar, soot blown across the water.

The boat that had moored up from theirs was already gone. The cupboard was growing bare, and they did not head into town.

Chapter 25

Theo Miller went to see Seph Atkins and her lawyer.

She wasn't being held in the police station. It wasn't cost-effective.

They met in an office just south of Holborn. Marble floors, fishbowls on low glass tables holding green branches without leaves that coiled and looped into themselves like angry snakes, something Theo struggled to imagine had ever lived in nature. A waterfall within a glass wall behind the receptionists, a security gate guarded by Company Police, Tasers on the left hip, guns on the right. Vagrants could be Tasered on sight in this part of the city – they caused emotional distress, and emotional distress was basically assault.

Theo tried not to stare, to imagine what it must be like to wear silk and have a resident's permit for Zone 1. He stood quietly in front of the reception desk, hands clasped, satchel over his shoulder, and the receptionists ignored him. He coughed. No response. He said, "Excuse me?" and the receptionists looked up, all three of them, simultaneous, outraged at his audacity. Then the nearest fixed her face in a radiant smile, daring him to think he'd ever seen any other expression on her softly toned features. The transformation was so sudden and complete that Theo nearly jumped, flinching from the brightness of her polished white teeth. She took his fingerprints, a credit rating, gave him a free chocolate in the shape of a heart, a leaflet about civic–corporate partnership and told him to wait.

Theo ignored the leaflet, listened to the words around him, eyes half-closed, satchel in his lap.

"When people say monopoly they don't understand the way our economy works. No one has a monopoly on supply and demand – but the money to fuel growth must come from a dynamic, central source which carries not just a responsibility for economic, but also for cultural growth within the . . ."

"I do the law to make a difference. I really do. We're giving so much back to the nation . . ."

"No. Downstairs. In the lobby. Yes, in the lobby! We need to talk now. *Now.*"

"Government raises taxes to subsidise business. That's what economic planning *means.*"

The lawyer sent her secretary down to Theo after keeping him waiting barely twenty-five minutes. They did not speak in the elevator up to the twelfth floor, and the secretary did not meet Theo's eyes.

An office, larger than any at the Audit Office and smaller than any other in the building, a painting on one wall of great bands of red and orange colour, perhaps a sunset, inverted, or a spilt drink seeping into canvas or the colour of the artist's anger and conflicted love, it was all very . . .

"Mr Miller. Thank you for coming down so quickly." A woman, five foot five, sepia-brown skin, rich and warm, doe eyes and a bun of woven silken black hair, dressed in charcoal skirt-suit, sheer tights and black pumps, a chunky black watch on her left wrist, a gold bracelet on her right.

By night Mala Choudhary practised Muay Thai. She won most of her fights but found those she lost more exciting. She used to do MMA, but it had too many rules and the wrong kind of machismo – the kind that never learned. Her mother calls her a chubby pumpkin, because her legs are muscled and her hips are broad. She secretly didn't do very well at university, but what does that matter when you excel in the real world?

She's going to be a partner soon. She smiles, and Theo Miller tastes something liquid and hot in the roof of his mouth, like car sickness, while standing still.

"Just before we begin, I will be recording this conversation, is that acceptable?"

"Fine."

A tablet, laid down on the glass table between them, a glimpse of words and images; is that the blasted remnants of Dani Cumali's head that she swipes away, quick, searching for more pertinent things?

"Thank you – yes, please send Ms Atkins in."

A command issued to her watch, Theo thought for a moment that Mala Choudhary had gone mad, but no, the watch records her heartbeat, steps walked, calories burned, emails received and of course links to her assistant's assistant, for all matters where her assistant is busy with more important assisting.

They waited.

Theo felt his fingers ripple, once along the desk, looked to see if Mala had spotted the movement, saw no sign, put his hands carefully in his lap, folded into a fist one over the other so tight it hurt.

Seph Atkins entered the room. She wore a white shirt and blue jeans. She had no jewellery, no make-up, knew that their absence made her handsome. She glanced at Theo, turned her attention to Mala, smiled a smile of tiny white teeth, glanced back to Theo and paused.

Stopped.

Looked again.

Theo stood up, nodded. "Ms Atkins."

"Ms Atkins, this is Mr Miller," exhaled Mala, smooth as single cream, pulling back a chair for her client. "He's from the Audit Office."

Seph sat without taking her eyes off Theo's face. Mala swung her tablet round, tapped tapped tapped, looked up with a burst of practised brightness, all smile and eye, announced: "Shall we get down to business? Our office has done a preliminary assessment of the case but before sharing our conclusions I was wondering where the Audit Office was currently at in processing this matter?"

Through the dry heat in his skin, a familiar phrase to carry

102

him through. "We have conducted the initial assessment, and are looking at premeditated first-degree murder as our initial—"

"Mr Miller I have to stop you right there, we will of course not be accepting that charge in this case."

Theo met Mala's eyes. Her eyes were easier to meet than Seph Atkins', and there was that within them that stirred a memory of something resembling . . . was it anger? He wasn't sure. He found it hard to remember having felt anything of anything much for a very, very long time.

"We are confident of success in a first-degree charge. Ms Atkins entered Ms Cumali's house for no other purpose to kill her. Her motivation was—"

"Self-defence."

"Ms Atkins had a gun. No fingerprints were found on it; Dani Cumali certainly did not clean her fingerprints off the weapon after she was dead. The room had been searched, the bullets were fired at close range to centre mass, there was no attempt to disable, Dani was . . ."

He stopped himself.

Uncoiled his fingers, aching in a clump in his lap. Looked away. Felt Seph Atkins' gaze on him still, silent, smiling.

Words from Mala Choudhary. Second-degree, manslaughter, there are mitigating circumstances you see, Ms Cumali was in fact – if you'll look at these documents yes there – a history of criminal activities of . . .

Theo half-listens.

There was a case he worked once, a boy, seven, was run over by three teenagers. They hit him, then rolled over him four more times, laughing, and he died. They filmed the whole thing; it was great, it was hilarious it was . . .

But the teenagers had money, and the boy was autistic and assessed as being unlikely to contribute very much to society. Then it turned out his mother was an immigrant anyway so it wasn't like the boy was even a citizen just a scrounger on the nanny state, and that had been Theo's first case, his first proper homicide as a senior auditor and how much had that cost?

How much had the boys paid?

He thought . . . if he closed his eyes . . . maybe £35,000 each?

Maybe a little more, because they'd also damaged a neighbour's car, and it was a Volvo.

"If you look here you'll see that our initial assessment of Dani Cumali's life was that actually she was barely worth £17,000, and that's with the societal cost of her demise thrown in, she was in fact a burden on the exchequer and I have seen reports from her managers saying that she was a disruptive element, even with the good fortune to have got parole she was . . . "

The parents had paid their children's indemnity, and one of the kids had been sent off to boarding school on the Isle of Man. The other two had been grounded for a month. They'd also paid for a discretion clause, and no records were retained.

"A drug user, there are reports that Cumali had been found with—"

He stood up. "Excuse me," he barked, cutting through Mala's flow. "May I use the bathroom?"

"Of course," she replied, leaning a little away from the desk, surprised, reassessing. "All the way down on the right."

"Thank you."

He marched through the office, beautiful, glass and acrylic canvas, comfy sofas in a comfy break room for people to put their feet up and choose a magazine from the extensive and frequently updated collection of lifestyle guides, adventure fables and fashion gloss; the kind of office every kid raised through every corporate–educational partnership school dreamed of working in. Even in Shawford they'd been shown pictures of Budgetfood's corporate HQ and three students who'd completed their Gold Enterprise Certificates were taken on a tour as a special treat.

He locked himself in a cubicle in the bathroom and felt
he felt

once upon a time he'd had these feelings he'd felt things there'd been a case a woman raped repeatedly by her partner, that was before they changed the law so that rape within relationships was just a misdemeanour because frankly common sense the indemnity had been £7800, but he made that every week with extras so he paid it and did it again

and again

and again

and she

"You've already got the previous case file, just use that!" exclaimed Edward. "We can't be clogging up the system!"

what happened to her she jumped in front of a train she

Theo had felt something then, hadn't he?

The old guy beaten to death in his flat the kids who did it couldn't pay the indemnity but that's all right the Company sponsored them, put them on its Special Securities team, they're doing well now they're big shots in the world of private peace solutions . . .

Dani Cumali with her brains blown out not like her case is special not like it matters more or less or differently or

The man called Theo Miller stares at a grey toilet wall and is grateful that it is not a mirror.

A swoosh of door. The door is heavy, with a furry strip at its bottom that picks up grey felted dust. Footsteps. A tap. A squelch of soap. The tap stopped. A hot-air dryer, rippling skin like tissue paper in a storm. Stopped. No footsteps. No door. Theo waited. Silence in the bathroom. Theo opened the door of the cubicle.

Seph Atkins looked at him through the mirror, hands framing the sink on which she leaned, smiling. "I saw you," she breathed. "I saw *you*."

"Ms Atkins, you appear to have the wrong bathroom, this is the—"

"At the enclave. You were in the door. You made like a heron."

Not turning, she straightened up, stuck her arms out to the side, elbows bent at ninety degrees, stood on one leg and waggled her tongue. For a moment she wobbled there, eyes popping, then relaxed, beamed, and walked away.

In the office, Seph Atkins did not speak. Mala Choudhary talked and talked and Theo pretended to listen.

And at the end Mala said, "Well that was all very interesting. If you persist with this first-degree nonsense we will of course take you to court where I have no doubt you'll lose, meanwhile there is the discretion clause ... "

Theo's face flickered, the first movement it had manifested for nearly an hour. Seph Atkins examined the rim of her fingernails, cut short and lacquered an unnatural shade of natural pink. "The discretion clause. Yes. Talk me through that."

"My client is interested in ensuring that no records of this matter are kept and that all files are removed from the system, I believe if we look at previous judgements that a standard cost is £45,000 for a case of this kind ... "

"£45,000 for manslaughter," he retorted. "£80,000 for murder."

"As the charges are going to be manslaughter," Mala breezed on brightly, "I don't think we need to consider the worst-case here."

"The judge will decide if—"

"Mr Miller," she cut through, harder than he'd heard her speak before. "It will be manslaughter. Now £45,000 and that's the expunging of all records including police, and Dani Cumali's death will be registered as drug overdose ... "

"It's an extra £700 to alter the death certificate."

"There'll be drugs in her system." Mala shrugged. "She was that kind of woman."

Seph Atkins watched Theo, who did not look her in the eye.

He walked back to the office, very, very slowly.

Chapter 26

Edward Witt came to Theo's desk, which was unusual and did not bode well.

" . . . fucking Cumali case why isn't it cleared why haven't we got . . . "

As the words rolled over him, it seemed to Theo that he was hearing, not language, but shaped sound on the air, and it was strangely beautiful, even calming. His serenity only appeared to enrage his employer, who had decided a long time ago that his own presence was terrifying. Years of protein shakes, teeth-whitening treatments and secret acting classes with an unemployed actor called Reg had given Edward the physicality and voice to dominate a room.

"She sells sea shells on the sea shore!" he snarled at the mirror every night, trimming nasal hair with a pair of fine steel scissors. "The shells she sells are surely sea shells!"

Dozens of management guides had taught him that the secret to success wasn't about being right, merely about appearing to be more right than everybody else. He knew he had the intellectual and physical prowess to cow anyone before him. Grown men had been reduced to tears by Edward's cutting wit. He seduced women to prove a point, and could bully the gates of hell into opening, if it suited him.

But where others flinched before Edward's wrath, Theo sat implacable. He was implacable when delivering good news, implacable when receiving bad. He endured rage and condemnation, insults that should have had him walking from the office

107

in disgust with a tilt of the head as if trying to discern a hidden secret, not in the words, but in the soul of the man who threw them. He smiled politely without humour, spoke when spoken to, worked without complaint, achieved nothing spectacular and never failed beyond average. He was ... harmless. There was almost nothing more to be said about him, and that caused Edward a great feeling of unease.

Over the years this unease had built, reinforced by Theo's repeated failure to show any reaction to Edward's management style whatsoever. If Theo was aware that Edward's anxiety on this point had grown into animosity, he showed no sign of that either, and this passivity made Edward's fury all the greater, so that he barely found himself speaking to the other man except in roars, barks and sarcastic snaps, an undignified yapping dog rather than the prowling wolf he believed himself to be.

And now he was doing it again: howling in Theo's face, spittle flying, waving papers in front of the other man's nose, and fuck-ing Miller just didn't fucking seem to care the total ...

"There's actual cases with actual profit on the desk! There's actual indemnities that will bring something for the fucking department so you get your head out of your arse and fucking get the Cumali job cleared – I've got Mala Choudhary on the phone, do you have any idea what Faircloud Associates does, they're the Company, do you understand, they're the Company, the people who keep the lights on the water running the petrol in the pumps and you want to give them shit over some drugged-out little patty-line whore and—"

Did Theo flinch?

Edward stopped dead.

He had never seen a reaction on Theo's face before and ... was that a flinch?

Probably not. Stone again. Impassive, patient, stone. He didn't even smile that nervous smile of stupid boys hoping that if they show willing the abuse will stop. Nor did he scowl, or glare, or retreat inwards. He simply waited, like pebbles before the sea, for the storm to pass.

"Close the Cumali job, and get on to a case with some real fucking money in it," Edward hissed. "Or I'll get someone else to do it."

He threw the papers down across Theo's desk and stalked away.

It was a great gesture, really dramatic, other people would have at the very least run outside for a shaky cigarette. But Theo stacked the papers in a pile and returned to his computer screen. Later Edward had to send his secretary to get them back, as there were documents in there he needed.

Chapter 27

Once
                   this was before he learned how to grow a beard
    the boy who would be Theo was taken to a party in London
by the boy who was actually, in fact and from birth, Theo Miller.

"It'll be great, just the ticket. You need to be thinking about
corporate sponsorship – you'll never make it, never achieve what
you need to achieve and

    well yes you could wear that but tell you what and I say this
with the greatest possible love why don't you try wearing something else – you know you're roughly my size let me see if I
haven't

    splendid! Splendid! We'll drive. No, as in my father's driver is
going to collect us and he'll take us to ...

    ... a train? I've never taken the train before isn't it terribly
crowded isn't it full of people who are a bit ...

    isn't this exciting!"

The party was at a club in Kensington. Theo's father had some
sort of connection with the place – more than a member, less
than a founder, a giver of money perhaps, without the posses-
sion of the kind of excessive wealth that would make him a
distraction. Theo's father was not there. Theo's father was very
rarely in England at all these days, but Theo didn't seem to care.
He wasn't sure when he'd last seen his parents. He wasn't sure
it mattered.

    They arrived just after eight, two boys in shiny shoes, the boy who would be Theo hiding behind his dining partner, who swept up the stairs and exclaimed, "Come come come!" and like a dog at heel, the boy came.

A sickly smell of dried-out petals from a fish bowl on the entrance desk. You could leave your business card or take a chocolate liqueur from within the crispy blossom – but all the best treats were gone.

A man all in white bowing and smiling and nodding to the young gentlemen as they entered, of course, follow me.

Stairs that rose straight up towards a portrait of the queen, then split in two beneath her knowing stare, amused at a secret only she could know. Then the curving stair bent back on itself in two parts and reunited at a long landing where a ten-piece jazz band played, silver glittering off their coats, a crown woven into the hair of the lead singer, sweat on their faces, something hot and mad in their eyes.

A room that the boy who would be Theo assumed was a ballroom and was in fact a mezzanine. The great, the glorious, his tux is new, hem hem, her dress was shop-bought, tut tut, come with me come with me there are some people you simply have to meet there are ...

"I tell him why does he wear his Rolex on business it's just asking for trouble but he never listens the great lump he never listens to my good advice when I say that ... "

"Yes, of course. Now where is that in relation to Chiswick?"

"Trickle-down works – if I wasn't in this country there'd be at least twenty people who wouldn't have jobs – at least! – and that's not even counting the ... "

"Theo?"

" ... said to the sultan but of course, I mean of course you would and it's only natural that ... "

"I'm very strict there's just not enough time for me to be involved in the charities and well you do don't you, you do find that you're putting other people ahead of yourself!"

"Theo?"

"In Nepal actually and it was incredible the people the people are just well it's just so you have to be there really you have to be there and afterwards we went sailing round the Med ... "

"Theo?"

"Yes?"

"Are you ... is this ...?"

"Normal? Fairly much. Easier to do business eye to eye sometimes, lubricated by a little champagne. There are people here you need to meet absolutely, come with me your future depends on it now hello, this is my friend he's doing maths yes lives on the same corridor as me he's brilliant simply brilliant yes."

The boy who will be Theo stands on one side of the room and wonders what his friends would think if they could see him now, and for a moment remembers that he hasn't spoken to Dani for nearly nine months and wonders if she's okay, and then is given more champagne and some sort of nibbly thing on a penny-size lump of not-really bread, and forgets.

After a little while of watching, he realises that there are nearly as many staff as there are guests at this swirling ball. Not merely waiters, but personal servants – men and women dressed in white frills and black cotton who stand silently behind their masters and hold their champagne glasses, receive and give business cards, answer the mobile phone. It would be a terrible breach of etiquette for a guest to answer their phone during these matters, and when an argument breaks out over some detail of stocks or celebrity scandal, it is a woman with head down and eyes fixed to a point two feet in front of her big toe who checks for an answer on the internet and whispers it into her master's ear, who may or may not lie about the outcome, depending on where his opinions lie.

The young sweep around the old, and laugh, and hold their own glasses, and are absolutely fascinated by everything that these wonderful people believe and actually yes it's funny you should say that, I was thinking of going into corporate financing when I graduate did you say you ran a ...

The boy does not resent luxury.

At college his meals are cooked for him six days a week. Room cleaned. Shoes polished. He goes to the library and someone else puts the books away if he forgets. At the weekend he has money for drink, or can walk by the river without a care in the world, or take a bicycle out into the countryside and let the sunlight wash away the work, and when he returns to his soft bed

he is better

can work better, do what he needs to do, *better*, and one day

if he works hard enough, earning through his labours

one day maybe someone else will turn down the duvet in the corner of his bed and someone else will press the smell of cleanliness into his fresh-washed clothes and he need not scrub at dishes and argue with the water company and stand in line for the bus that never comes because these things are fundamentally

not the things he is best at

he can give

so much more to this world

so much more

if he's just given the opportunity to do it.

This is not an unfair position.

You must live your life first before you can help others, you must have the security so that you are not a burden, must have the space to be free to be able to make a difference to have that freedom – freedom is a thing which must be bought you buy the freedom you buy . . .

pension house home time learning skills friends

dancing dancing we spin the world spins all things in harmony the harmony of the heavens we are starlight stardust spinning fizz on the tongue kiss on the lips beauty bought at the gym silk and pearl and diamond and

He desires, and possibly – just maybe – he deserves

yes, *deserves* . . .

Something clatters in a room next door, a smash loud enough to briefly drown out jazz. Some heads turn; most do not. The boy looks and thinks he sees Theo through an open door. He approaches, weaving through the crowd unnoticed, and yes,

113

there is Theo Miller, laughing in his drunken state, cracked glass and spilt lobster at his feet, a girl crying, a teenager, and three boys staring with no laughter whatsoever in their eyes, and Theo may not be sober

but the boy instantly is.

He knows these faces, though he's never met the strangers who wear them now. He used to see them sometimes in the snarling boys who liked it when their dogs growled at passing strangers, because the dogs made people scared, and if people were scared of you then you were powerful, and if you were powerful, you mattered. Even if you didn't know what mattering was good for.

The girl cries, the boys glare, spilt champagne crystallises on the floor as silent, non-reproachful staff rush to clean it up. Theo laughs and doesn't seem to recognise the danger that he's in as one of the glaring party snarls:

you stupid fucking bastard why the fuck did you fucking

and another joins in

fuck him fuck him let's just fucking go can't fucking believe they let in

and the third stands silent, arms folded, and watches.

"Gentlemen, gentlemen!" chuckles Theo, wiping shattered shards of exploded ice off his sleeves, lifting his feet one at a time to check that he hasn't stood in anything organic. "It was a perfectly valid thing, I'm sure there's no harm done, the lady clearly wasn't interested in your ... "

"She's mine!" snarled the first boy.

"She's his," agreed the second boy.

I'm watching, the third offered silently, his eyes skimming the room, meeting the gaze of the boy who would be Theo, recognising for the briefest of moments a sobriety equal only to his own.

"Now I mean clearly this is just ... "

"My father sponsored her."

"His father sponsored her!"

"He paid for her tuition for her dress for her face — *for her face* — he paid and that means that I ... "

114

"For her face!"

"Sponsored and the deal was very clear . . . "

"A bargain!"

"A very clear deal and if she . . . "

"A contract."

"Fuck you." The girl, on her feet, the tears still running but her voice holding strong. "Fuck your dad." She peeled off one elbow-length glove, threw it on the floor, dragged at the other, one finger at a time, hissed in frustration at the slippery silk, got it free, threw it in the first boy's face. "Fuck you all."

Tried to run in her high-heeled shoes, wobbled, nearly fell, stumbled against the teetering glass-covered table, gritted her teeth. Raised her left leg so the back of her heel was behind her bum, peeled the shoe away, wobbled again, caught her balance. Raised her right, snatched the shoe off with enough force to break the strap across the top, flung it into the boy's chest. Raised her head, pulled her shoulders back, walked away through a pool of melting ice and alcohol.

The boys watched her go.

Theo Miller giggled, tried to stifle the sound, couldn't, burst out laughing. "Well!" he guffawed, and then, struggling to find inspiration through the champagne, "Well!"

The boy caught his arm, whispered, "Theo, we should . . . "

" . . . have her fucking head," growled the first boy.

"Her head!" agreed the second boy.

Still watching, mused the third. There is something we can all learn from this.

"Her father was joint signatory on the contract he'll have to pay now he'll have to . . . "

"Fucking pay!"

"If she can't keep her contracts she'll never work never work never even finish but also never work I'll see that she . . . "

"Her! Working for the Company?"

"She can clean the fucking floors no not even the floors she can – she *can* . . . "

"A contract is the most sacred thing which can . . . "

"Philip, I think you've got some lobster in your hair. Or is it crab?" Theo leaned in close to the first boy, a blast of alcoholic breath swimming across his face, then reached up and flicked a slip of shiny whiteness, glistening flesh, out of the hair above the boy's right temple. "There you go! All better now."

For a moment the boy called Philip looked into Theo's eyes, and the world waited on the tightrope, wondering which way the wind would blow.

He punched Theo. If he'd had the imagination for a witty put-down, he probably would have chosen that, having not punched anyone since he was twelve and remembering it being quite an awkward experience even then.

As it was, wit failed, and so he hit him, and Theo Miller dropped to the floor and lay on his back in a pool of mingling liquids and torn fishy flesh, stared for a moment up at the ceiling, incredulous, then laughed. He laughed and laughed and let his head roll back and laughed a little bit more, as his friend squatted down next to him and wondered if he was meant to intervene, and how.

Then the boy called Philip said, "I fucking challenge you."

He offered a few more words too, and they seemed to give him an increased passion for his theme. Most were terms of sexual abuse, but at the end they returned to the point. "I challenge you – get up you little shit – I challenge you!"

"Darling," chuckled Theo, "you can't. Duelling hasn't been legal since—"

"My lawyer will draw up the indemnity. We'll pay no more than £75,000 apiece. You can afford £75,000, can't you? Get up! Get up!"

Theo laughed. He laughed and laughed and laughed and . . .

On the following Wednesday a lawyer knocked on his door with the insurance papers to sign.

"Good afternoon. I am from the firm of Hatfield and Bolton and I have a preliminary indemnity insurance here for your perusal. You will see that it states that whoever should kill you should you be found deceased within the next two weeks will pay no more than £75,000 for the cost of your death and here also you will find the equivalent statement for the murder of one Philip Arnslade, assuming that your respective deaths satisfy the circumstances laid out in clauses three through eight of the—"

"I'm not signing this are you fucking kidding me I'm ..."

On the Friday morning, as he was walking home, Theo Miller was mugged by three men dressed in balaclavas, who beat the shit out of him and took only £10 from his wallet, leaving credit cards and another £40 in cash behind.

On the Monday the lawyer came again.

" ... and you will see a discretion clause of course which has been drawn up at Mr Arnslade's own expense, he is generously covering the legal fees in this matter, which have been substantial, to guarantee that the indemnity is worth no more than ... "

Theo Miller threw coffee over the papers, and if only he'd planned ahead and made two cups, might have thrown something in the lawyer's face.

Two days later he got a phone call from his aunty, whose dog had been killed, its mutilated body left on her car bonnet, head balanced on the stump of its neck on the path from the front door.

The day after that Theo Miller knocked on the door of his next-door neighbour, to discover him lying in bed with a swollen face and a split lip, torn almost exactly on the scar where as a baby his mouth had been gently stitched together, and Theo shouted, "You idiot why didn't you say why didn't you say this had happened you're such an idiot why didn't you ... "

Later they sat together in the kitchen. The floor was sticky with old spilt coffee, crunchy with shattered remnants of dry, uncooked pasta, ground into dust by weeks of neglect. The cleaning lady had given up trying to keep the place in order after someone boiled milk and eggs in the kettle.

Theo said to the boy, "It's stupid, of course. I don't even know the girl's name. But I walked into this room at the party and they were holding her down, and Philip had his cock out and was . . . it happens all the time. The contract doesn't say that you'll have to do anything, it's supposed to be charity, but if you take the contract away then what have you got left? You've got dreams, I imagine. You let yourself dream, think for a moment that there was something else, a different future, and then when it stops you realise that there's just this. Just this. That you've been bought as a whore for the master's son, and they have the discretion to destroy your dreams whenever they want to, and you have nowhere to appeal and nothing to . . .

. . . my father bought my mother, you see. She had dreams, and he bought them. Money buys dreams. But it didn't work out, and so he bought my stepmother and my stepmother is actually a very impressive woman but she knows, she understands that as long as she dreams of money, they'll be fine. They'll have a wonderful life. It's only if she dreams of something else that her world will fall apart. Only then."

The boy said nothing and thought briefly of Dani Cumali, felt a sudden surge of terror, panic even, and shifted in his seat and winced at the pain, and in that moment of distraction forgot again.

That night Theo Miller called up the lawyer, who'd thoughtfully left a card, and signed the indemnity. "Tell Philip Arnslade that I'm going to blow his damn brains out."

"Mr Arnslade will be most relieved," replied the lawyer.

118

Chapter 28

"Your grandmother?"

"I'm afraid so."

"I had no idea, it's so . . . "

"Sudden?"

"You have a grandmother, Mr Miller?"

This is clearly a startling idea for her. Theo Miller is an artefact of the Criminal Audit Office; to imagine he has any existence beyond it is a struggle.

"Had. I *had* a grandmother."

Theo gives his excuses and wonders if human resources are cross-checking as he speaks, looking for records of any previous absences. They won't check if the grandmother is real – that's not their job – but they will look through his work history and do a quick count of just how many grandmothers have died during his employment.

None thus far. That's a good sign. There are several in the office who've lost at least three. And no one credits Theo with much imagination. He's never given them reason to credit him with anything of anything much at all.

"And when do you think you'll be back, Mr Miller? The limit on compassionate leave for this sort of thing is forty-eight hours for a domestic case and seventy-two for a . . . "

"Forty-eight should be fine. Thank you."

"Of course. I'll have your payslip updated. And . . . I do hope the funeral is nice. When my grandmother died the priest had a double booking, and started giving the eulogy for the wrong dead woman."

"My grandmother was an atheist."

"Oh yes, but that's no reason to miss out on a church is it? Lovely bunch of flowers, music, the whole . . ."

It wasn't hard to find Dani's supervisor.

Seb Gatesman, twenty-nine, fiddling with his mobile phone round the back of a large, detached house on the edge of a park in Barnes, trying to take a photo of himself looking appalled, horrified *and* humorous all at once to send to his mate who had just suggested this thing they could do tonight, the most – you won't believe – like we're gonna totally fuck those bitches up it's gonna be . . .

"Excuse me?"

Theo Miller, dressed in a suit and tie, stood beneath the ash tree and smiled politely. The younger man was nearly a foot taller than Theo, with a carefully trimmed dark goatee that he secretly oiled last thing at night and first thing in the morning. He wore a white shirt and black trousers, and was proud of this because all the patty bitches who worked under him had to wear the jumper with the name on it, like the parole sluts they were.

"Excuse me?" repeated Theo. "Mr Sebastian Gatesman?"

"Who're you?"

Too early in the morning for Theo to be anyone important, the wedding party was still down the church. Gatesman was just here making sure his staff didn't fuck up the reception, the champagne bar the ice sculpture the chocolate fountain the diamond hidden in the wedding cake health and safety had given him such shit over that and he'd been like *it's the size of a fucking fist no way you could fucking* . . .

. . . but it'd be just his luck if someone broke a tooth on it.

"Mr Gatesman, my name is Theo Miller, I work for the Criminal Audit Office. I'm here about Dani Cumali . . ."

"Yeah? What's she done?" Seb Gatesman is keen for the answer to be bad. Hit by a bus, fell off a roof, gnawed by an unexpected llama, he'll take it.

"She's dead."

"Fuck off!" Not anger or sadness – just an outrageous joke being pulled, funny of course, it's funny but also in bad taste, mate, like, that's some bad taste.

"I'm afraid so."

"What the fuck? You're serious?" A flicker of something – perhaps relief – before the important thoughts hit. "That's the whole fucking rota fucking – I mean sorry, mate, like it's all very – but that's the rota that's – fuck! How'd she die?"

"She was murdered."

"Fuck *off*."

"You weren't made aware by your managers."

"No! Last to fucking hear anything, last of the—"

"Mr Gatesman, my job is to audit the value of the crime. To do so I need to ascertain information concerning Ms Cumali's past in order to profile the societal impact her murder will have. Did she have dependants, was she in good standing, were there outstanding debts which have to be paid, these matters can be ..."

A snort of derision.

Theo paused.

Thought that in another time, another place, this garden would be beautiful. Autumn leaves falling onto thick green grass. The twisted spine of the hawthorn, the tall sweep of the oak, acorns dropping, conker shells cracking open to reveal their shining fruit, the distant sound of water trickling from a stone fountain crusted with yellow lichen, fresh-cut flowers all along the windowsills, their perfume drifting through the cold.

The only ugly thing, he decided, was the face in front of his, but that was the face he had to deal with and so:

"Mr Gatesman? Your insight would be most useful for my audit."

"She was a patty, straight off the line. Twelve years or something, she was lucky she got this job, the company picked her up cheap too, you know what those women are like, once they're in a way of thinking, there's nothing, like she's lucky she got what she got."

"Did she have children?"

"Don't think so. Dunno. Look, I'm her supervisor not her dad."

"What was her job, exactly?"

"Cleaning. Also went on a few catering gigs to clean the glasses and unload stuff."

"Where?"

"Anywhere we needed staff, got a lot of big contracts, corporate stuff. Doesn't take much to clean a glass, even a patty is good for that."

"Anyone she disliked or who seemed to dislike her? Anything stand out about her behaviour or the behaviours of others towards her?"

A shrug.

"Any friends?"

Another shrug, and sensing that maybe this wasn't quite enough: "Look, man, she was just a patty, okay, I mean like is it such a—"

"I hear that a lot of patties – women like Ms Cumali – are sold for sex to wealthy clients."

A series of expressions cross Seb Gatesman's face, rippling like wind across a flag.

First, default: indignation, fury, clownish, comical, he's outraged how could you even – if you weren't such a stand-up guy and I wasn't so reasonable I'd

This phase lasted a few seconds, then died before Theo's steady blinking gaze.

Second, cheeky: hey, actually, you know what, you and me, you and me, men like us, we're men of the world we know how it and it's not illegal so long as you pay for the indemnity is it it's not illegal it's just expensive and if these girls they want to make a pretty buck then well who are we?

Finally: a shrug.

In answer to most things, Seb Gatesman has a shrug.

Does it matter?

Does any of this fucking matter?

And despite himself, another flash across Seb Gatesman's face, for there was a night not so long ago when a girl came off the patty line and he sat her down and said, "You've had it tough I get that, but here we help our own if they help us if you play ball with me I'll . . . "

Fuck me that had been one hell of a – she had totally known what he needed and . . .

Standing in the autumn garden, wet leaves beneath his feet, popped red berries crushed underfoot on the flagstone path, Theo watches the journey of the mind across Gatesman's face, and feels suddenly hot, and wants to be somewhere else, and has to force himself to keep looking the other man in the eye. "Was . . . Ms Cumali part of this arrangement?" he blurted, moving his brief-case from one hand to the other, feeling suddenly short, awkward against the lounging sprawl of Gatesman.

"Nah. Look I'm not supposed to talk about this, will this be in a . . . "

"The report is about Ms Cumali's murder, not her work. Unless it's relevant I don't see why you need to be . . . "

"Only I've got family I've got—"

"If you cooperate, I'm sure I can keep your name out of this. Now the arrangement, the . . . uh . . . the providing of physical services to wealthy gentlemen . . . "

"Some women do it. It's a choice."

"Ms Cumali didn't participate?"

"Nah. Coulda made a couple of quid if she'd played it right, but you could see she was trouble, sometimes you can get paid for that too – a biter a screamer there's a market for everything but when supply outpaces demand . . . "

Once again Gatesman's thoughts deteriorated into a shrug. Economics: what's a guy to do? What's a stand-up guy to do?

Theo grunts: "I need to know Ms Cumali's movements for the last two months."

"Uh, I don't know if like I can . . . is this like . . . part of your audit? Only I've never heard of it being so . . . "

"Have you ever been audited, Mr Gatesman? As victim or perpetrator, I mean?"

A shifting of weight that wants to give way to another

shake of the shoulders, and wisely doesn't go through with the motion.

A silent conversation, conducted in great detail in meeting eyes.

Seb, phone now forgotten in his hand, wondering what Theo knows.

Theo, matching his gaze, and at the back of his mind a few words blurted by Dani while he tried to pretend she didn't exist, and they hadn't been children together, and that her daughter wasn't also his.

I've got this boss. Gatesman. I got dirt, and now he's fucking scared of me. Embezzling from his bosses, naughty. He's scared and I can ask for any job I want, and I said – I want into the Ministry. Get me into the Ministry.

The Company has no problem with Seb sleeping with his charges, using them for his own power and sex. In many ways, that just makes it easier to turn a profit, get them used to the idea that this is it, all that there'll ever be, break them early. They're just patty-line whores and anyway, using women, it was a story as old as time, no point punishing natural instincts, not when Seb's performance indicators were so positive.

But corporate embezzlement . . . for such a crime Theo had handed out indemnities that cost more than murder.

And Seb looked Theo in the eye and saw the truth of it, and looked away, remembered the phone in his hand, put it back in his pocket, and was for the briefest of moments afraid.

"So uh . . . not sure I can get you the last two months but I could maybe see if . . . "

"Her pay record should include details of her shifts, yes?"

"Yeah I guess that . . . "

Theo's head turned a little to one side, and the other man didn't meet his eyes.

"Did Ms Cumali ever request a specific shift?"

"Yeah. Sometimes she asked for stuff."

"Did you give it to her?"

"I respect my employees," intoned Gatesman – shutting down now, fear will have that effect, "so if I could help her I would."

124

"What shifts?"

"Some office stuff. Cleaning after hours. Said she liked the quiet."

"Which office stuff?"

"Government buildings, that sort of thing."

"Which buildings?"

"Ministry of Civic Responsibility, mostly."

"Doing what?"

"Cleaning."

"Anything else?"

"Not really."

"Anything leap to mind, small details, it can be so easy sometimes for these things to be . . . "

"She wanted to be sent to this swanky do, couple of weeks ago. Big house, something corporate."

"Did she say why?"

"No."

Her exact words were in fact: You don't fuck with me, I won't fuck with you, you fucking get me?

Seb Gatesman had understood and given her what she wanted. For now. One day he'd make her pay – he'd make her fucking suck his – but not yet not until he'd found where she was keeping the pictures he needed to get the photos off the bitch before he could

"And where was this corporate event?"

"Some place . . . Danesmoor Hall."

"And this was recent?"

"Coupla weeks ago. You know it's a busy job, we've been really . . . you know. You know. Dani murdered. *Murdered.* It's not every day that you get – I mean you hear but you sure she didn't top herself?"

"Very sure."

"I guess it can happen to anyone and a patty I mean more than others you'd think wouldn't you – who's paying for the funeral?"

"I don't know."

"The Company isn't liable for that stuff, you know. We don't do flowers or nothing."

"You've been very helpful. If you think of anything then . . . "

"Yeah, I mean, yeah, of course. Like. Yeah."

That was the only eulogy Dani Cumali would receive.

Time is

       time was

              Theo closed his eyes and tried not to think too much about time

Walked away from Seb Gatesman because there was nothing to be done, and that was how the world was.

Theo Miller sits on the bus and despite himself, no matter how hard he tries to stop it, words well up from a burning place inside, and in his mind's eye he sees –

Lucy's face, he doesn't have a very clear image, it's mostly fantasy really, but whoever she is, she's just a child and there's Seb Gatesman standing over her, a biter a screamer there's a market for everything there's a market for . . .

       Theo Miller watches the still surface of the canal in the dead of winter night, hands in his pockets, and nearly turns the engine back on at the thoughts he cannot stop from

sees his father, when they took him to the patty line

         his mother, getting on the train to Dorchester, I think I'll have a better life somewhere new, it's not much but I just don't want to be part of this any more it's not

Somewhere in the north there's a place where they lock up girls like Lucy Cumali, worthless patty-line whores who'll never amount to anything and they've got to help pay their way haven't they, there's a market for everything, there's a market for . . .

       Lucy, Lucy come on it's for the cost of things you want to help us pay for the cost of things and he said he'll be gentle since it's your first time since you're so young he'll be so . . .

Dani: she's your daughter.

She's your daughter.
She's your daughter.
SHE'S YOUR

Sitting on the bus, Theo Miller puts his head in his hands, closes his eyes and in an instant finds himself auditing the value of his own life.

In a rare fit of humour he decides that the cause of his death is "murdered in jealous sexual rage", and laughs into his fingers, and still can't make the value of his life worth more than a bedsit in Holloway, excluding stamp duty.

Chapter 29

The *Hector* spent a night in Cosgrove. The boat they'd seen before was moored next to Neila's, but the lights were off, generator silent and no one home. Neila went to the water pump and found it iced up. When, after a few hits with a wrench, the handle began to move, air chunked and water did not flow. No one was manning the diesel station, and the hoses were dry.

Wrapped in scarf and hat, glove and coat, they went looking for someone in charge, knocking on the shut door of the brick house that guarded the lock gates. No one answered. Neila sucked in breath and said, "Let's tie up properly and come back later."

They tied off to bollards, hunkered down by the stove to eat and listen to the radio.

Next morning went to look
   no one home.

As the sun went down went to look
   no one answered.

At 8 p.m. Neila stepped outside to get another log off the roof from under the tarpaulin and saw a light burning in the house by the lock.

"Theo!"

They nearly ran, Theo clutching his side beneath his coat, back up to the lock gate, hammering on the door.

A woman, thin white beard beginning to sprout from between the squashed plum of her chin, answered.

"Yes?"

"Hello ma'am good evening ma'am we're looking to buy some water and diesel and also to empty the waste tank ma'am . . ."

"Now?"

"We're heading north, Nottingham, it would be—"

"It's two quid a litre."

"For the . . ."

"Water."

"Ma'am, two pounds for the—"

"It's better than what you'll get further up the canal. I'm fair. Others aren't fair. I'm fair. Do you doubt me?"

Neila hesitated, blinking in the light of the door, Theo a huddled shadow behind her. "And how much for the diesel?"

Daylight robbery I have never I have never been so in all my days it's not how it's not

Theo strapped the lock-box shut on the roof of Neila's boat and let her talk, snapped the padlock in place

what does she even think charging that much we're a community we treat each other as – she can't set prices like that it's absolutely

Neila's rant paused only briefly as she popped open the waste tank, the flood of shit and chemicals slamming into her face, making her eyes water as she slid the pipe in.

And the way she spoke, the way she looked at me did you see the way she looked at me – well if she'd said something I would have just given her a piece of my mind

Theo flinched as the stench of liquid faeces hit him, carried by the faint southerly breeze.

Around the boat thin ice was beginning to form, millimetres clouding into centimetres, he prodded it with a stick and it buckled and cracked into thin wedges.

Never coming here ever again never even going to bother to

"You all right?"

129

The woman from the hut, she-who-sold-overpriced-diesel, stood behind the beam of her torch, looking down the towpath towards the *Hector* and its ranting captain.

Neila rose, the pipe in her hand vibrating as waste sloshed through it, mouth open mid-expletive. "I brought you ginger biscuits," added the woman, shuffling towards the boat. "Keep you strong."

She laid a foil packet on top of the boat next to Theo and patted it fondly, like a baked pet. "Well," she added. "There it is."

Walked away.

Neila and Theo stood in silence as the stars burst out across the sky.

In the morning the ice cracked easily when Theo poked it from the stern of the boat with the end of a broom handle. Neila hummed and hahhed and wasn't sure if they should stay and wait for it to melt or whether they risked being trapped here if it thickened and in the end

they stayed

and ate ginger biscuits.

By two in the afternoon the ice had retreated a little, and Neila took three starts to get the engine going, and insisted on steering just in case, just because, and they headed towards Northampton.

Chapter 30

Time is

　　　　There was a Theo who lived in the past; there was
this man alone whose life is worth no more than a single bed in
north London and he is . . .

　not the man who Theo is now.

　　　　Because the man called Theo is

　　　　　　walking to school with his baby girl, her
hand in his

　the first day at school she comes back and babbles, babbles
about all that it was and he is a little sad when she's not looking
she's so grown-up already it was so

　and the man called Theo is

　　　　　　disappointed in her first choice of boyfriend, but
that's fine these things happen, it's not fate or destiny she can
make her choices and learn from her mistakes and he will be
there for her if he is needed without forcing her to choose and

All these things, of course

　are not real.

Lucy Rainbow Princess was sold to a fashion company special-
ising in parties for parents who knew their kids were destined to
be on the stage and have million-dollar smiles and be the envy
of all the other children at school

　Lucy Rainbow Princess was arrested while drunk when she
was twelve

　spent her days forging five-star reviews for online retail companies

burned the gym to the ground
laughed at the flames
there's a market for

Lying awake in the dark, Theo Miller tries not to do maths, and can't stop himself.

If Lucy Cumali was born in March, at full term, she must have been conceived in July of the previous year. These things aren't exact, so +/− two weeks either side of her actual conception date to account for premature or delayed birth, that's a four-week window of opportunity. Assuming that Dani was having sex with Andy the national average − once a week, rising a little for the age range or the fact that Scotland seemed to do it more −

call it 1.4 times a week, adjusting for menstruation

odds were that during the likely conception window Dani Cumali could have had sex at least 4.2 times

4.2 is a ludicrous number how do you have sex .2 of a time although there'd been some encounters back in the day but . . .

Call it 4 times within the probable window of conception.

And only one of those times had been with Theo and he was so certain . . .

Even though memory is not always . . .

Four times. That means there's only really a 25 per cent chance that Lucy is his daughter.

In Tulse Hill, Theo Miller, the one who did maths and then pretended to do law, stares at the ceiling and does not sleep.

On the canal, Theo watches the reflection of fire on water and knows that if he does not find Lucy Cumali, he will waste away to a shadow, and there will be no colour in the sky, and he will never feel the touch of rain on his skin again.

Chapter 31

At the Ministry of Civic Responsibility the security man said:

"Ah here we go, Dani Cumali, cleaning staff, outside contractor, worked the night she – yes yes here it is logged in on and logged out on all here all written down proper proper as they say."

And Theo said, "I'm auditing her murder, there's financial irregularities in the assessment – we have to cover ourselves against liability for a misfiled claim against the prosecution if . . ."

They gave him access to the CCTV records because he seemed a nice man, utterly harmless, and why wouldn't they?

Sitting in a booth behind the security office.

Fast-forwarding endless film of working day.

Stop talk cup of coffee machine is playing up again and

oh my God he said she said he said shall we go to the

WHY DOES THIS ELEVATOR ALWAYS TAKE SO LONG hey it's here now bing!

holding hands

letting go

Lives lived at high speed a moment of tenderness is

gone

a flaming shouting match you stupid stupid how could you how could you be so

sorted now smile on the way to the

For a few weary moments Theo finds himself fixating on the potted plant in one corner of the screen. If he watches it long enough, will he see it grow?

133

Then he realises he's drifting to sleep, and shakes himself, and stands up and gets bad coffee from the bad coffee machine, and returns to the desk, and forces himself to sit right on the edge of his chair and try again.

topping up the fruit bowl

sneaky playing with the phone under the desk no one will notice if

laying down the law on a matter of

lights go out

lights turn on somewhere else

go out

turn on.

Dani walks in.

Here she is.

Alive.

Dani is alive, only a few weeks in the past, right in front of his eyes.

He leans in so close his nose skims the screen, slows everything down to half speed, watches her turn on the spot, swimming through a digital fog.

She wears cleaning uniform, a new badge pinned to her chest.

The uniform is blue, but Theo only knows this because he's seen it before. On the screen it could be anything, any different shade of grey.

For a moment she looks at the camera, she might be looking at him, and the shock of it is so great he falls back in his chair like a man punched in the chest

and realises he wants to look away

and forces himself to watch.

Dani arriving at the service entrance, filling in paperwork on her first day, yes she's been checked she's got the − hold on it's right here it's . . .

Big duffel bag full of clothes to change into and cleaning products because she likes to bring some of her own she often thinks the stuff you have here is, well . . .

The security guard searches her bag on the first two days, then

134

gets bored and gives up and smiles her through, known now, how you doing luv how you

Dani cleaning.

Desks.

Computer screens.

Taking the trash out.

Scrubbing the toilets.

Scouring the sinks.

Emptying the grounds from the coffee machine. Who'd have thought something that made a drink that bad had anything organic in it?

She leaves the trash bags by the lift, to take downstairs with her in a big bundle of white.

Collects them as the last act of her work.

Goes into the lift

downstairs

emerges

vanishes off screen

reappears a few seconds later on a different camera

vanishes

reappears

puts the trash in big green bins round the back of the building and is

the same

the same

the same

three – four – days

Theo's nose drifts back towards the screen. Even the face of Dani cannot keep him awake, dead Dani dead, he didn't actually see her die he didn't see her face with the bullet in it until the photo came but he knew and still has a place to doubt the truth

dead Dani dead.

On the fifth day she gets into the elevator with three bags of white trash

leaves the camera

emerges

135

vanishes

emerges

goes to the bins with

two bags of trash.

Theo sits up, head foggy, mind adrift, looks again.

Two bags of trash.

She puts them in the bins and vanishes.

Stays out of camera shot for nearly five minutes.

Re-emerges, swiping her security badge out at the service door and

does not look at the security camera and

leaves.

Theo scours the cameras.

He can't see can't find any sign of

the third bag.

Looks again.

Arrives, cleans, collects the trash, gets into the lift, gets out of the lift, turns the corner with her three bags of

re-emerges into the camera shot carrying only two.

Theo went downstairs, following half-seen geography captured on CCTV, stepped into the dead zone in the lower corridors, pipes overhead, foil wrapped around the heating units, walls that had once been painted green, then yellow, and were now a chipped collage of both.

Walked through the place where the cameras didn't see.

Found the room on his second sweep.

Inside: a shredder, a photocopier, a stool and a sign showing the price of postage and packaging for oversized letters nine years ago. Very little of the equipment had been used for a long time. A single fluorescent tube shone overhead, flanked either side by two broken friends. A big green bin behind the shredder contained the soft tattered strings of graphs and documents long ago destroyed, letters and numbers forming strange dunes as he ran his fingers through them. He dug down into the paper, not for any particular reason other than the pleasure of sensation, and found the newspapers.

He pulled them out.

Trashy tabloids, free at the local Underground station, 40 per cent advertising, 50 per cent celebrity pop-talk, 8 per cent sport and 2 per cent rumours of death and environmental catastrophe in less important places than here.

affair scandal actor pop icon party drunk exposed footballer pregnancy sex naked downturn argument divorce

He pulled out a wedge and checked the date. The last was from a few days ago, and once he dug deeper, he found nearly thirty copies.

He drifted back to the security booth, replayed Dani's movements on that date.

Arrive

upstairs

clean

vacuum

take the trash down

three bags in the elevator two when she

He froze the image just as she vanished out of frame, thought about what he was seeing. Her entrance and her exit both took her past the room with the shredder. He zoomed in on her arriving, exiting, looked at the duffel bag slung over her shoulder.

Bulky both ways in, but on the way out the shape had changed.

Sat back to think.

Began to laugh, and had to stop himself abruptly when a guard popped his head inside the booth to make sure he was all right.

In the evening.

He looked up "Danesmoor" from an internet café in Bermondsey.

Ancestral home. Nice garden. Areas open to the public four days a week, guided tours on the first and third Sundays of the month. Family seat of the Marquess of Mantell, title currently held by Philip Arnslade son of Helen Arnslade wife of . . .

He stopped.

Got himself another coffee, even though the first was still buzzing through his mind.

Sat back again. Looked up Helen Arnslade. A picture of a woman, mid-sixties, posed formally besides a bust of her dead husband, pearls at her neck, hands clasped, proud of her home, dedicated to her duty. The captain read: "Lady Helen Continues to Set the Standard for the Shooting Season."

The photo was from several years ago. On the next page was an image of her son, proudly sporting a double-barrelled shotgun and a felt cap. He couldn't find anything more recent. No interviews, appearances, social media; just silence and a formal picture of a woman with sealed lips who knew how to throw a party for men who liked their meat bloody.

There's this woman, her name is Helen, she's seen the pits, she's got the . . .

Dani hadn't said anything more about the woman called Helen. It was a common enough name. In its way. He looked at the picture of her son, forced himself to stare.

The face was familiar to everyone, in the distracted way of someone everyone knew without knowing how. The minister of fiscal efficiency had long been tipped for the top job; tipped so long that people were beginning to speculate he had other plans altogether. Something in the Company, perhaps. He'd worked for the Company before politics. The Company liked to share its expertise with government; things were so much easier when you spoke the same language.

Light brown hair on a face of long curves drooping down towards a winning, stapled smile; a swell of forehead above the eyes, a sudden drop into sallowness, another burst of bone below at high cheekbones, a long droop into the cheeks and a final, triumphant protuberance of expression at his lips, as they danced, delighted, around phrases like:

"The ongoing strong economic growth in the services sector is a direct consequence of cutting taxes to those ordinary decent working middle-class people who give so much to the nation."

Theo had seen that face when it was younger. It had been the face of a man who couldn't understand why a woman whose education had been paid for by his father didn't appreciate the full nature of her commitments.

Philip Arnslade pulls the trigger by the river, and a boy dies, and as he dies, the boy who will be Theo thinks he falls too, watches the sky wheel overhead, feels the bullet in his lung, drinks blood and cannot breathe, the grass is wet and the earth punches into his back as he hits the ground and he cannot move can't believe that he cannot move as Philip Arnslade of Danesmoor Hall walks over and

Philip Arnslade is a king, born to rule, and nothing stands in his way.

As the night settled

Theo returned to Sidcup.

Three women guarded the estate, as always. One had a child on her lap, another lost in thought, or prayer.

"Who are you?" demanded one, and immediately another:

"I remember him. He was here when Dani died."

Hostility, plain and clear, one woman reaching for her pocket, the child sat bouncing on her mother's knee glaring, her face a fixture of compressed concentration and dislike, he had no idea one so young could find such depth of feeling in her soul.

"I was Dani's friend," he replied, hands folded in front of him, back straight, head down. "I knew her from Shawford."

"Could be anyone"

"Can't trust"

"Could be one of the filth"

"Men!"

"Fucking coming here and giving it"

Theo blurted, "I'm Lucy's father."

The women hesitated, the child's face flushing brilliant red with the effort of rage she was putting into this moment. Then her mother put a hand on her shoulder, and all at once the infant relaxed, beaming proudly into her parent's eyes, asking with her

139

suddenly lightened smile, delightful eyes – Did I do well? Did I hate well enough?

"Come with me," said a woman and stood up, nodding at her sisters of the guard, and Theo followed.

They walked through the estate. No lights shone in the windows, no creatures stirred. Far off, the sound of the motorway; across the stubby grass, a torn plastic bag, a tumbled can oozing fizzy drink. A banner was slung across three different windows, huge and torn by the wind, the letters sometimes visible, sometimes twisted into obscure tangles as the stitched-together sheets on which they were written caught together.

JOBS JUSTICE AND

He couldn't make out the last word.

"Dani was one of us," the woman grunted as they walked together towards the door. "She was a patty from the women's line. We tried being with the men, but when you spend your days in the women's prison, in the men's prison, these things – you spend so much time thinking about what it'll be like that when you actually try to be together it's hard, sometimes, to see what's real and what's not. So here we are. Sometimes the queen of the patties sends us a few things. She's got a court in the north. We have to stick together, us sisters, that's what the queen says. What's your name?"

"Theo."

"Theo what?"

"Theo Miller."

"She never mentioned you."

"Did she mention someone from home? Someone she grew up with?"

"No."

A little laugh that vanished instantly. "That's me too."

She shrugged. None of her affair.

From an open window a sudden rising of a voice, female, coming high and shrill, reaching a crescendo of fury

gurgling away

dying.

The woman walked, and seemed undisturbed.

The rage rites of the patties were something Theo did not enquire into.

Coming to Dani's door

shut

lights out

no sign the police had been

or gone

or cared.

She said, to no one in particular, "I stalked a woman called Naomi. I stalked her for five years. I told her I'd rape her, with a bottle, with a stick, I described it all so she'd understand. I sent postcards to her sister the day her kids were born, congratulating them on the birth and telling them to enjoy their kids while it lasted. I thought it was funny. It was funny. It was very, very funny."

Sighed, waving at the door.

"The police said they'd send someone to clean the blood, but no one came. We're saving up for some bleach."

Theo walked inside. The woman followed.

Up the stairs, pushed open the door

the stench of brain, rotting flesh it was still on the floor bits of her brain on the floor it hadn't been real until this moment Theo

guessed at a bathroom and managed to vomit into the sink before it was too late, acid in his nose, up his nostrils he was . . .

The woman stood behind him, waiting, arms folded, leaning against the wall, lost in her own thoughts. There was no water in the taps to wash his puke away, but she didn't seem to care, and he felt ashamed.

Theo returned to the bedroom, tried again.

The room had been searched. Drawers opened, mattress turned over, cupboard torn apart, clothes ripped out. Had that been the way it was when he stood in this door, looking on the feet of Dani's corpse?

He thought that yes, it had been Seph Atkins who searched the room and had she found . . .

"Has anyone touched the window?" he asked.

His guide shrugged.

The window still half-open, letting in cold air, taking some of the stench off.

There was no way to avoid Dani's blood, the sprays of the policemen as they'd squirted something orange around the body. He looked out of the window, down to the hedge below. If you'd been fast, you could have thrown a mobile phone out of the window at the right angle to land in the privet hedge, a desperate act at the sound of footsteps, an act that acknowledged in an instant that it was too late, you were done, nowhere to hide.

"Papers," he blurted, turning away. "Did she have any papers?"

The woman nodded, once, and led him down to the concrete back patio behind the house. Between the overgrown brambles and stinging nettles, someone had cleared the space for a crooked child's swing, the parts salvaged from a skip and strapped back together with tape and long, string-wrapped branches. Someone else had drawn the outline of a rat's corpse in pink chalk.

A metal bucket, knee-high, stood in a corner. The ashes were cold. Discarded half-matches formed a halo around the edge.

He sifted through the blackened crumbs of paper, found a white corner.

OF THE LATEST VALUE ON
PRODUCTIVITY TOWARDS
MAKING SAVINGS IN THE

The words vanished into char.

"She was down here a lot. Burning things. People joined her. They liked the fire. Sometimes the biters would come, the zeroes, and they'd sit and rock and scream and that. Neighbours hated it, but we respect those things round here. You gotta get it out of your system. You gotta let it out. You gotta let it go so you can keep going."

"You've been very helpful."

"One of ours let the killer in, of course. One of ours did it for the cash. I get that, we could all do with the dough, but when we find her . . . are you really the kid's dad? For real?"

"Yes. I am."

"You should do better. You should."

Theo cycled home, and the route seemed shorter tonight than it had last time he made the journey.

Chapter 32

Neila drew cards the moment they moored on the outskirts of Northampton, where the canal divided towards the River Nene.

Knight of cups, ten of cups, the Fool (inverted), nine of swords, the High Priestess, three of cups, seven of wands, the Tower, the Hanged Man (inverted).

She stared at them long and hard, realised she didn't know what they meant, couldn't find any comfort or meaning in them. Usually, no matter what she drew, there was something that gave purpose, direction to her life. Today her mind seemed frozen, trapped, looking at images without meaning. For the first time in her life she drew nine more.

Four of cups, Temperance, the Chariot, the World, six of staves, the Stars (inverted), four of swords, six of swords, the Hanged Man (inverted).

A guard from the university was at the side of the boat within ten minutes. Who are you? What are you doing here? I'm from the business school. There's a business school next to the station, we have to keep an eye out because this is a protected space for our students; we promised our students that they'd be safe here . . .

No.

Our students do not cross the canal.

They don't go to – are you joking with me, lady, are you – no, of course they don't go to . . . we abandoned the northern campus two years ago because we couldn't guarantee the safety of

87 per cent satisfaction rate, as you're asking, 94 per cent in

the arts. We lost a lot of lecturers, though, when the new system came in. They said that the criteria meant they had to be nice to their students, instead of making them learn. They said that the less homework they gave, the better their overall assessments. The better their overall assessments the more money they could make. Everyone's gotta eat.

Ginger biscuits? Really? Well as you're offering I mean don't tell anyone it's just

oh thank you these are the best they just really

look, I don't mind you staying but the evening shift guy he's going to be because this is a protected space it's a place of safety so

just to let you know.

And don't cross to the other side.

They moved the boat away from the bright glass walls of the business school, the men in black who prowled its edges. At the mooring point they found the narrowboat they'd seen a few nights before, an old woman stood with a blowtorch pressed against the air intake, cursing under her breath.

Neila went to help, smiling, hello again, and revved the engine as the woman pushed fire into the intake, and after a little while the engine reluctantly spat into full, chugging life, and the woman said thank you kindly but it's getting dark now

can I offer you tea

and Neila said thank you but no, no, I'll be all right, I've got . . .

And stopped herself before admitting to the existence of Theo, making a brew in the *Hector*.

In the evening, barely an hour after sunset, there was a sound like the howling of wolves.

It came from the darkness to the left of the canal and filled the sky above the streets where the lights had been cut off.

Blood between their teeth, chins craning to the hidden moon the children raised their heads and howled

howled

howled!

And in the darkness the others answered and shrieked their darknesses to the sky, the sound echoing off the water, the cry of the hunter, the predator that drinks the hot fresh juices from a still-beating heart

hoooowwwwwwwllllll!!!

Around the business school, the security men shut their students in and told them to wait until the buses came, secured with metal plates against reflective glass, a driver who kept a stun gun lodged between handbrake and gear stick

hoooooowwwwwllll!!!

Neila did not sleep, and neither did Theo.

At 1 a.m. they met each other, both going to the kitchen sink for a little more water.

Theo said, "There's a queen of the patties. They say she was one of the first, the oldest – the first woman they ever condemned to make burgers on the patty line. Half the meat they use is wasted anyway, but it doesn't matter. The government subsidises the companies that run the prison, to make sure they make a profit so they can carry on being efficient rehabilitators, says it's better that way, cheaper in the long run, so the companies don't worry if they waste stuff. There's mountains of minced meat at the back of the yard, the flies are so thick it looks like a living thing. My dad died on the patty line, but the contracts say that the government can't sue for negligence and why would they? Only a patty. Only another patty."

Little bodies darted by the window, little figures ran along the canal.

They sat together, close to the half-orange embers of the stove, as the voices were raised around the town, screaming at the dark.

"The queen says it's good to scream. Good to rage. If you don't get it out of your system then you're not being honest to yourself. You're just pretending that everything is okay. That this . . . this shit, this nothing-nowhere you've got, this dream that you swallowed whole when you were a kid because dreams weren't for the likes of you . . . you pretend that's okay. You live

146

your life as a grey one, one of the zeroes who'll die alone begging for Company scraps, because you didn't have the guts to look at yourself and say yes. Yes. This is fucked-up. And no. No. This isn't my fault. This was done to me. The world . . . did this to me. Accept that, she says, and you have seen the truth of the patty line, and the only thing that is right is the screaming, the raging, the burning and the truth of the flame. And when you've done that, then you can find yourself again, and the quiet place inside that will let you take control. That's the creed of the patty queen. That's what she told them, that's why they have these prayers . . . "

Blessed are her hands blessed is the water beneath her fingers blessed are the ones who blaze blessed are those who wait in shadows . . .

Neila warmed her hands by the stove and murmured, "All it is is screaming. That's all they do. It doesn't change anything."

They sat in silence a little while.

Theo said, "You sleep, and I'll wake, and in an hour I'll sleep, and you wake," and Neila nodded and lay down on the couch without another word, and pulled the blankets that covered Theo over her head, and didn't notice his smell on them, and slept for an hour, and woke feeling refreshed, and they swapped and just after 4 a.m . . .

. . . little hands thump thump thumping against the side of her boat thump thump thump not hard just a patter of flesh thump thump thump palm against steel, a dozen, two dozen, three, the children went running

the youngest barely three years old, carried by her elder sister they ran along the pavement in their torn shoes and flapping rags, not howling now, but tip-toe tapping in the darkness

The slapping of their hands against the boat woke Theo, a jump-start, and he pulled the blanket tight and looked like a man in search of a weapon, but Neila shook her head and whispered:

"It's just the children. Just the children. They'll pass. They'll pass."

And the children did, but before they went

A smash in the night!

Something metal!

Someone fell

a squeak of voices and

another crash, hollow across the water, and more disturbing perhaps a ripple against the boat, a gentle rocking, what has disturbed the surface of the canal so much

but then that too passed.

And Theo slept, and Neila waited, watching, until it was her turn to sleep again.

They rose at sunrise and found a child, dead, face down in the water. Where she'd fallen the thin ice had cracked, then begun to seal back around her, keeping her in place where she'd landed. She wore blue rubber boots and a huge red puffer coat. Her hair was black, in two bunches held up with plastic dragonfly-adorned clips. The blood from the wound in her scalp had been trapped in the ice, retaining its crimson brilliance. Neila stared at the corpse and thought she was going to cry. Theo stared at the body and thought: probably about £120,000, £130,000 at a pinch, depending on her manner of death, add an investigation cost of course these things can spiral out of control unless you're thoughtful about the fiscal consequences of . . .

And stopped.

And for a moment thought he saw Lucy there.

Thought he was going to be sick, and despised himself and everything he had become.

The locks on the doors into the narrowboat moored beyond theirs were broken. Potted plants on the roof had been smashed, spilling black, rich soil down the sides and onto the towpath. Someone had cut the rope to one bollard, but missed the second or not been bothered by it, so the boat drifted, bum out, away from the child in the water.

Neila went round to the prow, knocked tentatively on the half-open metal door, called out the old woman's name, pushed the door back, peeked inside.

The woman sat in the half-gloom, her face illuminated by the rising daylight through the portholes.

There was remarkably little blood on her face or on her hands. Remarkably little on the kitchen knife she still held clutched in front of her. Neila looked, and wondered if maybe the blood wasn't real, and decided it was.

She called the woman's name again – Marta, Marta, can you . . . ?

The woman didn't stir.

"Marta, it's Neila. Marta are you . . . are you hurt? Did they . . ."

The woman didn't raise her head, and held the knife close.

Theo peeked in behind Neila.

Saw the old woman.

Saw the blood.

Looked away.

At the sky and the water, at the city and the business school behind them, gearing up again into full swing, at the girl floating face down in the water.

He stepped inside the cabin.

Crossed slowly to the woman.

Squatted down in front of her.

Put his hand over hers, cradling the fingers that held the knife.

Her eyes drifted to his face, and her fingers tightened on the handle.

"Blessed are the mothers," he whispered. "Blessed are the children. Blessed is the dawn on the day of release. Blessed is the mist that rises by the river."

Her eyes dropped down again, her lips hung loose on a crackle-boned jaw.

Theo took the knife without a word, laid it on the counter to one side.

Burned-down incense sticks sat in a blue ceramic holder on the fold-down dining table. A half-finished copy of a romantic novel about a family in the south of France lay on the couch. The kettle on the stove had boiled itself dry, leaving a steaming scar on the ceiling above.

The woman stared at nothing as Theo held her hands.

He waited
waited
waited
as all things waited
for the woman at last to blink, look him in the eye, feel his skin on hers and say, "They came onto my boat."

Theo nodded once, squeezed her hands, let go, walked away.

Neila called the police.

Theo said, "I can't be here . . . if the police come . . . "

She replied, "There's water at Nether Heyford. I'll find you, I promise I'll find you . . . "

To Neila's surprise, the police came.

Marta had comprehensive security coverage. She turned out to be rich, had chosen to live on the canal with savings from managing space on cargo vessels. She'd sold her house, her second home in the Cotswolds Community, most of her ninety-plus pairs of shoes, her ex-husband's wine collection, and now she sailed the waterways for reasons that no one knew. Because she loved it, perhaps?

And in the night the children had come and they had broken into her boat and she had panicked she'd simply panicked and . . .

They used long hooks to fish the girl out. It took two strong men to haul her onto land, ice water streaming from the tops of her boots.

"It's all right, love," said one of the coppers as they handcuffed the old woman and led her away. "Kid you popped was one of the children. Everyone knows you get a discount for that sort of thing."

Marta cried silently when the man said that, though she hadn't wept until that moment.

When the police were gone
Theo didn't come back.

Marta's narrowboat drifted, stern out, and after a while Neila

150

realised no one was coming for it, so she climbed on board, slid along the narrow edge of the boat to the rear, threw a rope to shore.

Tied off.

Had a look at the smashed door, shattered lock, couldn't see an easy way to repair it, thought of getting a new one for when Marta came back.

Couldn't think of a way to make that work out, didn't know if . . .

Let herself inside.

Cleaned up a bit.

Righted a smashed picture frame, Marta and a child, maybe a son?

Swept the glass up, threw it away.

Cleared out the stove, made the bed, put cups back in the cupboard, straightened everything out, didn't want to do anything more, felt intrusive, felt that what she was doing wasn't even close to enough.

In the end, she put a note in the window.

ENGINE TROUBLE — WAITING FOR REPAIRS

The note wouldn't buy Marta much time before she exceeded her permit to moor, but maybe someone would come and help save the boat before the scavengers split it open and stripped it down.

At sunset Theo did not appear.

Neila slept badly.

There was no howling in the night.

The streets were silent, except for a voice, raised shortly after midnight, a child singing in the dark, somewhere beyond the water.

*What shall we do with a drunken sailor, early in
    the morning?*

151

Hey ho and up she rises,
Hey ho and up she rises,
Hey ho and—

As suddenly as the voice had begun singing, it stopped, and was not heard again.

"Cut his throat with a rusty cleaver," sang Neila under her breath as she turned the lights down. "Cut his throat with a rusty cleaver . . ."

By the water
to the north
the man called Theo thinks he hears singing in the distance but can't make out the words.
"Blessed are the ones who walk," he whispers under his breath as he trudges, head down, hands buried, through the night. "Blessed are they who remember and fear . . ."

In the houses where the children live
the school burned down and the parents had no place to go there is only
the moon
the night
the howling at the sky
A girl is dead and the children are silent in the corners of the crowded rooms.

In the police station Marta said, "I won't pay for an indemnity. I won't pay. I won't pay for the indemnity. I must pay some other way."
And the coppers shake their heads in disbelief, and one brings her a cup of tea and sits next to her and whispers, "You don't want to go to the patty line, luv. Not at your age. You won't make it a year, it's the work you see, it's just the work, round here you gotta make Cornish pasties and I like a pasty I do lovely jubbly

but the fat you know the fat? You take a bite and the fat it just burns like – you don't want to get burned. It was just a kid you killed. Just a kid. She wasn't going to be nothing, you don't have to – it was just a kid. Pay the indemnity. They're giving you that discount anyway!"

And in the office above the cells:
"What do you mean, two sets of fingerprints?"
"Two sets on the knife, and this second set you got there's a . . . "
On the table in front of the man in charge, a kitchen knife, the blood dry, white forensic dust on the handle where another man's hand gently prised the weapon away from an old woman's fingers.
They wouldn't have bothered to fingerprint it at all if the old biddy hadn't been quite so peculiar about her need to be punished.

In London a phone rings.
"Mr Markse? We've found a fingerprint and you won't believe who it . . . "
The clouds skim across the moon.

On the towpath Theo stops suddenly, dead in his tracks, and sees a heron. It stands on one leg where a ledge creates a shallow step of water, waiting to strike with its raised claw, and does not move or turn its head.
He stares at it for a very, very long time
then raises one leg
and makes like a heron.
For a little while.

Chapter 33

The police had an inventory of items removed from Dani's flat
  toothbrush hairbrush shoes bedside cup
  splatter evidence blood evidence fingerprints DNA not that
anyone would
  A confession has been received, and given the low estimated
value of the indemnity against Ms Cumali's death, it is not considered necessary at this time to run any more tests on . . .
  Theo went through the list, hunched in the low light of his
bedroom, until he found her mobile phone.
  He called the station.
  "Paddington Safelife Policing?"
  "I'm from the Criminal Audit Office – if you could – thank
you that is . . . "
  Holding music, a distortion of a tune he thought he once knew
from his childhood. Or maybe all music just sounded the same
these days; it was hard to tell.
  "Hello? Who am I speaking to?"
  "Hello, yes, my name is Theo Miller I'm from the CAO audit-
ing the Cumali case. I just had a couple of questions . . . "
  "Auditing?"
  "Yes for the audit I'm—"
  "What do you need?" Brisk, bored, the copper was mid-email
and now he's got to deal with this, his shift is ending and he just
knows his missus has ruined the dinner, she always does if he
gets back soon though he might be able to stop her from making
it worse.

"The inventory gave a mobile phone as being part of Ms Cumali's possessions. I'm wondering if I can drop in tomorrow to access it?"

"Why do you need—"

"There's a suggestion of cyber-crime which might affect – you know how it is if the defence find this stuff before we do they can argue an unfair indemnity against the value of . . . "

"Hold on. Hold on. Just hold a moment will you if the . . . "

More music. Electric guitar. Electric keys. A song about discovering how sexy you are and hoping all the women will notice your starlight smile your million-dollar sparkle your sky-high . . .

"Mr Miller?"

"Still here."

"I don't have any record of a phone."

"In the file I'm holding . . . "

"No, no record definitely I've just—"

"It says that—"

"There's nothing entered into evidence there's no sign that I'm sorry but you might be looking at the wrong – what's your serial number?"

"I'll cross-check with the office tomorrow thank you you've been very . . . "

Lying awake, watching the ceiling.

If he closes his eyes he can for a moment imagine the world above, he is rising like an angel, spreading wings of light and dancing, dancing in the clouds, ice-cold crystals on his skin and yet it doesn't hurt, thin air in his lungs and yet breathing just makes him lighter, soaring, naked, beautiful, liberated and free.

And all the people of the city they fly too, the dreamers and the sleepers, the staring children and the distant old ladies drifting before the TV, they close their eyes and soar, majestic in golden light, they dance around each other like mating songbirds, wings tucking in close as they twist and twist, ribbons of DNA across the moon, meteors ripping the stars in two as they . . .

there's a market for everything

She's your daughter. She's your daughter. She's

Sits up gasping for breath, had dozed and not even noticed it, sweat and terror and

lies back to sleep, and does not dare close his eyes, and is scared to dream.

Chapter 34

Fifteen years before, in a pub in Oxford:

The duellists' insurance papers required witnesses.

The boy witnessed Theo's; the real Theo, the one who actually believed in something. Anything.

Simon Fardell witnessed Philip Arnslade's. They signed it at a pub round the corner from St John's on a drizzling afternoon. The rugby club were in, and had trained most triumphantly and roared and cheered and clawed at the backside of any creature that passed, sex, age or willingness unimportant.

After they had signed, the boy sat with Simon Fardell to discuss details.

"The indemnity gives each party five shots. We have to make sure that the terms aren't violated. I have these guns from home which I think would be appropriate, we can guarantee they fire true and of course the indemnity doesn't cover us so I've drawn up a formal letter of protest requesting both parties to cease which we can sign and file in case the police attempt to give us an accessory charge, and the lawyer assures me that—"

"I haven't seen the letter . . ."

"Don't worry about that it's really an irrelevance, the police won't actually bother — and the discretion clause means that if it did go to court both parties would be subject to litigation regardless of who survives and I'm training to be a lawyer you know are you . . ."

"Maths."

"Really? Who's your sponsor? There's a whole section of index-based market leveraging which is—"

"I don't have a sponsor."

"Oh. I just thought . . . I mean you seem so . . . "

"I self-funded."

"Really? Never would have guessed. Anyway, as I was saying the discretion clause so neither family can sue in open civil court or defame litigate or libel the surviving party of the . . . "

At sunset, by the river, in the far-off half-dream of the past, the boy stood with Simon Fardell by the thin, reedy banks of the Thames and held a gun between two fingertips, and had never held a gun before, no not even with his dad doing all the things they said his dad had done, and Simon tutted and exclaimed:

"The safety here, you see, you take a grip, two hands underneath – have you never really done this before? Now sight down here, two points see two on the barrel that's it now we're at thirty paces which is how far they will be and – shoot!"

The boy shot, and missed by a mile.

"For goodness' sake, squeeze the trigger just squeeze it, breathe out and . . . "

"Are we allowed to do this, I mean the noise, won't the police come, isn't it . . . "

"I know the chap who owns this land. Don't worry about it, the farmers around here, the people, it's fine so now deep breath and exhale and . . . "

The boy fired, and this time he hit the edge of the target tacked to a high-packed hay bale.

"Good! Better! Now, fire a few, get a feel for it, don't lock the arms, don't fight the recoil that's how you – excellent! Would you say that this weapon fires straight?"

"I . . . yes. I suppose I would."

"You'll need to sign the release here for the documents it's – good good good so here's your copy and here's mine and I'll just test my gun and of course we'll lock the weapons up afterwards, two boxes two keys, prevent tampering, photo evidence all part of protecting ourselves against – God that's a great gun, the kick of it it's just so . . . "

"Does it have to be these guns?"

"What do you mean?"

"It seems . . . you said it was a .45 and I thought maybe they'd use a lower calibre, maybe .22 I mean that way they could . . . "

"What a curious idea!"

"This duel, I mean forgetting that it's illegal for a moment, forgetting that it's . . . "

"Illegal but affordable."

" . . . illegal it seems to me that the cause of the fight is so I mean it's just so ridiculous isn't it fundamentally it's . . . "

"Philip doesn't feel it's ridiculous. Nor does your man Theo."

"But it is; it is you and I can both see that it is can't we? You seem . . . very smart I don't mean that in a – but very smart and I mean don't we have a responsibility, a civic responsibility, a responsibility as friends I mean for God's sake we're talking about one of them dying!"

"We're committed now. The papers are signed."

"What if we swapped the bullets?"

"For .22s?"

"For blanks."

In Shawford the sea rolls against the shingle, the chalk cliffs crumble, Dani Cumali sits on a bench dedicated to D. WRIGHT, 1944–1999, HE LOVED THE SKIES, and stares across the water and cannot remember why she sat down, and does not wish to stand.

In a time yet to come, Neila threw another log onto the stove, and closed the door as it began to hiss, two parts steam to one part smoke.

In the dreams of the man called Theo, he hears his daughter, roaring.

And in a field outside Oxford, two boys stood holding loaded guns before a wall of hay bales, waiting at the centre of the universe.

Simon Fardell, even aged twenty, looked like the man he

would grow into. His place had been sponsored by a company that would soon be simply the Company. He went to lectures in a three-piece suit because he knew he needed to stand out, to make an impression. It was all about thinking ahead; he had his three-year plan, his seven-year plan and his twenty-year objectives he was . . .

. . . in many ways a very handsome boy who would grow into a handsome man. He didn't play any team sports but worked out three times a week, kept his fair hair cut short at the sides and back, had a tiny, slightly beakish nose above a small, tight smile that flashed and faded like lightning, a notch in his chin and blue eyes which he knew were unusually dark, unusually beautiful.

"Blanks?" he mused, and the boy who would be Theo, crooked and small, smiled uneasily and realised that he knew nothing about people, or human nature, and was actually really bad at remembering faces and he should try and learn some sort of method for dealing with that.

Simon laughed, and slapped the boy on the shoulder and exclaimed, "You do have the funniest ideas! Blanks! What an incredible idea. Let them fire their five and then . . . well blanks! Yes I suppose I see how we could . . ."

That night the boy slept with the gun under his pillow and it was really uncomfortable so in the end he put it in the drawer by his bed.

And in the morning, before the sun was up, he borrowed a bicycle and pedalled out to the field by the river, with Theo Miller by his side, and they didn't speak, and they did not go to the open-faced barn with the hay bales but stood before a line of beech trees as the sun rose and the dew melted through their shoes, and it was remarkably cold for the time of year and Theo wished he'd brought more clothes but as the sun rose higher it became hotter and hotter and he realised he was sweating a waterfall and . . .

Simon and Philip came on foot from up the drive, their car

left, engine running, by the gate, this wouldn't take long, and as they went to load the guns the boy looked into Simon's eyes and saw him smile and nod and understood that to be an agreement, a confirmation of the pact they had made, and he nodded back and loaded the gun.

Can it be a bullet if there is no lead? A casing to be ejected, gunpowder but no death, he loaded blanks, five shots in total, and took the weapon to Theo and said, "Good luck," and Theo did not smile and did not flinch and did not nod and looked like he might be sick.

And the boys stood back to back, in the traditional way, and at the command of Simon, they walked fifteen paces apart in opposite directions, and at a word

"Go!"

They turned and fired.

Theo was slightly faster, he saw Philip flinch, but then Philip shot and missed, and Theo fired again, and Philip did not fall, and they fired again, and again, and on the fourth shot

Theo staggered.

He staggers and the engine of the passing barge goes chunk chunk chunk chugger chugger chugger chugger and the man who is called Theo feels the tear in his side sewn together with cornflower-blue thread and hears gunfire in the engine chugger chugger BANG

in a field beneath the shadowed light of the rising sun Theo Miller staggers, raises his gun, fires once more, but he has had his five shots, and still Philip comes, he has one shot left now he comes closer and closer stands over Theo and the boy shouts

... sounds without words or meaning ...

and Philip lowers the gun and pulls the trigger.

Theo Miller died in the ambulance.

The boy rode with him, held his hand until the paramedics pulled him away, cried and shivered and at last sat in silence.

The paramedic said, "Nothing you could have done. It took out his lung then the abdomen; he was bleeding heavily I think there was nothing it wasn't your fault . . . "

Time is
         days are
               passing and yet the winter is
time is frozen and it is the nature of time that sometimes

The boy sat outside the morgue, and called Theo Miller's parents.

His parents were away, out of the country. They were always out of the country. No, the maid didn't know when they'd be back. No, she couldn't contact them immediately. Yes, she'd pass on his message, ask them to call. Was it . . . was everything . . . was young Mr Miller was he . . .

The boy hung up and sat in a white corridor outside an unnamed door, locked, a vending machine at the bottom of the hall offering sugary drinks and dried fruit snacks, a couple of porters gossiping as their patients drooped and slumbered in wheelchairs, saline bags suspended above their heads. Oh I *know* she's just the worst she's just the . . .

The boy waited and didn't know what he was waiting for.

When Theo's parents called back, it was a bad line from far away.

"Hello! Hello? Yes, I'm Mrs Miller. I was given this number and told to call it – who are you?"

"I've got bad news."

"What? Speak up it's a terrible line hold on I'll just go outside and . . . yes, that's better, what did you say?"

"Mrs Miller, I've . . . got some bad news. Earlier this morning Theo was . . . there was an accident and Theo is . . . "

"What? Is he in hospital? What?"

"Mrs Miller, Theo is dead."

"Say again? What was that? Listen this line is terrible is it your end can you . . . "

"Theo is dead."

Behind the silence someone is laughing. Mrs Miller is outside a restaurant, there's music playing, there's gossip and life and a car revving a very expensive engine *vroom* they make the sounds different for different nations the Italians you see they like to know that their engines are powerful *vroom* it's all part of the

she drops to the ground

holds the phone

listens to the world

"Are you sure?"

"Yes. I'm sorry but he . . . "

"What happens now?"

"I don't know."

"Is there . . . there are things that need to be done. There are . . . what happens now? Who are you? What happens now?"

The lawyer came.

"The indemnity has been registered and confirmed. Mr Arnslade will pay £75,000 to cover the cost of the alleged felony against Mr Miller and in addition, as a token of commiseration, he's adding £15,000 without prejudice for the family of Mr Miller or a named charity without in any way such gesture being an admittance of liability. The discretion clause and mutual agreement between the parties ensures the case will not result in a criminal record and all parties involved are barred from further discussion, dissemination or in any way from referencing the manner of Mr Miller's departure."

There were nine people at Theo Miller's funeral, which was held discreetly at a small church in Cumbria, near a stone cottage which the family had liked to holiday at when Theo was a child.

No one from the university came, apart from the boy.

He thought perhaps Theo's stepmother would scream at him, attack him, rage at him, how could you do this how could you let this happen how could you be so . . .

. . . instead she held his hand like she was comforting him, like he was a brother who needed her support, her only surviving son, and Theo's father gave a short speech about a tragedy that could not be undone, and the next day the two of them left for their apartment in Vienna and never came back.

Return to Oxford. Exams were done the results came and Theo's name was still on the list, he'd got a 2.1, all that gin and still got a 2.1 fancy that, and no one seemed to realise that he wasn't there to collect it; that his name when called would be spoken at an empty seat.

The discretion clause worked its magic. When you weren't allowed to talk about a thing, sometimes it was just easier to ignore it, pretend it had never happened. Theo Miller vanished and people wondered where he was, and those who knew . . .

. . . did not answer.

The boy went back to halls, began to pack, not sure where he was going, not sure what he was meant to do now.

Realised, as he packed, that Theo Miller's room was untouched next door. No one had come to take his things, no one had asked him to leave, the rent had left his account automatically, somehow in the notification process his bank hadn't been informed, the discretion clause had frightened the morgue or the police from doing their thing.

The boy packed his stuff, went back to Shawford, three trains and a bus, arrived at the station with no one to meet him but . . .

"We should go to the beach together. You bring blankets, I'll bring booze."

They lay on the beach together, Dani pressed to his side, and the boy tried to say something, to apologise, to explain that he'd cocked it all up, that his dream was dead too and more, his dream had always been a lie, always, he'd thought perhaps he had a future and it had never been true there was no future there was no dream only guilt and failure and regret and the distant memory of promised light.

And Dani said:

"They didn't extend my contract. No point. They've got other kids coming up through the programme now, give the job to some sixteen-year-old, not like they need much training, let them work until they're twenty-one then give them the shove before they have to pay full wage and you just keep thinking, don't you, you keep thinking ..."

The next morning there she was, with Andy. She was going to dump him. She knew she would. It was just ... really hard. Because once he was dumped, what was she supposed to do?

What was she supposed to do?

Their eyes met, and he walked on by and did not look back.

Went to the train station.

Threw his phone out of the window.

Took three trains and a bus.

Back to Oxford. Back to the safe place that had always been a lie, he never should have been there, he was never going to make it. Some mad fantasy of his patty-line dad, some hilarious criminal's joke.

At the careers centre the woman said:

So maths but no sponsor?

Internships, perhaps, a couple of years of unpaid internships and you could absolutely ... do you have any contacts, or does your family have any contacts who might be ...

and your father is

I see

for

driving the van.

Well I'm not saying it's going to affect your career prospects, not at all, it's just that ... well, people might see and be somewhat ... you know.

And most people who do your course
have sponsorship
   the banks
         the defence firms
           the Company
       it's all about derivatives about the way in which
money works, about
  well.
        Well.
               It is so good that someone like you thinks
of applying.

The day before he had to go
  Back to Shawford, perhaps. Back dragging his heels, too edu-
cated to work down the chippy, too tainted to work in a bank.
  Back to . . . wherever the hell he was meant to go next, head
full of numbers and wallet full of £17.28.
  He used a knife to force the lock to Theo Miller's room.
  Let himself inside.
  Sat on Theo's bed.
  Flicked through his clothes.
  Opened the envelope from the university reminding him
of his new degree, congratulating him on his success, inviting
him to attend the graduation ceremony. Unanswered emails
on the laptop, which Theo had never properly password-
protected. Interviews. Prospects. Future shimmering like
dawn's first light.
  Ran his fingers down the black gown on the back of Theo's
door, longer sleeves than the boy had ever had, a scholar's sleeves,
indicative of great academic promise, a badge of honour and . . .
  Picked it up.
  Tried it out for size.
  Swirled, feeling the sleeves flap limply around his body.
  Stared at his face in the mirror.
  Pushed his hair back from his forehead. Wondered how he'd
look with a beard.

Found Theo's passport in a shoebox at the bottom of the cupboard.

Sat a while longer on the edge of the bed.

Put the passport in his pocket and went to the local pharmacy to get some new photos taken.

Chapter 35

A few days after Dani died, Theo returned to work.

His grandmother's funeral had been very sad very sad indeed but also it was her time and he didn't really want to talk about it . . .

Which was a relief, as no one wanted to talk to him about it either.

A few good cases had come through. A wealthy landlord had burned alive a former tenant who was harassing him for the return of his deposit. The case was especially lovely because it turned out the tenant was a trustee for a charity that helped terminally ill children visit petting zoos and all in all . . .

. . . £600,000, maybe even £700,000 for the murder?

The accused's lawyer would probably barter it down to £590,000, but even so, it was an open-and-shut case and best of all, the killer could pay, it was bonus time at the Criminal Audit Office.

"My grandmother died last month," mused Charlotte Burgess as they stood in the food queue together at lunch. "Her last words were 'I should never have kept that damn cat.'"

The two of them considered this in silence, and Theo ordered the jacket potato with cheese and beans.

£6700 for the investigation costs because they had to do a test on the knife after the coppers decided that the

yes well the thing is she had two kids and also helped at the local community centre so that's an extra £15,000 for the you robbed a man with insurance the policy covers a minimum indemnity of £20,000 well that's just how it works with

knock off ten grand because actually the guy was asking for it and

He submitted the Cumali case in the afternoon. After due consideration, charges were dropped to manslaughter, and the indemnity set at £84,000. If Edward was pleased, he didn't show it, and Mala Choudhary sent Theo an email congratulating him on his good sense.

Theo cycled home faster than he'd ever ridden before, swerving through London streets, a driver opened her door to shout at him you stupid bloody wanker what the hell do you think . . .

He was gone before she could get to the juicy bits.

He picked up Dani's phone from its hiding place above the spice cupboard in Mrs Italiaander's kitchen – the phone she'd thrown from the window, the one the police hadn't found and lost – and cycled to Streatham Hill. The sun was already down, the air cold enough to make the grass crackle beneath his feet.

Found a bench.

Sat in darkness.

Turned the phone on.

There were three numbers called – his and two he didn't recognise.

He dialled the first unknown number.

The phone was answered after two rings.

"Heya honey, what can we do for you tonight?" A voice trying hard, a little too hard, to exude sultry allure.

"Uh . . . I don't really know. Who am I speaking to?"

"It's Salome. Can I take your name?"

"Salome . . . who?"

A switch, a drop from sultry to something altogether more regularly seen down the pub. "Do you want me to get the missus?"

"Where are you?"

"Where are *you*?"

"I'm sorry, I don't know what number I've called."

"Wivelsfield."

"Wivelsfield?"

"You seriously don't know?"

"No."

"We're a massage parlour and luxury club experience, mister."

"Right."

"*Luxury club experience.* For men, yeah? With massage? Jesus."

"Oh. I see."

A slight shuffle on the other end of the line, an attempt to reassert a certain sensual musicality to the whole conversation, failing. "So you uh ... interested?"

"I don't think I am right now, thank you. Do you know a woman called Dani Cumali?"

"She's not one of ours. Look, I've got to go, there are other callers, the lines are like, you know ... "

"I just need to know if—"

"If you're not buying then ... "

"Can I ask—"

"Bye!"

The woman hung up.

For a while Theo sat, holding the phone, bewildered. Thought about calling back. Wasn't sure what he could possibly say.

He dialled the second unknown number.

Waited.

Waited.

"Hello?"

"Hello, who am I speaking to?"

Silence.

A rustling, a motion, a beep.

"Hello? Hello? Is anyone ... "

The line was dead.

He called back.

The phone rang, then stopped immediately.

Rang again.

Didn't get past the first ring, before it was silenced.

Texted instead, went through various drafts, threats and challenges, wheedles and appeals to a better nature. Chose the least offensive of them all.

I knew Dani Cumali.

Hit send.

Counted to thirty.

Rang.

The phone rang a very long time. One ring before it was going to go to answerphone, a man answered.

"Yes." He sounded tired, resigned, old.

"Who am I speaking to?"

"You first."

"My name is Theo."

"Theo what?"

"Just Theo. You?"

"Faris."

"Is that . . ."

"Just Faris."

"Fair enough."

"I can't help you."

"I just need to ask a few questions about— "

"Don't call me again."

A sudden blurt; a desperate burble of words before he could be cut off. "Dani Cumali was murdered by a professional hit woman. A firm called Faircloud Associates have bought a discretion clause to close the case. Dani's phone, the one that was registered to her, has been lost by the police. You were one of three people called from this device, which neither the killer nor the police found. One was a brothel. I am the other. I think it would be in both our interests to meet."

time is

flying when you're having fun

takes for ever when you're about to

have a needle shoved in your arm, it's just one of those things

*

171

The man called Faris thinks a very long time, then says, "I can meet you in an hour."

They met at a café near Vauxhall Bridge. The café was inside a licensed area. The bouncers checked Theo's ID and credit rating, waved him in.

Thwump thwump thwump the sound of bass. It hurts the ears, it's in the stomach, the kind of sound that lets you know how much food you've eaten lately, or if you had a liquid lunch, because you can feel it all vibrating, the soft inner sea inside your belly bouncing like the surface of the water before an earthquake thwump thwump thwump

An assault of colour.

Fuchsia, magenta, pink deepening down to red. Streaks dripping from the ceiling like blood. Across the floor, colder whites and blues, ultraviolet splotches on the floor lighting up the spilt gin and fluorescent paint, spinning green disco lights and sharp-tipped lasers burning on the retina.

Drugs too.

Theo looks for a few seconds before seeing the first pills, just there, on the table, a bit of something extra a bit of something to raise the night keep you partying stronger, harder.

If the cops catch you there'll be an indemnity of £9150 minimum but actually the girls taking it tonight

they can pay

And more importantly the licensed area has its own security, private security on a corporate contract. It's not that they endorse breaking the law. It's just that cops don't have any authority over licensed corporate business, because the law isn't about removing choice; it's about protecting it.

Eyes of bursting red, capillaries popping. Swollen noses, hysterical laughter, a woman sobbing in a corner, dress torn, a group of friends by the toilet door, one of their number bent over double, she didn't make it to the sink. Let it out, honey, just let it all out.

Women in patty-line overalls, mopping up noodle-threaded

puke. A parade of flesh in bikini and thong, the hottest new commodities, some are from the patty line looking to make a buck. Others too – this is just what they do. They want the money, dream of the money. Money makes the world go round.

Theo scuttles on as the security guards glower at him and his light wallet, sober face.

He found Faris in a section designed to resemble an all-American burger bar, complete with alcoholic milkshakes in chilly metal pint jugs that dripped slow condensation onto the tabletop. The sound of music was fainter here, muffled by curtains behind which waitresses in tight yellow tops and frilly white aprons negotiated with clients for more than the usual service, arms poked and scratched, veins like dead silver worms sunk into flesh.

Faris was tucked into a booth, halfway through a chicken burger with extra chilli, his beard stained with orange sauce, dark brown eyebrows drawn together. He glanced up as Theo approached, scowled, looked down at his plate, carried on with his burger.

Made a big deal of consuming it, every last bite, licking his lips, wiping his face with a napkin, spreading the detritus, putting the napkin down, picking up a single, skinny dry chip from the basket by him, taking a bite, half a chip gone, chewing with his mouth open, then the other half, licking his fingers, picking up another, watching Theo. His skin was the colour of monsoon earth, his hair was going badger grey at the temples and crown. His nails were buffed down to tiny, soft stubs. Two tendons stood out below his jaw and down his neck, like the lines of a suspension bridge.

He ate chips.

Theo waited.

Another chip and

another chip and

Theo waited.

Faris took another chip, and didn't eat it, but held it sticky in one hand and at last met Theo's eyes.

"So. Dani."

"Yes."

"When you rang . . . "

"I knew Dani."

"That seems . . . "

"Yes?"

"Stupid thing to say to a stranger if you're . . . "

"I figured we're both . . . "

"In it?" Faris's head turned a little to one side, the chip drooping between pinched fingers. "Shafted?" he added, running
through options, tasting the ideas. "Up shit creek?"

"Yes."

"How'd you get my number?"

"Found Dani's phone. Her other phone – the one they were
looking for the night she died."

A shrug. Faris supposed someone had to find it; there are worse
people than Theo. "Why'd you get involved?"

Theo hesitated, eyes drifting up as he ordered his thoughts.
"Dani Cumali has a daughter. She hasn't . . . hadn't . . . seen
her for fourteen years. She tried to blackmail me into helping.
Blackmailed her boss. He got her work at the Ministry of Civic
Responsibility. She stole documents. She'd get into the lift with
three bags of trash and leave with only two. In her last message to
me she claimed to have found something big – 'They broke the
world,' she said. I think she was looking for something to leverage
against her daughter's freedom, more blackmail. Her boss, he said
this thing – 'there's a market for everything'. Lucy – that's her
kid – she's on the patty line. Still a juvenile, it's all just writing
reviews, nothing . . . but you get stuck – these things – you get
stuck and before you know it . . . "

Whoomp whoomp whoomp went the music and the security
guards looked the other way and money switched hands and no
one cared, and none of it mattered.

Theo looked at the damp bowl of sagging chips in front of
Faris, and felt suddenly hungry. "Whatever Dani found in the
Ministry killed her. They sent a woman called Seph Atkins.

Atkins is being defended by Faircloud Associates. Faircloud Associates works for the Company, and the Company is in part run by a man called Simon Fardell. Simon Fardell is the oldest friend of Philip Arnslade, minister of fiscal efficiency. They have ... shared experiences. Dani, when she blackmailed her boss, made him send her to a place called Danesmoor. Danesmoor is the ancestral home of Philip Arnslade. I'm not sure what this means yet, I'm not sure what she found, and I'm not sure I want to find out, given that they killed her for it. But I am sure that if they killed once, they'll kill again. Before she died, Dani threw a mobile phone away – this phone."

He laid it on the table, an ugly brick in a world of neon.

"There were three numbers on the phone. One of those is yours, one of them is mine. I thought that maybe this might create a shared need to communicate."

He stopped, head turning a little to one side. Faris's lips were drawn to invisibility across his mouth, a paper cut where smile, scowl, anything should have been, as if he would swallow his own features whole. Behind them a waitress in a little white apron exclaimed in a bad Texan accent, "Oh hun, you'll just *love* the special!"

Faris ate a chip, picked up another, moved it towards his mouth, stopped, put it back in the basket, turned the basket so that the longest edge aligned with the bottom edge of the table, spun his empty burger plate so that the largest smear of ketchup was at the top, picked up another chip, ate half of it, put the other half back in the basket, leaned back in his chair and for a while

had absolutely nothing to say for himself.

Theo waited.

"I was a journalist," Faris announced, a tale told too many times, the meaning sucked away into only words. "I was done for libel. The indemnity was £329,560. Few years ago, government licenses the Company to collect taxes. It was part of mainstreaming the income process blah blah blah, that shit, business efficiency taking over from creaking public authorities.

Deal was, Company pays the government a guaranteed cool four hundred billion every year, just like the budget says they should, and the Company gets to keep any profit above and beyond that. They're not allowed to set the tax rates, not officially, but of course they're allowed to choose how they exercise their power how they . . .

. . . so they set the rates, I mean, it's not official but everyone knows that's what's happening because the Company are controlling the algorithms that do the maths and you can appeal if you've got the cash or time but who's got that except the rich guys and the rich guys are getting really good rates, I mean rates that would . . .

. . . and the Company is netting maybe six fifty, seven hundred *billion* a year. That's a two-hundred-and-fifty-billion profit and sure, there's some objections, people who are, like 'That's our money they're taking this is tax farming they're squeezing us dry' but who even listens to that stuff these days? And some bleeding-heart liberals start a petition and a few try to take the whole thing to court but it was the government who made this deal and you know what? That makes it law. That means no one did anything wrong.

Except Philip Arnslade, the minister of fiscal efficiency – he's getting two million a year from the Company for 'consultation services', and pays ground rent of a quid for a palace off Sicily, and that's corruption, I mean, that's proper, provable corruption not just mismanagement, cos you can't arrest someone for being crap but you can arrest them for . . .

But the Ministry said I'd misunderstood the tendering process and was bringing them into disrepute, and their lawyers took it all the way to the appeals court, and I lost when I couldn't pay my barrister. By then I was broke anyway. I got five years on the patty line, but because of my CV I was sponsored out by a copy-writing company, given four years six months proofreading washing-machine manuals. My parole finished two months ago, and they decided not to keep me on at full salary. Cheaper to pull people like me from the patty line instead."

Theo sat silent, one elbow nudging a pool of beef fat that had solidified on the table to a translucent smear.

"My daughter's paying for me at the moment. That's how I get by. She works for the Company, does their marketing for the pharma side of things. I can't get sponsorship for benefits; my record means I'm an unsound investment. They keep telling me to fill out the form again. That's what I do, mostly. I fill out the forms. I also help some of the others fill out the forms on the sly, you'd get into trouble if anyone found out that ... that's how I knew Dani. She wanted all these forms done, trying to find her kid. No chance in hell they'd let her see her, but ... she kept on trying. Gotta hand it to her. Waste of bloody time."

"Was that it? Was that all she wanted?"

The chips are getting cold. Faris's gaze is lost to some other place.

"If a Company man kills a stranger, he pays less than an ordinary citizen. He's worth more to society than other people – no point penalising the successful for a lapse in judgement. Wouldn't be efficient. So that's it. That's our world. Eat your fucking chips and deal with it, right?"

A defiant chip, defiantly consumed, if George Washington had eaten his fries like this, the War of Independence would have been over twice as fast.

"This isn't new," mused Theo. "Everyone knows how the system works, everyone knows that's just ... how things are. The Company makes a profit to keep things efficient, it's better that business profits than ... than ... " Stopped himself, couldn't even remember the words he was supposed to say.

"Yeah," grunted Faris. "All of that crap.' Another chip. Then a thought, a flicker almost of something excited, alive. "You heard of the queen of the patties?"

"Yes – a little."

"She's got this enclave somewhere up north, a place for the ones who dodge parole to run to, somewhere even the Company can't be buggered to go, no point in it. The queen says this country is a slave state. That there aren't any chains on our feet

177

or beatings on our backs because there don't need to be. Cos if you don't play along with what the Company wants, you die. You die cos you can't pay for the doctor to treat you. You die cos the police won't come without insurance. Cos the fire brigade doesn't cover your area, cos you can't get a job, cos you can't buy the food, cos the water stopped, cos there was no light at night and if that's not slavery, if that's not the world gone mad if that's not . . .

. . . but we got used to it. Just the way things are. Just what the world is. Sometimes you think – people go missing, and how are there so many patties now? You do the smallest thing, and I mean *the smallest* thing, and you go to the patty line, that's the law now, and who wrote the law? Who paid to get the guy to write it? This thing Dani said – 'They broke the world.' Yeah. Yeah they did. So? So the fuck what? That's what I said to her. That's what I told her to her face." A little sigh, no more chips to play with, nothing left to do. "One day I'm gonna go see this queen of patties. I'd like to hear more of what she has to say."

"What did Dani want you to do?"

"Said she could destroy it. Said that we hadn't seen the half of it. That the four hundred billion that the government got in receipts from the Company, like, three hundred of that just went straight back to Company contracts anyway. Paying the Company for the bin men and the cops and the academies and the private hospitals and the prisons – paying them cos it's cheaper to pay the Company you know, cheaper to . . . but actually it's not, it costs a fucking fortune, so they've got this problem, yeah, they've got all this stuff they need to do if they're not going to have a revolution, but people are skint and the more skint they get the more pissed off they get and the government sure as hell isn't gonna spend to get them out of the shit and . . . "

He stopped, mouth curling like he'd bitten the tip of his tongue.

Theo waited.

"Anyway. Dani said, 'You don't know the half of it.' Said she had secrets. Could take them down. I didn't believe her. Told her where to go."

"Philip Arnslade? Danesmoor? Did she mention them?"

Another shrug. Faris sat back, hands resting on a gentle paunch of oil and margarine pushing at the bottom buttons of his thin blue shirt.

"What did you do?" asked Theo.

"Laughed. Told her to get lost."

"And?"

"And she sends me this picture. It's one of those ones taken on a phone camera, bit crap, light's shit, but there's this bulldozer, big yellow thing, and these guys in yellow jackets and white helmets and one guy giving a thumbs-up to the camera. And this guy with the Company T-shirt at the back texting like he's not even paying any attention, and I'm like, so what the fuck is this? And she's like, look closer. So I look closer. This is something she's swiped from the Ministry of Civic Responsibility, said they were going to destroy it, destroying evidence, she said, so I look closer. I look real close. And it takes for ever to spot it, I've got soft in my old age, I used to be . . .

Anyway.

And then I see it. Right on the edge of the field, where there's a ditch. Thought it was just a shoe, but look really close, real careful, and it's not a shoe. It's a foot. Sticking out of the field. It might belong to a kid. And these guys they're just standing there, just smiling at the camera, and they've just turned over the whole fucking field, I mean, they must have found it, they must have found the body unless . . .

So I say it's Photoshop it doesn't mean anything, but she's like, you have no idea.

You have no idea.

It's so much more.

With this, we can take back the world.

She made it sound so real. She made it sound . . . for a moment I thought maybe there'd be something – I mean, maybe something I could do, something important that perhaps . . . but it wasn't real, of course. That sort of thing isn't ever real. So maybe she published and maybe she said that some guys who worked for the Company dug up a field where there was some-one's foot, but I don't think it matters. We got taught not to care. It'll pass.

It'll pass.

I told her to leave me alone. And now she's dead and I'm ... "

What is he?

Faris is terrified is what he is. His hands are shaking. Even though his mouth finds the words he can't meet Theo's eyes he is ...

"I made a phone call. After she called me I made one phone call. I called my daughter I said look there's this thing there's this thing I heard there's this thing and ... "

Now the terror seeps into his words, the tears into his eyes.

"She told me the Company knew what it was doing, that they were great for business great for Britain that ... then a man called Markse knocked on my door, I mean like, five hours later, and asked if I knew Dani Cumali. I said no, I'd never heard of her. Not a clue. Just carried on as normal. I'm still carrying on as normal, that's how you do it. I'm just ... nothing's changed. Why would anything change when you've got nothing to ...

If I can't find the queen of the patties, then I keep thinking I'll go to Cornwall. It looks beautiful down there, even in the winter, though they say the winters are shit and actually on the TV you never see ...

... but how long does a winter last, really? It just feels long but how long does it ... "

His words ran away to shaking nothing, and he shrank into the curve of his shoulders and stared at emptiness and spun sesame seeds around the greasy edge of his plate, and spun sesame seeds, and spun sesame seeds.

Theo opened his mouth to say something reassuring and kind, but the words were meaningless. Instead: "Are you being followed?"

Faris didn't answer.

"Are you being followed?"

"My daughter ratted me," mused Faris. "I told her this thing, cos I was worried about her, and she went straight to the Company, she told them about me, about Dani, she ... she says it's for the best. That the only way I'm ever going to pick myself up, make something of myself, is if I get back in the normal way of things, make myself an attractive business prospect again, not some done-out outsider. That I had to get realistic and stop pretending I was some kind of martyr. That this was the way things worked and it was for the best, stop being old-fashioned, everyone has a good chance so long as they just ... "

Faris stared into the distance and did not speak again, and Theo waited a little while, then stood without a word, looking around, heart pounding, and walked away.

Marching away from Vauxhall Bridge the man who is now Theo Miller thinks

he thinks and his thoughts are

stone.

Harder than the stones that roll back into the sea.

Two men follow him. They are remarkably easy to spot, but the moment they realise he's seen them, they start to run straight towards him, leather shoes and chopping-board hands. Theo feels a sudden surge of contempt, wants to laugh in their face, lets them come on a few paces, and turns and runs.

He thought maybe he might have to run, and now he runs and he is fast – he had no idea he was so fast, he's run by himself for so long that he hasn't really got a sense of these things – but turns out all that time, all those early mornings and long, late nights when other people were living, had some upside after all.

The man called Theo runs.

Running changes the city. Sight and sound blazes into slithering sentience, the river is moving black popping with reflected lights of sodium orange, white, green and yellow. The Thames slurps its way down the thin tidal beach below the high walls of the embankment catching on muddy sand, belching wet gloop, the sky is a brown smear stained with bruised rushing clouds, buses unnaturally slow as they crawl across Westminster Bridge; the Houses of Parliament are all illuminated acrylic blaze and deep recesses of shadow, strips and nooks of blackness where only the pigeons can penetrate.

He runs and for a moment isn't sure who he's running from.

He's a reasonable man in a reasonable world, he hasn't technically done much wrong, running will only make it worse; they can go to the police station, there is a rule of law there is . . .

Theo runs without hesitation.

And for a little while, he feels free, alive, on fire. He can't remember the last time he felt so full of blood.

He thinks, too late, that perhaps it is a mistake to commit to the path that runs between St Thomas' Hospital and the river, flagstones singing, wobbling and free where the mortar has eroded away, once you're there it's hard to turn off any way, but as his feet ring out he glances back and sees the two men, puffing and huffing behind, one already at a half-jog, half-stagger, overweight and out of breath.

Laughs, and runs a little faster, just because he can.

The security cordon at the London Eye forces him to cut inland, away from the river, past rows of shops selling tourist food: noodles in cardboard boxes with wire handles, slices of pizza adorned with three thin slivers of black–grey mushroom, a kebab shop that offers authentic awful; only a London kebab can burn your mouth so particularly, leave that aftertaste at the back of your nose, it's an authentic city experience!

He looks back again at the British Film Institute, the faces of the latest idols exploded to two-storey monuments, edited black and white portraits of bygone goddesses smoking the latest branded thing, drinking this season's newest whisky, as the lights sweep back and forth across the technicians rolling up a trampled red carpet.

He can't see his followers immediately, so slows and stares properly, and sees them nearly a hundred yards off, puffing and

182

pushing through the crowds huddled around the burrito vans, tourist gazes riveted to the licensed skateboarders who range beneath the painted walls of Waterloo Bridge, or drinking and arguing over the price of dim sum.

Perhaps whatever Dani found isn't important enough for his pursuers to try very hard.

Perhaps you just can't get the staff these days.

Theo slowed to a walk, head down, hands in his pockets, turned into the crowd coming out of the National Theatre and let it carry him away, towards Waterloo Station.

By the river in Oxford Philip Arnslade is shaking, shaking, trying not to laugh, or maybe cry, he holds the gun and stares down at the body of Theo Miller and had prepared something really smart, really witty to say but doesn't have it so he just . . .

but Simon Fardell, his number two, leans over the expiring form of the boy as the breath leaves his lungs and says, "I suppose we should have brought something for the pain."

And shakes his head

and walks away.

After, in the ambulance

Theo Miller can't speak, is gasping for air, tries squeezing tight the hand of the boy who will become Theo, and for a little while he does this, and then his grip becomes loose, and cold, and wet, and the paramedic says

"nothing you could have done it wasn't your fault"

but with memory

like a night on the beach as the sea washes the stones

the man called Theo thinks perhaps that's not what he said at all.

Perhaps

now that he's rewriting the past and everything he thought he knew about it

perhaps the paramedic looked him in the eye and said, "It's your fault. There's nothing to be done. It's your fault."

And the boy who would be Theo looked into the eyes of his friend, and saw in that instant that his friend knew what had happened to him, and for all his good nature couldn't help but agree.

Chapter 36

Neila sailed north.

She had sailed for many years by herself, and sometimes it was hard, but in her heart it was easy, and she was fine.

She was fine.

When she was young, and still finding who she was, she'd wanted to matter. To her friends, family and to the world. She wanted the world to tell her that she was of value, that her actions had some meaningful consequence that people could generally see and perhaps even admire. Such actions didn't have to involve saving children from burning buildings or adopting stray kittens. Kindness, compassion, bringing joy to others — these were surely all worthy of appreciation, and she strived to live by them.

And the world said, "Fuck right off thank you what we really want to know is what kind of implants you got for your tits and backside."

That had been confusing, for a little while, but she'd joined the rat race and got great tits and a great backside, and the world had seemed generally content with her, as long as she played the game.

Right up to the moment when she hadn't, and the friends she thought mattered to her, and made her whole, had told her that they didn't like hanging out with someone who wasn't like them, and what did she even think she was doing in those God-awful shoes?

The years that followed had been hard. The Neila she had

believed herself to be turned out to be more frail than she'd thought. The self-confidence and charisma she projected was only that, a veil draped over the gossamer of her soul, and when the veil was torn, so was she.

She'd bought the *Hector* on a whim, with some romantic idea about life on the canals. She'd stuck with it, because having decided that this was a thing she cared about, the idea of admitting that she was wrong would be the last blow to any notion of who Neila was.

Who she aspired to be.

And over time she had found a certain something that kept her going, rituals and repetitions that drove her north and south, through the Midlands and along the old coal ways of the country.

She was fine.

She was alone, and she was among the communities of the water, and she was fine.

Then she sailed with someone else and it was . . .

easier

simple

different.

Every hour of every day she'd sworn she'd throw Theo off at the next lock. She did not need another person. Other people would only make her world unsteady, rip apart without even meaning to the woven confidence she'd created around the frail cocoon of self. Other people were a goddamn mistake.

She cranked the gate on the lock, her breath coming out in great huffing clouds

Pushed her back against the long timber braces

heaved

heaved

heaved

paused to catch her breath as the gate swung open.

Returned to the *Hector*

started the engine

sailed into the lock

gunned the engine down to idle

186

climbed onto land
heaved
heaved
the lock gate shut
waited
cranked
heaved
drove
heaved
cranked
drove

After four lock gates the shirt beneath her jumper was soaked with sweat, and her fingers were blue and white at the tips, and more than anything she wished the man called Theo was there too.

She sailed and did not see the man called Theo.

A desperation a terror she

Three of coins, king of coins, the Tower, nine of cups, ace of cups, knave of cups, the Priest, seven of swords, the Hanged Man (inverted).

Seeing the Hanged Man land on her table, she nearly choked with relief, and kept on sailing.

At Norton Junction she came across the *Poet's Rest*. The coal barge was moored just before the turning into the Leicester Section and had no coal for sale except a couple of secret bags stored beneath the floor of the deck, which the owners gave to her at best discount because she was a friend, and they knew each other of old.

Neila sat in the cabin and cut the hair of old Mrs Lude, whose long white tresses hadn't been touched for nearly two years, and who let only Neila cut them, and who burbled excited to see her friend and exclaimed:

The flowers! So beautiful in the spring but first the snowdrops the snowdrops as they emerge the whiteness beneath the trees

187

the bluebells in the forest

the daffodils, first sign of spring, great fat bunches of daffodils getting everywhere how the bulbs spread how they

the bees as they come to life for the lavender the . . .

and Mr Lude sat at the back and read his newspaper and smoked terrible, disgusting cigarettes that turned the roof of the cabin sticky and brown, and pretended not to enjoy his wife's endless happiness.

Once, Neila heard it said, Mrs Lude caught a sexually transmitted disease which damaged her brain and left her perpetually upbeat, but if she caught it from her husband then it clearly hadn't achieved the same effect on his disposition.

Anyway, Neila didn't believe a word of it. Some people were just delightful. Some people simply saw beauty in the world, even the winter, for the winter was nothing if not a promise of spring.

Neila cut her hair, and did an okay job at it, and Mrs Lude was ecstatic, and Neila returned to her own boat quickly, a bag of coal on her back, and sat up with one light on and watched the towpath, and did not see Theo.

Lucy

Rainbow Princess Lucy Cumali where are you now in his dreams the man called Theo watches the water and sees in its reflection . . .

father and daughter there was so much he missed but in his dreams he holds her the day she is born he holds her and she is sleeping and so tiny yet oddly heavy too and there's that thing that babies do that weird strength when they hold your little finger in their fist and they're so strong it's just incredible they're . . .

In his dreams Theo can skip over certain details. Someone else can clear up the baby poo. He heard that it can come in every imaginable colour, someone he knew once said her child's poop was bright blue.

In his dreams Theo pushes Lucy on the swings

picks her up from school

hides £1 under her pillow when her first tooth falls out, keeps hiding £1 until all her milk teeth are gone even though she long ago stopped believing in the tooth fairy

helps her do her maths homework, he'd be good at that

(very few fathers are good at that he knows this really but he'd be the exception because of how he'd respect her as a person as well as love her as his child)

Someone else can tell Lucy about puberty all that business with sanitary towels and tampons. Obviously he'd help out if wanted, but not intrusively – by this time Lucy is becoming her own woman, she should be allowed to make her own choices and just know that her dad is there for her to love her no matter what.

Funny thing. In his dreams, Dani isn't there at all.

Neila sailed, and out of the darkness there he was.

A man sat on a bench by a lock, and did not smoke, and did not drink, and had no bag, and wore a coat very similar to the one that Theo wore, wool and fine and dark. For a moment her heart soared; but then look again. Not Theo. This man's coat fitted him, and he had black leather gloves, and wore black leather shoes and he studied nothing much in particular until the *Hector* sailed into view, and then he studied it very much indeed, and studied her standing at the back, and as she approached he rose and called out, "Neil Madling?"

Neila slowed as she neared the lock and didn't answer. He stepped a little closer to the edge of the canal, watched patiently as she hopped down towards the low bollards, began to tie off, quick and sharp with the fraying blue mooring line.

"Mr Madling?" he repeated when the first rope was on. "My name is Markse."

"Neila," she replied sharply, and the man called Markse looked again, and was briefly embarrassed, and nodded once.

"I do apologise, ma'am. Is this your barge?"

"It's a boat, not a barge."

"A very beautiful vessel. Is there anyone else on board?"

189

"No."

"Do you mind if I check?"

"Yes."

"Ah. I'm afraid I may not have—"

"I don't know you."

"I am . . . still currently just with the Ministry of Security, I am—"

"There's no one on my boat except me."

"May I look?"

"Why?"

Markse hesitated, studying her face, watching as she tied off the second line, stepped back onto the boat, one hand on the rudder, holding tight, an instinctive comfort. She glared into his silence, and for a while he seemed to contemplate several different answers before with an almost-shrug declaring, "Because in Northampton you helped a woman by the name of Marta, who stabbed one of the children in the middle of the night. You told the police you were alone, and Marta told the police nothing, but on the knife there were two sets of fingerprints. The second of these belong to a man called Theo Miller. I think he's on your boat. May I come on board?"

He came on board, starting at the prow and walking through to the stern.

"Well, I do apologise for taking your time it would appear that—"

"So get off my fucking boat."

He got off the fucking boat, stood on the bank, hands in pockets, smiling patiently. He was, Neila decided, a deeply ugly man, too tall, too thin, too pale. His hair was thinning on top, prematurely, and he didn't have the grace to attempt a comb-over but just let the few limp strands that remained droop around his pale, pin-poked face. His nails were buffed and polished, a gentle vanity, and as Neila looked at him she realised she had seen him in the cards, and he was the Tower, and he was destruction, and he was the eye of the storm.

They looked at each other and understood each other perfectly.

"If you meet Mr Miller will you tell him that I called? It concerns his daughter.'

He held out a business card.

It had his name and a telephone number on it, and that was all. She took the card, put it in her pocket and turned away.

He waited a moment to see if she would look back, and when she didn't, he nodded once and drifted back down the canal.

Three hours later, she found Theo, sitting on the frozen grass by the water.

He'd walked nearly fifty miles. In the end the cold had slowed him, and the thirst had brought him to a standstill.

She slowed down, let the *Hector*'s momentum carry her past him to a stop.

He looked up, slow and tired, saw her looking back and smiled.

Wordlessly, she opened the stern door to the cabin, and he climbed on board.

Chapter 37

Nine days after Theo Miller's body was buried in an unrecorded ceremony beneath a beech tree the headstone was removed and smashed.

The boy who would be Theo watched, and didn't speak, because this too was part of the discretion clause, this was what they had agreed to, no name, no body, no sign that Theo Miller had ever died.

Fifteen years later the man called Theo Miller cycled to work and the work was:

value of property stolen: £13,492

value of life taken: £93,410

value of rape: £8452

value of sexual harassment: £3451.50

value of

the cost of doing

he said go on, you know you want to you're just playing hard to get you're just

victim's impact statement was not as fluently written as we'd hoped so only £7590 for the price of

the three kids obviously unable to pay and too young for sponsorship but the eldest was picked up by a private security force, they say they think he has a great deal of potential and want to see if he can handle an assault rifle before subcontracting him for special operations and . . .

fifteen thousand seven hundred and ninety-two twenty-nine

thousand four hundred and eighty-seven fifty-one thousand nine hundred and twenty-three

It occurs to Theo that he has been selling slaves for the last nine years, and knew it but somehow managed not to understand that this was his profession.

Chapter 38

In the morning two men on motorbikes trailed Theo to work, and behind them a van idled in heavy traffic, and never quite seemed to get where it needed to be.

Theo wondered how they'd found him, and thought that maybe Faris had betrayed him too.

There wasn't much to betray, but there were security cameras, credit checks, fingerprints on a linoleum table. He'd have found him, if he'd tried.

He wondered why they didn't just arrest him then and there, and when they didn't, he began to pack.

In the office no one talked to him.

At lunch he ate alone, and took an apple to his desk to finish working while his corner was relatively quiet.

When he cycled home, the motorbikes were on him again.

He went for a run and at the bottom of the hill a man sat reading a newspaper and the same man was there when he came back and it was . . .

That night he made stuffed aubergine with feta cheese, lentils, tomatoes.

While eating the doorbell rang, and Mrs Italiaander answered. A few moments later: "Mr Miller, there's someone to see you!"

He opened the door to his bedroom, fork still in one hand, looked down the stairs towards the man waiting in the corridor below.

"Mr Miller? My name is Markse. Might I have a word?"

*

They spoke in Theo's room.

Markse, cramped, constrained from his usual presence by pressing walls, perched on the chair by the desk. Theo sat cross-legged on the end of the bed, a half-eaten aubergine on a bright blue plate on the top of the duvet; a single unwise motion could cause a disaster of sauce and cheese.

Markse looked around the room, taking his time, trying to read some sort of personality into the closed wardrobe, the way Theo had arranged his keys and wallet next to the laptop, the bicycle helmet hanging up by the towels on hooks behind the door, the not–life, a room without a heart, just a place to sleep and eat, no more.

Shook his head, looked away, smiled at the floor, and kept the smile on his face as he looked up at Theo and said, "Do excuse my visit, but . . ."

"It's not a . . ."

"From the Ministry of Security, I work for the Nineteen Committee I don't know if you . . ."

"Anti-terrorism."

"Indeed, yes that is part of our – but terrorism is a broad remit these days. Anything which causes fear, in fact, and fear is . . . I read your report into Dani Cumali's murder. I had no idea that the Criminal Audit Office was so diligent."

Theo shrugged. "I could tell that the case was more than it appeared. Auditor's instinct."

"So not a personal interest?"

"I dislike it when people try to pay less than their due."

A smile from Markse. He shares this view. This is clearly a meeting of noble minds. "The Nineteen Committee was investigating Ms Cumali for a potential security breach. Documents stolen, dabbling in government business. She was in contact with certain elements who are not contributing to society. We think she had a second phone, contacted a man called Faris. Do you know a man called Faris?'

Theo shrugged.

"I'm afraid I'll need an answer."

"I met him."

"In Vauxhall?"

"Yes."

"Why?"

"His name came up. I thought he might have useful background information about Dani Cumali."

"How did his name come up?"

"In the course of my investigations."

Markse's smile, again, a little wider. They understand each other now, indeed they do, and what bliss this knowledge brings. "Do you like your work, Mr Miller?" A casual enquiry, eyes going to another place.

"Yes."

"You've been very diligent."

"The indemnity system is much better than alternatives. Much more efficient."

"Cambridge, weren't you?"

Blood colder than the ice on the canal, time is time was time when

　　　　　　　　it's your fault

　　　　　　　　　　a boy dying in a field shrouded in mist a

time when

"Oxford," Theo replied, voice matching the stiffness in his spine.

"Oxford of course, sorry. I went to Oxford too – you must have been there in ... "

"Fifteen years ago."

"Fifteen, fifteen ... roughly the same time as Philip Arnslade, yes?"

"We were on the same course."

"Really you were both ... ?"

"Law."

"Law together in Oxford! Know him well?"

"Not really. I was working, there wasn't time for many friends, it was ... "

"But if I was to mention your name?"

"I don't know. I suppose it would be flattering to think that he remembered me. Do you know him well?"

"We've met a couple of times."

"I didn't realise that the Nineteen Committee and the Ministry were . . . is this connected to the case?"

"Would it matter if it was? So long as the payment is made?" Markse shifted on his awkward chair, pleasantries passing by, back to business. "A phone was taken from the scene of Ms Cumali's murder. A phone and a memory stick. In the course of your remarkably thorough audit, did you find any sign?"

"No."

"But you found Faris."

"Yes."

"I would have thought without the phone . . . "

"As I said. I asked questions."

"And met in Vauxhall."

"Yes."

"What did Faris say?"

"That Dani Cumali believed she had information with which she could blackmail the government. That she was single-minded and determined to get her daughter . . . I can't remember the daughter's name . . . to get her out of some sort of place where she was incarcerated. That she kept on saying she'd found something big. It made me think that it was likely that Ms Cumali had been assassinated in order to keep her silent, which I find frustrating in light of the manslaughter plea entered in the case. Assassination is an entirely different auditing process, through different channels."

"You're very thorough."

"My work is important."

"So is mine. In normal circumstances I'd say you were a bit of a fruit loop, Mr Miller. Is that fair? You earn a reasonable government salary but lodge in a house in Tulse Hill; you don't have any friends except the occasional community gardening companion; you don't interact with your colleagues at work; you almost never make a mistake except the occasional lapse towards overcharging for a crime; you went to Oxford with the leading lights of the day and yet have never sought promotion or played upon your connections, and your pursuit of this particular case borders on the ... what does it border on? If I were to take you by your file, Mr Miller, I'd say there was something almost autistic about you. Is that fair? Socially autistic, perhaps, the child bullied at school. No after-work drinks, no meaningful interactions, maybe you don't understand how these things work, maybe you laugh because you hear others laughing but that's not ...

... but that would be wrong too, wouldn't it, Mr Miller? Because you're not pursuing this out of some ... neurological quirk that makes you so extra-extra-specially dedicated where everyone else would have just taken the money and run. You're not digging because the only thing you know is dirt. It's something else. My job is to find out what that something else is. I'm hoping that it's harmless; I'm sure you understand."

Theo said nothing, staring down at his hands.

Theo stared at nothing.

"Do you mind if I ...?" A nod, a gesture. Theo stood, held his arms out as Markse patted him down, found nothing, smiled, sat down again, gestured for Theo to sit. Theo didn't.

"Of course I had people watching Faris, in light of Ms Cumali's threats. You met him and then you ran. Why did you run?"

"Two people chased me. I don't know what else you're meant to do when that happens."

"You could have assumed they were with the authorities."

"I am the authorities, Mr Markse, and they weren't with me. Given that you managed to work out who I was, why didn't you just arrest me?"

A little shrug. "Because as you say, Mr Miller, you are the authorities. Why would I arrest someone who might be on my side? I'm going to search your room now. A couple of my colleagues are outside. One of them will sit with you downstairs while you finish your meal. We'll try to keep disruption to a minimum."

*

198

Sitting in the living room, he finished his dinner because it would be a waste to leave it, and a man in grey tracksuit trousers sat silently with them, and they watched a TV programme about rebuilding ruined houses to rent them out as holiday homes and ways in which you could use an accent wall to really set off the space with a vibrant colour against neutral shades.

After, when Markse was done, he stood in the living-room door as Mrs Italiaander pretended she had something terribly important to do in the kitchen and listened with all her might, and Markse said:

"We didn't find anything Mr Miller, but we appreciate your help on this, your cooperation. I do wish you the best."

And when Theo went back into his room, just before midnight, it was a turned-over disaster, bed against the wall, mattress torn and slashed open, pillows on the floor, the screen of the laptop cracked. In the end he slept in a bundle of dirty clothes piled up in one corner of the floor.

Chapter 39

"My daughter isn't . . . "

"He said your daughter."

"Why does he it's not it's not . . . "

The closest Neila thought she had seen Theo to crying. She's put him by the stove, fed him, given him water, tea, watched him drink, starving again, he'd run away and was starving what did he think would happen?

As they bobbed in a nowhere place between towns, moored by spikes driven into the frozen earth with a heavy metal hammer, Neila gave him Markse's card and now he paced, turned and twisted like smoke in the wind.

My daughter, he said, my daughter why did he say my daughter how did he she shouldn't be she shouldn't

And stopped, and sank onto the sofa and looked like an origami man crumpled at the bottom of a traveller's bag.

They sat a while in silence.

And the time was . . .

Neila put her hand in his, squeezed it tight.

They sat.

And the moment was . . .

Theo closed his eyes.

Spoke to the darkness.

"I have failed so many people. I have failed . . . everyone who ever mattered to me. My father died on the patty line, my mother ran away from all things, I thought the bullets were blank and Theo died and my friend she was . . .

... the patties burned they burned it all everything was ash and the lady ran towards her son and my daughter ran from me and ..."

Turned the card in his hand, one word printed and a telephone number, thick card, black edge.

"When we get to Leicester, I'll make the call," he said. "I'll ... but you pretend that you didn't — it's important that you didn't although I suppose now ..."

They sat a while, in silence.

Neila held his hand.

Later, she cut his hair by the light of an LED lantern on the kitchen table, and all things considered it was one of the better cuts she'd ever done.

The phone rings in London.

"Markse."

"It's me."

"Theo?"

"You said my daughter."

"We should meet."

"What about my daughter?"

"Where are you?"

"If I—"

"Where are you?"

"Leicester."

"I'll be there tomorrow, 9 a.m."

"The woman I'm travelling with, Neila. She's not ..."

"Theo. Listen to me. She's not part of this. We can still — they haven't found out what I did yet — we can still solve this."

"9 a.m."

"Yes, at Kings Lock on ..."

Theo hung up.

The canal at night.

In his dreams the man called Theo stands on one leg in the middle of the river, and still hasn't caught any fish.

Chapter 40

At the office, the morning after Markse searched his room, even the security guard wouldn't look Theo in the eye. When he went to access his email, a sign appeared saying his password was out of date and he needed to contact IT.

IT were away for training. The entire department was on a surprise trip to Slough for a creative thinking and imaginative problem-solving development day, hosted by a manufacturer of face paints whose son had been done for child molestation and was looking to get a discount.

Theo tidied his desk, took a few paper files down to the canteen and sat in the window to read. He hadn't been in a window for a very long time. There had been no sunlight in his working life for nearly six years, and at this time of year it could become hard to remember what it felt like, washed to silver-white, playing through the glass, warming his skin. It was, in a way, one of the nicest days he'd had at work. No one questioned him and no one spoke.

A man sat on the other side of the café and stared at him
just stared
visitor badge around his neck
and that was okay too.

Theo went out for lunch, bought a coronation chicken sandwich.

Afterwards, he returned to the office and went for a piss.

While inside the toilet cubicle, he climbed up onto the top of the toilet bowel, pushed up a ceiling panel above his head, fumbled around between the loosely laid cables until he found Dani's phone, retrieved it, put it in his pocket, flushing the toilet on his way out and washing his hands carefully with soap and water.

On his way home, he cycled down to Westminster Pier, chained his bicycle – probably illegally – to a high iron lamp post, walked down to the wharf and caught the River Bus heading towards Blackfriars. He stood at the back, where the noise of the engine was loudest, turned on Dani's phone and made a call.

The station were slow to answer but got there in the end.

"Paddington Safenight Policing, how can I help you?"

"It's Markse."

"Who?"

"Markse," he called out over the roar of water and foam and the lashing of the wind. "From the Nineteen!"

Holding music. The same holding music as last time. Theo's heart rushed as loud as the water foaming below, he didn't turn his head, didn't look to see the man on the deck above watching, just stared at the city moving behind him, stared and waited and listened.

The superintendent, when he came on, was far more solicitous at the idea of Markse's name than he had been when Theo had called as himself.

"Markse? What's that dreadful fucking noise are you . . ."

A soar in his heart, a laugh in his chest. "Sorry, very loud where I am. Just needed to check on the files from Cumali's phone. Do you still have a copy?"

"You said to—"

"I know what I said, but do you still have a copy?"

"Yes, but we were going to—"

"Still do that, but first you need to send them to – and this is important are you – send them to this email address write it down then destroy it – so it's gx7pp9 – did you get that it's gx7pp9 at . . ."

Theo gave him the email address, barely bothering to pitch his voice to sound remotely like Markse's own, letting the roar of the wind carry the sound away, letting it fill him with strength the smell of the river the cold on the air, and the policeman said:

"Look, Markse, I don't need you checking up on me like this I've got enough with the ..."

"Thanks for your help!"

Turned off the phone.

Counted backwards from twenty.

Nearly laughed out loud.

Leaned over the railing to see the vortex of water churned up below, the wake washing out towards the high stone walls of the embankment.

Let the phone drop into the river, to be crunched by propeller and nibbled by grey fishes that dwelt in the spinning mud.

Chapter 41

Theo stayed on the boat to Canary Wharf, changed to the Underground, headed down to the bulbous white spot that had been the Millennium Dome, bought an overpriced ticket to the first thing that was on that night, waited in the queue, pressed in with bodies – mostly screaming young girls with huge bunches in their hair and boys in leather trying to be cool.

Bought a wrap that tasted of salty goo and wet paper.

Let the crowd heave him into the auditorium, blues and lightning-whites, lasers flicking through the smoke-filled air, a scream, a roar, ear-bending as the band came on stage. They were a Japanese girl-pop group, seven of them dressed in tiny black skirts, white socks up to their knees, they swung between covering their mouths when they laughed, little-girl giggles and shakes of their immensely long black hair, to thrusting their hips forward and exclaiming, "I ain't taking no shit from this world!" to the adulatory screaming, whooping, shrieking, crying, frothing of the audience.

Theo moved with the crowd, up and down, side to side, a motion of its own, let it carry him, let it spin him around the stage, flowed with the rhythm of the people until he found a boy with a mobile phone sticking bright and easy out of his back pocket, tears of joy running down his face, streaming through the UV paint drawn in whiskers from the corners of his lips

stole his mobile phone very easy, really, his father would have been proud his father would have been . . .

his father would have

Drifted to a corner of the crowd, where the ecstasy of the moment was weakest and the floor was sticky with beer.

Logged into an email address – gx7pp9 – and the only email apart from the ancient "welcome to" was brand new and came straight from Safenight Policing Ltd, police force to the stars.

Theo is

maybe in his heart he was always a criminal, maybe he inherited something from his father after all, maybe he just likes it maybe he . . .

He stayed until the end of the gig, left with the crowd, pushing, shoving, sobbing, laughing, let them spin and spin and spin, down to the station, a heaving mess on the Jubilee Line, got off the train at Stratford, got back on it and headed back to Canary Wharf, ran for the DLR, then changed his mind and ran for West India Quay, up the stairs three at a time, caught the DLR heading towards Bank, saw a man panting for breath running after him, saw the man miss the train . . .

Got off at Westferry and ran.

Ran for the canal, for the darkness, ran in the wrong kind of shoes but who even cared?

Ran for the terraced streets of Victoria Park, where the CCTV cameras hadn't grown.

Ran for the bustling traffic, Vietnamese takeaways, evangelist churches and frozen-food shops of Mare Street.

Ran for the hipsters' coffee shops for the sodium lights for the squirrel bulbs hanging with bare, twisted filaments of life, for the place where the enclaves and the sanctuaries bumped almost nose to nose, the darkness of those who couldn't pay pressing up against the floodlights and barbed-wire walls of those who could.

Railway arches and trains that screamed and screeched in the night, flash pops of ultraviolet fire off the wheels

the used-metal yards

the yoga studios and vegan cafés

the drug clinics and trash yards for those who had nowhere else to go boarded-up windows and fresh new signs – it was the perfect place to be as the night settled into the cold.

Theo Miller ran, leaving his followers far, far behind.

An all-night internet café near Dalston Kingsland. The market a few doors up had been caught selling dog, rat, monkey and bat meat again. Several arrested stallholders objected to the charges, saying it was part of their culture, it was how things were.

(Indemnity of £17,820 for the initial crime plus for the repeat offence they could be looking at ...)

The internet café windows were pasted with posters for a dozen different plays and gigs. R 'n' B, rap, music from the Congo and Nigeria, songs of freedom, songs of love, something by Chekhov, a show by kids, a panto starring that woman off the breakfast shows, you know the one, not the weather lady the other one yeah with the really big ...

Theo opened the email from the police service and went through the life and times of Dani Cumali.

They'd taken her phone, dug through her files. She'd managed to borrow a laptop pinched by a kid in the enclave, they'd torn it apart and now here it was, a full report from the cyber division complete with emails, photos, phone calls, text messages – far too much for him to digest in a single night.

But he had a feeling he knew where he was going.

He read.

And for a moment Dani Cumali was alive again, and sitting at his side, speaking the words that were on the screen, watching him, her hand on his shoulder, a guardian angel painted in blood, a ghost who whispered, *she's your daughter*, and every time he thought he might drift towards sleep, she squeezed, and it hurt, and he jerked awake and kept on reading.

There weren't any videos of Philip Arnslade.

No records of crimes committed or corruption planned.

Just the odd email from the Company, a few photos.

You fucking bitch. You fucking speak a word and I'll fucking kill you.

A text from Seb Gatesman.

You're safe, she replied. *Touch me and you won't be.*

Messages in and out, nothing from Faris, nothing that would have been anything other than places to go, people to see there was nothing but . . .

(The man called Theo is aware that time is growing a little peculiar, things which he thought were in the past turn out to have some pertinence after all and there was a time when he sat on the bench with his best friend, two children by the sea drinking the cheapest beer they could buy, the only beer they could buy, canned hangover with flat fizzy bits.)

You just make like a heron and maybe one day you'll catch some fish.

A cormorant can count to seven. Put a ring around its neck and send it catching fish and it will remember that the seventh it catches will be its to feast on.

Owls are actually very stupid birds, but when something moves! That's when evolution does its thing.

Chugger chugger chugger goes the boat.

"You want to swap?" asked Neila. "You must be freezing."

"I'm all right, but thank you."

"More tea. Peppermint or ginger?"

"Peppermint, please. How far are we now?"

"A few more hours. We'll moor on the edge of town give me a shout when you see . . . "

jerking back to reality, Theo reads as the sun comes up, another three quid for another hour, he reads and this is all that there is to be done now this is all that . . .

At 8.45 a.m. he found it.

An unsent email, sat in the drafts, no address at the top.

Dani wrote it twenty minutes before she died.

She's your daughter. Save the mother. Go home.

Theo stared at it for a while, then shut down the computer, walked to the nearest cashpoint, took out all the cash he was allowed, pushed his credit card down the nearest drain and went to find a train home.

Knave of coins, the Devil (inverted), the Priest, seven of wands, three of coins, the Fool, three of cups, king of coins, the Hanged Man (inverted).

Neila said, "I don't like the word 'mister'. It's weighted down with this idea, this baggage like you say 'Mr Smith', and there's this idea isn't there in your head immediately of what Mr Smith must be because the word, the gender identifier, it imposes so many cultural ideas about strong and right and reliable and . . . "

Theo made pasta with spinach and mushroom sauce.

" . . . once stopped at customs – this was when I could afford holidays – and they said 'We are going to search you' and I asked why. They didn't give me a reason, but they took me to the men's room. The men's. I was so . . . I said I'm not . . . And I begged them I was crying I was just – but what the system says matters more and I . . . "

They ate in silence, counting down the hours until the morning. Low brick houses, white window frames, roads without trees, pawnbrokers, betting shops, a bit in the centre of town for the parents to take their kids shopping for £1 water pistols and a pot of paints that the baby would eat in the car back home. A theatre, abandoned, squatters sleeping in the place where the fly bars once had been, cardboard mattresses laid across metal beams and in the musty, mousy warmth of the orchestra pit.

"I don't ask anything," Neila mused as they sat together by candlelight. "Loneliness is a state of mind. You have to want something, to be lonely. You have to need some sort of reassurance, someone to tell you that this is who you are. I'm not lonely. I don't want anything. I don't need anything or anyone to tell me that . . . you know that, don't you? You know that's how I . . . "

They held hands, watched the fire melt.

Theo said, staring into flames, "There's a place where the

words stop. She did this and it was ... and then we stop. It was terrible. It was barbaric. It was beautiful. You understand. And we do. We know. Our lives exist in many different, contradictory states, all at once. I am a liar. I am a killer. I am honest. I am fighting for a good cause. I am burning the world. We want things simple, and safe, and when they aren't, when the truth is something complicated, something hard, or scary, we stop. The words run out. Everything becomes ... "

Sound died on his lips. A dead place where he once thought he had the answers and where now he isn't so sure.

"It's how it happens, of course. The worst of it. Not 'My neighbour has been taken to be burned alive, their house stolen, their children dead and I am so, so scared to speak of it.' Just 'They went away. Just — away.' And we smile. And everyone else is as scared as we are, and knows what that smile means. Is grateful that you didn't make the terror real. Thankful that you haven't caused a stink. Because it would hurt ... someone. Someone who isn't a stranger would get hurt, if we ever managed to speak the truth of things. If we ever had the courage to say what we really think, even if it destroyed who we want the world to think we are. Who it is we think we should be. There would be too much pain. So we say nothing. Things just ... trail away into a smile, which everyone understands and doesn't have to mean a thing. We are grateful for that silence, for the thing that can't be expressed. To fill it would be a terrible thing."

She put her head on his shoulder, and they sat together a while longer, waiting for the morning.

At 8.45 a.m. Theo perched on a stool on the prow of the *Hector*, a hot mug of tea in his hand, watching the sky.

At ten minutes past nine the man called Markse appeared, walking around the bend of the towpath, hands free at his sides, coat open, head up and eyes bright.

He didn't slow when he saw Theo.

Stopped in front of the boat.

Smiled.

Said, "There you are. Shall we?"

Theo nodded once, stood, folded the stool neatly against the wall of the cabin and followed Markse into the morning.

Two and a half hours later he returned, hands buried in his bulging pockets, chin tucked into his chest, and said, "Sorry about that. I have some pastries, if you'd like one?"

She had a cherry Danish. He had an almond croissant with margarine. Afterwards, they refilled the water tank and sailed north, towards Nottingham and the Trent.

Chapter 42

The man called Theo bought a ticket to Dover.

He paid in cash, a baseball cap covering his eyes, head turned away from the CCTV camera above the desk.

The ticket seller exclaimed, "If you use a card and register with our reward traveller scheme you can save up to 15 per cent on every trip you make with a value in excess of—"

"No, thank you."

"Do you want to receive our special offers for—"

"No."

"How about buy one get one free on our latest range of—"

"No."

Her face fell, and sulkily she pulled the handle that spun the small metal plate that gave him the tickets.

He took the slow train.

It ran once every two hours, and was standing room only for non-gold-club-membership passengers. Sitting on bags was not allowed; it constituted a health and safety violation. Music played faintly, a soul-numbing assault on reggae. He stood head down, eyes up, avoiding the security cameras in the creaking, stinking carriage as it rattled south. Metal grates on the windows offered limited protection against the ragers, the children and the wild women who haunted the edges of the tracks as they chugged out of Blackheath. Condensation from the breath of the passengers, elbow to elbow, dripped waterfalls off the inside of the glass. Outside Sevenoaks three children stood on the tracks, staring, staring at the driver, daring him to mow them down.

The youngest child held a bicycle wheel in her right hand; the eldest carried a baby. The driver accelerated towards them, as he'd been trained to do, and they did not move, and did not move, and did not move, until at the last minute, in a breach of all guidelines, the driver slammed on the brakes, knocking people in the carriages to the floor, indignant screams and shrieks; one woman twisted her ankle, another man dislocated his shoulder as he grabbed, and missed, a handrail.

The driver put the brakes on too late, but that didn't matter to the children – they'd done enough, they'd won their victory, and they scampered away delighted as the train picked up speed again and waved at the passengers inside the secure carriages as it rattled by. A couple waved back.

At Sevenoaks men in white shirts got off, and transport police got on, started checking IDs. Theo moved through the carriages slowly, a man looking for the toilet, and that bought him time to Tonbridge, where he got off the train and circled behind the police, pressing in between two teenagers with a pair of sticker-stamped guitar cases.

At Bethersden a woman stood on the platform, holding out her hands to the open doors of the train. "Jesus!" she shouted, and then threw her head back and roared, "Jesus! Jesus Jesus Jesus!" And then lowered her head and murmured, "Jesus. Jesus the Jesus the Jesus the Saviour Jesus the Jesus the Almighty Jesus the—"

The doors closed, cutting her off, but the lack of audience didn't seem to deter her.

There was a replacement bus from Ashford.

Theo used elbows and brute forward momentum to get on, pushing children and old men aside. People scowled, cursed him under their breath, but did nothing more since they were doing the same anyway.

Familiar countryside outside the windows.

Tough grass clinging to the chalk slopes of the Downs; patches of forest, beech and oak, ash and sycamore, the red and brown leaves billowing away in the salty wind off the sea. Oast houses on the edges of little black and white flint-walled villages; commercial estates pressing hard against reedy rivers which had broken their shallow banks. A chalk figure carved into the hillside above the motorway, a rider galloping away, hair billowing in the wind. Recent years hadn't been kind to the hills of Kent. The only work came from the companies which were owned by a company which was owned by . . .

. . . and with no one else offering much in the way of employment, the companies had made certain demands on the local civic and political leaders – not demands exactly – requests – *suggestions*, that was it, suggestions. And when the workers had rioted the police were called in and by then the police were owned by the Company too. When it's your job, it's your job yeah, when it's your wife and kids and look, cops have rent to pay too . . .

Of course heads had been cracked.

Of course they had.

And the hospitals, run by the Company, hadn't been willing to treat the men and women who'd rioted since they were only going to cause trouble, not within the charter to treat violent people. There's funding to think about.

Now there were just the ragers and the zeroes left. The screamers, the ones who tore at flesh, the ones left behind when the sirens stopped. Sometimes they scraped a living, picking fruit in summer or stacking shelves in the towns that had been smart enough to obey when the Company spoke, but at night they returned to the empty places whence they came and howled at the moon, and good people learned to look the other way.

High fences cut the motorway off from the surrounding hills, as the bus idled in traffic jams for petrol stations, tailbacks on the Dover Road. Coastal–commercial partnership towns, two-storey terraced houses with paint scraped away by the sea, concrete front gardens and British flags flying proud, chippies on every other corner, the freshest fish you'd ever eat, seagulls circling the rubbish bins, orange-brick company offices and a shuttered-up library. A castle on the hill, layers of different worries built into its architecture. Once a keep whose soldiers rode inland to govern unruly natives. Then a wall circling the keep, with towers looking towards the sea. Then earthworks built for cannon, waiting for an invasion that didn't come; then bunkers cut into the cliffs against bombardment, then nuclear shelters built all the way down, cold and dark, silent except for the endless drip-drip-dripping of water through the chalk, some people fainted going inside, knowing that if the torch went out, they would never be found.

A port.

Cranes, huge concrete car parks with painted lines to guide the way.

Ferries inching in slow past the sea wall, the smell of diesel on the air, queues back to the overspill car park in town, next to the old Roman ruins where once there had stood a temple where men sacrificed in blood to an ancient spirit, half Zeus, half a pagan being that no one dared offend, even if they didn't believe.

At Dover there were no buses running to Shawford.

He went to the taxi rank, but the drivers refused to take him there.

"Budgetfood pulled out. No one goes there any more," explained one. "No good, no good at all."

He thought of hiring a car, but they wanted his name, ID, credit card.

He tried hiring a bicycle, but they wanted the same.

In the end he walked.

It wasn't so far, really.

Nine or ten miles, a little less if you cut inland, but he knew the cliff road best, the cliff road was just for pedestrians, less likely to arouse questions if you kept close to the sea.

Theo walked.

Chapter 43

Beneath the White Cliffs of Dover, where the chalk bends towards Hellfire Corner, and the smell of the docks gives way to the billow of the sea, there is a moment when the land breaks free of the town, steps into fields of wheat rippling in the wind, the ocean stretching like a prisoner set free, the sky infinite.

Theo walked.

A sanctuary village, above the bay.

They'd built a fence around it with a locked gate, sealing in the houses that rolled down towards the water, the crab pools, the waterfall sheering to the shingle beach, the pub with its bright flags and overpriced kale salads with extra-virgin olive oil.

"Stop! Stop right there! You!"

Theo stopped, half-tangled in brambles, circling the path that surrounded the razor wire. A man and a woman, dressed in black, came running towards him, panting for breath up the slow slope of the path.

"You!" the man managed to gasp, wheezing, and when that word seemed to take his stamina, the woman picked up where he'd left off.

"You! What are you doing here?"

"I'm walking to Shawford."

"Why?"

"It's where I'm from."

"But what are you doing *here*?"

"I'm walking to Shawford. Is there a problem?"

"This area and the bay is protected land. You can't come here."

"It's protected land inside the fence. I'm outside."

"But you're near the fence!"

"But not inside it."

"You're looking inside!"

"I'm not walking inside."

"People have seen you and complained!"

"I don't think I can do anything about that."

The two guards hesitated. Technically this was true; Theo could not stop people looking, if looking was what they chose to do. Then the woman exclaimed, struck by a bright idea, "We'll walk with you!"

"To Shawford?"

"Round the edge of the village."

"If you want."

"That way people will see!"

"I suppose if they . . . "

"And they'll feel safe."

"If you're sure."

"Do you want an apple?"

"Pardon?"

"I've got some apples. Oh – and some fudge. Do you want fudge?"

"As you're offering . . . "

"Take them, please. I can't move for apples and fudge. It's the locals. You as much as look at someone funny and they give you apples and fudge."

"And tea," added the man, falling into step on the other side of Theo, as they continued to track the line of the fence. "I've had to start carrying my own teabags, decaffeinated. What I do is – they make the tea, and when they're not looking I whisk their teabag away and put mine in so that I don't die young. Do you want a teabag? Caffeinated, I mean, not decaf."

They walked together beneath grey autumn sky, a military escort around a village where the school always had a summer fête and a harvest festival, and the delivery man only ever served organic.

217

"Once we had some ragers come up from Shawford," mused the woman as they swung past a white lighthouse, the light long since snuffed, barbed wire on top of the wall, HOME SWEET HOME painted above the door. "I thought we were going to *die*."

"Die!" agreed the man.

"I thought, this is it, they've come to tear this place apart and I'm not paid enough, pardon me saying, I'm not paid enough to be fucking massacred for a bunch of rich wankers who don't—"

"Don't say wankers!"

"Affluent clients who don't ever look out, don't leave the walls because if you leave the walls . . ."

"Never leave the walls!"

"There are people if you leave the walls you see . . ."

"But thankfully the Company came, they sent a helicopter with tear gas and a machine gun . . ."

"I wouldn't call it a machine gun."

"A machine gun it was—"

"There were rubber bullets."

"I saw the bodies, those bullets weren't—"

"It's what our clients pay for, you see."

"They pay to be safe!"

"Protected."

"So that's why."

"Are you sure you don't want some fudge?"

In the end Theo accepted two apples, four teabags and some fudge. It seemed rude to say no.

Five miles further on . . .

The wind off the sea blows away all doubts, it blows away the past and the smallness of this world, it tears open the sky the fields ripple like water; it blows away the tiny cramped-up prison bars that you built across your soul the wind is . . .

Theo isn't sure he has the words for what it is. It is a thing he cannot express. If he could express it, he might have to say what else the wind purges from his soul, and he can't imagine saying these things out loud would make anyone happy.

Walking past an abandoned golf course.

A monument to pilots who died in a war, buddleia growing from between the cracks.

A trapdoor down to an unknown place beneath the cliffs, a single KEEP OUT sign nailed to the posts, rusted and ancient.

A village close enough to the water's edge that sometimes the sea came up through their toilets, through the basements where once the smugglers had hidden their goods, chimney stacks crumbling and semi-detached retirement homes slanting a little to the side as the land gave way.

Great stems of pale brown and bright green grew from the peppered stones where they met the edge of the land, spiny, spindly, no flowers or leaves, just a forest of stems heading upwards. An empire of snails had taken up residence amongst these stalks, their shells spirals of blood red edged with black, imperial yellow dotted with white spots, flashes of blue. A single tree had managed to grow in that muddy area where stone met farmer's field, and over the centuries its roots had spread beneath the land, sprouting in shrubs and spindly white-barked children. Someone had put a tyre swing inside the den it made of its own umbrella branches. Theo ducked beneath the canopy of leaves, a habit, a thing from his childhood, he had come here once and it had been . . .

That was in the time before he was Theo Miller, and these things should not affect him any more.

He walked through the village, and the curtains twitched, and grey eyes peered at him from behind the netting and through the cracks in the doors, and no one moved, and no one spoke, and no one walked along the edge of the water.

He saw the pier at Shawford before he saw the rest of the town, sticking out into the sea before the curve of the bay.

Several spans had cracked, fallen into the water. Now Dory's Café lurked at the end, cut off from the world, lights out, and the fishing deck was swamped for most of the year, unusable as the waves crawled in.

A small rose-shaped stone fort marked the edge of town, built by Henry VIII a few months after he realised he'd pissed off the pope. Black iron cannon, the ends plugged with red bungs, pointed out towards the sea. No flags flew, and the gates were barred.

On the hill above the houses the Budgetfood Estate was silent, vines breaking through the loose corrugated-iron walls. No lorries came, no lorries left, and grass pushed up through the cracks in the pavement.

He walked into town, past the seafront apartments where the old folks had sat in long bay windows to watch the yacht club and the passing trawlers, along the shopping street of boarded windows and street lamps with no bulbs in them. Baskets still hung from some of the lamps, the soil long since washed away, the exposed roots rotted to wisps. On the walls of the local Indian takeaway someone had graffitied, WILL YOU MARRY ME? but if an answer had been given, it hadn't endured.

The paddling pool was empty. There were poked holes where the crazy golf had been, a scar in the tarmac where the ice cream van had stood. Somewhere deep in town he heard the sound of raging, a man's voice soon joined by a woman's, soon joined by a few others, a call and response of unseen faces rising in fury.

Theo shuddered and was briefly afraid, and scurried on.

A man sat on a bench opposite the place where Budgetfood had once run "Microwave Meal Fridays", discount days when it offloaded its inferior goods cheap for the town. The man had thin ginger hair, a round, smiling face stained red by the wind, a great belly and tiny legs. He smiled affably at Theo as Theo walked by, and didn't move.

Silence on the high street.

Silence outside the church.

Silence where the arcade had once jittered and tittered its twinkly songs, its come-yea-golden salutations into the night.

Silence by the old railway line, the copper cables taken up and sold for scrap, the pylons rusted overhead.

Silence on the bridge that looked down to the dry-tiled swimming pool

Silence in the bingo hall, painted cobalt blue, a domed roof above a shuttered concourse.

Silence on the shore, except for the beating of the sea as it pulled a little more of the land back down into its depths.

The town was dead except for the man on the bench and the sound of rage from the inland streets.

Theo followed memory through a ghostly map, and went to the detached two-up, two-down on the edge of a caravan field where, as a child, Dani had lived, and knocked, and heard no answer and immediately felt stupid, and went round the back to the garden overgrown with brambles and stinging nettles, tried the back door, found it open.

Fading light from a settling day through the kitchen window.

Empty cupboards and empty shelves, an empty place where the fridge had been.

Tiles behind the sink, he'd painted them with Dani, a childish thing in bright pinks, purples, blues and yellows. It had been part of a community art project, a summer fête for the kids, they'd caught the perfect moment; both still young enough to be welcome at the kids' fair, and old enough to have decided that mucking around with paints was cool again.

That had been a few years before the night on the beach, the sound of the sea and pebbles in Theo's back.

He went upstairs.

Dani's room.

Her parents', though only one had ever slept in the bed. The mattress was gone, the frame remained, as did a mirror on the wall.

He went down to the front hall, was surprised to find some mail, curling up and crinkled. The gum had long since faded and the contents came out easily; he read with barely a glimmer of guilt.

An offer for a discount eye exam.

A letter from the GP commanding Dani to book and prepay for 10 per cent off her smear test.

A series of ever-more-threatening letters from the council, demanding unpaid taxes and charges.

A leaflet inviting the people of Shawford to come to a town meeting about Budgetfood's proposed withdrawal, explaining that without this industry the town would die. It would simply die.

But Budgetfood had enough workers coming up through the patty line. It wasn't economically viable to stay in a place where they had to pay national minimum wage. Cheap food came at a price, after all.

He searched the house by the failing light, and didn't find anything interesting.

By the time he finished, he was working by the light of the torch on his mobile phone, SIM card in his pocket.

There was no electricity. No lights shone in the streets.

He let himself out the way he'd come in, and wandered a few roads over until he came to the house where once he'd been a child, almost the twin of Dani's, and finding the front door locked, went round the back, and finding that locked too, broke the glass panel above the handle and let himself in.

Chapter 44

There had been a day his mother phoned.

"I'm selling the house and moving to Dorchester."

"You're . . . why Dorchester?"

"A job. I've got a job there, I'm going to be a care assistant."

"You've never cared for—"

"A care assistant – the pay is £8.20 an hour I will look after the old women and I will help them shower and use the bathroom and eat and . . . "

"Mum I'm not sure that it's such a—"

"And I'll start again. I'll start again in Dorchester."

"Where is Dorchester? Is this really what you—"

"I'll start again. You should think about what that means. I want you to remember this. It's never too late to start again."

When he became Theo, he only ever called her on a pay-as-you-go mobile phone, and never from the same place twice.

"Hi, Mum, how are you?"

"Oh. You know. It's all pretty grim."

Said affably, without much interest. Things are bad. They've been bad a while. Why would you bother asking?

"Hi, Mum, how are you?"

"Well my back's given out."

"How are you?"

"My wages have been cut and I'm very lonely. You know."

"How are—"

"I don't know why you bother to ask me that, what do you think I'm going to say, that it's all puppies and roses?"

"What do you want me to say instead? What else is there?"

Their conversations became shorter, except for sometimes when she explained about how someone had said something about something else that she thought was stupid. She never asked how he was. She never knew that he was called Theo. She never called him and after a while . . .

He thought that if he called her, she'd be grateful to speak to him, and they'd be happy for a few minutes.

After a while, he thought that she might be dead.

There was nothing malicious in thinking this. She needed to be someone else. When his father was taken away, so went the woman she had been, leaving only a body behind. He needed to be someone else too; in that they understood each other perfectly.

There was probably a bit of love left, somewhere. It simply hadn't been a priority for either of them.

An empty house in a silent town.

The furniture gone, every room seemed bigger, the windows smaller, looking out on to something less exciting than he'd remembered.

There was a smell of damp. Someone had ripped out the boiler and left the pipes wide open, but the gas and electricity had stopped a long time ago, and in the living room there was still that mark on the wall where he'd once thrown a plate and it had dented the plaster. He couldn't remember why he'd been angry at the time.

He lay on his back on the place where his bed had been, stretched out across the floor, and studied the ceiling. Constellations shone luminous green-yellow above, glow stars bought in packets of twenty-five which he'd meticulously pressed into the shape of the galaxy above his head, and, not knowing what to do with the rockets and UFOs that came with them, added some space battles too, fleets roaring across the universe in endless pursuit.

His phone beeped, battery getting low.

He turned off the torch and lay a while longer.

Time is . . .

When he left home to go to university he couldn't wait, it was the most important thing, he was stifled by everything to do with . . .

. . . and he didn't just leave home, he left his father's crime, his mother's . . . whatever his mother was . . .

He left Dani's despair and the taste of over-salted microwave meals, you could get ten for £2 on a Friday when they had their reject sale it was

And now that he is back

In this place you cannot hear the sea, but there is still a memory of something that might have been contentment.

The man called Theo thinks that tomorrow, when he leaves, he will not remember the thoughts that now run through his mind, glue him to this spot.

And the man called Theo remembers the day he put his father's name into the Criminal Audit Office's system, to see if he was still alive, still on the patty line, maybe even up for parole.

He wasn't. He was dead in an unmarked grave behind the prison after a spill in which two chemicals shouldn't have mixed, a fire that gutted B Wing of HMP Elmsley by Dazzling Beauty and Skincare. Seventeen people died in the blaze, and Theo hadn't heard about it, and four weeks later they reopened for business. The prisoners on B Wing made jewellery, plastic gems and studs, barbells and hoops. His dad, before he burned alive, had specialised in vaginal gems. Theo hadn't realised there were such things.

And the man called Theo thinks that there are some wading birds which can stand motionless on one leg in a river for over . . .

And the man called Theo thinks that time is . . .

      Is not . . .

        Is . . .

          . . . getting harder and harder to keep track of, as time goes by.

A knocking on the door.

Theo jerked awake, listened, waited for it to go away.

The knocking came again.

It didn't seem urgent. There was no breaking of glass, howling at the night.

Three knocks, then waiting, then three knocks again.

He went downstairs, holding the phone like a weapon, a thing to smash into faces. A figure against the half-moonlight framed in the front door's frosted glass. He undid the lock from the inside, opened the door on the chain, just like his mum had taught him.

"Yes?"

"Are you Theo? Dani sent me."

Chapter 45

The girl was no older than eighteen, and sat cross-legged on the floor eating cheese and onion crisps from a bag in her pocket. Theo sat opposite her. Between them a USB stick.

Around mouthfuls of potato wafer: "I knew Dani from the prison, she was nice you know? She knew what she wanted – you don't get many people what know what they want and that's something that inspired me, you know, like real inspired. I'd like to know what that's like, I mean, being certain about things, like who I am and what I think and what I'm worth because that's the first step – you got to know – and Dani did. I don't know shit. That's what everyone said," a huge gap-toothed grin, another fistful of crunch, it's funny this, isn't it? Everyone says she doesn't know shit and that's a really funny joke, look, trust me, just because you weren't there you don't understand and so . . .

"I got out a few months ago. Parole company sponsored me, like with Dani, but they said I was pretty that I could make a few extra quid if I slept with the old men and the old ladies and that. And I said no, fuck that, because I'm trying to know myself and I don't think that's the sort of thing I'd do, and Dani told me that I shouldn't, she said that it would be . . .

So they terminated my contract, removed my sponsorship. And there I was without a job but Dani, she worked real hard, got me this job in this club down in Wivelsfield I mean, yeah, it's a sex club, only it's like run in this semi-detached house in this really dull street. The missus, she drives a Honda, but I don't do the sex. That's the deal. I'm the cleaner. All that stuff has got to be kept clean, I mean, you should use barriers on everything because you get tearing, and the vagina's got some natural protection against STDs, the fluids and stuff that are secreted which help clear things out, but still, you know. So I take my work really seriously, even the straps and that because you get bodily fluids and chafing and that's the blood barrier, it's all about the blood barrier, so yeah I'm . . .

Anyway, Dani called a few days ago, like, last week or something, and asked me to do her this favour. She gave me cash to buy the time off and my boss was real understanding cos she used to be on the patty line too and she was like 'You won't be sterilising dildos for ever, my girl!' only she didn't say my girl, that's sorta what you think she's saying but she doesn't say it out loud, if you get me.

And Dani's got this memory stick she needs to hide, cos it's got serious stuff on it. So she goes down to the club late one night yeah and leaves the stick in the laundry and I pick it up, and there's money and stuff and I'm like, cool. Then I get this phone call, and she's crying or something, like properly scared and she says she's being followed and watched, and I owe her, you know? I owe her. She saved my life, back on the line. She saved me. So she says I need to wait a few days, then take the money and the stick and go to this place called Shawford and wait. And I'm like are you fucking kidding me, screamers and ragers no thank you but she's like it's okay, it's okay, they won't hurt you if you stay small if you stay broken they recognise the broken ones, the broken things, they don't hurt them who are already hurting, and I'm like fuck that shit fuck right off . . .

But I owe Dani. And two days after that the club is raided, I mean like, it's torn to pieces it's just the most

and that's when I knew that maybe Dani wasn't lying. That maybe she was in shit, because the local superintendent he was with the girls every other day and even his wife sometimes came down so . . .

But these guys, the ones who tore the place up, they weren't like normal coppers – I got interrogated! Me, I got put in this room with a man called Markse and he was all like 'Tell me about Dani Cumali' and I'm like, don't say a word, like not even hello, cos if you start to talk to them that's how they break you, and in the end he lets me go, not worth bothering with.

So I get the memory stick and I'm on the first train to Dover, which is like the most expensive thing I've ever done ever, and then I walk and I'm waiting at this place, just waiting it's the shittiest thing I've ever done but also sorta the best. The ragers leave me alone, mostly. One night they started screaming and they were real close, and I pissed myself, like, actually pissed myself – not bad, like, not a lot of piss just a little bit, like less than a teaspoonful I reckon. Then I started screaming too, just screaming, and it felt good. I'd never done nothing like that before but I was crying after, I screamed and then there was nothing left and I just cried and it was the best thing it was . . .

They don't bother me now. They've got this guy, this boss bloke, he goes to the sea every morning and rages at it. Just rages at it, cos of how he was born into this shit, and he didn't ever find no way to make his life good, and he rages at the sky cos it never helped him, and at the earth cos it never carried him somewhere else, and his raging it's . . . it's sorta good, you know? It's like going to church, only different like. Sometimes I scream, it's like praying, but different.

Anyway. Tonight's the last night I'm sticking in this place. Fuck knows where Dani even is, I've got stuff to do . . . but tonight I come home.

See there's someone in the house.

And there you are. There you are."

She finished speaking, twisting the crisp bag into a knot, then unwound it as if surprised by her own destructiveness, smoothed it out on the ground between them. Stared at the USB stick, looked up at Theo, then away. "Missus already reopened the club, mind. Says she's still got a place for me, says there's a market in Wivelsfield, and I'm like real diligent; that's economics that is that's knowing your business. Says no one else bothers to put the plastics in the bin marked BIOHAZARD. I'm gonna . . . "

She stood up, unfolding in a single motion, long skinny legs in dark blue leggings, pale face turned towards the door.

Theo stayed sitting cross-legged on the floor. "Thank you for the—"

"I did it for Dani. Dani was good to me. She was like . . . she was good. Is she dead?" An afterthought, a thing which was probable but which the girl hadn't wanted to ask.

"Yes. She is."

She nodded once, sad, at nothing much. "I thought maybe she might be, way she was acting it was all . . . was it quick?"

"I think so."

"Did she die cos of that?" A nod towards the memory stick.

"Probably."

"Why? No – don't tell me. Don't tell me. I got a life I gotta live. I got . . . I got this person I need to be. I gotta find . . . I'm gonna go now. I gotta get back to Wivelsfield."

"Thank you for the . . . "

The girl was already going

going

gone.

Chapter 46

Once upon a time Neila was a man called Neil, and she worked out down the gym six times a week and drank protein shakes and was going to have the surgery for her arms, to make them properly, you know, but one day she realised that all of this, all of this was because she was in the wrong body and the protein wasn't making it right because not only was her body wrong, the soul she was trying to force herself to be

the place inside her flesh where she fitted the light of her heart

she had shrunk down so small beneath the muscle mass that she hadn't been able to see that the shape of her soul was a woman, blazing with light.

Theo stands at the back of the narrowboat, one hand on the rudder, and for a little while Dani Cumali is with him, disguised as a cormorant that keeps following the boat. It follows like the albatross followed the ship at sea, and for a while it was discomfiting, but now he knows it is divine.

On the patty lines they sing their songs
   We are the ones who
                   we are the fallen who
                        we are the dead who
                             we are the dirt beneath
                                    ours were the dreams that
                                        we were the ones who

We lost the
      we lost the
            we broke the
        blessed is the key in the lock
blessed are the children, for theirs is tomorrow, and their hands
make the world anew.

Chapter 47

Theo slept on the floor where once his bed had been.

The cold kept waking him. He huddled into the furthest corner from the window, buried himself inside his coat and slept.

Once he thought he heard music, a tiny sound, sung in a child's voice.

"Together we march, together we sing, happy in our community. The children play, there are igloos on the green, happy happy happy, the aliens make noodles . . . "

He thought he was dreaming, and the thought that he was dreaming seemed very alert, and wide awake.

He curled up tighter, shivering, and the singing went away.

A little before dawn the screaming started again. A morning chorus, a rising prayer, the hidden people of the town turned their faces towards the mirrored sea and wailed. Not a song of rage, not for the rising of the sun. They called out the long sound of the whistle that marked the end of the factory day. They sang the closing of the metal gates across the forecourt. They shrieked the rubber on road of the last lorry driving away. They called to the sea, and at their sound Theo jerked awake, and bleary crawled to the bathroom and tried the tap, and there wasn't any water, and so he walked to the front door and opened it a crack as the eastern sun bounced off the ocean at the bottom of the hill, and as he opened it, someone grabbed his hand from outside, pulled him forward and off his feet, and kicked him in the head.

*

The screamers, the ragers, the ones who got left behind, they feast on raw fish torn from the sea, they pick at the mussels that cling to the edge of the pier. There are no children born here, but they cling on, cling on, cling on like the sucker-flesh they feast on.

Hands pulled Theo through familiar streets.

To say he was beaten was probably unfair as that implied a plan, implied that there was some sort of . . .

Instead they hit because it was what they did.

And they smashed the windows.

And threw stones at the wall.

And tore at their hair and hit each other and scratched at their own skin as often as they bothered to kick him, when they remembered he was there, thrown in a corner of what had once been the back room of the pub where the ex-sailors went to drink away their landlubber days.

He stayed huddled, most of the time, and hoped no one noticed him, and for a while that seemed to work, as the four men and women turning through the room seemed equally as occupied with clawing at the last remnants of wooden panelling around the bar, cutting their arms lightly with glass and fighting over a bag of slightly mouldy bread stolen from the back of a shop down the way in Ramsgate, smuggled out through the fences and down the muddy causeway, as with beating him.

Sometimes someone saw him, and remembered that he was there, and kicked him or pulled his hair or trod on a vulnerable-looking joint for good measure, because why not, and then they'd lose interest and go back to trying to rip out the bathroom sink with their bare hands.

After a while even the ragers were calm, their morning rituals fulfilled, and they sat on the floor of the gutted pub, thin burgundy carpets peeled back to brown strings stretched like tripwires across the floor; the mirror gone from behind the bar, the bottles smashed and handles wrenched off the taps.

Still a slight smell of stale beer hung on the air, embedded in the fabric of the walls itself. As the sun climbed higher and swept across the floor, it was easy to imagine the place that had been before, and remember the time Theo's dad came down here for a pint with . . .

A pint with . . .

It might even have been Jacob Pritchard, king of the coast, back in the days when boys were just boys.

Theo lay in a corner, and was for a while forgotten.

A man stood over him.

Thought about things for a while.

Then stamped on his abdomen, just to show willing.

Stood a while longer.

Said, not unreasonably, "You were Dani's mate, yeah?"

Theo opened his less swollen eye, and looked at the man through the fold of his arms as the pain blurred vision and the light from the sea turned all things into grey shadows against its brightness.

"Hard-faced bitch she was, but we had some laughs. Wasn't surprised she ended up on the patty line. Always gonna be the way."

The figure before Theo drew a penknife, squatted on his haunches, toyed for a while with pushing the knife into the top half of Theo's left arm, rocking the point back and forth against his sleeve, not applying pressure, not releasing the weight, just mulling a proposition, before getting bored again and instead digging the rusting point thoughtfully into his own leg, slow and long, then releasing it with a sigh as the blood began to flow.

"Shouldn't laugh. Maybe the patty line was better, a smart move, she was always smart. You were the dumb one, right? Yeah – that's right – Dani and her dumb friend. Wasn't your dad some sort of nutter? Or am I thinking 'bout somebody else?"

The blood from the man's leg seeped into familiar shapes carved by a dozen other indentations, a network of streams and rivers that had dried deep, muddy brown in the fabric of his once-blue jeans. Little crimson drops began to run down his exposed ankle into the hollowed-out rags of his shoes.

He didn't seem to notice, or care.

"She got knocked up, didn't she? Kept trying to tell me that the vermin was mine. No fucking way I said, not mine, not my fucking problem, you think she's my problem then you've got another . . . what happened to that kid anyway? What happened to her?"

A thoughtful prod of Theo's shoulder with the point of the knife when he didn't answer, then another, a little more insistent.

"Dani's dead," whispered Theo through the bundled-up cocoon of his own pain.

"Is she? What was it – drugs?"

"Murdered."

"Boyfriend?"

"No. The Company."

"Seriously? Seriously, you're not just – shit. Hey that's something, to say that's a real . . . "

From the back of the building a sudden howl of fury, met by another, the sound of gasping men, a fight breaking out, something cracked, something smashed, someone fell, screamed in agony, true agony now, a bone broken, something cut.

The sound subsided.

The man with the knife listened, waited for it to fade away, the distant whimpering of a broken body crawling towards the dust, then turned his attention back to Theo, smiling broadly.

"What's your name?"

"Theo."

"Theo, huh? Didn't think . . . but what do I know? Never stuck my nose into the business of . . . come on then."

He folded the knife away, hooked one arm under Theo's, pulled him to his feet. Theo moaned, unable to keep down the sound, half-fell, was caught on the man's shoulders, let himself be dragged, feet trailing, out of the pub into the blazing light of day.

The pub looked straight onto the shingle beach. A criss-cross of tattered grey British flag bunting still swagged the pavement in front of it, waiting for a brass band to play below, the souvenir shop to reopen and sell bags of shells imported from Thailand for only £2 a kilogram.

In the brilliant outdoors light Theo saw the face of the man who carried him, and thought he knew it. Somewhere, through the cuts and the scars, the intricate dot-to-dot patterns of scabs and half-healed wounds drawn through the ears and cheeks, nose and lips, there was a recollection, a name.

"You were Dani's boyfriend," he whimpered as the man carried him towards the sea. "Your name is Andy."

The man called Andy gave him a hoick as he began to slip again, beamed brightly, exclaimed, "You ever been mad at something, Theo? You ever properly lost it?"

Theo grunted in reply. Andy carried him onto the shingle, laid him down at the top of the slope that tumbled towards the sea, thought for a moment, then with an easy kick pushed him, so Theo rolled like a sausage down to the edge of the water, landing in a curled-up groan of pain where the sea darkened the stone to deeper brown, the detritus of his fall forming small mounds of rattling pebbles against his side. Andy slipped down behind him, the shingle scuttling away beneath his weight, landed easily on his haunches. For a while he sat there, rocking a little, as the water came in and brushed against his toes, thick white foam hissing and popping as it rolled back out.

Theo turned his head away from the incoming tide, let the cold salt seep into his coat, his clothes, chill his fingers, and waited, eyes half-shut, and didn't have the strength to bother with imagination.

After a while Andy said, "You gotta stick around and look after what you got. That's what it is. You gotta say fuck you to them who tell you to go you gotta believe in what you have you gotta stand up for your family and the little guy and for the . . . "

He stopped as suddenly as he'd begun, opened his knife, stared at the bloody blade, closed it, opened it again, washed it in the salt water, dried it on his sleeve, closed it, put it away.

Rocking on his haunches, like a man at prayer, he watched the sea.

"Sometimes we go on raids. Me and the lads. We go pinch things, sometimes we dance around the village up on the cliffs to make the rich people scared, it's funny that, funny ha ha. Last time though, bastards called a helicopter on us. Didn't even let us get the dead, funny, funny ha." Watched the sea. "Murdered, huh?"

"Yes."

"You and she, you like . . . "

"No."

"No?"

"No. We weren't. Once when we were kids, we were . . . but that was fifteen years ago. She's just someone who . . . I just thought . . . it seemed like that maybe this might matter, that maybe it was . . . I lied about who I was. I've been lying since I left this place. I pretended to be stupid, I stole this kid's degree and kept my head down, you just . . . keep your head down and . . . "

Stopped. Words hurt, breath hurt.

Rolled a little to one side to see if that would make things better. When it didn't, groaned, rolled back. Andy watched in silence.

"You ever screamed?" he asked at last. "You ever howled?"

When Theo didn't answer, he leaned forward, breath brushing the salt on Theo's face. One hand slid over the exposed left side of Theo's ribs, as a lover might hold their beloved close, found a part tender and swollen, pushed. Theo's eyes bulged, his body curled in and away from the pain, he spat salt and spit, but the scream stuck somewhere in the mess of his throat, and with a tut Andy let go, shaking his head sadly.

"Gotta learn to let it out," he chided. "Gotta listen to the truth of the thing. Seems like guy like you needs to get a bit of the rage. You don't do the rage, you not gonna know what matters."

Shook his head again, chuckled at a distant memory. "I met Dani at the factory. She did the maggot nets. I did packaging – you have to make these cardboard templates which wrap around things like you know your sandwiches? When you have a sandwich you open up the packet and it just folds out so neatly, it's

238

the perfect size and shape. That's what I did. I was great. I was the shit, I was ... but they had this kid who they didn't have to pay full wage to so when I turned twenty-five they were like, the kid knows everything you do, and I was like, I've got talent I've got skills I've got ...

But they sent me away. Next thing Dani is knocked up, and she's like, it's yours, but we'd stopped going out by then we'd stopped being – I was like, fuck that shit babe fuck that I don't care who the fucking dad is cos I can't deal with some ...

Too late for an abortion by then, course. Couldn't pay for it even if. Didn't have health insurance, she has to borrow cash to get to the charity hospital in Canterbury but they don't have beds so she phones me and is like, my waters are breaking, and I'm like, fuck, and by the time I get there she's given birth to this purple thing in the car park and I'm like ...

... babies stink. And like, when a woman gives birth, she can like, crap herself there was like blood and crap and baby stink and it was ... "

Rocking, rocking by the sea, he drives his fists forward suddenly, both, knuckles down into the gravel, bone cracking, blood and bruising, rolls forward, rolls back, rolls forward, rolls back. An animal groan, a moan, head twisting to the side, back arch, curl, arch, curl. Then silence a little while. Theo lay, half on sea, half on shore, and watched through his one open eye.

"I went for benefits, and they said my case was a hard one and they'd put me on £53 a week. I had to have a sponsor, my sponsor was the dentist my job was the biological waste too you'd get these bags, these little yellow bags, of teeth.

I'd put them in the incinerator every night, kids' teeth, but also old teeth and broken teeth and yellow teeth and black teeth and you'd get the roots too I'd never seen a root before but it's long and covered in the bits of meat that get pulled out when it does, like it's furry you know?

I wasn't talking to Dani. Her dad had a stroke, and she pinched some medicine. You shouldn't do that shit, shouldn't get *caught*, they gave her an indemnity, she couldn't pay. Sent her to the patty

239

line making kids' shoes and before she went she came to me with this baby and said, you gotta look after her you gotta, but I was like, she doesn't even look like me, and she tried leaving the kid on my door, can you fucking, she left the kid who was . . .

They took her away, anyway. Dani first, then the kid. Good riddance I said good riddance and . . . "

He reached over, caught Theo by the back of his head, rolled him over, pushed his head down into the rising water, into the softer sand and, biting little stones of the low-tide beach, held him as he twitched and gagged and writhed and gasped, chuckled and let him go.

Theo flopped back onto the stones, gasping for air, tried to crawl away, couldn't move.

There they stayed a little while longer.

"She got out, in the end. Dani, I mean. Went crazy trying to find her kid, was like, where the fuck is Lucy? – that's her name, Lucy – and I was like, fuck if I know, and she was like, she's your daughter she's your daughter how could you do this to your own fucking daughter, and I thought maybe . . . I thought maybe . . . "

Tears in his eyes? Spray from the sea. Salt from the rage, the pain, the rocking and the blood. Theo found it hard to judge. Maybe none. Maybe all three together, now rolling down the red, scarred cheeks of Andy.

"She punched her parole officer. That was it. Back on the line. Never got free. Out for a few weeks, she'd steal stuff, go back on the line. Got into crack. I didn't see her. I was like, I don't want to know, I just don't wanna, and after a while she shut up, pissed off, let me think. Fuck it's so hard to think sometimes it's so hard to know anything, I know things when I scream then I know then I know what's inside but the rest of the time it's just . . . Never surrender never surrender that's the way you do it. Never admit you're beaten never let go of justice truth justice making right that's all that matters now blessed are the it's justice for the . . . "

"Lucy is my daughter," he mumbled.

Andy stopped rocking, thought a while, shrugged, didn't move.

"I didn't know, I thought . . . she's probably your daughter.

240

She's probably your daughter, Dani didn't lie if you do the maths if you ... "

Andy feinted towards him, hands, feet, head, and laughed as Theo flung his hands up to protect himself, curling up in the expectation of pain. Andy uncoiled, enjoying his merry joke.

Laughed a little.

The laughter faded.

A jerking half-chuckle.

Then silent again, apart from the washing of the sea.

At last, Andy mused: "Sometimes I'd think, maybe the kid was mine. I'd think that for a while, and I'd think, so what? So fucking what? Doesn't fucking matter. But couldn't stop thinking it. Couldn't get it out of my head. Tried shouting her name, but that didn't stop it hurting. Usually, you put one pain over the other and you forget the thing that hurt and it's better, I mean, it's better it's how you get ... but it didn't get better. It doesn't get better. I don't know."

Salt on his face, between his toes, in his fingers, Theo blinked at Andy against the light and couldn't work out what he was seeing on the other man's face, or what he saw through the brilliance of the ocean-reflected sun. "It doesn't matter," he croaked. "It doesn't matter. Dani said she's your daughter and Dani is dead so this is all ... "

Words rolled down.

Nothing more to say.

Andy watched the sea, Theo watched the land.

Andy said, "Lucy is my daughter." Rocked a little while by the sea. "Lucy is my daughter. I got that, one night. I got it when the raging stopped, when I cut my wrists but didn't die, men shouldn't do that, men shouldn't die, Dads shouldn't ever ... that was when I got it. Lucy is my daughter, and I left her. I left her. I fucking left her."

Tears and blood, rolling into water.

"If she's your daughter, will you ... you gotta find her and tell her that ... she can't live like we do. The sea the sky the earth they never carried me I hate them for letting me be born for

241

making me breathe I hate them I hate – but she gotta love 'em. If she's your daughter you gotta find her, you gotta help her be something which isn't . . . you know. You know."

Shook his head. Stared at his hands.

"You'd best be going."

Salt water ran out of Theo's nose.

"There's a queen, somewhere in the north. They give her prayers, blessed is the sky blessed are the falling leaves blessed are the daughters who – there's a queen. The queen of the patties. If the kid, Lucy, if she wants a DNA test or something like that if she wants it . . . "

The sea rolled in and they lay in silence.

"Nothing changes. Nothing changes. That's just the way it is and you fight against it just the way it is you go places and it still doesn't change and you ask what the point of . . . "

Silence again, watching the sea.

"You walking?"

Theo crawled onto his hands and knees, waited a while, stood up, slipped, sat on the shingle, crawled onto his hands and knees, stood, swayed, waited a while, looked towards the land at the top of the curve of shingle, the town obscured by stone, only blue sky above.

"Don't come back," mused Andy. "Don't come back. Tell Lucy it's on her now. She's got to make something she's got to . . . tell her I'm . . . don't come back."

Theo crawled, hand and foot, up the slope of the shingle.

Andy watched the sea.

After a while he stood up, waded hip-deep in, letting the muddy swell knock against his balance, grit fill his shoes. He closed his eyes, and punched the water, screamed and wailed and hurled his fists, his arms, kicked out beneath the foaming waves he screamed and screamed and punched and punched and

Theo walked away.

Chapter 48

Walking inland.

Didn't feel like the cliff path again didn't think he could make the hills, there were stairs cut into the chalk but even then . . .

Fell by a windmill which had stopped spinning a long time ago.

Lay on the ground as the sun turned towards afternoon.

Walked crusted in salt shoes and socks and shrivelled-up feet. A USB stick inside his pocket. It wasn't wet. That was a miracle, divine intervention, he thought he saw something in the flight of seagulls, thought there was meaning in the way they turned overhead.

He came to a farm and dogs barked and a child shouted and a man came charging with a shotgun which probably didn't work, but Theo ran anyway and fell in a ditch and hid there a while as the sun moved towards night.

At sunset came to a village with a little church where all the people prayed and a little square outside the church where there were stalls to sell childhood teddy bears to raise money for the fight against cancer and a pub where the landlord knew everybody's name.

But the pub landlord took one look at Theo and absolutely did not have a room for the night, so he walked on until he came to a house on the edge of town which doubled up as the dentist's, and the dentist came out and said, "You're in trouble?" and led him inside and sat him down in front of the electric fire in the living room as the TV played far too loud, and gave him tea and bread and said, "You can sleep in my son's room. He's gone away now. He wouldn't mind you sleeping there. I'll phone him to make sure."

And the dentist went into the kitchen and tried phoning her son, and he didn't answer, because he never did, and he didn't reply to her texts, but that was okay, if he cared about someone sleeping in his former bed she was sure he would answer, absolutely he would.

Theo sat on the floor in front of the fire as the dentist watched the weather, a channel broadcasting nothing but temperatures and wind speeds, ocean currents and storms brewing in the Carolinas, no mention made of Kent, and accidentally he fell asleep in that place, and woke in the morning to find that the dentist had put a pillow under his head and a blanket over his shoulders, and had washed and dried his socks and laid them out by his shoes, along with a cheese and pickle sandwich and a set of rosary beads.

The rosary had belonged to her son too, but he'd forgotten to take it with him when he left home. One day, she knew he'd reclaim it.

"I give kindness to strangers. The Lord teaches us to give kindly, that's how we find grace."

The vicar came round to check in on Theo, and told him that Jesus was his salvation, and to give thanks. The dentist made tea and whispered, "I didn't believe, but my son he believes, and I find that since he's left home believing brings me closer to him. Believing makes me . . ."

"You're very kind," mumbled Theo. "You're very . . ."

Time, when your face is all smashed up, is a little . . .
the ice on the canal
It creaks it cracks before the prow of the boat he hadn't even noticed how deep the cold went into the marrow his fingers are blue the ice
Even thin ice can puncture the hull, can sink

a narrowboat. They drown as they sleep they wake the water rushing down their noses it is

Even Neila dies, sometimes, in Theo's dreams and time is . . .

From the room next door, mystic words:

"P2, P3, M1, M2 . . . M2 . . . P2 M2 . . . "

The dentist pulled back the top lip of her patient and tutted at what she saw.

"Mrs Trott, I did tell you that this day would come."

The high whine of the electric drill, a whimper of pain.

Neila turns over the cards.

Four of coins, Temperance, ace of staves, Death (inverted), king of swords, the Emperor, ten of staves, eight of cups, the Hanged Man (inverted).

The Hanged Man is a complicated card. Restriction, letting go, sacrifice. Trapped between heaven and hell, perhaps supporting the heavens, maybe plunging into hell. Only the Tower is a trickier card to handle when it's drawn.

Indecision. Martyrdom. Suspension of all things, a failure to act, the need to look at things from a new perspective, a willing victim a . . .

Neila doesn't like the word "victim".

If you're "willing" then how are you a "victim"? Victim is the denial of choice, it is . . .

From the banks of the canal, shrieks of laughter through the night. She looks up from the cards, Theo from the stove, and they listen.

The laughter is the heady wildness of the poisoned mushroom, the crimson berry, the wild things who run naked through the dark.

Neila turns out the lights, and for a while they sit in silence, peeking through the porthole.

The convoy rolls past, trucks blazing with light, a hundred, a thousand bulbs flashing and blazing, rattling along the nearby road, turning the gently falling snow into a bubble of white. The revellers are dancing, writhing, kissing, falling, sleeping, shrieking, laughing, they crawl across the tops of the over-heavy vehicles and over each other, stepping in eyes and on bellies, glass bottles smashing on the tarmac below, they laugh and laugh and laugh

and keep on driving, no one entirely knows where, a wild hunt through the night.

Sometimes, secretly, Neila hears the people scream at the side of the canal and wants to raise her voice in chorus with theirs, to join the singing, the singing of the ones who have lost. But she knows that if she does, she will be an animal. Only animals howl at the moon.

In a dentist's house in a village with no name, no walls and a church in a little square, Theo sat at the computer and slipped Dani's memory stick into the slot.

There, laid out in neat little boxes, was the mother lode.

Flicking through files.

Video, taken from a strange angle: two men in a high-ceilinged room, or maybe it just seemed that way because of the plant pot the camera was hidden in. They drink port from little crystal glasses and behind them is a painting of a man with one hand resting on the turning globe, and they are Philip Arnslade and Simon Fardell, and Simon says:

"The problem with the excess is that ... "

"I entirely understand."

"Under these circumstances, for the sake of the business."

"It's a relief, really."

"If they don't pull their weight."

"I've always said ... "

"We can't always guarantee ... "

"The site at Wootton ... "

"Entirely in hand. You're doing the right thing, Phil. You're doing the right thing."

A door opened, someone came in, the two men switched immediately, golf and the weather, the camera stopped filming.

*

From the dentist's studio next door:

"You can't gargle what do you mean you can't gargle look it's NO THAT'S CHOKING NOT GARGLING IT'S LIKE THIS YOU ..."

Photos on a screen.

A factory behind, a pit in front.

The bulldozer has nearly finished filling in. The sheer horse-power of the machinery makes the bodies seem like fabric things, easily bent, easily pushed, no sense that this was once human flesh.

On the canal:

"Neila? Have I said thank you? Have I said ... did I ever say anything which was ... is there anything I can say which is ... "

Neila turned over the final card and sighed, and looked up into the face of the man called Theo and smiled. "No," she replied. "No."

On the computer screen:

Finances. Data, numbers, they run down the screen projected profits margins of opportunity the number of ...

A list of names.

Wootton.

King's Badby.

New Roade.

St Cecile on the Neve.

Lower Ayot.

Little Fife.

Twinmarsh.

He looks them up on the computer, and sees only the factory buildings and high walls of the patty lines.

Looks again and sees the long, dug fields of earth behind the factories, where fresh grass is beginning to grow.

The dead weren't given names, but the last four digits of their National Insurance numbers were visible, along with the crimes for which they were indicted and the value of the indemnity they had failed to pay.

Theo washed his face in the bathroom sink, put the memory stick in his pocket, and let himself out of the back door of the house as the dentist berated a crying child.

Chapter 49

Following country lanes for a while, until he turned north and found the River Stour.

Long reeds tipped with black ends and sharp spines, slow-running waters through boggy marsh, midges, an apple orchard, a town where they sold hog roast and methane.

An empty village where the pub sign swung gently in the breeze.

Not tracking the river as much as he'd thought, the wetness of the land pushed him through little villages and around enclaves where sometimes the screamers screamed and the rich locked up their cars.

A tiny town, no name, no gate, where two people sat in their front garden, naked, and watched Theo go by. Another woman, naked, stood behind a living-room window, hands on hips, and in the full resplendence of an autumn sun shimmering cold across her bare, goosebumped flesh, glared at the walking man as he passed by.

Soon they'd have a party, soon there'd be another night for flesh and seeing what new flavours could be best licked off another man's skin and it would be . . .

. . . but for now the sun was still up, so they waited for the evening and Theo walked.

He wasn't sure if he would find the place he was looking for.

Doubted very much if the man he needed was still there, but still, sometimes you had to put everything on a wager.

He turned off the path where it met a slightly larger country lane, followed it down to the river's edge, paused to wash his face again, dribble icy water down the back of his neck, listen to the swaying of the red-leafed trees, smell the mould behind the church.

Crossed a fat, belching A road, a railway line where the trains had stopped.

Walked up a hill to the valley's edge, to a village of two houses and a corrugated-iron farm. There were gates on either end of the road, in and out of town. The gates were built in two parts, the outers heavy black metal, the inners swirling iron, reclaimed from a manor house, the date of construction still visible amid the roses blooming and songbirds soaring in metal, lovingly restored.

He knocked on an outer gate, and a panel swung back instantly, a man glaring through the peephole.

"Yes?"

"I'm looking for Mr Pritchard."

"He's not here."

"But he *lives* here."

"No."

A little sigh, a shifting of bruised, aching bones, flat, blistered feet. "I'm looking for Mr Pritchard, it's very important."

The peephole slammed shut.

Theo knocked again.

The peephole didn't open.

He called out, voice bouncing back at him from the high metal gate, "Tell Mr Pritchard that I'm Mike's boy. My name is Theo. Tell him I'm going to destroy the country, the government and the Company."

No answer.

He slunk down, back against the concrete blast wall that encircled the little cluster of thatch-roofed houses, and waited.

Slept a while.

Woke hungry.

Slept a little bit more.

250

Stirred with the crunching of boots, the play of light against his eyelids, bright against the thick dark of cold autumn night bitten with the taste of winter.

A man in a green waxed coat, dark blue rubber boots and a pair of tatty blue jeans stood over him, face half-lost behind the glow of torchlight cutting into Theo's face. A long-tongued mongrel dog sat patiently beside him, waiting for orders, tail beating slow and rhythmic against the ground, breath steaming a little in the air. Behind the pair, two more men stood, arms buried in black woollen coats, faces hard, ready to kick out against any who dared their disfavour.

"It *is* you," mused the man with the torch. "You look like shit."

Theo, shielding his eyes against the glare, squinted up. "Hello, Mr Pritchard."

"You'd better have a cuppa."

The gate was opened at a nod, and Theo followed the older man inside.

"You take tea, right?"

"Please."

"Milly! One cup of proper tea for our guest here, and I'll have that herbal shit – it's past my bedtime you see, if I have even a sniff of caffeine after 3 p.m. I can't get to sleep and it's my bowels too – you wouldn't understand but when you're my age you'll see. Sit down, sit down."

"Thank you I'm . . ."

"Someone do you over?"

"In Shawford."

"Ragers?"

"Yes."

"Town went to piss. After Budgetfood pulled out, place with such a fine tradition of smuggling too but they couldn't hold it together, it's all gone downhill, it's nice to have a place to call your own though isn't it, this place – biscuit?"

"Thank you."

"Digestive?"

"I'll eat anything."

"Hungry? Milly! Our guest is hungry! Knock something up, will you?"

"You knock something up!" came the reply from the kitchen, down the end of a low-ceilinged, wood-timbered hall.

Jacob Pritchard chuckled, eased back into his padded chair with a creak of spine and sinew, smiled brightly at Theo.

Flames in an old iron fireplace; soot in the chimney. Various prizes for darts on the mantelpiece, getting old now, a few newer trophies for bowls. The stuffed head of a gorilla above a rocking chair, its face wrinkled in disapproval. The face seemed old, wise; it was not angry that it had been killed, severed from its body, stuffed, pickled and suspended on a living-room wall in Kent. It was merely exasperated that there was a species out there that thought this was the acceptable way of things.

A single fat-bodied fly crawled weakly at the edge of a window-pane, too exhausted from days of endeavour to find its way to the open crack at the top.

Jacob Pritchard, king of diesel, prince of cheap booze, sitting in a padded brown armchair, had grown old. His once-dark hair was tied in a thin ponytail, the peeling-back strands revealing the bright pink scalp underneath. His great hands shrank into his chicken-skin arms; most of his teeth were fake, and he kept them in a clear green jar by his bed at night.

His mind would be the last to go, and he knew it. Always assumed he'd go mad like his old mum had, but no, he'd be awake until the end, as his body failed one bone at a time, so it went, so it goes, you can't beat time, not even him, not even Jacob Pritchard.

"So," he mused, studying the bruised figure in the chair opposite his. "Little Mike's boy, all grown up."

Theo shrugged, and it hurt.

"All strapping man, all bringing down the Company, yes? All heroic causes and towns full of ragers and knocking on my door in the middle of the night. Yes indeed grown up, but maybe not the way your old man would've wanted. So how'd it work out for you, being Theo Miller? Did he have a good life?"

"Mostly."

"Mostly – mostly – a joker – *mostly* he says and I say to you mostly is not what brings you to my door, sonny, it's not the truth of matters as they now stand. It's not why we're here so why are we here, Theo Miller? Why would you come knocking, and what trouble do you bring?"

"I have proof."

"What kind of proof?"

"All of it. Everything. Company Police shooting runaways, gunning down screamers and ragers, clearing whole enclaves out to send in the patties to remove the scrap metal, the bricks, the pipes – everything. I've got the maps of the mass graves behind the prisons, the records of how many people died cos the hospital wouldn't let them in, the starvation figures for Wales, the murder rates for Newcastle, the ... "

Jacob Pritchard rolled his lower lip in, puckered his cheeks, stared up at the ceiling, then shrugged. Where's his tea? Pritchard called for tea and tea hasn't come. In his more tempestuous days this would have been cause for some remark.

"If you can't work on the patty line, you're a burden on the state," Theo mused. "You have to be fed, be given clothes, you have to be ... but there are jobs, dangerous jobs, sometimes it's easier, cheaper ... at New Roade they process radioactive waste. The oldest patties, the ones who aren't any use, are sent into the rooms with the spent fuel rods. They're given these overalls, but real kit costs, so they just let them work until ... then they break the bodies down and put them in these heaps and wait a few years and ...

At King's Badby they process jet fuel. There's these conditions you get, these tumours, but the Company contracts don't say they have to provide medical help. It got left out of the deal. The government deliberately left it out of the deal, Philip Arnslade and Simon Fardell, they were at university together. They're best friends. One for the Company, one for the government, but the Company pays for them both.

And when they run out of labour, they send Company Police into the enclaves, and they grab anyone who looks at them funny. Where'd you think the beggars went from the city? Where'd you think the drunks, the kids who throw eggs are? Why'd you think there aren't more people in the ghost towns that the Company left behind? Where'd you think they all went?"

On the canal, Neila said, "Tea? We're down to camomile, which I don't even like, but it's all that is . . . "

In the prison, in the past, the man who was Theo's father reached down into the bowels of the machine and realised, too late, that something was still moving, felt the cog, felt the lock, the first brush of metal and then the squeeze it burst through his hand like a bullet through a melon and he screamed and screamed and knew that he could pull his arm free and didn't dare because if he did he would have to look at the place where his hand had been and he . . .

In Dorchester the woman who was Theo Miller's mother helped pull up Mrs King's trousers, sweeping thin faeces off the inside of her thigh with a Wet Wipe and popping the fouled tissue into the bin, and said, "Mushy banana for supper lovely mushy banana you like banana don't you you like it?"

But Mrs King didn't answer. She never did talk, really, except for when she wasn't allowed her cigarettes.

By the fire, Jacob Pritchard said, "So?"

Outside the churchyard, the unnamed grave of the real Theo Miller is cold and overgrown. The first winter snow has fallen, the grass is stiff and cracked with frost there and the body is just bone in the thin coffin.

*

Jacob Pritchard shifts in his seat, wiggling an old ache in his lower back, and says again, "So? So what? Everyone knows this shit. This shit has been happening for years. This ain't nothing new. So you got some shit. Funny – it's funny, I like that, very funny – dead people, enclaves cleared, slaves locked up on the patty line, yeah, that's a thing but what about it? I'm comfortable. I'm peachy. Most people are. Few thousands die . . . well shit. Most people are scared of the ones who aren't like them anyway."

Silence on the canal.

Silence in the firelight.

And of course, there it is. There is the truth, the one that has been waiting for Theo, and the ghost of Dani Cumali, their whole lives.
    Everyone knew.
    So what?

Then Theo murmured, "You're right. Of course. Everyone knows. I've known. I send people to die, and I knew it. I've always known. No one ever says it. We stop before the hard things. We never finish saying anything that might matter at all. And you're right. That's how it happens. That's how it always happened."
    Looked up. Met Jacob's eyes. Smiled.
    "My friend left me a message – save the mother. I thought she meant *her*, I thought I had to save her, but she was already dead. Dani went to a place called Danesmoor. There's a woman there called Helen, she's Philip Arnslade's mother. Help the mother, Dani said. And sure, Dani stole stuff from the Ministry, but she'd been pinching things for weeks before she got herself sent to Danesmoor. That changed everything. Something there scared the Company enough to kill Dani. Kill my friend."

255

"Boo hoo hoo kill my friend; well bugger me, Hamlet."

Theo smiled at nothing much, nodding into the mesh of his fingers. Without rancour: "I don't think bodies pushed into a field are enough to make people care. Or maybe ... maybe that's unfair. Maybe they care. But caring isn't the same as doing something, and doing something is hard. It's very, very hard. But the Company is made of people, and people are weak. They are cowards, like the rest of us. They wear a nicer suit. I'm going to destroy them all, one at a time, until there is nothing left, and the cities can burn and the sea can turn red with blood, and when it's done I will make a better world for my daughter." Thought through those words, looking to see if there was anything wrong with them. Couldn't see it. "That's all."

In the room where they keep the children before they're strong enough to be useful or pretty enough to sell, Lucy Rainbow Princess clicks through to her next review. "Came in perfect condition and is everything I wanted. Would 100 per cent recommend."

Pauses, head on one side, thinks for a moment.

Types at the bottom: "Until it broke, 24 hours after opening the box. Fucking shit."

Hit send.

She'd be punished later. The night would be hungry and cold. Someone had said once that her sentence was nearly up, but then it hadn't been, it had been extended for ... she wasn't sure for what. Someone said she should see a lawyer, but no one would come, so here she was. This was what life was. This was all that her life would ever be. But for now, in her own way, this was a little victory.

By the sea, the screamers screamed at the waves, which foamed beneath the beating of their fists.

In the prisons, the patty lines kept on rolling rolling rolling

*

The golf club swung and the ball went wide, carried by the wind

A child scratched the art on the wall, wicked child you wicked wicked

The girl said, no, no, I don't want to, I don't want to, please, I don't I don't I just please stop please it's not . . .

By the fire, Jacob Pritchard weaves his fingers across his belly and thinks about his past, his future and the man before him, and murmurs, "Not sure I want to bring down the system, not sure I do at that. I do just fine, I do, I do just fine with my wall and my gun and my dog we are safe, see, men like me, the Company — it'd buy the petrol I brought in cos I never robbed them, nice cheap stuff, no VAT, they do right by me, I do right by them so you see . . ."

Then the woman called Milly was in the door of the room, and Jacob looked at her and had nothing but a heart full of love, and saw that in her face which did not approve of this line of conversation, and sighed, and said, "You can sleep in the spare room, but if you get blood on my shit I'll do you. Only bothering cos I liked your dad, a good man, him and me, we went way back, we went all the way."

In the morning Jacob Pritchard gave Theo a car, stolen, plates changed, a Tupperware box of egg-and-cress sandwiches, five hundred quid in used notes. "Don't come back," he explained, affably, as Theo climbed into the driver's seat. "Come back and I'll drown you in tar." And smiled, and shook Theo's hand cordially, and watched him on his way.

A bouncing plastic toy wearing the colours of Watford FC by Hairworks swung from the front mirror, thumbs up and right foot raised to boot a ball towards victory.

It was annoying for a time, and then, after a little while, it wasn't any more.

Part 2

Chapter 50

Lady Helen Arnslade, Marchioness of Mantell, seventeenth of that name, sat before the portrait and said:

"An eye for an eye, a tooth for a tooth?"

Her great-great-great-great-great-grandfather-in-law, who'd served under the Duke of Wellington and damn well shown those pesky Indian natives whose flintlock-fuelled culture was morally superior thank you very much, shifted uneasily against the stiff wooden frame that held him high above the unused fireplace of her tower room. Flakes of oil paint drifted down from his mighty whiskered face as he considered the problem.

"I suppose," he mused, "that it's much the same as the divine right of kings ... "

"Precedent," she agreed, pulling open and shut, open and shut the white dressing gown that swathed her grey, thin body. "Or do I mean proportionality?"

"Is the monarch the state, is the state greater than the sum of its people, are the people really the best judges of the value of the state and ... " pondered Lord Arnslade, eleventh Marquess of Mantell, one hand resting on the turning globe, another on the golden handle of his sword, his favourite spaniel frozen, eyes wide and frightened, mid-gambol at his feet. His family had earned its title, so the rumours went, not for mighty military service but for questionable sexual liaisons with a monarch who probably should have known better. Several centuries later he knows these things are all culturally relative, but still ...

"I do still love him, of course," mused Helen. "But can love not be loving by going against his wishes? Can you not ... " She paused to scratch at the eels coiled in her hair, which, while perfectly acceptable guests, still sometimes got on her nerves when she was trying to concentrate on more important matters.

"You're talking about making decisions for other people," the Most Honourable Marquess concluded sagely, feeling on safer ground here – making decisions for other people was something he excelled at.

"I suppose. But then isn't that the whole point?"

"The moral framework ... "

" ... well yes there's the ... "

"The whole issue of how ... "

"Are my ethics of an acceptable standard to ... "

"Having conviction is more than most people ever really achieve, of course."

Lady Helen hesitated, staring up at her long-deceased, paint-frozen relative, and for a childish moment realised she was chewing her fingernails, a disgusting habit that had been ground out of her decades ago, ridiculous that it was back now. "I don't think I have conviction," she said at last. "I used to, but I don't think I have anything like that any more."

Lord Arnslade strained, wishing that the painter who'd captured him in oils hadn't given his chin such a haughty upwards tilt, it was giving him a right crick in the neck now, and though his eyes could naturally follow anyone around the room no matter where they wandered, most of the time he was most comfortable studying the cornicing, which upon consideration he considered to have been rather poorly done. All this made thinking about the serious issues – the deeply concerning matters – that were now before him that much harder.

At last he concluded, a little shower of dust trickling down from the back of the canvas with the effort of it: "Action is belief."

He felt very proud of himself for having expressed this, essentially condensing his entire life story to three deeply sage words.

Lady Helen looked less convinced, and he felt the globe turning beneath his fingers slow as her confidence waned. Hastily, before the moment passed him by, he added, "Also he is a total shit, if you think about it, and probably has it coming."

"But he is my son. Granddad? Can I call you Granddad? He's my son. He's my son. He's my . . . "

But Lord Arnslade was just paint and canvas again, the harsh light of the overhead chandelier bouncing off his thick dark curves, the spaniel still waggy-tailed and wide-eyed leaping for ever at his feet, and there was blood in her mouth, and Lady Helen realised she needed to wash her hair.

Chapter 51

Theo Miller drives.

He sleeps in the back of the car.

Eats egg-and-cress sandwiches.

Reads on the old laptop of Jacob Pritchard's younger son, who long since upgraded and fled abroad to Spain, where things were a different kind of easy.

Records of deals done, of lives sold.

He wonders where Lucy is.

For a little while thinks about praying, and realises that he is praying to his daughter. She should not be God, she is *not* God, and yet he feels this urge to bend his knees and pray, pray for . . .

It's a stupid instinct, so he gets back into the driving seat and keeps going west.

"Hi, Edward Witt, Criminal Audit Office, I'm . . . yes that's – no I can . . . "

He sits in a service station off the M40 and enjoys being his boss, for a little while.

"No, still here thank you – yes it's about Lucy Cumali that's right Cumali you might also have Rainbow Princess it's – that's the one thank you. Criminal Audit Office, yes so I'm looking at a request from a lawyer on behalf of a corporate entertainment company enquiring as to the value of her indemnity is it . . . I see. I see. Yes. No that's more than I think they were expecting it's . . . can you send me that file? Thank you yes my email address is . . . "

*

264

He read Lucy's file while eating a kebab in the passenger seat of his car, pulled up in a high street that sold birthday cards, burgers, scones, second-hand mattresses and not much else.

A corporate entertainment company was interested in buying her parole.

The governor warned that she had an attitude problem.

Not a problem, replied the company. Our girls get to be very pliable, very soon. It's all part of the training.

A road, sweeping down a V carved between two chalk cliffs, breaking out into crimson-leafed forest, pillowed mounds of darkness, hammer ponds and running brooks through hills where the sun only sometimes managed to peek out from between the leaves.

He ate at a pub and rode their Wi-Fi connection and the menu was red cabbage and wilted spinach and Chantilly carrots and roast lamb and giant Yorkshire puddings and after twenty minutes the community Company officer came and asked him for his ID and if he worked nearby because you see the people here had paid their Company tax and there was a surcharge for visitors.

In the night he sat on a hill looking down towards the village, and saw a flash of firelight as the first torch was lit, followed by another, and another, and another.

The Company support team stood by with sand buckets, health and safety you see, but otherwise didn't intervene as the people of the town walked out in robes of black, flaming torches held aloft, went down to the edge of the town and circled its boundaries three times, twice clockwise, once anticlockwise, and spoke their prayers.

Protect us, Lord, from the evils that come in the dark protect us from the world that claws at our edges protect us from change and from pain and from evil and from . . .

After, they went home to play Xbox.

*

Theo didn't have the paperwork to enter the Cotswolds.

He hid the car on the Oxfordshire border, driving down the path to an abandoned industrial estate and tucking it into the deepest corner of the dark. Then he waited for the grey hour before dawn, and sneaked across on the footpaths with a pair of kids, dodging into the hollows of great-bellied trees to evade the patrols who swept the area in beams of white, looking for intruders.

His guides, fourteen and sixteen, brother and sister, made their living by taking strangers across the border. They knew where the motion sensors were, and the flight paths of the drones. For only two hundred quid they could get you a month pass to the Cotswolds, complete with 5 per cent discount at this big manor house where once a president had stayed, or maybe a military dictator, they weren't sure. They were all the same anyway.

He paid fifty quid for their skills, and didn't ask if they had family or if they'd be okay getting home. By early morning he'd reached a village of old stones and running water, a mill silent by the stream, narrow stone bridges criss-crossing through the village, a manor house offering spa experiences and corporate dining.

He washed his face in the stream, waited for the sun to climb higher, descended to the tea room to order a scone and a pot of Earl Grey.

"You're here for the walking are you?"

"Yes, the walking. My family have a cottage in Chipping Campden."

"Beautiful around there, beautiful. So how long have you been . . . ?"

"I entered a few days ago. I like to come here at this time of year – fewer people. You can walk for hours and not see . . . "

"Of course! It's not like the Lake District around here!"

An entrance pass to the Lake District was sometimes affordable even by people who weren't on the Company payroll, and there were some corporations who still insisted on sponsoring Boy Scout trips up the mountains too. Not that anyone had any problem with Boy Scouts, not really, it was just that people like that ... cluttered things. They made everything feel terribly ...

... cluttered.

"I was thinking of visiting Danesmoor. I heard that the paintings are ... "

"Remarkable, yes, remarkable do you know the ... ?"

"Arnslade; of course. I work at the Ministry – he's such a good boss, I mean you'll know of course, but such a pleasure and ... "

His hostess, blue and white striped apron, green beads at neck and wrists, beamed, and topped up Theo's cup with a little more steaming tea, milk in first.

One cream tea later, a family of three arrived, bright blue matching hi-tech jackets, matching red walking sticks, matching immaculate, mud-free boots. Theo watched them from the corner of his eye, waited for the child, a boy of seven, to be particularly obnoxious and vile, then stood up, swept by, and stole the father's travel bag. The entire exercise was ludicrously easy.

Sat on the edge of town, he rifled through the contents, stealing clothes, water bottle, money, credit card, papers.

Threw the rest into a gully, kept on walking.

A flock of grouse scattered down the side of the hill; a horse with wide brown eyes trotted to the edge of the field, inviting nuzzling, sugar cubes, company.

A town where a single church sang out a joyful peal of bells to the rising day.

A village with an autumn fête in full swing, the children laughed and played and spun around the maypole, there was face painting, giant bubbles drifted through the air, home-baked goods for 50p to raise money for a local charity, a fair for old cars, polished to perfection, 1930s two-seaters, tops down, men sat on the shining black leather seats exclaiming, without being allowed to actually drive, "Parp parp parp!" giggling with childish delight.

As he moved on, he passed a red phone box which had been converted into a station for CPR defibrillator panels.

A tourist shop selling hand-painted china, a thousand whisk-ered cat faces.

A security post manned by a member of the Cotswolds Appreciation Corporation, who scurried out as Theo passed and blurted, "Can I see your pass, please?"

"Of course just . . ."

"Where did you enter?"

"I prepaid at Blenheim. It was part of the tour, I have the receipt somewhere just here for . . ."

"If you don't have the proper paperwork then you can't – we have to protect the Cotswolds for the residents, for paying vis-itors, the purpose of the . . ."

"Here." He handed over the stolen paperwork, smiled and waited.

"Says you're with a family," the man muttered at last, cautious.

"Yes; they're still in town, enjoying the fair."

"Where are you going?"

"We parked the car back on the hill. I'm going to pick it up; my wife and son don't want to walk it's . . ."

He stumbled on the words, picked himself back up, smiled.

The man returned his papers. "Have a good trip, sir. The Cotswolds are the perfect place to enjoy the English countryside without anxiety or bother!"

Theo nodded, and kept on walking.

After a while it started to snow.

He looked down on a land turning from green to white, and it was beautiful. It was one of the most beautiful things he thought he had ever seen, and as he stared across the slow slopes he said out loud, "So Lucy, you may not like walking holidays but surely even you can appreciate . . ."

And stopped himself.

Put his hands in his pockets, lest they grow cold in the empty, biting air.

Kept on walking.

"Hi, Edward Witt again. Yes, the Cumali case – I was wondering yes I was thinking could I maybe talk to her, it's just

268

no.

no I understand of course.

Of course.

You have to . . .

Well thank you. Sorry to have bothered you I'll just . . ."

Theo sits a while, and stares at nothing, and only moves when the cold becomes unbearable. In the valleys below, the bells are singing a joyful song, and somewhere there is the laughter of children, behind the walls.

Theo reached Danesmoor on the early afternoon of his second day of walking.

Paced around the great stone wall that cut it off from the rest of the land.

Paid £19.50 for the entrance fee, showed his Cotswold papers, hoped no one cross-checked, for by now surely the theft would have been reported.

An old woman in a heavy lambswool coat sat behind the counter in the gatekeeper's lodge, and did not cross-check his papers.

"There's tearooms by the stable," she barked, handing him his receipt. "We close at 4 p.m."

Theo thanked her, walked up the neat gravel path, framed by yew trees carved into clownish spheres, towards the front door.

A beautiful house.

Three storeys of light brown stone, pitched grey roof, smaller windows on the top floor, servants' quarters. A series of stone arches and pillars had been raised at the end of the garden, mimicking something Roman. Beyond, forest began to intrude into the tended knee-high yew mazes and cherub-capped fountains.

Approaching the house down a gravel path, he found white doors standing half-open despite the cold, a blast of heat from radiators tucked away behind carved wooden facings striking his face as he went inside. A wooden sign in the shape of a pointing hand directed VISITORS towards a staircase, and a plinth invited him to remember that Danesmoor was a working family house, and guests were welcome only to appreciate a fascinating historical and cultural heritage.

Black and white marble floors, locked together in geometric squares and triangles to create a map of a madman's chessboard. Plaster ceilings, adorned with horsehair carvings of Greek gods and heroes: Hercules fighting a lion, Persephone reaching out towards fading summer as Hades dragged her down into perpetual night, Venus and Mars locked in an embrace, the Goddess of Love glancing a little away from her husband's shoulder as if catching sight of some other entanglement more interesting than the limbs of the God of War.

Paintings. Lords, ladies, their spaniels and babies, the dynasties that had gone before. A statue of a woman, veiled, weeping; a marble carving of a boy throwing a javelin, muscles tight and buttocks bare, head turned to one side as if, at the moment of truth, he had heard a voice cry from the crowd, but it was too late now to stop the spear's flight.

A roped-off route for guests to walk, little stands explaining the significance of this room or that flowerpot, the history of a fireplace, the craftsmanship of a chair. Theo wandered, and was the only wanderer, while outside the snow grew a little thicker, until he came at last to a sign that said NO ENTRY and, trying the door handle, found it unlocked.

The private family rooms of Danesmoor had all the painted grandeur of the public areas. Portraits still hung on the walls, but on the mantelpieces above the pink-veined fireplaces were photos of younger men and women, drunk, tongues waggling at the camera or dressed up in heroic swatches of leather and paint for a stag do. On the sofas, tattier, softer than the sculpted furniture in the rest of the house, out-of-date newspapers, magazines ringed with coffee stains, the sound of a TV somewhere below playing a reality show in which the contestants had to eat bugs, or a snake's heart, or their own vomit or some such, to win prizes and the adoration of the texting crowd.

TVs in most rooms, playing at empty air. Once Theo heard

someone move, and ducked through a white wooden door disguised as another piece of panelling which turned out to hide a
toilet, complete with a bottle of bleach on top of the cistern and
a waste basket containing a collection of old tampons wrapped
in tissue.

Footsteps passed by, and he waited, and when they were gone,
he let himself out and continued wandering.

A room
    potted plant a portrait above a long table he
    knelt down by the plant and looked up and saw in that moment
the image he had seen in a film on a USB stick, where once
Simon Fardell and Philip Arnslade had stood and said, "The
problem with the excess is that . . . "
    Another room.
    Crystal glasses, the port decanter had been refilled, thick
purple liquid behind shimmering glass. A white cat with a black
spot at the top of its tail, curious, brushed against his ankles. He
stroked its head, rubbed under its chin, tickled its belly, until, too
excited by this play, it flicked out joyfully at his wrist and nearly
scratched him, at which point he pulled back, and it grew bored
and slunk away, a king disappointed by a courtier.
    A flight of stairs. A bin filled with blue latex gloves, a golden
drinking chalice on a table next to a half-drunk bottle of Diet
Pepsi. Light fading through the windows, the end of the day; a
man ringing the bell in the courtyard outside to summon the
tourists away.
    A noise from the corridor. He ducked through a closed door
because it was there, shut it quietly, pressed his ear against the
wood, listened, waited, heard footsteps pass, let out a breath.
    Looked around the room.
    A single bed, long dressing table, a mirror, a picture of a cat,
ginger, hackles raised, painted in oils, hissing from the wall.
A TV, the volume turned down, showing a programme about
organising garden parties. On the dressing table – pills. Over two
dozen bottles, orange plastic, containing fat ones thin ones square

ones round ones, big red horse-pills and small yellow stubs that vanished under the tongue, and boxes in which these pills could be laid out in order – Monday morning, lunch, dinner, bed; Tuesday morning lunch dinner bed Wednesday morning lunch

Someone was halfway through filling a box, and had been called away by something else. Theo picked up a pill between thumb and forefinger, rolled it around, put it down, turned to go.

Saw the door, big black key in the lock, the sound of a radio playing static-cracked Russian classical music from the other side, something triumphant and brassy.

Hesitated.

Went to the door.

Tried the handle, slowly.

The door was locked.

Turned the heavy iron key, felt an oiled latch slip back.

Tried the handle again.

Pushed the door open.

The stink hit first the stink it was like . . .

He gagged, turned away, closed the door, caught fresher air.

Put his sleeve over his mouth, opened the door again, looked.

The sound of the radio, high and proud, a chorus of children's voices raised in triumphant song. A double bed, carved wooden post in each corner, no curtains hanging from the frame. At the end of the bed was a low, long bench for sitting on and taking shoes off, or leaving books on or for a sitting cat, he wasn't quite sure. On one wall was a picture of a man, one hand on a turning globe, a spaniel leaping in perpetual surprise at his feet, its eyes wild as if to wonder what cruel fate it was that it would be caught for ever leaping, never catching its prize. A single lamp was on by the bed. In the shadows to its left was an armchair, upholstered in thick, itchy thread woven with pale roses. A woman was in the armchair, eyes closed, head on one side, yellow-flecked spit on her chin where it had rolled from the corner of her mouth, fluffy slippers on her feet and a thick dark blue dressing gown around her frame. A blue cap had been pulled over her head, capturing the white fluff of her hair; her nails were cut to translucent stubs, and where her legs emerged beneath gown and nightie, brilliant blue-black veins throbbed and spidered over her chalky flesh.

The smell seeped through arm and cloth pressed over his mouth, there was no denying it, no pretending that there wasn't vomit in a bowl just visible under the bed. No one had bothered to remove it or change it, it was just vomit, a bowl full of vomit.

he closed the door again, thought he might puke, didn't, took another deep breath, opened the door, tried again

a yellow stain in the centre of the bed, old urine, new urine, brownish smear of faeces too but the woman sitting by the radio didn't seem to mind she was just

sitting.

Asleep perhaps or maybe

He looked again, and her eyes were open, drifting up to the ceiling, her head rolled back. She made a little noise.

Uh uh uh.

Perhaps language, of a sort.

Theo closed the door, didn't lock it.

Stood for a while with his back pressed to the wood, the key pushing into the base of his spine, and it seemed to him that there was a story to be told here. There was evidence which would be very easy to deny there was ...

Theo opened the door, one more time, to the room where the old woman sat.

Crossed the floor.

Squatted down in front of her, trying to ignore the fact that if he rocked back too suddenly he'd sit in puke, trying to exhale into the stench.

Took her hands in his, held them softly, waited for her drifting eyes to drift down to him, pupils far too wide, tongue loose in her mouth, the flicker of her gaze somewhere in the vicinity of his but unable to stay still.

"Lady Mantell?" he whispered. "Ma'am? My name is Theo."

"Who the hell are you?"

A sudden leap of noise from the room next door, a man in the open door pursued by a blast of TV, a cheerful chorus of, "So

273

with her customised bunting in place it's now time for the final touches as . . . "

The man standing in the door to the stinking bedroom wore black T-shirt, blue jeans, carried a tray of baked beans on toast and a flask of sugary orange gloop.

For a moment the two men stared at each other, wondering which way the next twenty seconds of their lives would go. An instant, perhaps, in which there could have been some bluff, some bluster, but no sooner had Theo begun to formulate the lie than it was too late, the opportunity to deceive had passed them by.

The man dropped the tray and lunged for a grey button on a thin cord by the door.

Theo threw himself across the room, caught the man's wrist before he could press it, kneed him hard in the stomach, not really knowing why or if it would work, he'd never kneed anyone anywhere before, but he had a knee and the man was in his way and so he

kneed him and it didn't really go as well as he'd hoped because the man gave a little grunt and then caught Theo by his left ear and tugged. He'd probably been aiming for hair, but in the scramble ear would do, and it hurt less than Theo thought it would do so he resisted and tried instead with his free hand to dig his thumb into the man's eyeball, he had no idea where that idea had come from it just seemed

the man let go of Theo's ear, caught his wrist as he went for the face, and for a moment there was an awkward push-pull of strength as neither knew quite where they were supposed to go from here, teetering with arms locked and fingers scrambling, bodies swaying until their balance broke and the pair tumbled down, Theo pinned beneath the larger man. The fall smacked the breath out of his body, smashed a bowl of baked beans beneath his left ribs, orange gloop and white ceramic shards smattering across the room. He lost his grip on the man's right hand, and now the man had found a brilliant thing to do with elbows, tucking his left elbow under his body and letting his whole weight drive it down, point first, into Theo's belly.

274

Theo tasted half-digested sandwich in his mouth, gagged, curled and writhed and couldn't get any breath inside, and the man sensing this snarled in expectant triumph and punched Theo across the face. He couldn't punch very well; there wasn't any room to draw the fist back and release, but it seemed to make him feel good so he did it again, a ring on his third finger slicing through Theo's cheek, warmth spreading inside his mouth as the pain knocked through to the back of his head, and again, and again and

then the woman in the dressing gown hit the man over the head with the remnants of the dinner tray, and his eyes went wide and his weight buckled to one side, and she hit him again, then dropped the tray, followed immediately by dropping herself, sitting with her legs curled up under her like a child picking daisies, and her eyes rolled up again and her mouth drooped open, but Theo

pushed the man off him, caught the fallen tray and hit him again and again and again and

at some point realised that the man wasn't moving, and there was blood on the floor, and it wasn't Theo's and

and wondered if he'd killed a man and

and if that man had a daughter and

Theo dropped the tray, crawled across the floor, felt through the blood on the man's face, found a pulse.

Felt around his skull, couldn't feel anything that had buckled or caved.

Looked into his eyes, saw that they were open and looking back, but the man didn't move, didn't speak, little gasping breaths, wondered if there was something he'd broken if there was

wanted to apologise, thought it was stupid

stood up

fell down

something inside him was, if not broken, then certainly turned around and he'd not really had time to heal from Shawford, he'd not really known what he did he'd not really stopped to think about

Crawled to the woman sitting on the floor.

Held out one hand.

"Lady Mantell?" he breathed.

Her eyes drifted again to his face, danced this way and that, fell away, rose, fell away again.

"Helen," he murmured softly. "My name is Theo. May I take you away from all this?"

Chapter 52

They stole a car.

For a moment Theo wondered if he'd have to hot-wire the thing. He'd read plenty of reports of people doing it, a minimum of £550 if you were caught hot-wiring any vehicle over an estimated road value of £3275, it was also likely that you'd be charged for . . .

But the man he'd beaten had some car keys in his pocket, so that made things easier.

He found a coat in a wardrobe, wrapped the ribbon-faced woman in it. He put her carer in the recovery position, eyes still open, that didn't seem right that wasn't normal that wasn't

took the car keys

held the woman gently under the arm

led her away.

A car in the staff car park.

A little Nissan that smelled of chips and sporty deodorant.

He put the woman in the passenger seat, and she didn't object.

He sat in the driver's seat, turned the engine on, and the moment he did the radio came up, far too loud, a Michael Jackson number, he turned it off quickly lest it upset the woman, and she didn't seem to care either way.

There wasn't a barrier to smash triumphantly as he drove out of the car park, and the woman on the ticket desk didn't look up from her mobile phone as they passed, which Theo found a little disappointing.

Chapter 53

He parked the car on the edge of a town whose name he couldn't find. Sodium light shot up the spire of a red-brick church. A large shop selling light fittings resembling mallards and soup bowls painted with puppies' faces cast white light out of its long windows onto the street. A fish and chip shop was still open, selling mushy peas with English mint, beer-batter fish, and chips three-times cooked in duck fat. Theo looked at his face in the mirror, and saw bruising and a long cut from a stranger's ring.

The woman slept.

He drove on.

Four miles from the Cotswolds border he saw the first sign: POLICE SEARCH IN EFFECT. EXPECT DELAYS.

He pulled off the road into a farmer's field, where a herd of fat-bellied cattle regarded him suspiciously for a while before forgetting and returning to the business of eating the wet winter grass.

The woman was still sleeping.

Theo watched her a while, and wondered what the hell he'd done.

Washing his face in a brook.

Somewhere upstream there was probably a dead sheep or something, so he didn't drink the water, just washed the blood away, which upon consideration was probably worse.

When the emergency fuel light came on, he drove the car to

the edge of a ten-house village built around a small manor house that now hosted poets' retreats. He shook the woman awake gently. Her eyes opened slowly, the pupils shrinking down tight as light met her face. Her gaze fixed on him for a moment, confused but steady. Then she said, "I need socks."

Theo licked his lips. "Okay. I'll see if I can find some."

"Thank you," she replied, and closed her eyes, and went back to sleep again.

Theo walked into the village.

Found a house with no four-by-four parked outside.

Tried the front door.

Found it unlocked.

Went inside.

Climbed stairs of soft cream carpet, leaving muddy boot tracks behind him.

Brushed past the pictures of family friends and family cats.

Used the toilet, because it was there, washed his face in hot water, found it sensational, wondered if he should have a shower, decided against it.

Found the bedroom. Stole some socks, trousers, shirts – armfuls of the stuff, he didn't even know why he took so much.

Shoved it into plastic bags that he found in the kitchen, in the cupboard that held the washing machine.

Helped himself to bread and last night's roast chicken, saw that this was a family who kept their ketchup in the fridge rather than the cupboard but seemed to just leave mayo standing wherever they wanted – odd that, very odd. He was at a loss to understand.

Walked back towards the car.

A curtain twitched, but he kept walking, a man with nothing to hide, and no one shouted, and the wind pushed the fallen leaves through the narrow cobbled lanes.

279

Chapter 54

They hid in an old stone hut where once the shepherds had tended their flocks, and which now only the kids and the teenagers used, the bored ones from the village come to drink beer and smoke pot and maybe try this sex thing.

Theo laughed despite himself as he kicked condom packets and crunched-up aluminium cans out of the way, remembering for a moment a night with Dani on the beach, cries of "Ow it's really cold is there more blanket ... my bum's gone to sleep!" At the time it had been as close to magic as his teenage brain could really ...

... but now it was something else and for a little while Theo chuckled silently as he laid the old woman down on a bed of stolen clothing, resting her head out of the wind, and as she slept, he put two pairs of socks on her feet and, having nothing better to use, another two on her hands, to keep her fingers from going blue.

For three days

"For three days," mused Theo as they stared down at the ice encasing the *Hector*, thin for sure but even thin ice could do so much damage, "or maybe it was only two? I think that perhaps it was ... "

For maybe only two days

They hid in that stone cottage on a hill.

Theo drove the car as far away as he could, abandoned it in a field when even fumes wouldn't keep it moving, walked back along the paths. That took nearly four hours, and when he returned it was dark and he was cold and soaked to the skin, not by rain but by a falling dampness on the air that made him shiver uncontrollably. The woman was awake, watched him arrive with the setting sun fading behind his back and said simply, "Come here."

He'd lain down on the bed of stolen clothes, and she'd pulled a stolen blanket over him, and held him tight, and soon she was shivering from the cold that radiated off his soaking clothes, and after a while they were both warm, and Theo slept, and so did she.

The next morning she threw up and couldn't hold even dry bread down and squatted behind the hut and shouted at him not to come near her, not to look at her, and for a while he hid behind the stones and covered his ears as she heaved and shook and choked and spat and coughed orange liquid out of her nose. The act of vomiting made her bowels go too, her bladder her . . .

And then she called, "Pass me some clean clothes – don't look!" and he passed her some clean clothes and didn't look, head turned down to the grubby earth, and she changed in the cold and returned wearing the clothes of a woman much younger and far fatter than she and without a sound lay down beneath the blanket and waited for Theo to lie down too, so that she might take some of his warmth, which before she had so preciously given.

And she slept.

And sometimes, but not very often, Theo slept too.

Until one evening, probably on the second maybe on the third day, a group of kids appeared at the door of the hut and stared, confused, bewildered, to find it inhabited, and muttered amongst themselves, for they had meant to come here and do such naughty things as open bottles with their teeth and maybe dare each other to touch their own vaginas or penises or something truly dangerous like that and it was going to be . . .

But here were two people, a man and an old woman, lying on a pile of filthy clothes and it was obvious to the kids that these were intruders, interlopers, bums, because even the most intrepid walkers of the Cotswolds Ways used licensed glamping sites.

So they muttered amongst themselves and scuttled back to the village, and one – the second-biggest and most brave – threw a stone at Theo that bounced off his shoulder, and Theo woke and saw the child, and the child shrieked and ran away.

Theo shook the woman and whispered, "We have to go we have to go there were ... *we have to go ...*"

And the woman opened her eyes wearily, and saw the shadow of the children running down the hill and grumbled, "Very well."

And climbed to her feet, pulling her blue cap back over her short white hair, rubbing yellow flakes from her eyes.

They walked, the woman leaning on Theo, one arm across his shoulders, each step a gasp, her weight swinging from side to side. Their only direction was the opposite of that in which the children had run, until finally the woman stopped, looked up the hill, looked down it, turned to Theo and, craning her neck a little to examine his face more particularly, said, "My name is Helen."

Chapter 55

Sirens in the night.

Police.

People – family people – heard rumours of bums, of interlopers on the hills of . . .

Theo said, "How fast can you walk?"

And she replied, "Not fast enough it's not going to be . . . but I know a . . ."

They stumbled through the settling dark, the sunset sky overhead a purple-blue pillow that stopped abruptly at golden-red sheets thrown up from the western horizon, night and day competing violently for who would triumph at the final bell.

The sound of dogs, dogs howling, and once Helen fell and Theo caught her, and once Theo slipped in mud and Helen hissed, "Come on!" and he struggled up, half-breaking into a run, down a path towards a stream, the forest whispering overhead, getting dark now, too dark, the trees hemming in all things, a prison that hid the howling dogs from sight that made the sound of the police bounce this way and that; a place where men could die and the earth would take their bones and none would ever know that it had happened here, a place where –

A voice called out from the darkness on a ridge overhead: "Helen! Lady Helen, can you hear me? Are you . . . ?"

Helen pulled Theo behind a tree three times their width, an ancient monster of gutted wood inside which a dozen creatures played, and the light of the torch passed by, but the barking of the dogs grew nearer.

"Come," hissed the woman. "Come."

Theo hauled her along, following the direction of her pointing fingers, whispered commands, along a path by the stream which he could barely see, twigs catching, mud rising to his ankles, they scrambled along until the darkness was so thick that Theo could only see the half-blackness of the trees a moment before walking into them, the stream a roar, he kept on missing his step and half-sliding into it, but always Helen hissed, "Come on! Come!"

Downhill, and down a little further, and then a light ahead, a yellow glow on a porch, and he hesitated but she did not, so he staggered on, and briefly the world was lit up blue as a light swept through the trees to his left, he hadn't even noticed the road coming close, didn't know where north was or what land he walked in but Helen seemed confident. Stepping over the now stride-wide stream as it entered a neatly mown garden, a plastic buggy for children to play at truck driver in, parked beneath a plastic swing, a car on the gravel before the door, little latticed windows beneath a thatched roof, a ceramic sign in the shape of a swan paddling on the river by the door: WELCOME.

Light behind the windows, thin curtains drawn. A floodlight turned on automatically as Helen reached the porch. She checked over her shoulder, then rang a bell, tingalingaling, an old black button with a real bell inside, nothing digital, not round here – nothing that did not conform to the standards set down in the Cotswold Corporate Community Charter.

The door opened.

A woman, younger than Helen by some thirty years, a green woollen jumper and bright purple leggings, stood in the frame. Her hair was brilliant red, bundled into a mess around her head. Her fingernails were painted black, her eyes were bright green, and as she recognised Helen with a little gasp of in-taken breath, a child scurried out from the room behind her, saw the older woman in the door and exclaimed, "Aunty!" running forward to wrap her arms around Helen's mud-soaked legs.

*

A hurried conversation in the front hall.

"They said kidnapped they said—"

"Not kidnapped. My son has done something – I need your help I need to . . . "

"Are you sure because you look and who the hell even is—"

"His name is Theo, Kirsty please listen to me listen to me look at me do I look insane to you do I look . . . "

"No, but they said, I mean I saw you and—"

"They drugged me, my son – please the police are coming they are going to knock on the door please trust me you always trusted me your mother trusted me you know that I—"

"The police but this is—"

"Kirsty. For . . . please."

"I . . . wait upstairs."

She led them upstairs.

A ladder into a loft.

The loft was full of ancient trunks. Memorabilia from a bygone age. A grandfather's gramophone. Models of toy aeroplanes built by relatives whose dexterous fingers were long since turned to bone. A scythe, rusted red. A bird's nest, fallen to the floor from the rafters, the tiny white shells cracked, their babies long since flown. The ladder folded up behind them, and Theo sat with Helen on a trunk, and they waited.

The old woman's head drifted to one side, rested on Theo's shoulder.

A car pulling up below.

Maybe two.

Doors slamming, soft thunks in the dark.

Doorbell, tingalingaling, cheery come-on-Christmas sounds, a merry welcome to the hearth.

Door opening.

Voices.

Concerned.

Have you

No officer no I haven't

this man is

285

I'll keep an eye out for

Lady Helen – it's very

I know, a close family friend. I'll absolutely . . . is the search..
do they think she's . . . ?

We don't know ma'am but if you

Of course, officer, of course, I'll give you a call if I see anything
be safe

you too, you too.

Door closed.

Car doors opened, closed.

Engines.

The cars drove away.

They waited.

After a while

A broom handle knocked against the trapdoor to the loft.

"Okay. You can come down now."

They took turns to use the bathroom.

Theo went first.

In the living room beneath Helen and Kirsty talked, and he
wondered what they were saying.

The shower curtain was translucent, painted with whales
blowing water from their spouts, a bright red ring of crabs
scuttling along the bottom, eyes boggling, claws snapping at
dancing fish.

When he emerged, swathed in towel, Kirsty stood at the door
with her gaze averted, a bundle of clothes in her arms. "These
were my husband's. They might fit. You can change in there."

She nodded once and said nothing when he thanked her.

Helen had a bath.

Theo and Kirsty sat in silence in front of a black iron stove, the
TV on low in the corner of the room, the child enthralled at the
rare treat of a late-night movie, her mummy should have guests
more often if she got to stay up late like this.

Theo stared at his hands. Kirsty stared at his face.

286

From upstairs, the sound of water.

In the corner, the TV.

They waited.

Finally, Kirsty stood up, shot a look towards her child, another to Theo, then left the room.

Returned a few moments later with a plate of bread, cheese, ham. Put it down on the coffee table between them.

Theo ate slowly, stomach turning.

"Mummy can I watch another can I watch another please Mummy please I want to watch another I want to ... "

"One more and then it's bed – it's already a long way past your bedtime this is a special treat, do you understand? And I want you to be good when it's done, I want you to be very very good tonight it's ... "

Mother and child sat together in a corner and chose a cartoon. Theo watched. In the end, they chose the story of Bobby-X, an ordinary high-school kid who is secretly a ninja spy working for the Company to help stop the evil anarchists before they can destroy innocent children's lives. He supposed it was quite good, in its way.

Upstairs, a plug was pulled.

Water drained away.

Theo and Kirsty waited in silence.

Helen came downstairs.

She was wearing clean pyjamas and socks. A towel was wrapped expertly around her head.

She took in the room, the cartoon, and at a cry "Aunty!" shuffled over to the child to hold her tight and exclaim how wonderful it was to see her and how she hoped she'd been good at school, good with her mum.

The child scowled, but yes, she'd been good just like everyone wanted her to be ...

"Bed!" barked Kirsty.

"But Mum ... "

"You're not going to behave badly in front of Aunt Helen, are you?"

"No, Mum."

"Bed!"

Mother and daughter hurried away.

Helen sat in the seat that Kirsty had vacated, and examined the half-consumed plate of ham and cheese in front of her. After a while, she reached out, made herself something resembling a sandwich, put it on a napkin and took a careful bite from the corner. The bread was thick and tough, took a long time chewing. She worked, swallowed, laid the napkin back on the table, folded her hands and looked at Theo.

"So," she said. "We should talk."

Chapter 56

"Family is everything," Helen said.

"Family is everything," whispered Dani Cumali to the winds that shred the ghosts.

"Family is everything," muttered the father of the man who would be Theo as they severed his hand at the wrist.

"Family never did very much for me," muses Theo Miller, the real Theo Miller, the one whose grave has no name.

They sit by the fire as Kirsty puts her daughter to bed, and Helen declares again, sacred words to steady her soul: "Family is everything."

Her voice, tired, ragged around the edges. Theo wondered how much the words were costing, how much she remembered of the days before the forest, hot baths and this house, or whether she could still remember the smell of urine and puke on the bedroom floor.

After a while she leaned back in her chair, arranging words slowly around ideas, piecing them together as a child might tentatively try some new mathematical formula, or an artist compose with unusual paints. They came slowly at first, then a little faster.

"My son has been poisoning me. He has been . . . no, that's not the place to start. I have this condition. My kidneys. Really, I feel absurd when I say it, you always think it'll be something like the heart that gets you rather than bloody urine. It's manageable. Not treatable. Just manageable. But after Philip found out – after he started ... treating ... me, it was ...

My friends would visit, people I've known since I was ... and they'd talk to me in that stupid little voice, that stupid 'Oh Helen isn't it lovely yes it's so lovely you're so lovely well we're going now.' Even though I wasn't there, even with the drugs, I still knew. They put it in my drink, at first. Sedatives, mostly. Some other things. My son didn't come to see me. He had people for that."

A pause, scratching at the skin on the inside of her right arm. It flaked in little white mounds of damp flesh, forming ridges under her nails. If she noticed, she didn't seem to care.

"Family is everything. I was born into wealth. We were what you would call the landed gentry. My father was a sir, my mother was a ma'am, and we lived in desperate poverty. It was desperate poverty because we had a manor house in Devon, and the upkeep of the place was eighty thousand a year. My father farmed the land nearby; to not farm the land was to let it spoil, and to let it spoil was to destroy the essence of what the land was. What it means to have land. What it meant to our ancestors. My mother worked as a manager at a call centre handling telecoms complaints. Between them they brought in around sixty thousand, which was spent on stopping the roof falling down – and the roof was always falling down – repairing the tractor, paying labour, providing electricity, water and heat for a family home containing seven bedrooms, five receptions, three kitchens, eight bathrooms and a billiards room, though no one enjoyed billiards except me. They took out loans, mortgages, and every few months let visitors come in for a fee, in order to raise a little more cash. But they were very badly organised; they never promoted it properly and never managed to turn the house into a business. Sometimes people turned up to the official open days. Usually people would just drift in at random, assuming that you were living in a public museum. My brothers hated it, and once George even threatened a man with a shotgun, and was arrested and had to be got out by his godfather, who was the magistrate. We couldn't have afforded the indemnity. If my father had been willing to let someone else do the farming, if he'd not resented the idea of any other kind of work, then perhaps we could have saved something. But quitting wasn't what men like him were meant to do.

By the time I was sixteen, my older brother was off at university, where he got a 2.2 in economics, and my younger was thinking of joining the army. I knew that we were in trouble, so I'd set up little events – fêtes and open days and trips for the local scouting group – to try and raise some cash. I'd get a few hundred quid too, but it never meant anything. Not in the grand scheme of things.

I tell you this because it's very important that you understand – we never considered selling the house. Never. And we never went to the pound shop either. Frugality never occurred to us as an option. We still wore the best clothes, attended the best events, ate the finest food. We had no conception of alternatives.

Attempting to run the estate in a more businesslike manner, hosting weddings, conferences, that sort of thing – it wasn't what you did. The house, the lands, the title. This was why we were born, our purpose, and we would see it all destroyed rather than dream of leaving our home. We felt, I have to tell you, very sorry for ourselves. Surrounded by silverware and the weapons of our grandparents pillaged in colonial wars, my family and myself would very calmly and simply state that we knew precisely how the people on council estates felt, except that they were lucky because they could get emergency corporate sponsorship, and we weren't eligible.

When I was twenty-three, my father died, and the estate passed to my brother. He moved back immediately – it was his duty – and continued to run it into the ground. It wasn't ever said that I needed to go, but it was obvious. He was the master now and naturally Mother could remain, but siblings were ... well it smacked of something medieval, shall we say. Successors at the dinner table, with opinions ...

I moved out, got a job selling perfume at the local superstore pharmacy. I wasn't very well educated. It had never seemed like something that a girl needed to be. But my name still got me into the right places. When people asked what I did, I said I was a perfumer. Perfumer is an acceptable business for a daughter, as are vintner, equestrian and extreme sports. I met Jeffrey, my husband, at one of these parties, and lied to him about where I really worked until the day after we were married, and he laughed and forgave me instantly and we were very much in love.

Very much in love. It is important you understand this too.

Of course I had a duty to perform here, at Danesmoor. Jeffrey knew I understood what these things meant. I valued family as much as he did. It is incredibly important that these things are preserved, it is as vital as any library or work of art. We are the history of this nation, we hold within us part of its culture, which if it is destroyed is the death of a piece of Britain that everyone, no matter what, loves for its beauty and its charm and its essential Britishness. These things must be protected, and to do so, of course, I had to have boys. The line passes down through the boys, not because of sexism but because that is the culture, the history, the truth of who we are. I will not say anything else on that.

I had two sons and two daughters. My youngest daughter is married. My eldest died. My youngest son runs a trekking company in Arizona. My eldest is Philip. He inherited Danesmoor when my husband died, eight years ago. You will know him, of course. He is the minister of fiscal efficiency. He owns an island in the Mediterranean. He doesn't use his title. Everyone calls him Mr Arnslade, because if he was Your Lordship it might seem elitist. People are very anxious about that sort of thing in government. They don't want to draw attention.

I am the only family left in Danesmoor, but the estate is run by a steward called Fish. Fish isn't his real name. I don't know his real name. He never told me. He arrived a few years ago and took over everything, and I caused a fuss because the estate had been a thing I managed, and it was going well, but Philip said . . .

There wasn't much for me to do after that.

Fish wasn't a bad manager he just didn't

I felt like a foolish old woman and I was being treated like . . .

Do you know a man called Simon Fardell? He's an old school friend of Philip's, and they went to university together. They went to Oxford do you know

you do.

Simon is a shit.

I'm not saying this to excuse my son. My son is also a shit. But Simon was the shit that blocked the toilet, if you'll pardon my saying so.

Naturally he assumes he isn't. Most people assume they aren't shits. It's just good business. That's what it amounts to. Business is good. Good is business it is

Anyway.

They would meet in Danesmoor. They'd have long weekends together, there'd be drink and I'd sit with their wives in the other room, that's how this works. Philip is married to a useless trophy creature. I know that I'm his mother and it's my job to dislike anyone my son marries, but she really is a vacuous little nothing. I quite like her, in a way. Being so empty-headed means that, unlike my son, she isn't a shit. She's just too useless to be anything better. Simon's wife is far too good for him. Her name is Heidi. I think he hits her sometimes, but she always says . . . when it's good, it's really good, and when it's bad, he always says sorry afterwards and that's how she knows he loves her. I always thought I'd tell her to run away. It's a very easy thing to say, much easier than anything that matters – but I never mustered the courage. We'd sit, us women, and drink tea and read magazines about holidays and handbags, and in the room next door the men would carve up the country and that too was just part of . . . how things are. How they have always been.

And one weekend I walk into the room while the men are talking to look for my mobile phone, which I'm always putting down somewhere, and they're talking about mass graves.

They don't call it that, of course.

They use the words 'excess labour reallocation', and I think well, excess labour reallocation isn't it wonderful if a little sad when your boys are all grown up.

But then they stop speaking when I enter and I wonder why, surely reallocating labour isn't that bad after all, but they're now pretending they were talking about anything else. Anything else at all. And I'm a little bit curious, I'll admit, but don't really think about it, except I do.

I do.

Because I know Philip's face.

I know when he's . . .

Once, when he was a young man, he got into a duel at university. He shot another boy. Killed him. I was mortified, but all he could talk about was the cost, and Jeffrey indulged him of course, paid the indemnity because it was that or let his son go to the patty line, so of course he paid but . . .

There was a look in Philip's eye, a thing that reminded me of that day he came home with an indemnity and blood on his shoes, and I thought . . . hello, I thought. Hello, my boy. What have you done this time?

It didn't take long to find out. I wasn't being nosy, not at first. I was just . . . drifting into the study. Then I was just sitting at his desk. These actions I could explain as being casual deeds on an innocent afternoon. Even when I started rifling through his files, I thought, this is just a mother being interested in the son who she loves.

Which of course was a lie.

I knew he'd done something, and I wanted to know what, needed to know how bad things were, without ever admitting this to myself. When I found the files, I was almost disappointed at how easy it was. In his own home he hadn't bothered to hide anything. Numbers of beggars rounded up from Birmingham city centre and sent without trial to the recycling yards for 'rehabilitation through labour'. Number of illegal immigrants caught on the last sweep, divided by age and gender, sent to the patty line for 'indefinite reintegration'. Companies who make dangerous products – chemicals, oils, fuels – don't like to pay for their workers. Patty labour is much cheaper, but sometimes it's hard to find. And when the patties can't work any more, they sell them off cheap to another company, which is owned by a company which is owned by a company which is always owned by the Company. And when you can't sell them, when they're too broken to buy, you have to find an economic use for them.

It's not that they're shot.

Lined up against a wall.

They're just starved to death.

Or set cleaning radioactive equipment.

Or beaten because they can't work a seven-day week.

Or locked in solitary confinement until the noises stop.

It's not murder.

It's corrective rehabilitation integration. It is the individual repaying their debt to society through labour. Labour benefits business. Business is society. That is all.

These things take some time to contemplate.

And there were the documents. Paper, files, I even used the computer. A doddery old woman like me, fancy that I can click on 'Yes'; Fish would be amazed.

When my son sold the government tax service to the Company, a lot of people got extremely rich. I'd say there were over a hundred people who became billionaires overnight, and another thousand or more who are now millionaires courtesy of their shrewd investments. But that's all. A thousand people enriched and the Company now owns the country. A single stroke of the pen and they own everything. They own the law, the judges, the hospitals, the schools, the roads, the police, the army and the government. They own it all, and maybe that's good, maybe that's what we need, to be efficient to be ...

But it's not.

There are the obvious signs, of course. The mass graves behind the prisons. where they bury the ones who never got to see a lawyer before they died, whose sentences were always extended, always, because the paperwork went astray. The company that handles the paperwork is run by a company which is run by a company which . . .

The enclaves levelled because the people couldn't afford to pay their corporate community tax. The homes destroyed, the migrants who died on the side of the road, villages and towns wiped out because they didn't produce a decent profit margin for the Company. And then there's the rest, the casual murders that aren't even part of the plan, just happen on the side. The old people dying of cold in winter, heat in summer, because they can't afford to pay their energy bills and the Company doesn't make a profit on relief for that sort of thing. The dead in the hospitals. The dead in the cells. The police needed to save money to turn a profit, so the Company took over responsibility for reporting fatalities. The hospitals didn't have enough money for the morgues, but the Company owns a company which owns a company which . . .

We all knew, of course. Everyone knows, but no one looks. We don't look because if we look it makes us evil because we aren't doing something about it, or it makes us sad because we can't do anything about it, or it proves that we're monsters when we always thought we were righteous because we won't do anything about it. Either way, safer not to look.

I couldn't stop myself; it was my son. I needed to know, to see. I spent so long trying to find a way in which he was doing right. Trying to find something which said that this was good. Of course it's so hard to prove anything now, it's so hard to find anyone who doesn't just look at the facts and say that she who wrote this is a liar, there is no room for reason there is only . . .

Family is the only thing that matters.

My children are having grandchildren now. There will be more to carry the family name. Family is safety. It is love. It is a thing that you defend because it is the one thing which matters more than anything else, it is love in adversity, it is giving, it is that which lifts us up. It is the trust that spans the generations. It is the young who look to you to do them right. It is the old who look to the young to make a newer, faithful world. We carry humanity it is . . .

296

I bugged my son.

He's got security teams, of course, but in Danesmoor they left us alone, didn't bother to do any real checks inside the house, not when the threat was clearly going to come from elsewhere.

I stole documents, copied them, made a file.

Filmed his meetings.

No one suspected me – I am the lady of the house. I recorded everything. For three years I recorded everything, and didn't know what I could do with it. That's not true. I knew what I could do with it. I just never had the courage to do it. Maybe that's love. Maybe that's what it was.

They caught me, in the end. A man called Markse found one of the cameras I used, started a manhunt. I knew that he was going to fingerprint it and I hadn't used gloves because the idea was ridiculous.

All of it was just so ridiculous.

This was . . . a month ago, perhaps?

There was a do scheduled, all of Philip's Company friends, Simon fucking Fardell and his battered wife, all the best people, the mass murderers, out for a bit of a laugh, the shooting, the sport, Pimm's on the lawn. I knew they were going to catch me, and that would be it. I felt like such a stupid old woman. I had all the proof in the world, and I hadn't had the guts to do anything with it. Even with them closing in I couldn't decide, couldn't act.

Then I found my miracle.

Not a miracle, in fact. Not at all. There was a woman indentured to the catering company. I caught her trying to break into my son's study and I was angry, instinctively, my house, I was the lady, I was furious and then . . .

Then I thought for a little moment longer, even in my panic, and I realised – *she was trying to break into my son's study.*

And perhaps there was a reason.

I told her to come upstairs with me. Informed her, in my most imperious way, that if she didn't obey I would report her instantly and she'd go back to the patty line. She came with me, she was so angry and scared. I sat her down and made her tell me why she was trying to break into my son's study. I was trembling with excitement, but maybe she thought it was rage.

She refused to answer at first, but I could see it in her, the desperation, I saw the mirror of myself in her and finally she said, 'I think your son fucked the fucking country.'

I was relieved. To hear her say those words, I was desperately relieved, and I think she saw that. 'Your son fucked us,' she repeated. 'He's gotta pay.'

She'd found something, working at the Ministry of Civic Responsibility. Some sort of documents, she'd been stealing for months. Someone had asked a question, spotted that there were figures not adding up, that the number of patties going to a sewage treatment facility in Cambridgeshire was greater than the number being released, and wondered where the discrepancy lay.

She'd been on the patty line. She'd seen friends vanish, and when the patties asked they were always told 'reassigned' and no one questioned it because if you asked questions, you might get reassigned too.

But she'd begun to question. To suspect. That's why she'd come to Danesmoor. Blackmailed her own supervisor to do it. I was impressed, I liked her at that moment, I thought her supervisor sounded just like Fish.

'Why?' I asked. 'You're nobody. If you find proof of anything, what do you think you can do?'

'I can get my daughter back,' she replied. 'I can make them give her back to me.'

My heart fell.

I didn't need an amateur blackmailer. I needed a firebrand, someone who would save my family name, protect it, go out into the world and do right, right as the family should have done, right as is the right that is the responsibility of this place of . . .

But she had lost her daughter.

Family is everything.

Family is everything.

To lose a child, it is . . .

When my daughter died I spent so long trying to make it my

fault, because if it was my fault it wasn't just luck. It was the action of man, it was fate, it was God, it wasn't just a faulty car brake on a rainy day it wasn't just that it wasn't

and she isn't

sometimes I still think maybe it was a trick, and she'll be there

and sometimes in my dreams she is a presence who sits by me and is warm and kind and says that she loves me and I cry when I wake

and sometimes I spend days and weeks without thinking about her, and I am simply a woman without children.

That is who I am now.

I knew they would come for me, so I gave this stranger, this woman in prison clothes, a copy of everything I had.

I gave her everything and told her to run away.

The next day, after the party was over, Philip had breakfast with me. He hadn't had breakfast with me for months, maybe even a year. He was so important, always so busy, but that day he made time to have breakfast and I thought ... this is nice. This is nice. He loves me. Maybe it'll be all right, maybe there's something I don't know. And he was charming, the brightest and kindest I'd seen him for years, he really seemed to want to know how I was, said we should go walking together by the lake, like we had when he was young, that it'd been too long since we'd just talked.

There were sedatives in the tea, of course. I thought I was having a funny turn, but the turn never stopped. Next thing I knew Philip was nowhere to be seen, and Fish was at my door telling me I had to take my medicine, and I said that's stupid that's absurd I don't need any medicine

and he said yes, yes, your medicine your medicine

They put it in my food, in my water. I could taste it, occasionally, the bitterness of the powders masked by too much chilli.

They weren't poisoning to kill.

They just took away my mind, my intelligence, my freedom and my will.

I haven't seen my son since that morning. It was a beautiful morning. We ate in the eastern rooms, where the sun comes in. It was the perfect day I'd always thought my days were meant to be when I was a girl.

Sometimes friends would come over – Kirsty came a lot. They told her I'd had a stroke.

They told her that.

And they kept me alive.

I suppose that's Philip's thing. He stopped short of having his own mother killed when he found out what I did. I never found out what the woman did with the file. I assume she got her daughter back. But if she did, why would you be here?

Mr Miller?

Why are you here?"

Time is

Neila gunned the engine and it refused to tick over, cursed and muttered and opened up the cover and in the end had to put a hot-water bottle on the blasted thing before it would start.

In a stranger's house in the Cotswolds the mother of his enemy sat quiet before him, Theo pinched the tips of his fingers together beneath his bottom lip and tried to find words.

"I ... there was ...

... sometimes pieces come together and it's ...

So I used to be an auditor and while I was working on the job there was

Dani is dead.

Her name is Dani.

The woman who

her name is Dani.

She was murdered.

She was my friend.

Her daughter is my daughter. Her name is Lucy. Dani went to a journalist called Faris, I think she tried to ... But they got found out. His daughter was Company and she told them and that was ... They killed her, Dani, I mean. And I audited her

300

death. Her life is worth £84,000. She left me a message. 'Save the mother.' So I came to Danesmoor and saw you and certain things fell into place and

here we are.

Here we are.

I have Dani's information now. I have her copy of your file. She sent it back to the town where we'd grown up, so I could find it. She knew she was going to die, I think. She used me as a back-up plan.

I think you should understand that my life has been cowardly, futile and empty. You tell me that family is the most important thing in the world. You should understand that when I was a boy my father was arrested for theft, and died on the patty line, and I hated him because he wasn't there for me and never gave me anything to believe in. And my mum sort of . . . faded out, and when I was given a second chance, I blew it. I went to university and realised that all the dreams which I thought were mine were just some fantasy that couldn't ever come true, so I took the identity of a boy who I got killed – I killed him, I didn't pull the trigger, but it was me, it was my fault, he died because of me. I took his identity. I became Theo Miller and with that opportunity, that amazing chance . . .

I blew that too, you see. I couldn't ever find anything to care about. I couldn't understand why anything mattered at all. I didn't think there was any point to me. Just keep going. Just . . . go through the motions. I have spent my life sending people into slavery, and freeing killers because they were rich, or because the person they killed was poor, or an immigrant, or no good for society, and it was . . . I did it because it was a job. Because all I ever wanted was a job, and to be safe, and not cause any trouble.

I have led a thoroughly despicable life. Or rather . . . not despicable. My evils have been ordinary evils. My sins against the world are daily, little sins that no one would question. I am a normal man, and have done no wrong, and there is a place in hell waiting for me. That's

that's what I have decided.

That's what I think.

I want to get my daughter out. I've never met her. She's in an institution writing online reviews for sales products. She's never getting out. Kids like her don't. They get lost in the system. Dani's supervisor said . . . there's a market for anything. There's a market for my daughter. He didn't know that's what he was saying, but that's all I could hear. She's probably not my daughter. I want her to have a better life. Even if I die for it, it seems now of extreme importance that I do something in my life which matters. Our children matter. There we probably agree. I plan to destroy the Company, the government and the country. When there is nothing left except ashes, then I get my daughter out, and make a better world for her.

I am probably going to destroy your son. I came to find you because Dani told me to. She seemed to have some sort of . . . of centre, something in her that was . . . real, and mattered, which I didn't. I don't know why. Maybe she was just a better person than me. I have some ideas. Do you want to help?"

Chapter 57

Time is

The children play in the park, they run and play as the city burns because the fire is beautiful and the sky is huge and their eyes are full of light and

time is ...

Neila moored the *Hector* a few miles outside Nottingham.

She said, without fear or reproach, "It's an enclave town. My insurance makes it difficult to ..."

They sat in silence at the back of the *Hector*, looking towards the place where fields ended and bricks began, the low edge of buildings rising towards the empty shopping malls in the centre. Finally Theo said, "The queen of the patties once guaranteed me passage. Her word might still hold."

Neila bit her bottom lip, hand resting on the rudder, contemplating the river. Then: "Screw it."

They sailed on, towards the town.

She chugged down the middle of the canal, listening for every sound, whisper, bump and thump over the slow rattle of the engine. Fat wetlands gave way to streets of close-pressed houses, white chipped paint and boarded-up windows. A lone wind turbine spun in the distance. In an office block of grey lines and black windows a single light turned one rectangle of glass yellow. A sudden burst of tall red houses emerged from behind the overgrown hedges that hemmed in the canal, blue-black tiles curving up into little ornamental cupolas, before collapsing back down again into bungalows and lanes of grey. At Beeston Lock the water branched, wide river laced with blue-balustraded bridges in one direction, canal criss-crossed by silent railway lines and black brick arches in the other.

Neila stood at the back of the *Hector* as the water rose in the lock, and in her mind she counted steps to the kitchen knife, listened to the tock-clock of the winch in the gate as Theo turned the handle, wondered if she should tell him, it's heavy, iron heavy, the crank could be used as a weapon just in case, you never know, just in case it becomes necessary.

The boat rose, and she headed into the narrower, softer waters of the canal.

A bonfire burning outside Lenton Abbey, she couldn't see what fuelled it, just odd squares and hard angles breaking through the inferno, hints of black behind the smoke, the shape of figures moving around it, none turning to look at her as she sailed by.

Four children sat on the railway bridge, feet dangling over the sides. She sailed beneath them, waiting for them to spit on her, throw stones, laugh, shout, run for help. They didn't. They watched her pass, then scrambled to the other side of the bridge to sit and watch her emerge, waiting silently, kicking their heels, fingers spun together in their laps.

At Castle Lock there were seven people waiting for them. Two held battery torches; one held a makeshift flaming torch of rag and wood. No street lights burned. A generator rattled somewhere far off. The turbine eclipsed the moon. The night was silent as Neila gunned the engine down and drifted, out of reach of the first lock gate, watching the people on the bank.

For a while all were silent. Then a woman called, "North?"

Neila nodded, then realised the gesture might not be visible in the dark, so called back, "Towards Gainsborough."

The woman nodded, swept her torch across the boat, her expression lost behind the beam.

"Petrol?" she asked at last, a tired lilt to her tone.

"Not much."

"We'll take half."

"No."

"You wanna pass; we take half the petrol."

No antagonism, no shouting. A simple statement, the truth, two women discussing the hardness of stone, the wetness of water.

Theo emerged from the cabin, stood next to Neila, squinted as the light swept his face.

"We'll throw you a line," continued the woman. "Fill our buckets. Then we open the gate."

"No," repeated Neila, calm and ready. "I won't have enough to get to the next pump, and I can't pay for more than what I've got."

A shrug.

"We'll turn back."

"You're going north."

"We'll turn back," she repeated, resigned. "We'll turn back."

The woman on the bank hesitated, sensing a bluff to be called, uncertain where the cards lay. Then Theo said, "I was at Newton Bridge."

The torch turned to his face, caught it in a tight circle of white. The figures on the bank were still, waiting.

"I served the queen. My name is Theo Miller. If she has a court . . . "

Silence in the darkness. Silence on the water.

"We'll wait a little while," he added, glancing at Neila for permission. "Then go back."

Torches shone into their eyes.

Then three of the figures on the bank turned away and headed into the night.

Neila pushes the rudder this way and that.

Even the slow, tepid canal has energy, a life of its own. Take your eye off the current and you'll drift, bump into walls, into locks, break against the ice she

holds the boat in the middle of the water and waits.

Theo brings her tea.

Holds her in his arms.

She puts her head on his shoulder.

Shivers a while in the cold, until she is a little warmer.

Holds them still, in the middle of the water.

Dawn pricked the eastern horizon with a hot needle of pinkish red.

The sun rose behind the low clouds, then emerged for a moment, glorious, between a band of low and high, before vanishing again into the greyness.

It started to snow.

Theo sat with one hand on the rudder, waiting, while Neila pretended to sleep inside the cabin.

After a while Theo realised that he too was sleeping, and jerked hard awake.

A man stood on the bank of the canal, flanked by a woman and another man. His skin was pale olive-brown, his eyes were flecked coffee, his hair was curly almond, exploding around his head. He stood bent to one side, favouring his left leg, and moved with a long, dragging limp. Wore oversized jogging trousers and a grey tracksuit top, and didn't seem to feel the cold. He looked across the water at Theo and didn't smile.

"So," he grunted. "Still alive."

They moored.

Theo stood on the back, and didn't help with the ropes like he usually did, and put his hands in his pockets

then took them out

put them back

watched the man and the man watched him, and Theo was afraid.

306

Neila hesitated, but the momentum of the boat was already carrying them to the side, too late to turn back now. She watched Theo's throat, the involuntary curling-in of his lips, the way he turned his gaze away at last, unable to meet the man's eye, and thought for a moment, as she tied off, that Theo wasn't even going to get off the narrowboat, but they'd be stood there in the cold freezing their . . .

Then he looked up.

Seemed to reach a decision.

Stepped off the boat.

The man in grey walked towards him slowly, stood before him, thought about the world for a moment, lips twisting as if they might smile, then dipping as if they would scowl.

Reached a decision, and punched Theo in the stomach, once, hard and precise, a short distance to send the blow but placed to cause pain, and as Theo buckled forward, he reached out and caught the smaller man by the hair, pulling his head back, so his body contorted like a lightning bolt, every part bending away.

Theo didn't struggle or claw at his attacker.

For a moment they stood watching each other's eyes, before with a shrug the man let go of Theo's head and turned away, letting him fall to the ground to pull in breath. Neila moved forward quickly, caught him under the arm, whispered, "The wrench, or in the kitchen there's . . ."

He shook his head.

Put his hand on hers, grateful, warm, squeezed once, stood up, bending over the pain, and followed the man in grey along the canal.

The two men walked a little distance away, then turned into the city.

Neila stood on the stern of her boat, and watched the woman who watched her.

After a while the woman got bored, and flicked dirt out from under her nails with the stub of a dried-up stalk.

Neila watched.

The woman finished.

Cracked the stalk in two.

Threw it away.

Sat on the long beam of the lock gate, waited.

The two women regarded each other as the snow thickened, and Neila was shivering, and so was the woman.

Then Neila said, "For fuck's sake," and went into the cabin, and put the kettle on, and made two cups of tea, and offered one to the woman. "Want a cuppa?"

The woman hesitated, then smiled, nodded and followed her inside.

"Ever had your fortune read?" Neila asked as the woman made a direct line for the heat of the stove. "I'll get the cards."

Three hours later, the man in grey and the man called Theo returned to the boat. Theo carried a bag containing two tins of tuna, one tin of peaches in sugary liquid, a bottle of flat lemonade, a toilet roll, a biscuit tin and an object wrapped in oiled cloth.

The man's name was Corn. He joined them for supper and ate voraciously, and said almost nothing, except for once, when dinner was served.

"Blessed is her name, blessed are her hands upon the water, blessed is she the mother who gives life to the children in the mist, blessed are her hidden ways. Let the bars be broken let the journey end there is nothing at the end except darkness and the quiet place where all things fade amen."

The words, a headlong chant, a habitual stream. The woman whispered a silent "Amen" as they finished, and they ate, and when they had finished Corn stood and shook Neila's hand, and said, "Thank you," and walked away, and the woman followed, and they slept the night by the side of the canal, and no one bothered them.

In the morning.

Theo opened up the object wrapped in cloth and said, "It's . . . wrong . . . to have it on your boat and not tell you. Only half of the ammunition is live, the rest is blanks – it's easier for . . . I'm sorry I brought it on without your permission but with Corn there it was difficult to explain why the . . . "

"I don't want it on the boat. What happened, why is there . . . "

"I'll go. I'll go now and . . . "

"I don't want it on my boat," she repeated, knuckles white as she clung to the table.

"I'll go."

"Why do you have to have it?"

"To get my daughter back."

"You're going to kill . . . you're going to kill someone."

"You always knew what this was. You always knew. You always knew why I came here, you – I'm sorry, that's unfair that's making this . . . it's not about . . . I'm sorry. I didn't mean to . . . "

"Give me the gun."

He gave her the gun.

She'd never held a gun before. She was surprised how heavy it was, how cold the barrel was in her hand. Theo watched it for a while then blurted, "There's a woman. Her name is Heidi. She loves my daughter. She took her but she's married to this man, he took her, took my daughter too, and Heidi, she said that they had to protect her but he only agreed in order to

Heidi never had a daughter, you see. She never had a daughter and now she's got mine and that's . . . "

Neila stood up without a word. Went to the back of the boat, turned on the engine, held the gun over the water and

In the evening that bloody goddamn cormorant was still bloody bumping its bloody head against the side of the bloody cabin why couldn't it just

Theo made supper, and she didn't really eat, and conversation was stilted, and she didn't check the cards as they sailed north.

In the land of the dead
        in the place where the dead people lie
          the real Theo Miller

                  the one who actually fell on the
field by the river
           looks up at the world of men and is, in his own
quaint, deceased, skull-grinning way,
  mildly amused at the way things have panned out.

Chapter 58

Three days after arriving at Kirsty's house, Theo and Helen sneaked across the Cotswolds border at night.

They got out in the back of a horse trailer.

The trailer was owned by Kirsty's sister. She had two horses, one doing quite well for the season. Whenever the horses left the farm, a sheep called Mitts would stand by the gate bleating piteously for her companions to return, her own species ignored until at last the horses came back and the sheep would snuggle up against the legs of its favourite runner, which tolerated the intrusion as a lazy cat might tolerate the nuzzling of a toothless pup.

Theo and Helen hid under blankets at the back of the trailer, sheltered from the door by the horses as they rocked and swayed down the soft hills of the valley. At the border fence they were stopped, papers examined, a torch shone briefly into the back of the trailer, illuminating animal, tack and hay, and waved on.

In Oxfordshire Kirsty blurted, "I'm not sure about this, I don't think this is . . . "

"This is necessary. This is what I need to do."

"But what about Philip what about the hall I mean Danesmoor is – if you leave now it'll be . . . "

"This is important. This is absolutely what needs to be . . . "

"There are people out there. It's not safe. It's not safe out there you've seen the news you know that they don't even show the bad things – everybody knows!"

"I have to do this," she repeated, firmer. "It's what is required."

Theo watched in silence, huddled beneath a tree as the cold morning rain thickened to sleet, and Helen waited to watch as Kirsty and her sister drove away.

Theo tried to steal a car.

Stealing a car proved harder than reading about it in Audit Office reports. He remembered something clever about chips and Wi-Fi networks and maybe hijacking ...

... and then there was this thing you could do with a coathanger, wasn't there, but that was only on certain models and ...

Pull out the key socket somehow you sorta popped it out and then twisted the green and the red or maybe the yellow and the blue or maybe just maybe twisted everything together or did something with a hairpin to make a connection and ...

In the end Helen stole the car keys from a vicar she spotted putting them in his far-too-baggy jacket as he parked in his private space beside the church. Bumping into him and exclaiming, "Oh, my, sorry!" as she dipped a hand into his pocket turned out to be incredibly easy, and she was glowing with self-satisfaction for nearly ninety miles, until the wail of a police siren just outside Birmingham brought them back to reality with a hard thump.

Theo pulled onto the hard shoulder as the police car approached, M6 traffic rushing by.

Helen said, "Isn't that going to ... "

The policeman pulled up fifty yards behind, got out, walked along the edge of the turf, knocked on Theo's window, which he wound down.

"Excuse me, sir, do you have any—"

Theo slammed his foot onto the accelerator, leaving the policeman cursing and puffing, running back to his own vehicle as Theo pulled away into the traffic, peeling around the streaming cars before turning late and hard onto the slip road off the motorway.

The police car followed, but as Theo tore across the

roundabout at the top of the exit ramp, their pursuer vanished from the mirror, and another sharp turn pulled them into a petrol station a hundred yards further up.

"Out," hissed Theo, and Helen was already halfway out, scampering for the pavement.

They walked briskly together, away from the petrol station into the small, scraggly mess of single-storey white-walled houses that clung together on the edge of the motorway, shaggy temporary homes which had become permanent, with a tin-roofed church and Portaloo school, marching stiff and upright as if they belonged. Behind the sirens wailed and the police car swept into the garage to find their abandoned vehicle.

They walked, a village with no name, as the skies drizzled, then sleeted, then drizzled again. On a hill above were silent concrete chimney towers. A gate led to a public footpath climbing towards a mobile-phone mast. They followed the muddy route in silence. A golf club to the left, blue lights behind, and after a while a helicopter overhead. Theo gripped Helen by the arm, felt her flinch, hadn't realised he was holding so tight, relaxed, whispered, "Just walk. We're just walking."

"I know," she muttered, and they walked.

The mud path narrowed to the width of one person, brambles pulling at legs, then widened again to a pebbled thing that crunched underfoot, then split in two. Theo chose a fork at random, followed it down to a country lane, shuddering whenever a car went by.

Another path away from the road brought some relief, and they walked until they came to another village, smaller than the first, the houses white-timbered and spread apart, a flag hanging limply from the branch of a tree overhead, the café shut, the charity shop boarded up, the chippie still doing a roaring trade.

Theo bought fish and chips.

They sat a while on a little wooden bench as the drizzle blew in sideways, threatening something close to rain, and ate in silence. After a while Theo realised that he'd put so much vinegar on his chips that the paper bag was starting to tear through, and he

313

pulled off a strip of paper from the top to secure the greasy mess at the bottom before his meal ended up in his lap.

Helen ate one chip at a time with a little wooden fork, but struggled to find a decorous way to eat the fish, and eventually used her fingers, holding it by the tail to bite off chunks. There they sat, and no one looked at them, and no one asked any questions, and the helicopter vanished from the skies, and the rain gave up before it could really get going, and the sun began to set.

A cemetery, busier and neater than the village that protected it, spread behind a well-trimmed dark green hedge. White stones in perfect rows, a white pillar at its core. Monuments to soldiers fallen in battle. D. Aaron, d.1917. W. Acroyd, d.1915. E. Dwyer, d.1916. S. Gilson, d.1918.

FOR THEIR TOMORROW, WE GAVE OUR TODAY.

Theo looked down and saw that his legs were splattered in mud.

Helen's fingers shimmered with grease, and her lips were blue.

He murmured, "We can't stay here," and she nodded, and they waited by the bus stop to catch the fourth and final bus of the day, going north towards Stafford, and kept their heads down and eyes turned away from the CCTV cameras as it bounced and rattled its way through the country lanes.

They stayed in a room above a pub called the Stag. The pub advertised itself as being authentically historical, and the taps splurted and spluttered yellowish water into the sink. They stayed there because the landlord was impressed by Helen's accent, and needed a cataract operation, and had to stumble his way up the stairs by memory, and knew the feel of a £20 note more than he could remember the face of the monarch that adorned it.

At night Helen groaned and couldn't hide the pain in her belly, the slow pulling-apart of things inside. Theo tried to calm her, and when that didn't work, he lay awake with his hands over his ears and prayed that she'd stop, that the nightmares would pass, that she'd exhaust herself into slumber, and at some point this must have happened. They slept too long, and woke when the

314

sun was already high and their trousers still damp from scrubbing the night before, and their shoes squelched as they settled into them, and they walked.

"He was a terrible child really. At the time you don't think of it that way, you just say he's got high spirits – that's what you call it. If you call him terrible you have to ask yourself why, you have to blame yourself and no one wants to do that. It's the hardest thing in the world to say 'I am a bad mother, and he is a bad father,' it is impossible, it is devastating it is . . .

because if I am a bad mother then I am . . . there is nothing worse.

So of course Philip's not a bad child, because I'm not a bad mother. I'm not. I know this as much as I know anything, and the only thing I know more is that I love him.

Then he was a teenager, and I suppose he was well behaved as a teenage boy. He was always careful to hide the worst from me. He was indulged. He knew he could get away with things and I thought well in a way if he gets away with it I suppose . . .

It's very hard to deny your child in these circumstances. It's very hard to say 'I'll show you the stuff of life' if you don't really have the stuff of life in you. And I did not. Then when he got into a duel at university, I managed to tell myself that it was probably Simon Fardell's fault. He told me that the boy had done something awful. Hurt a woman or something. I didn't really believe it, but you make yourself believe because the alternative is much worse.

You're going to tell me not to blame myself, aren't you, Mr Miller? You're going to tell me that it's not my fault, the way Philip turned out.

Aren't you?

Aren't you?"

They walked a while.

Then Theo said, "I honestly don't know."

They walked a while longer.

"I think . . . some of it probably is your fault. I think it probably

315

is. I think it has to be someone's fault, at some point. Or maybe it doesn't. Maybe it isn't. There was a time when he was a child, but then there was a time when he was a man, and when he was a man . . . there must be a moment when you take responsibility for your own actions, and stop blaming the past and stop blaming . . . so maybe I don't. I don't think I can. But I think it's my fault that Lucy is in prison, and if it's my fault that the daughter I've never met is in that place, then it's got to be someone else's fault too. You have to be a bad mother, you see, if I am going to spend the rest of my life knowing that I failed as a father. It's not right. It's probably not even true. It's just the way I feel about it. Sorry."

A forest of falling leaves, slippery underfoot. Yellow and spotted browns and greys, brilliant crimsons and faded ochres, black-tinged curling auburns and vein-riddled purples, frost in the morning, a herd of deer looking up, startled from a field, before realising that the people passing by were no threat, and returning to their chewing.

A path down to a river, round stepping stones over the running water, green moss and yellow lichen, white foam caught in whirl-pools, a perfect hollow carved out at the bottom of a waterfall, a place where tiny fish played in the winter light.

Theo helped Helen wobble across, and for a while they sat by the water, listening to the wind through the trees.

Then Helen said, "Or maybe we're just both totally fucked in our own delightfully unique ways."

Theo considered this a while, then shrugged, and they kept on walking.

From a farm halfway up a yellow, treeless hill they stole two rusted bicycles that had been left behind an iron barn. Theo's bicycle didn't have any brakes. Helen's was stuck in third gear. They pedalled down the country lanes until Helen could pedal no more. Then they sheltered from the wind beneath the silent spire of a concrete plant, sand and dust blowing in their faces, and ate pork pies purchased from a corner shop in a village where they used to make pottery and now made nothing at all, a population of seven still hanging on, hanging on, and didn't talk, and didn't sleep.

"So how ill are you?" asked Theo when Helen threw up without warning, a vomit with no matter in it, just clear acid and yellow slime.

They sat on the side of the path, morning frost melting beneath them, breath puffing thick in the air.

Helen thought about the question for a while, then smiled, shrugged, murmured, "Some things they don't make a pill for."

On this she had nothing more to say.

On the third day they came to a statue of an angel set in the middle of a treeless, stone-pocked landscape. The angel was carved from white stone, and stood four or five feet taller than them, its wings spread out in thin spires of cracked lime to catch the wind, its face turned downwards in sorrow at the sins of men. Tears of red paint had been daubed onto its eyes; names had been scratched into the hem of its robe. T♥P. LAUREN & J 4EVR. THE DOOGLES. K, L ✱ W WER ERE.

A few hundred yards further on, a cairn of flat, faded stones, barely knee-high, grown a little taller over the years, built by travellers who paused to pick up stones and lay them on top of the uneasy structure, constructing a thing that might one day be ancient.

A sign stood next to it.

TURN BACK

They kept on walking.

At night, as they huddled down on the edge of a treeless moor, they heard the sound of a single voice raised in rage from a village below, which was soon joined by the barking of a lone dog, somewhere higher in the valley. The screaming went on for nearly an hour, before whoever it was ran out of breath or stopped to make a cup of tea.

Chapter 59

"Helen?"

Theo's voice was distant, carried away by starlight.

"Theo?"

He stared up at the sky, and couldn't remember the last time he'd seen so many stars. Not in Shawford, not by the English Channel, where light from both sides of the water blurred everything to an orange-stained muck of factory shite. Not in London, where the sky was an eclipsed line between grey houses. He half-closed his eyes, and tried to remember, and couldn't find anything that wasn't a figment of his imagination.

"There's something I want to ask you," he murmured, and was surprised to hear himself speak so calmly. "I think I can destroy them. I think I can destroy your son. But I might have to put you in danger to do it."

"Yes. And?"

"You might be hurt."

"My own son was poisoning me, dear."

"It might be bad."

A slight sound of movement in the dark as Helen shifted, uncomfortable and cold on the ground. "Well," she mused at last, and thought about it a little longer. "Well. I am a grown woman who knows the things to be said, and the things best left unsaid. I make my own choices, and that is all that can be asked. What did Dani say to you?"

"What?"

"When she died. Your friend Dani, you said she told you . . . "

"She said that Lucy was my daughter."

"And?"

Theo cast his memory back, struggling to find a thing from a very, very long way away. "She said 'Don't fuck it up.'"

Helen nodded in the darkness, and for a moment Theo thought he could hear her expression, hear the twitching of her lips. "Sound advice that. Stuff of sense."

Theo stared into an endless sky, and neither of them had anything more to say on the subject.

In the night in the dead of night in the dead place where the dead moved in the forest in the

A burst of torchlight an explosion of men and women they came from nowhere and they filled the world behind the torchlight they came from the dark they

grabbed Helen by the hair grabbed Theo by the throat they

there were dogs and torches and someone possibly had a gun but even if they didn't they were

and they shouted and pushed and pulled at skin and faces and there weren't really any questions in there just a lot of noise and that made it hard to answer and

they were pulled through the dark the dogs nipping at their heels the men half-running along gravel paths there was

a farmhouse where no lights shone and the skull of a sheep was nailed to the letterbox and there were

two trucks, the headlights on, the engines running, and

Theo was put in one Helen in the other he called out and tried to grab her hand, knew if he didn't that he really would be a failure the greatest failure in the history of mankind

but they pulled them apart and he went in one and she went in the other and when he tried to see where they were going, someone kicked him in the ribs and it really bloody hurt

so he did as he was told, and stayed on the floor, one leg tucked to his chin the other stretched out behind and wondered if these people knew what it meant to make like a heron and whether they

Dawn, grey through the square open canvas at the back of the truck.

Someone turned the radio on and it was really bad pop, the pop played at a disco for the old folks who used to be sexy back when flares were in fashion and before the moonwalk made all the young things scream.

Theo realised he was sleeping, and the thought was so astonishing that he jerked wide awake.

One man in the truck

no – a boy

– no! A woman. Her hair cut short, tall and skinny but with a face that could have been a boy if she'd wanted, could have been a youthful beautiful boy but look at her hands, long fingers around her rifle she is

Praying.

Her words half-caught, a whisper between the rattle of the suspension as they bounce through potholed, ravaged roads.

"For those who lived for those who died," she whispers. "For the children born to the sun for the ones who lie beneath the old man's moon for those who . . . "

Theo prays.

He prays to the dead, who he thought he was helping and was almost certainly letting down.

He prays to his daughter, that one day she will open her eyes and see the sun and there will be only radiance on her face.

Knows he's absolutely fine with dying, as long as it's for her.

Neila prays.

To those she wronged to those she helped to the world she thinks she helped build, not in any spectacular form not in war or stone or blood or iron or but in her deeds.

In her choices.

In the kindness bestowed on others there is a world somewhere where the children will be different from the kids of her days.

Dani gave up praying a long time before she died, but then, just before the end, there was a moment when she got on her knees to a deity unknown, to an idea that needed to be real and ...

If Helen prays, she keeps her prayers to herself.

They came to a place called Newton Bridge.

It had begun with a bridge across a river. The bridge was stone and mortar, and horses and carts went across it, carrying cotton, mostly, which they wove at the watermill, before the business-men discovered it was cheaper to pay for coal and build factories in places where the workforce was plentiful and less likely to go on strike.

Then for a while the bridge wasn't crossed very much, except by the shepherds who roamed the hills and the farmers who built the walls that divided the fields.

Then one day it fell down and stayed broken.

And then one day it was rebuilt, restored even, only a bit of ironwork underneath to give a clue as to the industrial labours that went into its repair.

And then one day the town got a sponsor, a company special-ising in executive glamping, and wooden huts were built on the edge of the village beneath the trees that spread morning shade and people came and drank red wine and it was all terribly lovely until the railway company stopped sending trains down the slow line.

And then the company left.

As did the doctor, teacher, vet, rubbish man, hairdresser, plumber, electrician – pretty much anyone, really, anyone who could get out, and only the buildings remained.

For a little while.

*

They pulled Theo from the truck with busy hands and roaring faces, which seemed unnecessary given he wasn't going anywhere else.

Pulled Helen down too, for a moment he called out her name but she was pulled away, up a street towards a grey concrete hall that maybe had been a library once, or perhaps some sort of council office where they sorted the tax and where now . . .

He couldn't see what now. Dragged down to the river, to the old watermill, pushed through a door onto a wooden floor, an abandoned bar where once they'd made cream teas or home-made fudge and where now the dust was imprinted with different shapes of trailing hands and doodles made with fingertips.

Locked the door.

Left him there a while.

Theo waited, knees huddled to his chin.

Shadows moved and though he couldn't see them moving, every time he checked they'd travelled a little bit further and he waited.

Theo waits.

The door opens.

Helen steps inside. Perhaps it's her face, or something of her dignity, but they're not in such a hurry to push her around.

Perhaps it's his face, and his lack of dignity, maybe that's the swing of things.

"Just tell them the truth," she murmured quickly as a man in an oversized tweed jacket and rubber boots picked Theo up by the arm. "Tell them the truth."

They led Theo outside, locked the door behind him, leaving Helen to watch the shadows. He wondered if she'd see them moving, even if he couldn't.

Pulled through tight, curling streets up a hill, past shattered windows boarded up with card, children in bare feet who squatted on the pavement and glared, past a patch of ground where geraniums grew amongst the potatoes, an abandoned fire station where now men sat cleaning rifles, a once-fine town hall where the merchants used to gather to argue about the price of wool and where now the old people sat with one tooth per length of pink gum and chewed on air and glared at the passing skies.

Up, to the top of the town and then a little bit beyond, feet stumbling on muddy paths, to a cottage between the trees.

The cottage lay within a stone wall. In the garden the owner grew tomatoes, the vines long since plucked, and potatoes, and carrots, and cabbage. On the windowsills there were nasturtiums, blue cornflowers and trailing crimson-streaked dangles of ivy. Above the low front door was a pottery sign which said HOME SWEET HOME. Solar panels sat on the roof of the house, a tendril of cable running from them and heading back down into the village. Smoke carrying the smell of burning wood rose from a crooked chimney. A woman was tending the flowers. Wearing yellow rubber gloves she squashed the plague of black-bodied aphids that clung to the green stems of the nasturtiums, squeezing and scraping in oily genocide. Her hair was a faded yellow, spread through with oncoming white. Her chin rolled down into a secondary flange of flesh that bobbed in and out of existence as her neck moved. Her shoulders were broad, her legs were short, she wore a dark red body warmer over a torn grey woolly jumper, a brown skirt that stopped just above her knees and green boots that started just below, revealing a hint of expanding, pasty joint. She didn't pay the men much attention as they deposited Theo on her garden path, but kept on tending her flowers, peering under leaves and fading yellow petals in her quest to exterminate her tiny-bodied enemies.

"Lady tells me you're looking for your daughter," she muttered at last, sparing Theo not a nod.

"Yes."

"How's that going?"

"Looking isn't as hard as doing."

323

"What's that mean?"

"I know where she is. I know which prison. But getting her out is meaningless, impossible, until I can keep her safe."

"Does she want to be found? Does she want you keeping her safe – keeping her anything?"

"Don't know. Maybe not. She can make that choice, if she wants to, when the moment comes. Least there'll be a choice."

The woman nodded at nothing much, scraped the last aphid from a flower, straightened up, wiped her insect-smeared fingers down her skirt, peeled away the gloves, draped them over the side of a plant box, and turned to examine Theo.

"Don't look like much," she mused. "Come have a cuppa."

Theo hesitated, and was duly poked in the back to follow her inside.

There was a wood-burning stove with an iron kettle on top, a smell of lavender and lace. The woman stood on a plastic orange stool to fumble on the top shelf of a cupboard, before bringing down a teabag. "It's not proper tea of course," she muttered as the kettle boiled and her escorts draped themselves around the low, sky-blue kitchen. "I think it has dandelions in it. Dandelions, it's just . . ."

A scoff, a half-guffaw, you know how ridiculous it is it's just . . .

"But it's what we have and tea is an important binding social ritual, so sit you down."

A hand on Theo's shoulder plonked him down in a wooden chair at a small square table in the centre of the room. A bowl containing almost-blooming winter bulbs sat between knitted table mats. A mug stained with tannins, the front depicting a penguin performing a probably impossible sexual act, was put in his hands. He sniffed the tea and flinched. Sipping, his host watched him. He drank cautiously, and then quickly, getting as much of the heat and fluid as he could without having to spend too much time with the taste.

The woman beamed, sat down opposite him, let the heat from her mug seep into her skin.

"I'm the queen," she said at last. "You're Theo, yes?"

He nodded.

"You can call me ma'am, or your maj, or Bess. If you call me your maj without looking proper about it, my boys will take you out back and beat you till you bleed out your ears."

"What's proper?" he mumbled over the lip of the mug.

"Proper! Respectful. Proper respect."

"But I can call you Bess?"

"Respectfully, yes."

"All right."

"And I shall call you Theo."

"Okay."

"So!" She slapped the table brightly with the open palm of her right hand. "Helen tells me that you're looking for help. Says you have information that'll take down the government, rip the Company apart and generally set things a-burning, is that about the short of it?"

"Yes, ma'am."

"Is it proper?" Theo hesitated, sucked in more liquid, tried to guess again at proper, at the mystic meanings of this word. Bess flapped impatiently. "Proper, proper, is it good, is it decent, or are you spinning me a yarn and are we gonna have to do the beating business?"

"I can prove that the Company is murdering thousands of people, imprisoning people without trial, all in the name of profit."

She shrugged. "So? Stuff like that never makes it to court."

"I know."

"Then you're wasting my time, yes?"

"I have financial records from the Company. Documents, records of—"

"This sounds like shite to me it sounds like – do you think this sounds like shite I think it's . . . "

"I have Philip Arnslade's mother. She is willing to testify against her own son. I can make the Company destroy itself, and in the process take down the government and all who sail in it."

325

Bess raised a hand, stopping the men who'd already begun to move towards Theo's slouching back. "Okay. Don't be boring."

Theo spoke, and by the way she listened, it wasn't boring.

Chapter 60

The queen of the patties, Good Queen Bess, her name isn't Bess of course she took it because it seemed nice, it seemed sort of regal, sort of majestic but also very down-to-earth, it was a name that implied a much grander name somewhere behind it but she wasn't grand she wasn't . . .

She killed her husband a long time ago. It was self-defence. She called the ambulance immediately, but he hadn't paid for the health insurance like he'd said he had, so the ambulance didn't come. He hadn't paid for a lot of things that he said he had. The money was a big part of how the troubles began.

That was when she was still a teacher. Things were different, back then.

"So why'd you come to me?" she asked when Theo's story was done.

"People are looking for us. Mostly looking for Helen, but also for me. We needed a place to go. Somewhere safe."

"This ain't safe. The police don't bother to come here no more, but sometimes the Company sends in the boys and shoot the village up a bit, just to keep things ripe. They used to try to take the kids, or the pretty ones, but we shot back and it wasn't a worthwhile economic investment. They think there might be some gas down beneath these hills, they want to dig it up, so they cut off the water, the electric, the roads, trying to starve us out. We are starving. It may look all lovely but they're starving us to death. We go raiding for grub but they make it harder every year. This isn't safe."

"I heard the patties had a queen, they say these prayers, blessed are the—"

"Even atheists pray when they're gonna lose a thing they love and know they can't stop it. It's the knowing they can't stop it that makes them do the whispering."

"They pray to you."

She shrugged. "They pray to the idea that somewhere in the north there's a place where the patties can be free, where we try again. They pray to that. I'm just sitting here."

"Will you help us?"

"Maybe. Maybe. I don't know about you, boy. But I like Helen. She's got class. They don't teach that, class, they don't teach it at all. Now some might say I'm just responding to a certain socio-economic stereotype, that it's the accent and maybe that's true, maybe it is at that, but I dunno. If she's willing to shaft her kiddy, that's something. You think she's got long left for this world?"

"I don't know."

"You think she knows?"

"Yes."

"But she ain't telling."

"No."

Bess beamed. "It's that sorta attitude that makes the aristocracy so goddamn sexy."

They took him back to the room where the shadows crawled, left Helen and Theo in the dark.

"How'd it . . . ?" asked Helen.

"Fine. Fine. I think . . . fine."

"Did she . . . ?"

"She didn't shoot us, did she?"

Helen laughed at nothing, and Theo realised just how stupid these words were, all things considered.

After a few hours, a man opened the door, gave them a bowl of thin potato soup each, and a couple of blankets, chewed a little around the edges.

*

In the morning:

"My name is Corn."

"Theo."

"I know."

"I'm very happy to meet you, this is going to be—"

"I was arrested for assault. I did it. He attacked my sister. I attacked him. I got eighteen years on the patty line. After nine, I broke out. Killed a guard when I did it. I killed him. I didn't mean to, and I'm not sorry I did it. It's just the way it went down."

"I see."

"You used to be an auditor?"

"Yes."

"Bess told me to help you. If you fuck us, I will make you eat your own fucking eyeballs."

"Right. Well. That's very clear."

In a cottage ten miles outside Derby, a laptop, a connection, a woman who once did a favour for a man and the man loved her and never forgot, and now she helps the patties, the runners, the screamers, the faders, the ones who pray to the moonlight through the bars.

"I made the jam myself," she murmurs, putting a plate on the table in front of Theo. "I won't tell you how much sugar goes into these things."

The jam is made from gooseberries. It is disgusting. Theo eats it anyway, as Corn watches. Helen sits by the fire, gossiping with the woman about condiments and cats and the weather and the state of politics and the problem with women's fashion and how underwired bras are just a tool of oppression all things considered.

Corn fiddled with a camera. A young woman sat in the window of the living room, framed in light, one foot up on the sill, knee bent, eyes turned out towards the brilliant winter sun, a laptop shut at her feet. Corn murmured, not looking up from the camera, "She's Bea. She does the machines. She's good. She's good."

329

There was that in Corn's averted gaze, the quietness of his speech, that made Theo look away.

By the first light of the new day they sat down in the kitchen, put a camera on a tripod, sat Helen in a wicker chair, a cup of tea by her side.

She took a few attempts to get it right.

"My name is Helen Arnslade, my son is Philip Arnslade, minister of fiscal efficiency. These are the names of the ones who died in HM Prison Lower Ayot, and whose bodies were put into the incinerator. Una Debono. Alice Turan. Janet Gantly. Rowena Ngongo. Claudia Hull. Michelline Heather . . . "

They stopped every hundred names or so for Helen to have more tea and Bea to check the camera. When the light faded, they had supper. Supper was porridge and gooseberry jam. Theo was too hungry to care what it tasted like, and had stomach ache well into the night.

They posted Helen's videos online, and the contents of Dani's USB stick two days later.

Waited.

For a few hours nothing happened.

Then for a few hours, the internet exploded.

Then they turned on the news, and nothing happened. GDP was up, unemployment was down, and the prime minister was heading off to the USA to visit key corporate innovators.

At 7 p.m. Corn tried looking up "Helen Arnslade" on the internet, and no results were returned by any search engine. He tried texting a message to the woman in the window with Helen's name in it, and the message showed as sent on his phone, and she never received it.

"Well," mused Theo. "I suppose it starts here."

Chapter 61

Bea had trained as a weaver.

"I liked to play with computers when I was a kid," she mused. "I was told I should do IT GCSE. The school hadn't ever taught IT GCSE before, and the teacher didn't know what it involved or how to teach it but I did it anyway I did it and I got a C and I was really proud of that but the school tried to pretend it hadn't happened. It looked bad on the statistics it was just . . .

Anyway I was good at art too but there wasn't any use for that, but then someone said why don't you go into textiles, people always need clothes. And they do but they don't want to pay for them and the moment you design something new someone's ripped it off so I designed this T-shirt I thought it was really nice actually and I put a picture of it up on my blog and next thing you know . . .

I mean it was a large company who stole it, someone owned by a company which was owned by . . . anyway, I was like, give me my royalty cos you've nicked my design, and they said that I hadn't copyrighted it and I'd hear from their lawyers and we had this meeting and the man called me a very silly little girl and on the way out I was so angry – I was just so angry – I scratched his car with my keys and the indemnity wasn't much, but the guy put his lawyers on me and suddenly it was so much more it was, like, everything I had. I paid, but my parents, they lost their home. And now I was in the shitter, and this guy, it just made me so angry that he'd got away with this stuff, that he could do it and next thing he's running for government and – get this – he said that rape, he said it's a thing, like if women don't take responsibility for

and I was so angry I just . . .

So I hacked his site. Redirected everything to a victim support charity. He made sure I got six years. He had friends at the Company, and the Company was funding the redevelopment of the courts, and the judge, well, his pension came from Company shares so . . .

They put me in a textiles prison. I got my own cell and everything. Special sponsorship. Made the T-shirt I'd designed for the guy who locked me up. Retailed for £8.99, big spring seller. Funny that. It's all very funny, isn't it?"

Data rolled between camera and computer, computer and internet. Bea watched a bar crawl towards completion and chewed her bottom lip. Helen sat by her side, waiting, polite and patient. At last:

"I like machines. People think if you do art you can't like machines, but I always thought they were wrong. I think people like to be right. And they like to be told that they're right. And they forget when they're not, because it makes them feel bad, and most of the time they're wrong."

Helen smiled and mused: "I have led an incredibly privileged life. I am not ashamed of being privileged. If you could choose privilege you would, of course – but what matters is that you understand privilege for what it is. That you know this and see that with it comes a duty. Duty is the reason is why—"

And Bea replied, "I used to have my own loom. But different looms have different effects sometimes you want to achieve other things you want to – you'd really destroy your son for duty?"

A slice of the knife across the white of the egg on her plate, cutting off a triangle. She ate, and eating gave her time to think, and Bea waited, and Helen said, "Yes. Because my son is a good man who knows the difference between right and wrong. He is a man who understands that he has a duty. He does not destroy the world for an island in the Mediterranean Sea. That is the only acceptable truth."

Bea looked like she was going to argue, but looked in Helen's eyes and saw the tears that were waiting to grow there, and put her hand in Helen's hand and didn't say a word.

Chapter 62

Corn had a car. It was one of only two that the patties had running. The car was old, and made of different cars. He said, "We take it to Northampton, then we have to change cars. If you enter London in something like this – the CCTV – they pick you up, you have to be driving something proper."

Helen made them sandwiches. The sandwiches were bad. The bread was thick and dry, and there wasn't any margarine. She stood in the door of the farmhouse, pushed them into Theo's hand and murmured, "Be safe, down there. Be safe."

Bea sat in the front passenger seat because she got carsick, and took turns driving with Corn. Theo sat in the back, knees together, hands in his lap, and watched the land roll by. Gentle hills and bursts of thick trees, the leaves spiralling up and away in great gusts of wind that whooshed and crackled through the branches. A church spire peeking up from an orange-brick village. A manor house where once, centuries ago, a woman had hidden her brother from the Roundheads even though she didn't believe in his cause, and where in another time the children had lounged in the setting sunlight by the still waters of the lake as the bombers went overhead, barely disturbing their tranquillity.

A petrol station where behind the counter a man with two dangling hollows in the lobes of his ears where the dress code didn't allow him to wear his jewellery met them behind the air pump and pressed key's into Corn's hand and whispered, "Blessed is her name, let the bars be broken let the journey end."

Corn squeezed his hand tight, and the man nodded, and scampered back to the shop before his supervisor could catch him skiving.

They found the next car parked two streets away from the garage. It smelled of dog and a tiny bit of dog vomit, but they wound the windows down and wrapped themselves in coat and glove, and headed south.

London grew at the bottom of the hill. Strange to think that the city had boundaries, strange to think that there was a place where it stopped that you could stand on this line and your left foot would be in mud and your right on concrete and to the south the grey towers reached up to prick the clouds and to the north the mud squelched on into the damp, stripped hills and . . .

Strange to think that this was how he was coming home.

Huddled in the back of the car with a couple of patties, a hat on his head and a scarf around his neck to hide his face from the CCTV, because they'd be watching, Bea said, they'd be watching.

They left the car in a car park in Archway, and walked down the steep slope of the hill. Houses of red and black, stained-glass windows above the shut front doors, little front patios not quite big enough to be gardens but too big just to be for the bins, no one seemed to know what to do with them, you could maybe fit in a rose bush but that was all but anything less and the space seemed bare.

Theo found this troubling. There didn't seem any logic in it.

He pulled his chin to his chest, his hands in his pockets, and followed Bea and Corn down the hill.

They stayed in a house with four bedrooms and nine residents. Three of the inhabitants of the largest room moved into the beds of the others to give Corn, Bea and Theo a little privacy in a space not much larger than the double bed that inhabited it. The air smelled of stale cigarette smoke and spilt beer. The kitchen floor crunched underfoot when Theo walked on it. On his second night he found a needle in the toilet. The residents were all from the patty line. A girl with pale yellow freckles beneath her eyes caught his revulsion when he opened the door to the kitchen to find a month of dirty dishes, caked in tomato gloop, piled up to the walls. She looked away, ashamed, and her shame made him feel ashamed, and she looked back and saw he was embarrassed and she smiled and said:

"It's hard. You clean it sometimes, but it just gets worse again. And when you've got nothing else, what's the point of doing the dishes I mean what's the point of . . ."

The next day he went into the kitchen, and it was spotless.

"It's great you've come," whispered the girl as they squeezed by each other in the tight, carpet-torn corridor. "It's really good to have something to work for."

Some of the people in the house wanted to scream, but this was London, and screamers weren't welcome in this part of town, they vanished, disappeared at the slightest sound of trouble, emotionally assaulting the neighbours was the charge, causing distress. So they buried their heads into their pillows and howled until they were half-suffocated, and that appeased them a little bit, for a while.

At 4 a.m. a man staggered in, his face coated with black, his hands coated with black, the smell of ash and the Underground on his boots, and he went into the bathroom and locked the door and fell asleep inside, and when they woke him with knocking in the morning his face was still black, but he'd got as far as washing his hands and didn't seem to notice anything else.

The next day Theo discovered that the original owner of the house was still there, living in the attic. "I used to be a banker," he whispered when Theo brought him tea. "I made four twenty a year, before bonus. But one day I went to the patty line, an investment opportunity, and I looked. I looked. And once I'd looked I couldn't forget, I couldn't look away, I tried to look away and it was like it was burned. It was burned. I don't like to go outside now. The guys downstairs look after me. They look after me. They look . . . everyone can see it. We can all see it. So now I'm here."

336

On the fourth day Theo caught the bus into the centre of town, pressed in with the old women and the children, the greasy-armed men in sweaty T-shirts, the travellers with bags too big for the luggage space who were glared at and who glared defiantly in return. He stood away from the one cracked security camera, head down, hood up, and did not watch the streets, and listened for his stop, which came fifty-five minutes later, just outside King's Cross.

He walked, unsure if this world was real, let alone familiar, a familiar place that he had known, up towards the canal, through the new buildings of silver steel and green glass, towers framed in skeletal shells, spined like porcupines; up to the restored old ware-houses that now housed arts and dramas, music and penthouse flats. He sat by a fountain that spat bursts of white foam in busy, regimented rhythm, following a programme of surges and falls, and decided that it was all the same and only he had changed.

A gym was on the other side of the water. Above the front door a picture of a woman with bad technique and a huge grin punched towards the camera. As the door opened, it revealed a counter where a bored man in red sold protein shakes, dumb-bells, yoga mats and memberships. Gym memberships were good for an extra £2000 on the cost of an indemnity, if you got murdered with one. Showed that you were really trying to look after your health.

Theo waited.

The sun set, and he waited.

At 8.25 p.m. Mala Choudhary emerged, her dark hair swept back, bright pink trainers on her feet, legs sculpted in black leg-gings, a bag slung across one shoulder, chin high and skin hot from exertion. She walked towards King's Cross. Theo followed until she caught a cab and vanished into the traffic.

The next day he waited outside the gym for Mala to go inside, then followed Bea around to the service door. Bea knocked four times, then waited, head down, fingers tucked into her sleeves against the cold, a penitent monk in a tracksuit.

The door opened. A woman with a plastic stud through her

nose, scar on her chin, dressed in burgundy T-shirt and white shorts, stood on the other side.

"Blessed are her hands," whispered Bea. "Blessed are those who weave and those who break."

The woman nodded once, without smiling, and let Bea inside. Theo waited.

Ten minutes later Bea emerged. She had a data card in her pocket, a copy of Mala Choudhary's phone cloned onto it. She had photos of Mala's credit cards, including the lovely Company platinum card for wining and dining high-value-indemnity clients – the mass murderers, arms and drugs dealers – in all the nicest places. The juicy crimes always paid the best. "It's nice in there," she mused as they walked away, the patty-line cleaner closing the door quietly behind them. "They have really nice hand lotion in the ladies' lav, and the towels are fluffy."

Chapter 63

There weren't any messages between Mala Choudhary and her bosses on her phone.

There weren't any messages between Mala and Seph Atkins either.

There were a couple of photos of Mala's cat. A lot of her children. Theo was surprised. He hadn't imagined she had kids or could spend so much time pressing them to her glowing cheeks, bursting with pride and excitement as she hugged them close. He hadn't imagined Mala Choudhary was capable of feeling much of anything in particular.

There was an online banking app on Mala's phone.

Corn flicked through its transaction history, a photo of Mala's credit cards in his other hand. At last he said, "This will be enough. I can get a guy."

"No," replied Theo. "It has to be Seph Atkins."

"That's not gonna be easy."

"It needs to be her."

"Why?" When Theo didn't answer, Corn half-turned from where he'd sprawled, feet up on the kitchen table, chair rocking back on the edge of tipping, to examine the auditor's face. "I don't need your shit. First sign of shit, her maj said, do him. Protect the patties, that's what she said. Just do him."

"Atkins killed my friend."

A half-shrug. Corn has lost plenty of friends, and it hasn't got to him. He's just fine.

"Atkins killed the mother of my child."

339

A slightly less emphatic half-shrug. Okay, so Corn's never had that shit go down, that's heavy yeah, but still, all the more reason not to bring your personal crap into this.

Theo's shoulders rolled forward, head down. "If . . . if it's possible. It would be . . . it would be better that way. I would like to try."

Corn stared into the distance for a moment, face empty, then nodded at nothing much and muttered, "We'll see."

Three days later Seph Atkins' phone rang.

This was unexpected and unwelcome.

She hadn't given this number to more than a couple of people, and they should know that she was in Cornwall, having a little me-time. She peeled slices of cucumber off her eyes, wriggled her fingers, wriggled her toes, marvelled at how, after barely an hour of luxurious nothing, they felt like different limbs, someone else's body. She was putting on weight, she knew it. Could feel things pressing against her belly which hadn't pressed before. She should eat less, but she really liked flavours. She didn't like her bum. She felt it was pear-shaped, but that wasn't a lifestyle thing, it was just . . .

Her phone stopped ringing.

Seph Atkins stared up at the cream-coloured ceiling as wooden flutes trilled earthy calm from the speakers behind her head, and waited for it to ring again.

It did.

She let it ring out.

On the third attempt she answered, having worked through the worst of her annoyance on call two.

"Yeah?"

"Ms Atkins?"

"Yeah?"

"Ms Atkins, I wish to hire your services."

"I'm on holiday."

"I've been reading your file."

"I don't have a file."

"A colleague at Faircloud Associates was kind enough to help me," the voice replied politely, an old voice, female, someone rich perhaps, a woman who knew what she wanted and wasn't used to hearing no. "You come highly recommended."

"I don't work with people I don't know. Bye."

She hung up, lay back and put some fresh cucumber over her now exasperated, weary eyes.

Twenty minutes later her phone beeped.

She ignored it, until at last thirst and an empty flask of icy water by her side provoked reluctant action. She grunted as nose flutes snuffled their way to a tuneless conclusion, white towels tumbled around her body, and checked her phone.

A bank transfer had been made in her favour, to the tune of ten thousand pounds.

She phoned her guy, the guy who was good at this shit, the guy who'd got into the databases for fun, not even for cash, and had him back-trace the transfer just to check what she already knew.

The funds had come from Mala Choudhary.

Her phone rang again. "Ms Atkins," said the same wealthy, old voice. "Is now a convenient time to talk?"

Chapter 64

Later, Seph Atkins would admit that she was driven by greed.

She'd not got into the killing business because she liked committing murder. Indeed, she found the actual homicide part of her job frequently boring and often disappointingly mundane. The tears, gurgling, wheedling, begging, the endless litany of bargains and pathetic offers made by the dying and the soon-to-be-dead as they failed to expire neatly with a single bullet, all of it dispelled any real sense that humanity was special, or more than just a fleshy, crawling animal.

And the parochial motives given for her contracts – "They looked at me funny" or "I just know he's gonna do me" or money – always money – left Seph Atkins feeling fairly convinced that the vast majority of mankind was either stupid, cowardly or self-obsessed to the point of myopia.

Seph loved money, of course. But too many of her clients thought of nothing else. They wanted money not because they had a good idea for what to do with it – a thrilling investment or the adventure of a lifetime – but because it, itself, was their goal, rather than a means to something more exciting. She liked money because the lifestyle it purchased her was indeed according to her desires and expectations. If the glossy mags and glitzy journos hadn't bridled at the thought of celebrating an assassin, she would have been all across the page 7 spreads and the mid-afternoon lifestyle programmes. From her weeks at the spa to her love of ska and Mozart, her polished skin and extensive holidays through the best of Renaissance Italy or the finest ski slopes of the Alps, she was indeed a woman to envy.

She spent a lot of time dealing with the law, of course. But it was so much cheaper and easier to confess at once and have an indemnity taken out against her crimes than it was to go on the run that she regarded the process of arrest and bail as merely part of her professional labours. Sometimes she was hired to be the invisible bullet, the killer who could never be found, but in cases such as the Cumali job, where the indemnity was never going to be more than £90K for the patty slut, it was simplest to just phone the cops and save everyone a lot of bother.

She should not have taken the job.

She didn't know her contact, but the transfer of funds directly from Mala Choudhary's account was enough to pay for next month's scuba diving, and the details when they came through seemed plausible.

So it was that Seph Atkins went to the races.

Chapter 65

Helen sits alone as the sun goes down, and reads the names of the dead.

The ones who'd died on the patty line

the ones who'd died waiting for a lawyer who never came

the ones who died in the hospitals, their corpses returned to their homes so the doctors could say they died in their beds, not under the Company's care

the names of the children

the parents

the ones gunned down for running away

And no one listened.

And no one cared.

And it was shut down before it could cause a scandal.

And she kept reading anyway, because her son had done this thing. He hadn't fired the gun or dug the pit, but he had done enough.

He had played his part, and she had made him and so

She read the names of the dead.

And there were so many, the names running one into another, that she didn't realise she'd said Dani's name until at least six or seven names later. For a moment it seems to her, as she stumbles, that time is . . .

Time is

        Neila sat with Theo and told stories as the river, too wide and broad for their little vessel, bumped gently against the side of the boat. She told stories and once she started, she couldn't stop. She couldn't stop speaking the words just fell from her, so many years of silence, so many years it all it being fine and she looked up to the horizon, and the horizon was burning, the country was burning and only on the canal was she safe, only here.

And she said, "My brother had depression, he had depression and we all told him to get over it, we told him to just try and see the good side of things I mean, the good side it was just . . . "

And in the villages around the canal the lights were dark and the streets ran wild and there was blood between the stones, but not here, not where the ice cracked before the prow of her ship, and terror gripped her heart and she blurted:

"You ask people, when they tell you something terrible, you ask them 'Are you okay?' Of course they're not fucking okay but what else are you meant to say. 'Oh you must be feeling shit you must be so shit you must be . . . '"

Theo is going to leave soon, she knows it. She can feel it and now that she's taken a passenger on board, now that her heart has cracked and she chose human company, chose again to have someone in her life, anyone at all, she is terrified of letting go. She feels as if she is spinning out of control, just turning in the current, unable to find a way to steer in a straight line.

By yellow candlelight she put her head against his shoulder and he put his cheek into her hair and their hands tangled together, warmth in the winter night as the fire burned down and Neila murmured:

"My brother is better now. He is who he is. He knows that now he doesn't hate himself he isn't angry any more he doesn't rage he isn't . . . "

And stopped a while, as the snow fell and the fire flickered and the light burned down to the bottom of the bowl.

"In tarot, the Fool begins the journey. With an innocent heart and a soul full of wonder he sets out on his wanderings, looking to explore the universe, delighting in all things, trusting in all things the Fool is a card of exploration, hope. As he journeys, he meets many things. The wise Magician; the Emperor and Empress, the Lovers, the Hermit, the Wheel of Fortune, the Hanged Man. The Hanged Man is the crossroads, is suspension, a choice that holds you back or will send you forward, a moment where all things stand on the edge. Sacrifice, surrender, martyrdom, treachery – in some drawings you can see it, a halo, there is an idea there of giving up something old to make something new, for others, half in sky, half on land, the world tree but you hang from it, Odin searching for knowledge, crucifixion, some see divinity others say they see Judas with a bag of silver in his hand. I don't see anything noble in it, I used to think there was but now I just think it is the world. It is the truest card that is, the world we travel and we wish and we dream, caught between sky and earth. But we are tiny and the sky is huge and sometimes we cannot be all we think we are. We cannot be . . . there are some battles we cannot conquer and we push and we push until and still we are here, suspended, we did this to ourselves. We did this."

They sat together a while, and in the darkness another boat passed them by, the wake tipping the *Hector* a little from side to side, before washing itself out.

"At the end of the Fool's journey is the World. The Devil, the Tower, the Star, the Moon, the Sun, Judgement, the World. Once I saw a card, the queen of cups, and I thought . . . it always seemed to me that I was there, that she spoke to me. Sometimes I catch myself making stories from the things that happened in my life, making stories of who I will be, and in these stories I'm always the hero or the villain because that way I made a choice, I made a choice and I chose to be here and there wasn't ever anything which I couldn't control, there wasn't a part of me that is . . . "

She stopped.

"Time is . . . "

Stopped. Didn't know what the words were that followed.

"Do you regret?" she asked. "Do you look back, do you look at – when you think about the time you've had and the things – do you regret? Is that what you feel?"

Theo thought about it.

"I think I would," he said at last. "If there wasn't something more important to do."

Later, Neila stood alone at the back of the *Hector*, hand freezing on the rudder.

The fucking cormorant didn't even bother to fly away when she flapped at it now, just sat there on the roof of her fucking boat, minding its own business in the most insufferable way.

And in the days before

Helen sat with Theo on top of a hill as the sun set over the vales. In the town below someone was screaming, screaming, until they were silenced. Queen Bess didn't hold with that sort of thing, not in her neck of the woods, but on the other side of the valley there were the tearers the ragers the faders the zeroes the

Helen said, "Is it enough? Theo? Is it enough? Have I saved my son?"

And Theo didn't answer, and things didn't seem to change that much after all.

The next day they too went to the races.

Chapter 66

Getting into Ascot was easier than Theo had expected, and just as unpleasant.

The first challenge was penetrating the Ascot cordon. None of them had the credit to get past the toll booths, let alone proof of identity for the car park. Public trains had stopped running several years ago, with only a private prebooked service for race days; £76 a ticket and a trolley cart serving champagne and hand-cut roasted vegetable chips from a boutique in Devon.

In the end they crept in under cover of darkness, following the railway track and hiding in the trees until the patrols passed, camping without fire in the bitter, falling snow, huddled together in a chilly bundle as they waited for the sun to rise.

Theo pressed close to Helen, and Bea seemed to share his concern, twining herself around the older woman as if she could will heat into Helen's shuddering bones. Helen was too cold to refuse, shut her eyes and nodded in gratitude, blue lips curled in on themselves as if she might suck in warmth.

No one slept that night, and every now and then a helicopter passed in the distance, and Corn hissed that they should have brought foil sheets or painted themselves in mud, and Theo wasn't sure what difference these things would have made, but it seemed important to Corn, so he didn't argue.

In the morning they shuffled down the shallow hill towards the railway line, light bursting golden white off the clinging frost on the stiff green grass. A few pigeons fluttered in the trees; something larger rustled away into the undergrowth. For a moment the land below them was radiant ivory snow, branch-grey and grassy green where the sun was beginning to drive back the frost. The station was a timber canopy, the perfect place for potted plants and a stationmaster who knew the locals by name; the station café sold sausage rolls, pork pies and clotted cream, and smoke rose from the mansions tucked between the drooping oaks. The memory of a great forest had shaped the land, and still lingered in ancient beech trees and scars of ivy cut through by roads and roundabouts.

They met a white van on the edge of Ascot, parked by a gate to an empty field overgrown with long, spined grass. The man at the back of the van stood arms folded, smoking a tiny brown cigarette, eyeing them up as they approached, nodded just once at Corn as they slowed.

"Yeah," he muttered and, looking again from top to toe, nodded once more and added, "Yeah. Okay."

He opened the back door of the van. A smell of mothballs and mildew rolled out in a cloud of fine, floating particles, and as Theo's eyes adjusted to the gloom he saw clothes, piled on the floor and drooping out of stained cardboard boxes pressed to the side. For ten minutes they shuffled around in the back of the van, breath steaming and fingers blue-white as they fumbled with furs and velvets, Helen muttering, "Of course the code is less stringent for the jump season . . ."

In the end Theo found a black suit that didn't look too ridiculous. Corn dressed in corduroy and looked remarkably like a man born to hunt, only missing a shotgun under one arm. Bea found blue silk and a fur stole; Helen clucked and exclaimed how wonderful she was, and Bea blushed, and Corn very deliberately and carefully didn't look at her, and grunted something about how yeah, you know, it was like, good yeah.

Helen rolled her eyes and chose a more conservative dress suit of chequered black and grey.

They took turns to change in the darkness of the van, doors closed, Corn and Theo, Bea and Helen, hunched over double, slipping and sliding through a sea of shirt and sock, trouser and skirt, squinting in the gloom. When they were done, Corn held out money to the man with the van, who tutted and shook his head.

"Blessed are her hands," he grunted, throwing the words at the notes in Corn's fist, a condemnation as well as a greeting. "Blessed are the ones who scream, for they have heard the truth and the thunder."

Corn hesitated, nodded, shoved the money back into his pocket.

The van drove away, and they hid their bags in a yew hedge by a field where the crows hopped over turned-up earth, pecking at straw, and, dressed in their finest, headed towards the races.

Corn muttered, "We're everywhere of course. We're everywhere, we're cleaning the toilets and mending the sewers and driving the buses and ... "

"Blessed are her hands," whispered Bea as they trudged down the hill, coat and skirts hitched high, nose blue, lips white. "Blessed are those who break the silence."

"Half the people we ask don't even know if the queen is real, they can't imagine it, anything changing. But the idea makes them feel better. That maybe they can do this really small thing, like this *up yours* to the world and maybe it'll make a difference, maybe they count. That's all the queen really is. She makes people think stuff they do matters. If you take that away, we're all just fucked really. Just totally fucked."

With every step towards the wide grass of the racecourse, the towering central stands, white barriers herding humans like sheep, Helen seemed to grow a little brighter, warmer, louder. As she grew, Corn diminished, words shrinking, shoulders curling. Bea seemed to feed on the older woman's confidence, slipping in closer and hooking her arm around Helen's as they neared the gate, happy relations on a wintery adventure.

"These things are seasonal," explained Helen brightly. "They do flats in summer, jumps in winter, and they also have the

shows – the last one I went to with my husband was spectacular. We came away with more trinkets than sense, couldn't fit
everything in the car, but the atmosphere, the people! They
come from Dubai, you know, from the UAE, they really love
their racing out there, they know their horses, the horses they
breed in that part of the world are just magnificent, incredible
stock." She paused, head turning a little to one side, looking back
on memories, shifting through time. "Then again, maybe I just
remember it that way because it was our last together. Maybe we
make these things more important than they were."

Bea said nothing and shuffled a little closer to Helen, holding
her tight. Theo stared at his shoes, tight brown leather, someone
else's, stolen. It was only after he'd chosen his clothes and the van
had driven away that he'd found the stain under his left armpit
where once someone had bled into the cotton, which bleach
and chemicals had managed to fade to a pale purple tideline in
the fabric.

As they neared the racecourse, the crowds began to grow,
pouring in from car parks and the private train, helicopters and
the airstrips. The sound of music drifted over the honking of cars
queuing for a place, wintery festivities, a promise of hot wine and
wooden market stalls selling amber, silver, home-made candles
and winter woollens.

The queue at the entrance gates was a sluggish shuffle, pressing
in through a narrow entrance watched by Company security in
fluorescent yellow and navy blue. Bea collected four tickets from
a woman dressed in grey as they waited, huddled on the edge
of cold and warm. Laughter and an indignant cry at an outrageous joke drew Theo's ear. As his eye swept across the crowd
he thought he saw, for a moment, a woman, tall with short light
brown hair, familiar in every way, and he wondered if he should
make like a heron, and looked again and wasn't sure he'd seen
her at all.

They entered the enclosures of the racecourse, Helen chatting
merrily all the way as if she had not a care in the world.

*

Theo had never been to a countryside fair, let alone a race.

Bodies swayed and spun around each other between aisles of wooden stalls with slanted roofs, yellow bulbs twinkling brightly behind the counters, walls of gingerbread, candles, packets of scented lavender, twee teapots in the shape of penguins, kittens and puppy faces. Sizzling meat straight off the grill, waxed-cotton jackets, hats with duck feathers in them, walking sticks, shooting sticks, an enclosure where you could buy luxury cars, luxury holidays, luxury horses and donkey rides for the kids. The piping bellow of winter music, a merry-go-round where white-painted ponies rose and fell, pink and blue plastic manes rippling in the wind; steaming hot mulled wine and chilled champagne, eight different kinds of hot chocolate and a stall selling Baltic amber and Venetian glass.

A temporary miniature town of ye-olde-timey delights, of money laid out on a whim, shopping that wasn't spending on trash, not at all, merely innocent delight in necessary things. A monument to another world where you still walked to church across the rolling English hills, dogs lapping at your ankles and the neighbours calling your name. A bubble in time fed on 240 volts had cropped up around the fences and walkways of Ascot, selling a dream that only money could buy.

On the sidelines a few reminders of quaint pleasures for the discerning customer. The duck-herding competition was more enthralling than Theo had expected. The sheep race seemed too peculiar to take seriously, especially for those runners who had teddy-bear jockeys sewn to their bibs.

Corn put a pound on a race, and lost when his sheep refused to budge, and was in a foul mood for an hour.

Helen gossiped with Bea as they entered the stands, and sat away from the most glamorous and beautiful of the crowds, the ones who knew everyone else and thought they were marvellous, just marvellous, in case there were those who knew her, and Theo watched, and waited as those shoppers who liked to be seen to care detached themselves from the wooden stalls and climbed the stairs to the wall of chairs that looked down towards

352

the racetrack. Horses, coats polished to a reflective ebony or pristine autumn brown, tossed their heads and flicked their tails, impatient, ready to run, dwarfing their jockeys as they marched towards the starting line, unfazed by the cheering of the crowd as a favourite entered the lines, or the poles and hedges before them. Theo wondered how they trained the horses not to care about the gaze of the thousands who looked down on them. Maybe at night they played the roaring of crowds at the stables, a cascade of cheering to lull them to sleep?

When Philip Arnslade arrived, it was not subtle.

First, his helicopter came in low and loud across the site, attracting a fair share of glares from those who were claiming to enjoy the white-clad, bell-jangling, stick-clacking circle of morris dancers.

Then his security arrived, faces like breadboards, feet splayed as if struggling to contain their bodies or souls within the confines of their suits. Then Philip, chatting to a someone who is definitely something, perhaps in oil, whispering confidential somethings sure to set the crowd a-tittering.

"Well," mused Helen as her son drifted and waved his way down to his seat. "He is predictable. Comes here for the sultans, of course, the emirs and the sheikhs. Can't resist a shiny thing. Always mistook having wealth for being cultivated. Not the same thing at all. Wealth buys a certain culture, it buys a certain . . . " She realised that Bea was staring at her, silent, frowning, and the older woman smiled and squeezed her arm and muttered, "I suppose these things are fairly arbitrary after all."

On the grass, the horses ran, the crowds cheered, and the sky threatened more snow, which did not come.

Theo sat on the other side of Helen, and watched her, watching Philip.

She didn't move, her arm hooked so tight in Bea's that the younger woman visibly leaned to the side, pulled down towards Helen's neck and face. Helen's smile didn't fade, but locked itself in place, an engraving on a skull, as Philip nodded and smiled, before settling into a seat in the centre of the throng.

Theo looked, and looked again, and saw Seph Atkins moving through the crowd.

Seph wore white. A white coat, hanging sleeves framed with fur, that stopped at her thighs. Tight white leggings, white knee-high boots, white gloves. Helen hadn't seen her. Helen didn't know who to look for.

Slowly, a woman in search of another drink, Seph turned through the crowd, and her eyes flickered over Helen, and lingered.

Theo dug his chin a little lower into his stolen, dusty scarf and whispered, "She's here."

Helen's eyebrows flickered, once, the thinnest of movements, and nothing else changed on her face. "Good."

"You don't have to . . ."

"Darling boy, don't be absurd. I hired the woman, didn't I?"

"This isn't . . ."

"What would your Dani Cumali do?" Theo looked away. "Well there." She tutted. "That's settled."

Helen rose, and began to walk towards Philip. Bea followed a few yards behind, and Theo stayed sitting until they were on the walkway down between the rows of seats, watching Seph.

Corn stood at the front of the stands, waiting for the races, turning now to look back at the crowd as the track lulled. Theo caught his eye and turned his head a little towards the figure of Seph drifting up the stairs towards Helen, Helen descending towards Philip. Corn nodded, began to move through the crowd.

For a moment Theo thought everything was going to fail. That Seph Atkins was too good at her job, too keen to get the work done, that it was all for nothing. Then Helen turned, stepped into a wide row of seats covered with cushions and draped with red blankets to swathe the viewers, pushed past grumbling knees and over leather bags, marched up to the nearest security man, who turned to block her path, and said, "I'd like to talk to my son, please."

Seph kept climbing, oblivious to anything else in the world, towards the bar. Corn followed her.

"Excuse me!" exclaimed Helen as security did not move, her voice loud enough to catch the ears of listening strangers. "I would like to see my son!"

Her indignation, loud and clear, caught the ear of Philip and his guest. He looked around, and his face at once opened like an evening primrose, before locking back down into a grimace that might have wanted to be a smile.

"Mother . . . it's so . . . Mother."

Helen stabbed a finger towards him, having to lean past the bulk of the security guard to do it. "You tried to poison me," she exclaimed, not with rancour but a ringing authority that sang out across the stalls. "You have suppressed evidence of mass murder and abductions on behalf of the Company and that shit of a friend of yours, Simon fucking Fardell. You have in short brought disgrace to your name, and I am thoroughly unimpressed."

Theo, drifting downwards, put his hand over his mouth to stifle a laugh, an utterly inappropriate, terrible laugh, and realised at the same moment that he genuinely liked Helen Arnslade, that he admired her, that he wished he had more time to know her, valued her friendship, and that her death would be on his hands.

"You should be ashamed of yourself, Philip Arnslade!" added Helen, voice rising in shrill indignation. "You should be ashamed of what you've done."

"Mother," murmured Philip, slipping past the guard to grasp Helen gently by the elbow. "It's such a relief to see you. Let me take you inside, let me take you . . . "

He led her away, while his wife pinned down his guests with a laugh and an anecdote about exfoliation. His security followed, and Theo and Bea followed them, Helen proclaiming all the way, "He sanctions the abduction of innocent people! Patties are held without charge! They are sent to die because they are economic burdens! These are the names of the dead – Kam Akhoon, Robert Ebutt, Ned Hayhurst, Dani Cumali . . . "

Philip swept his mother through a pair of double doors, cutting off her voice from the outside world, who tried texting their

355

friends about her, and thought the text had sent, and didn't really understand why they never got a reply.

They took Helen to a private meeting room. The racecourse had plenty, where the grand and the great could organise discreet encounters beneath grey ceilings, while projectors hummed and the coffee machine took for ever to produce something too hot to drink that burned the top of your mouth.

Theo waited with the throng at the edge of the roped-off corridor that led to the room, and utterly failed to drink a glass of overpriced white wine.

Waited.

Bea waited downstairs, watching the front exit.

Corn waited in the car park at the back.

So did Seph Atkins, huddled inside a hired Audi, smoking an e-cigarette with the window open an inch, releasing clouds of thick, blue-grey smoke that rolled upwards like an inverted waterfall through the window, and tasted of peppermint, and burned strangers' eyes, and drove away anyone within a ten-foot radius.

In the conference rooms, various raised voices, muffled and distant.

"Mother it's such a—"

"Tried to poison!"

"You're not stable – she's not stable – the medicine you were – kidnapped I can only imagine the trauma . . ."

"Don't shit me, young man."

"See you're not just – she isn't – it's not that—"

"How could you do it? How could you do it to all those people? How could you do it to . . ."

Somewhere in the conversation Helen started to cry. She hadn't thought she would. She hadn't cried when her husband died. There had been so much to do. Funerals to organise, wills to read, people to inform. She had duties to perform and she had performed them and crying would have been a ridiculous distraction.

Now she cried, a foolish old woman who no one listened to,

and was furious at herself for letting herself cry, even more angry with herself than she was with her son, and that just made her cry more until she could barely get any words out at all between her pathetic, useless sniffling.

Philip blurted, "Well you see, I mean really! Really, Mother this is all so terribly – and you're ill – so we'll take you home now. We're going to take you home and you can have your medicine and then ... "

At the end of the corridor, alone with a white wine and a mobile phone which sometimes he pretended he was using, Theo waited and watched the door.

Once, a security man left, speaking fast and urgent on a mobile phone.

Then he returned.

Then a man in a white suit, carrying a brown leather bag, arrived.

Then he left.

Theo thought he might throw up, and waited, and did not throw up, though the feeling didn't go away.

Outside, the crowd screamed and the horses thundered and the morris dancers leaped and the ducks quacked and money changed hands and the helicopters came and left and sheep went baaahhhh and the patties washed the toilets where someone had pissed up the wall and in the rooms behind the course a man whispered, "There's a market for anything. I can get you some very good-looking subjects on extended contract for just ... "

And time was ...

Theo wasn't sure what time was, but he knew it was rushing, running, racing forward too fast to perceive, and it was slower than anything he'd ever endured and he was going to close his eyes and wake up six months in the past and nothing would be different and nothing would have mattered.

And he knew that he had probably condemned Helen to die, and it was his fuck-up and his fault and it would all be for nothing, just like everything he'd ever done had been for nothing always and ...

357

After an hour and ten minutes the doors to the conference room opened. Two security men emerged, looked left, looked right, saw no immediate threats. Then Helen, leaning a little on the arm of a third, her face slack, eyes distant. Then two more security men, flanking Philip, taking turns to hold the door so that one always walked in front and one behind.

They headed, quiet, away from the crowds, towards the emergency exit.

Theo stopped fiddling with his phone and dialled the only number saved on it.

"They're coming," he said.

"Gotcha," muttered Corn and hung up.

Theo waited for the group to be almost through the emergency exit before ducking under the rope that cut off their route from the main throng, following them. The door at the end of the corridor led to a grey concrete stairwell, brutally practical against the fascinators, ice buckets and soft velvet of the main event. He could hear footsteps descending, voices muttering into radios. He followed, moving no faster than Helen could, keeping at a distance.

The stairwell gave out to the service car park, caterers' vans and patty transport buses. The brightness of the winter's day was harsh after the half-gloom of fluorescents. Clouds scudding across the sun promised snow later, but only seemed to fracture the light, not dim it. Theo looked across the car park and saw the huddle of security, Helen and Philip already moving towards an exit, where two black cars were pulling up, ready to collect their passengers.

He looked through the parked vehicles, and saw Seph Atkins because he knew she had to be there, a shape more than a face clouded in grey, smoke drifting through the inch-open window of her car. Looked beyond her, thought he saw Corn move behind a floral delivery van laden with wreaths of holly and yew.

Thought he saw someone else moving on the edge of his vision, and knew it was probably Dani, or maybe Theo – the real Theo, the one who'd died by Philip Arnslade's hand – and realised he was going to fuck this up again, just like he'd fucked up everything he'd ever done his whole life.

Helen was a few metres from the black cars, trying to say something, half-turning to look back the way she'd come. The security guard who held her arm tried to guide her forward, but her walk was unsteady, her will absolute. She mouthed something vague, words slurring, craned her neck, and saw Theo.

Their eyes met, and she raised her head a little higher, smiled.

Corn detonated the bomb.

The bomb was under a six-seater car that had brought dish washers from the local prison to the racecourse.

The dish washer who'd built the bomb had been put inside for arson, but that was only because the explosives had started a fire. Because of his special skills, he'd been sent to a chemical factory. When he lost an eye and the tip of his nose to acid, the inmates held their traditional party, a feast of scavenged tinned food and banging of fists on walls. He was one of them now, for ever disfigured and welcome in their tribe, and he was surprised to discover that he wanted to live.

He wanted to live, and concluded that this could only be because there was something left to live for.

At night he whispered prayers to the lady in the north, to her blessed hands, to the breaking of the cage.

He'd really enjoyed putting the bomb underneath the car. He'd enjoyed it so much that he'd scratched FUCK U into the tin-can housing, still smelling faintly of tomatoes through the ammonia, a little act that only he would ever appreciate. He liked blowing things up generally. Blowing things up for a cause felt . . .

. . . like something new.

The bomb, as bombs went, wasn't as spectacular as Theo had expected. Cleaning products weren't as good as the proper shit, its maker might have said. The sound of it hurt his ears, and the shock wave was a hot blast in his face like an air-conditioning vent for a big office building. But there wasn't fire. There weren't licking yellow flames, and though the security men went down to the ground, they dragged their charges down with them rather than being thrown off their feet, covering Philip's head with their hands, pushing him beneath the shrapnel of metal that splatted out from the wreck of the car.

For a moment Theo thought that was it, and hoped it was enough.

Then Seph's bomb, the much larger, much more professional bomb she'd put in the boot of her target Volvo, stirred into life by the shock wave from the less competent device, also detonated. Philip and his escort were already halfway to the ground, which is why the ball bearings as they flew through the air ripped apart only one of the guards, the slowest, the one who'd been last to comprehend his environment. The blast knocked Theo back against the emergency exit, slamming the breath out of him, and the three cars nearest the bomb didn't have time to wail before glass, chassis and pipe were ripped to pieces, the poked frames lifted up and turned sideways, rolled over until they hit their next-nearest neighbours, which howled and shrieked, lights flashing and black smoke tumbling from broken, greasy valve as rubble and shattered metal began to drift down around them, soft against the singing in Theo's ears.

For a few moments there was only the howling, the metal rain, black smoke.

Theo crawled upright, leaning against the wall, looking through biting acrid smoke for signs of life. One of the black cars that had been waiting by the car park gate had been knocked on its side. As he watched, a door opened at the top and a man, groggy and struggling to get a grip, scrambled up through what had now become the roof of the vehicle, swinging his legs round and flopping like an overweight fish onto the ground.

Of the security on the ground, one was dragging the shattered body of his colleague towards the waiting vehicles. Two more, crawling, bloodied, clothes burned, dragged Philip Arnslade, who staggered and blinked and seemed not to see or understand. A third crouched over Helen and didn't know what to do.

A grunt of engine, out of time, unearthly in Theo's muddled

senses. Seph's car zipped by, her fingers as white as her winter coat where she gripped the wheel. There was a thing on her face which might have been panic, and if she saw Theo as she rushed by, he did not seem to register.

Corn, slinking away.

Bea, upstairs, watching from a window, turned her face from the scene.

Theo, in the door, looked and looked, and waited for Helen to move, and she did not, and the smoke began to clear and the sounds of the world began to return, the sirens and the shouting and engines and now an alarm inside the building, evacuation, the racecourse evacuating, and Theo couldn't move, and couldn't see, and Helen did not get up.

Did not stand.

Did not move.

The phone was ringing in his pocket, and he didn't answer, and Helen didn't move.

The fire door opened at his back, and a man in a black suit with white gloves was there, a yellow bib hastily thrown over his jacket. He looked at Theo, and didn't seem to understand, and growled through a world gone mad, "Sir we're evacuating please make your way to . . ."

And looked at where his muster point should have been, and saw only wreckage, and was for a moment not sure what to do.

"Sir please . . . please make your way calmly to the front car park, where there will be . . . will be . . . do you need medical attention do you . . . ?"

He'd only ever been taught one procedure for an evacuation, and it hadn't involved there being a bomb round the back. His mouth went numb, lips stopped moving. Theo stared into his face, and thought he looked very stupid, and felt very sorry for him, and looked back to where Helen wasn't moving, and said, yes, yes. I'll go. I'm going. I'm fine. Yes.

And went back inside.

And followed all instructions to proceed calmly and quickly to his designated exit.

And did not answer his phone.

And knew he had not failed, and thought that Dani walked with him, and that his daughter would be ashamed of who he had been, and who he had become.

Chapter 67

Seph Atkins phoned the police eight miles outside Virginia Water.

She'd reached the conclusion it was the smart move. Making them give chase would only increase the value of the indemnity, and whatever had happened, she would be safe.

She would be safe.

She would be . . .

The racecourse put on complimentary transport for anyone who needed it, to their destination of choice. If you had passed through the Ascot cordon, you could expect a certain level of service, of discretion and respect. This wasn't the first time people had targeted them. People were so resentful, they just lashed out, lucky really that more guests weren't hurt, it was all so deeply unpleasant.

Bea and Corn took a taxi to Victoria Station.

They couldn't find Theo in the crowd, and he didn't answer his phone.

Five hours after Seph Atkins was taken into custody, the police came to Mala Choudhary's door.

She said, "But this is ridiculous, get your hands off me – get your hands off me!" and was for a moment so shocked that she forgot she was a lawyer, and punched a policeman instead. That got her Tasered and put in handcuffs, but at least the cop wound up with a broken jaw. She'd have been disappointed in herself if he'd got away with anything less.

*

On the canal Theo is ice he is ice there is ice around the boat there is ice in the morning which they crack with a hammer there is ice and the snow turns all things black and grey it cuts down vision it reduces the land to silence to

In the prison Lucy Cumali writes:

> ♥♥♥What I love about this product is that it does so much more than what it says on the packaging. Really transformed my skincare ritual!!! ♥♥♥

Last night her bunk mate was put on half rations for not complying with company-standard review practices. Her bunk mate is twelve years old, and weighs five and a half stone. They say she's a burden; a real economic burden.

Seph Atkins said, "I want my lawyer."
    And Seph Atkins said, "I want my lawyer."
    And Seph Atkins said, "I want my lawyer."
    And when her lawyer came, she said, "This is the wrong lawyer," and he replied:
    "I'm afraid Ms Choudhary has been arrested. There were funds found in your account which appear to have come from her. This impropriety renders her unable to conduct your defence and so . . ."

Corn and Bea went back to the house in Archway, and turned on the TV, and discovered that a wonderful celebrity couple were looking forward to twins – twins they'd be so adorable! – and that the price of Marmite was rising again, if you liked that sort of thing, but it was all right because there was strong growth in the banking sector for the ninth consecutive quarter.

Theo did not answer his phone.

In the police station Seph Atkins said, "Okay. Okay. Yeah, I was hired to do Helen Arnslade. I was given a time, a place where she'd be. They said she'd go to the races, and then leave by the back, through the car park. They gave me the number plate of the car she'd be driving. Said she was having a meet there, all hush-hush, and to do her when she left. That was my brief."

And her lawyer said, "And the money?"

"It came from Choudhary."

"I'm afraid Ms Choudhary is denying that she ever sent you a penny."

A shrug.

"You do see how this situation is complicated . . . "

Another shrug.

Three cells down:

"No check again – *check again*! Yes, I represented Atkins but I never hired her, I never . . . do my kids know what's going on? You don't tell them, you don't . . . you don't fucking tell them!"

In the hospital room Philip Arnslade stares down at the sleeping form of his mother and is for a while silent as the choices of his life, the mad, headlong rush of recollection – no, of something worse; of *introspection*, of that terrifying reliving of the past in the present, of looking back and asking the questions now that perhaps should have been asked *then* – floods upon him.

And at the end of it, a thought strikes him, and it is certain, and it nearly sends him onto the floor, but his security man is standing right behind him, and puts a steadying hand on his arm, and always seems to know what Philip needs.

"Fuck," whispers Philip Arnslade as revelation dawns. And then: "Fuck!" And one last time, to make sure that it's real, to run the question again and see if it returns the same response. "Fuck. *It was meant to be me.*"

Later, it started to snow.

Chapter 68

Neila and Theo sat together on the roof of the *Hector* as the snow fell, and in the distance watched Scunthorpe burn.

Neila put her head on Theo's shoulder. He wrapped one arm around her, pulling her close. The smoke was a beacon drifting off to the south, pulled high and thin by the wind. The flames were a spinning orange dance in the sky on the horizon.

At last Neila said, "So you did that?"

"In a way."

"You burned it all?"

"Not that place per se . . . "

"But you burned the country?"

"I suppose."

"And killed people?"

He didn't answer.

"To get your daughter back?"

No reply.

Neila shuffled in a little closer, enjoying his thin warmth, and for a little while longer they watched the flames.

"Cool," she breathed, letting her eyes drift shut as if she could feel the heat of the fire from the water's edge, warming through to the bottom of her soul.

Three days after two bombs went off at Ascot the British government froze the assets of the Company.

Philip Arnslade, minister of fiscal efficiency, made the choice unilaterally. It was within his power, after all, and the civil

366

servants who made the call were surprised to discover that they actually could make this happen.

The banks said: are you kidding me no way that'll destroy everything the Company is the banks the banks are the Company we can't just stop trading their assets this is …

So the minister of fiscal efficiency ordered the Nineteen Committee to exercise its emergency powers, which it did, and shut down the banks' computer systems.

The Cabinet, when they found out, exploded, and demanded in fairly short order that the computers were unlocked, the assets unfrozen and that Philip Arnslade resigned. Unfortunately, by that time Philip Arnslade had vanished for a vital meeting some- where – Birmingham, perhaps, or was it Hull? – and the calls they made to his phone went straight to voicemail.

By the time the Cabinet met fully at 2.40 a.m., they had all received the same file. They'd seen it before, of course, on the day it was released on the internet. Helen Arnslade, reciting the names of the dead. Names of places. National Insurance num- bers. Bodies tumbling into graves. Severed limbs and walking skeletons. There was nothing new in this. Even those who hadn't fully appreciated or suspected weren't as surprised as they wished they had been.

What was surprising was that this time the file came from Philip Arnslade.

The Company tried to kill me and my mother, he explained. *This has gone too far.*

The debate on whether to unfreeze Company assets and reopen the banks raged on until 9.45 a.m., by which time the files had been re-released to the internet, and the search blockers appeared not to be working any more. Cabinet chose not to act at this time. It seemed the least dangerous course.

Nine hours later, Philip Arnslade resurfaced in Wales, where he had taken temporary residence in a castle, along with thirty armed men and a news crew.

Chapter 69

The phone call that evening between Simon Fardell and Philip Arnslade wasn't recorded, but no one in proximity to either end of it could have missed the basic gist.

"Philip, it's Simon, and what the fuck do you think you are fucking doing? I will fucking burn you I will fucking ... I DIDN'T FUCKING TRY TO KILL YOU OR YOUR FUCKING MOTHER WHAT THE FUCK DO YOU all right all right. Okay. Let's just ... think this through, shall we? Let's just talk about this, let's just ... okay ... "

There would be no trial for either Seph Atkins or Mala Choudhary.

Seph Atkins confessed, cleanly and precisely as she always had.

"I was hired to kill Helen Arnslade. I was given a time and a place. I received payment from Mala Choudhary. No, I never spoke to her. That is all I have to say at this time."

For her own protection she was transferred to a high-security prison where the inmates made concealer sticks and foundation for fair and pale skin. Seph Atkins said not a word as they loaded her into the truck, not a word as they took her through the prison gates. She made no sound as she was strip-searched and dressed in the inmates' yellow jumpsuit branded with the logo of the cosmetic company and inspiring brand slogans – "Be the true you!" and "Inner beauty, outside."

On her second night someone tried to beat her up, just because that was how they showed who was boss, and their body was found face down in a vat of boiling pig fat. Seph was put into isolation, and transfer orders came from somewhere, and a van came to collect her, and some time after that the paperwork was lost, and she was not seen again.

Mala Choudhary said, "I didn't do it. I didn't hire her. I DIDN'T HIRE HER. I don't know how the money left my account. I've been robbed. I don't know how the Company money came into my account either. THIS IS A SET-UP can't you see this is a set-up you stupid fucking . . . "

And two days later she said, crying, "I did it. It was me. I did it alone. Will my kids be all right? They're at this great school, they really love it, and there's all these extracurricular activities they both really love music camp they really love it, they love music camp please don't take them away from the school. Please don't take them away from it."

She too might have vanished, but at the last moment, as they led her towards the edge of the pit on the outskirts of Dagenham, freshly dug and ready to be sealed over with a skimming of hot tar, she remembered that she was the South London Women's Flyweight MMA champion three years in a row, and she roundhouse-kicked the nearest guy in the gut and smashed another man's nose against her kneecap, and only as she turned to deal with the final bloke did he have the nerve to shoot her, twice in the leg, once in the belly, once in the chest, his arm sweeping up in an uneasy, jerking arc as he fired.

A further two bullets went astray. One severed the femoral artery of his colleague with the broken nose, who bled out in less than four minutes in the back of the truck. The other hit the wall of the empty, abandoned warehouse behind, and on the ricochet lodged in the ankle of the man doubled over his bruised stomach, who only noticed it five hours later and never walked the same again.

With all the fuss, they didn't properly bury Mala's body, and a dog-walker found it nine hours later, the vat of tar cold and set to a solid cylinder next to her carcass.

*

Somewhere from a castle in Wales, Philip Arnslade roars, "KILL ME KILL MY FUCKING MOTHER I mean she was an embarrassment, a problem yes, she was a real problem and I was embarrassed, I was personally embarrassed, I was . . . "

Markse has given up trying to get a word in edgeways, so sits patiently, left leg crossed over right, and flicks through the pictures of the dead, the pictures of the vanished, as Helen Arnslade's voice continues to drone its endless litany of corpses from the laptop on the coffee table.

"When my mother started with her shit, Simon was furious. He's always had a temper, don't you believe the things he says, he's always been a . . . but he was furious he said we should just have killed her when she betrayed us the first time, just kill my FUCKING MOTHER ARE YOU FUCKING LISTENING TO ME?"

Markse smiles, nods, and that seems to be enough.

"KILL MY MOTHER so I'm searching the country and we stop it, we tidy things up, yes, there's a scandal but it passes we shut it down by now Simon worries that I'm 'unreliable' and I think, hold on there matey, and then he PUTS A FUCKING BOMB IN FUCKING ASCOT fucking uses the SAME FUCKING LAWYER and the SAME FUCKING KILLER-BITCH to try and fucking kill me he doesn't even have the decency to try and cover it up 'liability' he said 'loose cannon' well I'll fucking . . . "

It occurs to Markse, somewhere in the midst of all this, that his employers – whoever they are now – perhaps lack some of the temperament that he would otherwise wish of those in high office.

Chapter 70

Five days after the banks shut down, Theo found Helen Arnslade.

The hospital was south of Greenwich, with a view up the hill towards the observatory and the green laser that shot out into overcast skies to mark the line of the Greenwich Meridian, dividing the world between east and west. He'd already searched every other likely hospital in London, and was about to try and force his way back into the Cotswolds when he stumbled on her, sleeping in a private, guarded room on the third floor, on a wing reserved for patients on life support, in comas or permanent vegetative states. She'd been signed in as Mrs Danesmoor, and no further notes on her condition were kept. Theo waited for the late-night cleaners to go on shift, and whispered to a sallow-eyed man with a mop bucket and a limp, "Blessed are her hands . . ."

And he grasped Theo's arms below the elbows before he could answer and hissed, "Is it true? Is there a queen in the north? Will there be a rebellion? Are we going to be free?"

Theo didn't have an answer, couldn't find anything good to say, so he lied. "Yes," he whispered. "Yes. It's all true."

The man wept, and as he stripped out of his uniform and passed Theo his access pass, the tears rolled down his blotched, sponge-cake face, and he gibbered thanks and prayers to an unknown deity, and Theo thought perhaps he should offer comfort, and didn't know what to say.

Instead, he cleaned the hospital.

He mopped floors, sprayed sinks, sprayed bleach around toilets, kept trundling up and down, shoulders hunched, feet shuffling the slow-motion shuffle of someone with nowhere to go, nothing to do, just going through the motions. It was a natural walk for him, he found, and comforting to a weary brain.

There were very few doctors, and only a couple of nurses on shift. The hospital was owned by a company which was owned by a company which was . . .

However that old song went. Somewhere at the top of the pile there was the Company. On the TV, Philip Arnslade faced the camera. The volume was muted, but subtitles took their best shot at an accurate rendition, lighting up his words in cyan on a black background.

The Company
Abused its responsibility
Government forced to
Reconsider its relationship with
Revoking contracts to

A few minutes later Simon Fardell's face appeared.

The stoppages
Hospitals
Banks
Schools
Buses
Trains
Supermarkets
Farms
Food
Water

. . . all the government's fault. If they seize our assets let's see who folds first let's see who's really . . .

The TV station was owned by a company which was owned by a company which was . . .

And at midnight it too went offline, when the video techs realised they weren't going to get their salary for the week, and they had to get to the shops before the last of the petrol and food went.

At 2.17 a.m. the man guarding the door to Helen's room in a hospital in Greenwich fell asleep, and Theo let himself in.

The light through the half-open blinds on the window was a pink-orange reflection of street light. A car passed below, the sweep of its beams running like a clock hand across the ceiling. Fresh yellow flowers were beginning to droop a little in murky water by the bed. A flask of water was empty on a tray, a bowl of stewed pears had not been touched, the custard solidifying to yellow concrete.

Helen lay, one arm stretched by her side, the stub of the other arm wrapped in pristine white bandage. An accordion of blue plastic and clear tubes rose and fell by her side, supplementing the progress of her lungs, the end of the machine plugged into a careful incision in her trachea. Her face was rounded, purple-brown; she wore surgical socks beneath the blue blankets, her toes peeping out the end. A sac of clear fluid was nearly empty on its hook by her head, the line running into a needle hidden somewhere beneath her loose green robe.

Theo leaned his mop against the wall, pulled up a huge padded beige armchair covered with plastic that stuck to skin and held the white tidemarks of previous sweaty inhabitants. The pump by her bed inhaled, clicked to full, exhaled in a long *whoosh*. Her chest rose, fell. At the foot of her bed yellow fluid drip-drip-dripped out of a tube into a plastic litre-jar, nearly full, of faintly bloodied amber liquid. Theo watched her.

> The packaging said that this was a revolution in a box, and it didn't lie! I really know what it means to make a difference now! *****

Lucy has a new bunk mate, after Moira became too thin to work and was taken away for reassessment. Hanna doesn't know who

373

her mum is. By day she tells Lucy that she's a stupid slag and even the men wouldn't bother to rape her. By night they lie together, holding each other tight, sharing warmth against the winter, and never speak of these things, and are silent, and it's okay to be afraid.

Blessed is her name, blessed are her hands upon the water blessed is the mother who gives life to the child blessed is the moonlight through the bars blessed are the whisperers of the hidden truths blessed are those who stood before the fire blessed is the heat of the ash blessed is

Neila said, "Navigating the Trent to the Ouse requires a licence. It's tidal where it meets the Humber, there's a two-day transit on the lock it's . . . "

Theo sat in the cabin of the *Hector* as she put his hand on the deck of cards and said, "Ask a question."

"I don't know what to ask."

"Think of something that matters. Think of Lucy."

A flicker of a frown, anger almost, which went as quickly as it had come. He closed his eyes, hand below hers, and let out a breath, and held the tarot pack tightly.

They waited

He cut the cards

dealt the top nine.

She turned them over.

He studied the arrangement on the table. "What does it mean?" he asked at last.

"Nothing," she replied, heart leaping, tears of relief and gratitude pricking the corners of her eyes. "Nothing at all."

Stood.

Went to the locker above the sink.

Opened it.

Removed the gun from inside, still wrapped in the same plastic bag it had been when Corn gave it to Theo in Nottingham. Said, "I was going to throw it overboard. I wanted to. I was so angry with you I was so angry. But I think . . . "

Put it in his hand.

"I think this is maybe where you get off."

Theo sat by Helen's bed, and Dani was there too, and so was the real Theo Miller, the one who died, and it seemed to Theo that the past was just a present-tense thing that happened in his mind as he thought about it, not real at all, and that the future could only really be experienced in the present too and thus probably wasn't real enough to worry about and that . . .

That he was very tired and that

Dani forgive me Dani forgive me I don't know any way to I will always be there is no forgetting there is no forgiving I just stood there I didn't listen I didn't think forgive me forgive me there was there isn't I shall never

Theo stopped praying when he realised that he was talking out loud, and looked down at the floor, and wondered if anyone had heard him, and when he looked up again, one of Helen's eyes was open and fixed on him.

For a moment they sat together, watching each other.

Helen blinked, slow, once, twice, waiting.

Twitched, with her one good hand, tried to move it, couldn't.

Twitched again.

Made a sound.

Uh – uh – huh.

The sound broke away against nothing.

Theo flapped, muttered, what do you . . . what can I . . .

Felt useless and dumb.

Rummaged in the bedside table. Found a piece of paper, a pen.

Put it carefully under Helen's hand, balanced on the back of a dustpan.

She took an age to write, and every second was an eternity, and it was over in a moment.

END

375

Theo folded the piece of paper over.

Put it in his pocket. Pulled another piece of paper from the pad. Put it under her hand. Her one good eye narrowed, and again she wrote.

END

Theo sat back in the armchair, and stared at the ceiling.

Realised he hated hospitals.

Hadn't known that until this moment.

At his feet the bottle of amber fluid was full, beginning to back up into the drain. No one came to change it. A pair of bellows inhaled, clicked, exhaled, and so did Helen.

He thought he should say something profound.

Thought he should find words that mattered.

Nothing came to mind.

He reached over, and unplugged the tube that ran into Helen's throat. Air whistled from the plastic. Her body rose, sank.

She didn't die.

For a while she lay there, and gasped.

Gasped, eye wide, fixed on him, blinking.

Gasped.

Wheezed.

Shuddered.

Gasped.

Didn't look away.

She took nearly an hour and a half to die.

For a little while Theo was terrified.

Then he was hopeful, because she wasn't dying, so maybe she would live.

Then he thought he should plug the tubes back in, and nearly cried because he didn't.

Then he was angry, because she was dying, and no one came, and no one cared.

Then he was bored, and was immediately guilty that he was bored.

All the time she watched him, and she struggled to breathe and did not look away from him, and after a while he held her

376

hand in his, and she squeezed it once, and did not die, and did not die, and did not die, but lay a wounded shell.

And in the end, she died.

There wasn't even a heart monitor to beep, an alarm to sound.

She exhaled, and a little foam popped around the hole in her throat, and she exhaled no more, and she died.

Chapter 71

Neila moored in an inlet of Keadby Junction, stood on the prow of the *Hector*, and watched Theo walk away.

In the afternoon that fucking cormorant finally pissed off too, stupid bloody bird.

It'd be back.

That was just the way things were.

Theo – the boy who would be Theo – sat by the sea with Dani Cumali, and she said:

"I'm gonna change things. This whole system is so fucked up, you know? It's so fucked up, and people are just like, you'll grow up and you'll learn, and I'm like, fuck yeah, like you've learned yeah? but you know what people are like. Patronising wankers. You gotta remember what matters, you've gotta ..."

Or maybe she didn't. Maybe Theo's making it up, now that time is becoming a little ... now that his memories are more confused than they were, now that he might have a daughter who probably isn't his and now that the life he built from a lie isn't anything that matters at all, everything is sort of ...

And Dani Cumali dies at Seph Atkins' hands, and her daughter's name isn't on her lips.

But as she dies it occurs to her that things would have been better if she *had* whispered Lucy's name, it would have been a proper way of doing things, and she is briefly annoyed that she was so busy being scared and in pain, and didn't manage to fit it in.

Not least because, now she's here, she finds nothing else really matters as much after all.

In a hospital in Greenwich, Helen Arnslade dies.

She does not smile, and as her body turns from a living thing into limp biology in a bed, Theo adds up the value of her life.

Approximately £5.8 million, give or take.

Assuming she wasn't hiding any undeclared medical conditions or didn't give excessively to charity.

He waits a little while longer, then gets up, and walks away.

And on New Year's Eve Theo Miller walks away from the canal, a gun in his hand, Neila at his back, the sun hidden behind snow-threatening clouds, and has only one destination in mind, and only one thought in his trigger finger.

Chapter 72

Nearly fourteen days after two bombs went off in Ascot, Theo returned to Newton Bridge.

The men came out of the woods with guns and shouting and rage and hunger in their eyes, and he let them shove him from one side to the other and kick and roar, and this time they didn't dump him in a cold, grey room, but dragged him straight up the hill to where Good Queen Bess was making an especially disgusting cup of camomile tea.

And she looked up as he was thrown onto the floor at her feet, and tutted and said, "You look like shit. Dog?"

It took Theo a little while to understand what she meant, until the strips of dried spaniel meat were produced, which he ate with his fingers off a blue and white willow-pattern plate.

In London, Markse said:

"There is good reason to think that Simon Fardell *didn't* order the hit on you or your mother, Mr Arnslade. There is footage of individuals at Ascot, including Mr Miller, which implicates them in the crime. Further, there is reason to believe that Ms Choudhary was not lying about having her financial information stolen . . ."

To Markse's surprise, this information didn't induce the gibbering relief he'd been expecting from the minister of fiscal efficiency. Instead, he found himself in the awkward position of having a grown man kneel at his feet, clutch at his trousers, exclaim:

"Oh Jesus oh fucking Jesus oh God I froze their fucking assets I froze their assets I thought Simon tried to kill me I did the only thing I could oh God oh God he's going to kill me!"

Markse wondered what he was meant to do next. In a career spanning the mundane through the petrifying, he'd never before had his employer cry onto his polished leather shoes, nor did he know quite what to make of this development.

Moreover, he hadn't been paid for ten days, and suspected he wasn't about to be paid any time soon. It had become apparent that the Company's contract for the collection of taxes hadn't included lump-sum payments to the government, but rather a constant trickling-in of weekly finances controlled and carefully managed to maximise the efficiency of investment over . . .

. . . he hadn't paid much attention to the details.

He was beginning to wish he had. The kitchen cupboard was getting quite bare, and the companies who delivered food to his local supermarket were owned by companies which were owned by . . .

And all things considered, the world was a mess.

And Markse couldn't abide mess.

Twenty-four hours later, Philip Arnslade unfroze Company funds.

The action came too late.

Of the estimated thirteen thousand people who had died in the electricity blackouts, water cut-offs, transport break-downs and failure to get access to clean drinking water and food, nearly nine thousand had been over the age of seventy, too old, frail or weak to make it to the resources on which they'd depended.

Another seven hundred and twenty had died when the police opened fire on rioters in Manchester and Birmingham.

Fourteen were Company Police, burned alive when their station was attacked. The crowds had danced around the building as they smoked and screamed, and kicked the still-burning bodies of those who'd thrown themselves from the windows, just to be sure they were dead.

In Shawford, formerly of Budgetfood, the ragers raged at the sea.

In the enclaves, the safe spaces on the cliffs, a man beat his wife to death for hoarding food. His indemnity would probably have been less than £100k, all things considered, but the police never came, and neither did the ambulance, and no one seemed to care.

At the Cotswold border the man babbled, "But the sheep are for the aesthetic the rural aesthetic they are part of the expected aesthetic of the—"

A woman hit him over the head with a shovel, and they left him for dead as they burst across the cordon to feast on fresh mutton and blood.

On the canal Neila watched the flames, and was grateful to be on the water.

A few trucks lumbered out of the processing plants with microwave meals and tins of food. No one was sure who was paying for this service, since the Company didn't seem to be taking responsibility for anything much, but it seemed like someone ought to try.

Philip Arnslade resigned.

"Markse," he whimpered as they led him to the helicopter. "Simon's going to kill me. I've broken it all. He's going to kill me. He's going to . . . "

"Now sir," murmured Markse, "I'm sure it'll all be . . . "

The roar of helicopter blades drowned him out as he pushed Philip on board. The minister's face was white as he stared out of the window, and on the ground below Markse felt he should almost be waving, smiling, a proud parent seeing a frightened child off to school. Markse was still watching the sky when, two minutes twenty-two seconds into the flight, Philip's helicopter exploded mid-air.

There were no survivors, and the spinning remains of a blade falling from the sky also killed a woman in the street below who was out looking for her cat.

No one seemed very interested in spending money on an investigation, and the funeral was held in private, an intimate family affair.

Chapter 73

Theo cycled through a country on fire.

The flames were distant, the paths were bumpy and rough.

The air was frozen winter glory, the sky was crystal blue.

In the morning the frost cracked underfoot.

In the evening he huffed out clouds of breath, and watched the golden peach of sunset tangle in the moisture.

Corn and Bea cycled with him.

Corn carried a rifle, slung across his shoulder.

Bea carried water, dried meat of uncertain provenance, a map and a torch.

Occasionally they left the cycle paths, and paused on little country lanes where the birds sang in the hedgerows and the signs pointed to villages of a hundred people, or to the North, or to the South, and didn't give distances for either of these ideas.

Sometimes they passed food trucks guarded by local police, their Company insignia stripped, or by local men armed with shotguns and fire axes.

Once they passed a doctor's clinic. A paper sign hung on the door. ALL WELCOME.

A woman pushed a pram away from the clinic, a child gurgling happily within. A woman with a Zimmer frame, bent into a right angle over her support, head bobbing up and down like a hungry deer to check her path as she walked, scowled at them as they passed by.

A queue snaked around the block to a broken hydrant from which fresh water flowed. A couple of teenagers had broken out boom boxes and were entertaining the crowds with home-made raps about revolution, love and how lonely it was smoking cigarettes by themselves cos no girl would give them sweet sweet lovin'.

The day before they reached the prison, they saw a TV on in a lit room, and passed a church hall where sleeping bags had been laid on the floor and tea was being served, and outside a wooden stake where a man had been hung to die of the cold, a sign around his neck: COMPANY MAN.

He hadn't been anyone senior, hadn't done anything wrong or exceeded the remit of his job. But his bosses had been faster getting out of town, and people knew him as the man who'd refused benefits when people didn't fulfil the economic productivity eligibility criteria, so when he'd vanished, no one had looked, and no one had come to take his corpse down for proper burial, until his wife found it two days later, and wept until her lungs spasmed in the cold, and she had to be helped home by her children, who understood only that they were big kids now, and everything had changed.

When they came to the prison, the gates were already open.

A wire-mesh fence enclosed a single-storey yellow-brick building laid out as a hexagon. Buddleia grew from the cracks in the wall, grass from the cracks in the concrete. A single basketball hoop stood at the back, never used. Small square windows, covered with white wire mesh. A guard post was a black-burned shell. The heavy blue-metal doors of the loading bay stood open, and a fox had already been inside and had a piss in the corner.

They left their bicycles at the main entrance, and walked inside. Speakers stood grey and silent. Cold morning light drifted through barred windows and frosted glass. Posters on the wall, torn in two, declared from loose beads of Blu Tack:

WORK FOR
REDEMPTION THROUGH
THE FUTURE IS
MAKING A BETTER
A scuttle of feet, a noise in the grey. Corn swung his rifle

round, holding it tight. Theo moved slowly down empty corridors, the bulbs dead, broken glass on the floor, doors knocked out of their frames. A workshop had already been gutted, the tools gone. A room of computers stood silent, screens shattered, the casings dented with hammers, chairs ripped in two, stuffing spread across the floor. In a dormitory a doll had been left tucked up neatly in bed, the only centre of calm in a world ripped apart. In a room of upended green chairs hung paintings in brilliant red and blue. Eyes, huge, gleaming. A child playing beneath a rainbow. A torn canvas where once there had been a picture of a house, smoke coming from the chimney.

A scuttle of feet, a whisper of voices.

Corn's hands tightened on the rifle. The night before, three men had emerged from the woods by their campsite, and for a while they had just watched each other, no one moving, no one speaking, Corn with rifle in hand, and after a while the men had left, and since then Corn had stood never more than a foot from Bea's side, and said not a word, and hadn't put the rifle down, even when he wanted to sleep.

Theo followed the sound.

Pushed open another door, another dormitory of bunk beds, grey metal frames and thin stained sheets. Mattresses were toppled onto the floor, sheets torn up, blankets pulled free. In one corner, the furthest from the door, a small igloo of mattress and blanket had been piled up, encasing darkness. He approached it slowly, crouched down a few feet from the narrow black entrance to this bedding cave. Said, "Hello."

The darkness didn't answer.

"My name's Theo. I'm looking for my daughter. Her name is Lucy. Is she here?"

Silence, except for a slight shifting of sheets within the wall of mattress.

Struggling to keep his voice calm, hold back the panic. "Her name's Lucy Cumali. Lucy ... Rainbow Princess. She was held here, she's about fifteen years old. I won't hurt you. I'm not angry. I just want to find my daughter."

"Gun!" whimpered a voice from inside the burrow. A child's voice, hard to tell boy or girl, too young to have definition.

Theo glanced back over his shoulder at Corn. "Would you mind waiting outside?" he asked softly.

Corn scowled, looked at Bea, who nodded. With a barely audible huff, he spun on his heel, marched out of the room. Bea squatted down next to Theo. "I'm Bea," she breathed. "We won't hurt you."

A hurried whispering within the den. A muttering of voices in dissent. A final settling on agreement. A stirring of sheets. Then a girl, nine or ten years old, emerged slowly, crawling on hands and knees. She wore several layers of jumpsuit done up over each other, but her lips were blue and her face was bone. At her back eyes blinked and bodies shifted. The girl seemed to think about standing, then changed her mind, and plonked down, cross-legged, a chief guarding the entrance to her territory, and glared at Theo and Bea.

"Food?"

Bea hesitated, then opened her bag, handed over a wrapped package of dry dog meat, a packet of biscuits.

The girl took it quickly, tried to hide her excitement, passed it back to hands that emerged greedily from within the tent, then turned to face them again, stiff as a sceptre.

"Gates got opened week ago," she barked. "Guards said they weren't being paid to deal with this shit, they had families to look after, so they upped and went. Couple of parents turned up too, like, busting in and that, but they only took the kids what mattered to them. Some of us ran away. Lot ran away. I said they were dumb. They wouldn't get nowhere. They'd just get into shit. So we stayed. We look after each other. That's what we do."

Theo licked his lips, waited on his haunches, seeing if there were any more pronouncements from this tiny monarch. When it seemed there were not, he glanced at Bea, then back to the girl, and breathed, "Lucy? Did you know Lucy? Is she here? I'm looking for my daughter."

"I knew her."

"Knew? Is she ... where is Lucy?" Bea's hand on his arm, holding him down even as his voice began to rise. He bit his lip, stared down at the floor, let out a breath, tried again. "Please. It's very important that I find her."

The girl thought for a moment, then nodded once, uncrossed her legs, rose to her feet and scampered past them, a light run, habit dictating speed. Theo uncurled and scampered after her. Corn jumped as they belted past him, but didn't leave his post at the door. The girl ran, knowing every twist and turn of the shattered prison, her domain, broken windows and broken doors, smoke stains up the walls from the kitchen, furniture overturned and cupboards stripped bare. She ran until she reached another dormitory, the door open and undamaged, and pointed, triumphant, proud of her success.

Theo followed the direction of her finger inside. Bunk beds, less damaged than those where the children huddled.

Sheets in disarray, thin and torn.

An explosion of polystyrene beads across the floor, from packaging ripped recklessly apart, he wasn't sure how long ago.

A photo on one wall.

The photo was new, stuck in place with masking tape.

Lucy glowered at the camera, daring it to make anything of her blotchy face, acne-pocked and starved of sun. Theo peeled the photo carefully away, turned it over.

On the back someone had written in neat biro.

MARKSE

Theo marches from the prison as the children look on and
   Corn is all what the hell what
   And Bea silences him and
   Theo strides past the gate past the bicycles makes it to the road outside
   And the children are clustered outside now, five of them, what's happening why is the man sad why is he angry there is

*

388

Neila has a compass on her boat, it points north. Somewhere in the north there is her soul, there is the centre to which all things return, there is the fall there is the sky there is

"I did my best," she whispers as the world spins and the cards tell only lies. "I did my best. I did my best. I did my best."

Mala Choudhary's kids are taken out of school now that Mummy is gone we can't pay for these nice things you see we can't afford to have music but it'll be all right it'll be

The real Theo Miller lies in an unmarked grave and laughs and laughs and laughs at the funny old way of things and

Theo made it fifty yards before falling down.

It wasn't a sideways tumble or a face-down flop.

He was standing, and then he was sitting cross-legged in the middle of the street, a sack of potatoes dumped from tired hands. Corn followed, still trying to understand. Bea shushed him with a hard slice of her hands, then shuffled up to Theo, sat down by his side.

Held his hands in hers.

Whispered, "Theo? Theo? What does it mean? What does it mean?"

The picture of Lucy, crunched to a broken tube in his fist.

"Theo? Talk to me. Tell me what it means?"

He looked up at her, and cried, and didn't say a word.

Theo didn't speak for two days.

He obeyed commands, and they cycled, and he did not speak.

And one night Bea lay down next to Corn on the frozen ground, and Corn held her tight, and that was good, and they didn't talk about it, and kept on cycling.

And then

When one of the TV stations was broadcasting again, its crew paid in vegetables, beer and promises, and the pundits were beginning to pundit and there was sometimes cabbage in the shops again, Simon Fardell held a press conference, and announced that the Company was going to commence a major restructuring programme resulting in the dissolving of several major assets and that all things considered he was grateful for the opportunity to reassess the corporate structure of

and there was Lucy.

There was Lucy.

There was Lucy.

There was

Lucy.

They watched it on the one working TV in Newton Bridge.

Theo hadn't spoken, and did not speak when he saw his daughter's face, and Bea thought she recognised it from the photo but couldn't be sure, and everyone else cheered and said it was great, it was the beginning of something amazing, and there was a party that night complete with bad singing and home-distilled alcohol that bypassed the digestive tract and went straight to the retina.

And there was Lucy.

She was

Lucy.

For a while Theo thought it wasn't her, but knew it was, and knew her face and there was

Lucy

Glaring at the camera, dressed in a silly duck-blue dress with a white collar

Heidi Fardell's hand resting on her shoulder

Lucy

Lucy who is my

SHE'S YOUR DAUGHTER

who is my

Lucy who is

who is

obviously there are the usual words there are love heart soul burning fire ice pain guilt grief there is

*

390

And Theo sees his daughter's face and walks into the bathroom and locks the door and kneels and prays to a god who isn't there he prays and prays as the tears flow

Blessed is her name, blessed are her hands upon the water, blessed is the shadow at the door forgive me forgive me forgive me forgive me

After

He went to find Bea, who lived in an attic above what had once been the undertaker's. And he sat on the end of her bed as she huddles, knees hugged to her chin, wrapped in wool and dirty cotton, and he says:

"I've got to go to London."

Bea's head tilted a little to the side, waiting.

"They have my daughter, they . . . I have to . . . I'm sorry. I'm very sorry. I thought maybe I could be a hero and then they . . . so I'm not. It turns out I'm not after all."

"Do you need anything?"

He shook his head. "I'll cut across to the railway line. If they don't arrest me on the train, they'll get me in the city. Bess will try to stop me."

She shrugged.

"I think . . . when I'm gone, this place won't be safe. Tell Bess. Tell her it won't be safe."

"Bess won't leave here."

"She might have to."

"She won't."

"Please, I . . . "

Stopped.

Stared at the ceiling.

Stared at the floor.

Stood up.

"When I get to London," he said, "they will tell me how they'll hurt my daughter. And I'll do anything to keep her safe. Anything."

Walked away, without another word.

Chapter 74

Theo sneaked out of Newton Bridge in the middle of the night, and no one stopped him.

He crawled through bracken, and when no one came shouting, he walked down the side of the road, and when no vehicles passed, he walked down the middle, following white broken lines. Once a drone passed overhead, scouring the countryside for runners, screamers, ragers, ready to shoot, or maybe just flying because it still had power and it pleased its owner to fly, and Theo just kept on walking, reasoning that there was no hiding from this eye in the sky, and so he may as well not bother. And if they saw him, he wasn't interesting enough, not a runner, not a screamer, so it buzzed on by.

In the morning he came to a motorway fenced off on either side to guard against the world. Two or three cars passed in ten minutes, and he followed it until he found a smaller road bending off to the west, towards a town with an empty market square and a hotel that offered Thai massage and Sunday roast. Two cars were pulled up outside, bare concrete between the door and the empty square where once there had been stalls selling bruised bananas and replacement phone screens. Theo looked for any sign of other life, and couldn't see any, save for a single woman, hair wrapped in a white towel, body swathed in dressing gown and flannel slippers, who stood on the balcony of the hotel and looked out and seemed astonished to see him.

He drifted to the station.

There was one train a day. By 4.17, when the train came, the empty town had produced forty or fifty travellers, waiting in silence on the platform. Theo couldn't pay for a ticket, but there wasn't a barrier, and no one at the counter to sell him anything or call him out for his crime.

The train smelled of broken toilet and diesel. He stood, face pressed to the glass, swaying as it rattled south towards York. No ticket inspectors boarded, and at York he changed to a larger train, growling engine and less pee, heading towards London, and waited to be arrested. People stood pressed armpit to armpit, nothing to hold on to except each other. An old woman had a duck in a bag. A young man held a baby, no carrier or straps for support, wrapped up in his jacket, pressed to his chest. No one spoke, no one met anyone else's eye, no ticket inspectors came.

At Peterborough there wasn't enough room for people to get on, and a fight broke out. The train began to pull away before it was resolved, leaving a woman howling on the platform, a door open. A man was pushed backwards out of it as the people crammed on board reached a collective decision, landing with a bone-crack on the platform below.

No one was waiting to arrest Theo in London, and he shoved through the open barrier behind a mother and her child and didn't even bother to feel guilty.

Walked.

Sat a while by the river.

Maybe even slept, until the cold started him awake again.

Walked again, to the Kensington toll. It was manned not by people in Company uniform, but men in suits, local residents who, as this service had lapsed, had decided to take up the burden themselves. Theo almost laughed at the absurdity of it, and approached the pedestrian gate. "My name is Theo Miller. I'm here to be arrested."

The man he spoke to raised his eyebrows, sucked in his lips. "Uhhhh ..."

Theo smiled. "Do you want to call the police, or shall I just go to the station directly?"

"I uh . . . don't know if the police are running a full service . . . "

"I'll just go and turn myself in then, shall I?"

The man thought about this for a while, then shrugged, nodded, and stepped aside as Theo passed through.

Twenty-five minutes later, Theo knocked on the door of Simon Fardell's Kensington home. A man with a bulge under his left arm and the look of one who punched bears answered the door. "Yeah?"

Behind him a woman's voice called, "Who is it?"

Before the man could answer, she appeared at the door, pushing her head through the gap between chest and door frame to scrutinise Theo, nose wrinkled up, eyebrows down.

"Good afternoon, ma'am. My name is Theo Miller. I believe your employers have kidnapped my daughter. May I come in?"

The woman was in her early forties, and her efforts – make-up, lipstick, surgery – to appear as if she were in her twenties only made her seem older. Her face was vaguely familiar, from the TV, perhaps. Her hair was dyed blonde, cut to a balloon that bounced just above her shoulders. She blurted, "Oh goodness oh my!" and for a moment looked like she might cry. Then, composing herself hastily, added, "Would you mind waiting in the kitchen?"

Chapter 75

A very nice kitchen. It was possibly the nicest kitchen Theo had ever seen, which probably meant the people who owned it were also very, very nice. Black marble surfaces, polished taps, two dishwashers, fridge with ice maker and crushed-ice dispenser, and a nozzle for filtered cold water.

Theo picked dirt out of his nails and enjoyed flicking it onto the floor.

He was hungry, and wondered if anyone would mind him poking around in the cupboards. A chubby woman in maroon and green sat with him, playing on her smartphone, one leg folded over the other, face contracted in a frown, her hair haloed with a gentle fuzz of spray. At night she dreams of pulling out her hair one strand at a time and finding, instead of a little bulb of white root on the end, two tiny beetles twined in love, which begin to untangle and scuttle away as she disturbs them, until she slams her fist into them on the wall, smearing them into black-red smudges.

In Kensington nothing much has changed, except now people really, really don't like to go outside the confines of the borough.

"Can I make some tea?" asked Theo, and the woman shrugged, so he put the kettle on and went through the cupboard above the sink in search of teabags until, with a huff of indignation, she opened a drawer by the fridge to reveal a panoply of herbs and brews.

The kettle boiled, but amid the lemongrass and lavender there wasn't any proper builder's.

Theo had ginger tea, and didn't notice if it tasted of anything much.

"So," he said after a while. "I heard that the Company is pulling out of all UK business operations."

She shrugged.

"Cos of the riots. And the mass murders. And all of that."

Another shrug.

"Heard Simon Fardell put a hit out on Philip Arnslade and his mum."

A little huff now, the woman getting bored with all of this. "Whatever," she grunted, eyes not rising from the movement of one busy finger across the greasy surface of her phone. "Just the way things work, isn't it? Just how it goes."

Theo smiled a paper smile, and drank his tea.

Markse stood in the door, a man in grey behind him. The woman glanced up, sighed, put her phone back in her pocket and left. Markse sat on a high chrome stool opposite Theo, the empty tea mug cold between them, laced his fingers beneath his chin, rested his face on their weave.

"Mr Miller."

"Markse."

"You look . . ."

"Where's Lucy?"

"Upstairs."

"She's here? In this house?"

"Yes."

"*Why?*" Fury, indignation, a sudden surge of violence inside Theo's soul he didn't realise he had left in him.

"Because Simon Fardell wants to hurt you, very much." Markse, uninterested in such things. "He blames you for Philip Arnslade's death, even though he killed him. He blames you for riots against the Company, for the destruction of property and wealth, even though they have been committing mass murder for nearly a dozen years. He's not wrong, of course, but even I find this ... " A pause as he hunted for the word, which he couldn't find. A half-shake of his head. "Personal is not good policy." The commandment by which Markse had lived his life – a sacred mantra.

"I want to see her."

"You can see Cumali's daughter ... *your* daughter ... "

Theo flinched, Markse smiled without humour or relish. A question answered; a suspicion confirmed.

" ... but there are some questions."

"Lucy first."

Markse's head turned a little to one side, contemplating Theo's face, listening to a sound only he could hear. Then, brisk, standing, straightening his grey trousers, walking towards the kitchen door.

Theo followed.

The carpets were thick, pale cream and not meant to be sullied by shoes.

There were black and white photos on the wall, great feats of architecture viewed from strange angles, fractals of metalwork and giddy tangles of timber and stone, a monochrome cat caught licking its paw as it sat on the wing of an aeroplane – it all probably had some sort of meaning, something about ...

On the second floor, a closed white door. Markse knocked once, then opened it with a click of latch, a round brass handle, cold daylight seeping through from outside, the sound of gunfire, far off and bitten down at the edges.

sofa

giant TV screen

wires across the floor

Lucy sat cross-legged in the middle of it all.

She wore pyjama bottoms and a green fleece jumper. She was shooting aliens. The aliens were half mechanoid, half insect, with six flailing limbs, guns held in four of them, and couldn't aim for shit. Lucy's gun fired pale purple bullets of light and every now and then she charged up some sort of special attack that made the screen shake and go briefly white and left many scattered pieces of dead things all over the place, but the landscape seemed oddly okay.

"Lucy," said Markse. "This is Mr Miller."

"Hi," she grunted, not taking her eyes from the screen.

"Mr Miller, this is Lucy Rainbow Fardell. She's been sponsored by the Fardell family. She had some . . . difficulties . . . but now the family are paying her way and keeping her from . . . well. Are you enjoying your game, Lucy?"

"Yeah."

A grimace flickered across her face as a new alien started lobbing something green and sticky that exploded in an emerald splash across the screen. She rolled behind cover, reloaded, came back up shooting, jumped, jumped again, landed next to a scuttling centipede thing that spat hot acid, killed it with knives, then ran to avoid another blast of digital gloop.

Markse looked at Theo; Theo stared at Lucy.

"Mr Miller?"

Theo didn't move.

An arm on his arm, gentle. "Mr Miller? We should leave Lucy to her game."

"Mr Miller?"

"Mr Miller?"

"Mr Miller?"

An alien died.

Lucy's eyes flickered up from the game, met Theo's.

A flicker of

                well she doesn't know what's on his face but odds are that weird look is just another weird fucking thing so

                  deal with it the way you always

      scowl

shrug

      look away

collect loot from fallen machine-alien corpses

      carry on.

Bang bang splat bang *wowzers*!

This is of course the moment when Theo is going to say something profoundly important, something to establish some sort of

"I hope you enjoy your game," he says as Markse guides him away.

Chapter 76

They took him to some place in east London, near the Mile End enclaves. It had been a wood workshop where they made bespoke furniture, nice dressers for you to put your pretty things in, bespoke handrails – really hard to make a handrail actually it took a huge amount of craft to balance the twist with the drop but

now it was a prison.

They gave him a grey tracksuit and white T-shirt to wear, shoes without laces, bright trainers he wondered where they'd found them and time is

Neila does a three-point turn on the canal. It's tricky, you can see the place where metal hull has rammed concrete towpath, but if she's careful . . .

And having turned she turns again to point back north, then realises that's ridiculous and turns again and for a while is spinning, spinning and time is

time is

the real Theo Miller, the one who died

now when they were in the back of the ambulance did he say

it's your fault

it's not your fault

it's your fault

it's not your fault

it's your fault it's your fault it's your fault it's

*

400

They gave him porridge with jam, which was remarkably nice, and they sat down at a grey table in a grey room and Markse said:

"What happened with Helen Arnslade?"

Theo's words were a drone from a script he's already read, bored, tired, enough. "She found out her son was hiding the mass murder and kidnapping of patties and people from the enclaves. The skint. People who wouldn't be missed. Petty crooks who got lost in the system. He was feeding slaves to Simon Fardell, the Company and the patty line. Helen wasn't impressed. She gathered proof and gave it to Dani Cumali. Her son found out and dosed Helen with drugs. Had Dani killed."

"And you and Dani were . . . ?"

"We'd been friends once."

"But Lucy is your daughter."

"Yes. Perhaps. No. She might be."

"She . . . might be?"

"Yes."

"You did this for . . . 'might be'?"

"Yes."

"Why?"

Theo thought about it for a long time. Shrugged. "I imagine . . . that after nearly fifteen years of playing along, keeping my head down and selling indemnities against murder, I imagine . . . something had to change. Something had to switch, otherwise I'm just . . . " Stopped, searching the air for the word. "I am, fundamentally, a failure. I've known this most of my life. Since I was a child, it was always clear to me that the world I inhabited was not one I had contributed to. Everything that was good, other people made and paid for with their own sacrifice. Everything that was bad, I couldn't control. All the ideas and dreams I thought were mine were in fact someone else's, and the more I talked about taking control, being my own man, all the things you're meant to say, the more I was talking to cover the very simple truth, that I wasn't. I am not. I made some choices, of course, but they weren't defiant acts of judgement. They were made because the alternatives were significantly worse. I coasted down the path I had with the feeling that it was the only path that was really before me, and when I chose to choose to do nothing, it felt like a kind of release, an admission that this was my life and I may as well live it. Nothing changed. Murderers walked free, people died and begged and grovelled and lives were destroyed for so little, for fear and anger and ... but it didn't matter. None of it mattered. Because it was just the way the world worked.

And then Dani

I just wanted her to go away, she wasn't

but she didn't go away and I felt that this was yet another case of the universe coming and depriving me of my choices of making me

and she had a daughter.

Probably not mine.

I did the maths and Lucy is almost certainly not ...

What do you think the point is of us, Mr Markse? I don't believe in God, I don't think there's a celestial paradise, and humanity appears to be a virulent species that destroys, strips and lays waste to the world and each other. Every day in every way we invent new methods for curtailing our own liberty. The pursuit of happiness, but there are so many happinesses to pursue that sometimes it's hard to say that this is me, pursuing this truth, because instead I could just buy and sell truth for £2.99 down the local chemist and so I guess

it didn't matter if Lucy wasn't my daughter.

It didn't matter.

It doesn't matter.

Just one thing in my life, if not for me then for someone else a choice

a choice

I wanted her to have

to wake in the morning and see the sky and feel

I wanted her to know that there is more than what she's been told. That she can find a value in herself, that mankind isn't just a plague species, that we can be better, aspire to better, that ideas have meaning, value, that there is another way of living, that we can give more and be more and exceed the limits that we think we have or that have been put upon us and that one day we shall build something better, something kind and that

Her world need not be defined by my mistakes, my failures, her world could be

But even there I failed.

And I look and it seems that she is condemned to be a slave to a path that is the only one available, just like her mum, just like . . .

I think that's it. That's all."

For a while they sat in silence. Markse waited for Theo to look away, and Theo didn't.

Finally: "Tell me about Ascot."

"We stole Mala Choudhary's identity. Her financial details. We used them to transfer money from Choudhary to Atkins, and from Faircloud Associates to Choudhary. Helen contacted Atkins, claiming to be acting for Choudhary, and contracted a hit against herself. We thought it was more plausible, given everything, if the target was Helen. Helen had embarrassed her son, gone on record testifying against him. It was not inconceivable that someone would want her taken out, maybe even Philip. Far more likely than someone going after Philip directly. Helen knew her son would be at Ascot. We stole a car a week in advance, parked it by the gate at the back, told Atkins that this was Helen's car. It's surprising how people come to the patty queen's cause. People want something to believe. We planted our own bomb near the car, as back-up in case Atkins didn't go for it. We just needed Atkins to be there, for someone to trace that connection from her to Choudhary to Faircloud to the Company. Then it was a case of making sure that Helen and Philip ended up in close proximity. If it went wrong, Helen would be dead or locked up drugged to her eyeballs. When I first met her she was . . . but she said yes. She said it was more important to make things right – that was her phrase, 'make things right' – than what happened to a foolish old woman. That was her too. 'Foolish old woman'. She was proud of those words. They were

403

something people had said to her a lot, and she liked saying them when she knew they were a lie. She knew a lot about herself. I found that inspiring. She had this certainty. Dani had it too. Our bomb wasn't very good. Didn't need to be. But it triggered Seph's. Seph's bomb was too good. We'd always known it might be. It's just ... that was always a risk.

Philip of course, he was ... I imagine they put you on the case, yes? A manhunt for whoever tried to kill the minister of fiscal efficiency?"

"They did. Seph Atkins stood out immediately; confessed for the discount."

Theo nodded at nothing much. "Figured she would."

"But her story didn't make sense, so I looked again. You weren't as good at avoiding the cameras as you thought."

Another shrug. "Good enough that you missed me the first time, though?"

A little nod of the head, a tiny acknowledgement.

"So what did you tell Philip?"

Markse sighed, stretched in his plastic chair. "That the bomb which had nearly killed him, and was most likely going to kill his mother, was planted by Seph Atkins."

"And?"

"I didn't need to tell him anything else. He already knew who Atkins was. He'd agreed to the murder of Cumali. Simon and he were friends, at that time. When we traced the funds in Atkins' account back to Choudhary, Philip rushed to a conclusion. I thought it unwise, thought it seemed too lazy for Simon to have used the same hit woman, the same firm to organise an attack on Philip, but he was already scared. His own mother was broadcasting his sins to the nation, and while we to a certain extent suppressed this, he knew it had done phenomenal damage to his reputation with the Company. He was a loose end, an inconvenience, and so was Lady Helen. It was not inconceivable that both would be easily removed, so he reacted ... precipitately. He thought by freezing the Company's assets he could bargain with them for an easy way out, hold the money hostage against his survival. The Cabinet only agreed because he convinced them that they were next, that the Company was going to come for them all, that it had already gone too far. In the end freezing assets was the only thing they could do, and it destroyed them.

By the time I had proof that you, not Choudhary, were behind the assassination attempt, people were dead. I hold you accountable for that. I hold you accountable for most of this. You talk about your daughter, about being a hero. I find that hypocrisy of the highest order. How many mothers, daughters, sons and fathers have you killed, casually, as a senseless side effect of your crusade? How much have you destroyed because you thought it would make you more than just an ordinary man?"

Theo didn't answer, didn't look away.

Markse sighed, rolled his head around his neck, tucked his chin in, bunching a little bubble of flesh beneath his jaw, then stretched again. Declared to the ceiling and the sky, "Of course, Simon did kill Philip eventually. It was personal. Amazing how quickly friendship disappears when money is on the line. An apology wasn't enough; the Company was dead. Everything they'd built together, for nothing. Philip knew it was coming, and I suppose I did too, but I didn't think Simon would move so fast. My department is receiving pay again, a 'restoration fee' from the Company. There aren't any strings attached. There aren't any conditions. We are choosing not to investigate Philip's death too hard because . . . we don't talk about the why. We just . . . don't look too closely. And we all get paid. The Company is closing up shop, but there are still companies which are owned by the Company which can be liquidated for some ready cash and Simon is not going to leave without . . . "

Stopped again. Stared at nothing. Asked an incidental thing: "Did you kill Lady Helen?"

Theo didn't answer, looked away.

Markse grunted. Said, "Tell me about the queen of the patties."

And he told him.

And Markse said, "How many people does she have?"

And he told him.

And Markse said, "What weapons does she have?"

And Theo

lied a little bit, because he could, because he knew this game now, he could sense the flow of it he lied just a little bit

Because somewhere on the other side of his city his daughter was alive and killing aliens.

And nothing else mattered any more.

Chapter 77

When Simon Fardell came to visit he didn't know where to begin. He just stood by the door and looked at Theo for a very long time and finally, because he seemed to feel like it, because he was angry and his world was coming apart, he kicked Theo a bit, and that made him feel better. He stopped when Theo's breakfast came up again because it smelled a lot and he stood by the door and

didn't really have much to say for himself.

Then:

"Theo Miller died fifteen years ago. I was there. So who the fuck are you?"

Theo crawled into a corner, pressed his head against the wall, licked acid from his lips.

"Philip shot him. He died. I remember it very clearly. I don't remember you."

When Theo didn't answer, Simon looked for a moment like he might do a bit more kicking, but that would have meant stepping over the puke on the floor and that was just uch, it was

So he leaned in close and whispered, "When I sell your daughter, it'll be to someone who really appreciates the things you can do to little girls."

Theo managed to get a hand around Simon's throat before security came in and stamped on him, and retrospectively Simon seemed more satisfied with this result than Theo could possibly be.

*

Markse sat on a stool in the corner of the room, the smell of bleach on the floor, a bottle of water at the end of Theo's mattress, and said:

"Of course my life, in my line of work you make choices. Certain choices you make – you understand this you make these choices, and well . . ."

Theo scratched at the sole of his left foot as Markse talked. The skin was soft and wet, came away in painless white flakes beneath his nails, oddly satisfying, like kneading pastry.

"I found myself asking, what would make this ordinary man, this harmless individual, go to such extraordinary lengths? Principle? For a while I thought that was it. Just principle. You were the kind of man who – if you pardon me saying so – seemed enough of a socially isolated individual that principle, yes, you could compromise a lot for principle, but then I thought . . . all those years working for the Criminal Audit Office, surely there were other cases, worse cases, where your sense of morality would have been more offended this was hardly . . .

So I looked again, and I thought maybe I'd got it wrong. Maybe the man who stands up for principle is a lie, because there was no evidence that you'd ever stood up for anything before. None at all. You were, in fact, a moral vacuum. Oh, not in a spectacular way. You were no more or less evil than anyone else in society, and in fact evil isn't even the operative word. Apathetic, perhaps. Yes, that's it. You were as apathetic as everyone else, and to square that now with your actions, maybe everything I had concluded was false and in fact . . .

So what was left? There seemed nothing in you to hate, you hadn't been rejected, didn't seem unhappy at work, didn't strike me as proud or motivated by irrationality, and when all these things were eliminated, at the very end the only thing it left room for was love. At the end it did do that. Of course my first instinct *is* love, when fear is discarded, the romantic angle, but when I met you that was clearly absurd. But as time went by . . .

Your acquisition of the Theo Miller identity was excellent. I couldn't have done a better job and I'm . . .

It wasn't that you made an error. It just that there had to be, there *had* to be something we'd missed.

We found his grave, in the end. The real Theo Miller. That led to the opening of the files and there he was, dead in Oxford, shot by Philip Arnslade, and I thought that's it! That's got to be it, but what does that have to do with Dani Cumali how does that possibly . . .

I still don't know who you are. I still don't. I thought perhaps someone else at the duel, someone else who . . . Simon Fardell says there was someone else there but can't remember anything about him. A 'scurrying nobody' was how he put it. I thought . . . that sounds about right. A scurrying nobody who everyone forgets, that seems . . . and I thought, here's this man who vanished and here's this new Theo Miller who lived and I looked at the years and there was a moment, this instant where I had Dani Cumali's life pinned to the wall and the life of the man who became Theo Miller on the other and there's Lucy's birthday, there she is and it's . . .

shitting hell almost exactly nine months

practically to the day

after Theo Miller died.

And I thought no.

No.

It wouldn't be – it can't be that simple it can't be that

But then how did you get Cumali's information? She must have known you she must have trusted you there must have been some sort of pre-existing – some sort of . . .

You must have known her.

You must have.

And even if the girl wasn't your daughter even if she wasn't then

But she was.

She was.

I just

It made everything more

And even if she wasn't I thought

I don't have any children. My line of work, it wasn't ever a thing which seemed . . . apt.

My office is funded by Simon. He sold a company that was owned by a company that ...

But I suppose we've always been owned by them, really. And my boss said, after Philip died, tell it to Simon. So I did. It's my job, it is required, I am a man, you see, used to a certain order in things. I told him about your daughter, and he was delighted. We picked her up that very day, took her to Simon's home, he fed her like a princess, he fawned over her it was ...

And I looked at him and thought, this man is going to ... "

Stopped himself.

Looked, for the very first time, ashamed.

"I think that perhaps ... there are some despicable things I've done, but perhaps ... but Simon has a wife, Heidi, and I think she can sense what he wants, knows that there is something in the way he looks at Lucy, and Heidi has been ... she's always wanted a daughter.

I am good at my job. It's important to be good at your job. It's very important. It's how we know we're ... good people. Because we work hard. We work hard and we do our best and ... I am very good at my job. You were good at your job too, weren't you, Mr Miller? If we are both good at our jobs, then it doesn't matter what these jobs are, because it isn't the consequence that matters, just the doing.

Just the doing.

That's how the world works. Everything is

        I thought that

              it's how the world is it's how

you just do

        what you can when the world is

how the world works.

What else is there?"

Theo didn't answer. He thought there was perhaps a moment when he might have had something to say, something about standing up and taking control and being ...

But he can't find it. It all seems very self-important, now.

"Are you Lucy's father?"

No answer.

"You don't even know her. It can't mean so much."

Theo looks for a moment like he might retch, fingers frozen mid-scrape along the damp heel of his foot.

"Maybe it is love," mused Markse, staring at the ceiling. "Maybe it is at that."

A while they sat, staring into their own places.

"Of course my work," Markse breathed. "Sometimes I look at the actions I've taken and

if I had a daughter, and if she was in danger then . . .

The threat, you see. The threat is itself a beastly matter, even if you never follow through. Here is your daughter, safe in the house of your enemies. Come now, or we will hurt her. We'll hurt her. We'll hurt this child. It is the vilest sort of

But what has to be done.

A question of the value of the thing. Of the balance. Once you have life on the line, even a child's life – especially a child's life, if you are willing to go so far. To kill a child.

The vilest thing.

What's your name, Mr Miller? I'm curious I don't think it's relevant it won't affect . . .

No.

Well.

I suppose –

that's fair, in its way."

At night the prison is cold and Dani Cumali sits next to him and says,

"Ow that's my arm it's ow mind where you put your backside you great"

Theo rolls over and stares at a concrete ceiling sprayed with seaside stars.

"And I'm going to get a better job, a new job, and then I'll be able to move away from here and actually maybe I'll move first to get a new job because around here there's nothing it's just getting the money you know getting the money to move so job first then"

411

He holds Dani close, and she stares up at the starlight with him and says:

"My bum's gone to sleep."

And he holds her closer still.

"Bloody mess, really. Don't know how it got there. Don't know what we did. Thought we had some control but actually I'm not sure we ever did not sure there was anything we could have done which someone else hadn't decided it's like when"

And does not sleep, as the sky turns, far away.

Chapter 78

He thought it was late at night, and it was early in the morning, and still dark.

They put him in a nine-seater car on the verge of becoming a truck.

Next to him was Edward Witt, face grey, looking a little nauseous. Next to Edward was Faris. The old man smiled limply, shook his head at an idea that Theo didn't understand, and looked away. The three seats opposite were turned to face them. Three security officers, two men and a woman, sat in silence and watched their passengers. The driver listened to Radio 2. Every fifteen minutes the broadcast was interrupted for traffic news. The traffic was bad. Sometimes they drove up the motorway on the hard shoulder, and no one tried to stop them.

Edward didn't look at Theo for a very long time, but wrinkled his nose. Theo imagined he smelled. He enjoyed imagining this. The windows were tinted, making the yellow street lights splay across the glass in thin little lines, starburst through a grate. The traffic news remained bad as they reached the M25 toll. Someone had driven off the road somewhere further along. A bus had skidded into a ditch. Maybe children had died; maybe they hadn't. Maybe it was a miracle on the M25; maybe it was a tragic loss of life. Either way, here was another hit from the 1980s, bringing back that warm, glowing feeling inside.

They stopped briefly at a service station. Everyone got out, so Theo did too. A security man stood by him without rancour. There were six cars in the convoy, men in suits, women in black leather shoes, tinted windows, four police motorcycle escorts. There were no other cars in the service station, and only one pump worked. Markse drank coffee, and didn't look at Theo. Faces glowed in the white light of mobile phones. A harried woman in laddered beige tights balanced coffee for twelve on a couple of trays, swaying uneasily back through the car park, yellow lights of the twenty-four-hour coffee stop behind her. Two men returned, laughing, bladders relieved, bodies relaxed; one man with his back to the world shouted down a mobile phone, but the wind carried away everything except the anger.

Edward stood next to Theo and swallowed espresso in a single gulp.

"You little shit," he said at last, not looking at Theo's face, eyes narrowed on a small gaggle of women huddled together with clipboards. "You've no idea what you've done, have you?"

Theo shrugged, and they got back in the car.

The sun was rising by the time they reached Newton Bridge, but the smoke hid the brightest of the day. Theo smelled it before he saw the remnants of the town, mortar dust and boiling tar, petrol and timber.

They pulled to one side in a narrow country lane, bouncing through the potholes as two yellow buses drove the opposite way. The windows were grated up; the prisoners inside were chained at the throat and feet. A handprint painted in scarlet pressed against the glass as they passed by.

The convoy waited, then moved on.

They parked in what had once been the car park for the local library, and did not pay. The noise of the bulldozers made it hard to hear the words that Markse spoke as Theo was pulled gently by the arm into the lee of a pale blue-grey wall. Sometimes rifle fire pitted out, to be met by machine gun; if there were voices raised, they were lost in the din. Theo stood, shivering in the morning cold, breath steaming, one side of his face dry and hot from the growing flames rising off the former town hall, the other chilled and cracked by the winter air. Faris, Witt, three or four more he didn't recognise, stood next to him, and none of them moved. One was a woman, in a smart beige trouser suit. She held Faris's hand, and if you knew she was his daughter, then it was impossible to see anything else in her face, and Theo was relieved that it was Faris's daughter who was going to die today, and he couldn't see Lucy in the line.

People milled on mobile phones, and somewhere behind, another burst of gunfire, louder, broke across the slow hill of Newton Bridge. A truck on caterpillar tracks rode over the gentle mound where the pub had been; someone shouted, "Clear!" and another wall burst, rubble and flame and far off the sound of a woman calling for something lost. On the other side of the car park was a low stream, rushing down towards the bottom of the hill, all white foam and mossy rocks, a babbling brook you might even have called it, a playful spout of the river that had once fed the mill. Theo watched the water. A group of men in dark blue fatigues, assault rifles in hand, jogged briskly by, and the sun rose higher, burning away the mist, and somewhere a little too near for comfort the whoosh of a flame-thrower spat and a man burned alive screaming screaming that sound screaming but all the screams did was let in the flame that burned out his lungs and that was the end of the screaming and

Another car pulled up, flanked either side by heavy four-by-fours. It stopped fifty yards from where Theo stood, and no one got out, and shapes moved behind the glass, and nothing else happened.

Theo's teeth chattered in the cold, and he wondered if the others were as cold as he was, and they probably were, but no one said a thing.

Footsteps.

A marching line of soldiers, weapons at the ready

a cluster of prisoners in between.

One woman helped another walk. Queen Bess could probably have walked by herself, but Bea hooked one arm under her elbow anyway, like a father escorting a bride to a reluctant altar. Both were coated in white dust; the side of Bea's face and hair was matted to a thick black-crimson mortar with blood. Bess saw the wall, and stumbled, and Bea caught her and held her tight, and they kept walking, and joined the line in front of the empty library.

Theo looked at them, and they stared dead ahead and did not meet his eye.

After a little while Edward fell down, and Theo helped him up, and Edward clung to Theo's arm and whispered, "All I did was ask. I just asked. I thought – I only asked."

Theo nodded, and kept a grip on the crook of his elbow, and behind them something went whoosh, and the town burned, and a bulldozer crawled over the remnants of the patties' little world and all things considered it died so easily, so easily, it died and

Theo closed his eyes and time is

       shivering in the winter cold time is

The click of a safety coming off a gun.

       Theo opened his eyes. Thought he would be able to keep them shut, was surprised to discover that he couldn't. Thought he saw someone move behind the glass of the parked vehicle opposite. Saw, but didn't entirely understand, a man in blue raise a pistol, and shoot Faris in the face. Faris fell.

Ching ching ching! £36,000 for cold-blooded murder, minus £2000 for not making your victim suffer needlessly, now what was the value of Faris's life, he had been on the patty line but wasn't currently a burden on the financial system, were there any health problems were there

about £92,000, Theo concludes before the body hits the floor. A deposit on a two-bedroom flat in Denmark Hill.

The man stepped past Faris's body, wandered down the line, back once, up once, down again, picked a target, levelled the gun at Bea's head, listened for an order only he could hear, shot Bea between the eyes. Stepped briskly past Edward, levelled the gun at Theo's head.

Waited, listening for an order.

Theo stared into the barrel, and was briefly confused but not scared, and was surprised that he wasn't afraid.

416

"Bang," said the soldier, repeating words heard through an earpiece. "Lucy is dead."

Then he nodded, turned to the queen of the patties, and shot her in the face and twice in the chest when she hit the ground.

Edward cried, and Theo waited and the man listened for instructions and nodded at something unheard and barked, "Right you lot. Let's get them buried."

They dug a pit in a field on the edge of town where sometimes cabbages were grown. Theo didn't feel the pit was deep enough – the crows would get the bodies in no time, a strong rain would wash the soil away – but the work warmed him up and the guards seemed happy enough, so he and Edward Witt picked up Bea. Edward lifted her by the feet, Theo under the arms. Her body swung awkwardly in the middle, hinging at the hips, bum bumping along the ground. That made Theo more upset than her blood on his hands, her broken skull and ruptured eyes, staring. A woman like Bea shouldn't have her backside dragged through dirt, she should be carried properly, he struggled to lift her, to haul her higher, but Edward didn't seem to understand, didn't seem to get why this was important, was just shaking and crying without making a sound, his silk suit ruined, spit flecking his mouth with every ragged exhale.

The burst bubble of Bea's head rolled back, one open eye staring up into Theo's face, the other shattered in blood, ink and lead. Theo thought if he met that gaze he would puke, and then couldn't look away, and didn't puke, and on a-one-a-two-a-three, swung her body down into the pit, went back for Faris's corpse, then for Queen Bess, then a few more were added to the tally: a couple of men who'd tried to fight, a couple of women who'd been caught with loaded guns. £83,000, less if they'd resisted arrest. £52,000 for the man who'd shot back. £145,000 for the woman who'd died with her child in her arms. At least one or two middle-management figures in the Company would have to forgo their annual bonus to pay the price of this, if it ever became known. If anyone cared. That was all. The rest would be written off against tax.

Three black cars stayed in the car park at their backs as they moved the bodies, and the doors did not open

and when they were finished, a bulldozer came and shoved a great pile of earth onto the gentle bump where the bodies were buried, and Theo didn't understand why it did that because it disturbed one edge of the pit, making it all lopsided, and if the crows weren't coming before, they'd definitely come now

and the fire turned the midday sun pink and red, black smoke from the burning village spinning and twisting in the cold wind, making his eyes water, spit slick the inside of his mouth, and he wondered why he didn't puke and didn't cry and didn't fall to the ground screaming and then they pulled him back to a car and put him in the back although this time they didn't make him ride with Edward, who was a bit hysterical, and they drove away from the smouldering, flattened remnants of Newton Bridge, where the trucks were already grinding the dust to earth.

Chapter 79

Still alive.

They kept him alive and he didn't understand why he was still alive.

And the question once asked

is Lucy

is she

is Lucy is she

where is

is she safe is she

my daughter where is

He tried not to ask it before but now it comes again, it comes in the day it comes in the night it seeps into every part of him makes him rock and shake and pull at his hair he whispers it first then asks it out loud then paces muttering under his breath then slams his fists on the door hammers and punches and screams and

WHERE IS MY DAUGHTER?!

and tears the sheets off his bed and wraps the pieces around his wrists until his fingers go numb and realises that he can imagine hanging himself hurting himself this is how it happens he knows he's seen this before on the patty line you smear your own shit up the wall to get someone's attention you throw urine across the mattress you cut yourself on the

the first time he cut himself he used the smashed glass of the light above his head, and sat in darkness gently bleeding, and felt a bit better, and felt very good indeed when the guards came in and put his head in a sack because that was progress that was someone taking him seriously now

WHERE IS LUCY WHERE IS

Markse sat on a plastic chair opposite him in a pale green room without windows, and stared at the floor a while as the clock went tick tick tick tick

tick tick tick tick

and at the end looked up and said, "The Company is selling 85 per cent of its assets back to the government. They're paying £781 billion for it all. We're going to be bankrupt for years. Simon's got a house up north. He's going to sell it and move to Monaco. They have good tax laws in Monaco, he'll be able to keep a few billion in profit and ..."

Stopped.

Couldn't raise his head.

Said, "The Company has holdings in Monaco of course. They have an understanding with the Italian and French governments. Rehabilitation through labour is a popular way of making cheap goods for export and I believe they are going to take Lucy and—"

They'd cuffed Theo to the chair, but he still managed to rip it from the floor and get halfway across the room, stretching out for Markse's eyes, before the waiting guards kicked him down.

A while, sitting in the dark.

Rocking in the dark.

They took away the lights because he'd smash them to pieces they took away the mattress the sheets

they

he can still hurt himself though he knows but now he sits in the dark and

"She's your daughter," says Dani, knees huddled to her chin, arms wrapped across her shins, sitting next to him in the perfect blackness of

"She's your daughter.

420

She's your daughter.

She's your daughter.

Don't fuck it up."

Theo stared up at the place where the ceiling probably was, and in his mind he filled it with stars.

"What are you going to do?" she asked. "What are you going to do? Theo?"

"Not my name."

"I know."

"Not my name."

"Name of someone better. Someone better. Be someone better. What are you going to do?"

Theo closed his eyes, and watched the stars spinning across the vacuum of his mind.

On a day without a name, like any other, like all the rest, they took him to a room with fake plastic flowers in a blue glass vase, and gave him a cup of bergamot tea, which he sort of liked despite himself, and handcuffed one hand to the side of his white wooden chair, and said, "Would you like a biscuit?" and when he didn't answer, left a plate of cookies on the table anyway.

He waited.

A clock showing the time in three different places ticked away. He wondered what the other two places were, or if the clock was just there to screw with his brain. Somewhere, far off, women's voices were raised in song. They were singing to their infant children, *the wheels on the bus go round and round, round and round, round and round*, but the acoustics of wherever they were distorted sound, made it a distant prayer, priests crying out to an angry god, *round and round, round and round*.

The door opened.

Heidi Fardell stepped inside. He knew her from the photos, remembered her answering the door to Simon's Kensington house.

She wore a bright blue jacket and matching skirt. She wore flesh-coloured tights and a white scarf. The red nail polish on her right hand was beginning to chip. When she had applied mascara, her fingers had shivered, and she sat as far away from Theo as she comfortably could, without removing her chair altogether from the vicinity of the table.

Thin lines crinkled in the nooks of her eyes. The red lipstick brought out the hatched contours of her lips. Her voice, when she spoke, was at first broken and inaudible, then stronger, ready for command.

She said, "Lucy is well." Theo stared until she looked away, swallowed a lump of tepid weight in her throat, then looked up again, matching his gaze. "I thought it was important that you knew that. I thought it was . . .

Simon wanted you to see her, of course, next to him. Wanted you to know that . . . Were you Theo Miller's second, in Oxford? What was your name?

He wants to burn it all, of course. He was so angry he was just so . . . he had to kill his best friend, he had to kill Philip, good business, but the queen of the patties, he just said she needed to die she needed to be, for what she's done you see, for trying to . . . stamp out dissent now so that when the Company comes back, and it will, and he's just so very . . .

Lucy is . . . when they first told me about her, I thought maybe, actually, she's being used by these men, but I'll look after her, I'll make sure she's happy and doesn't know that there's this . . .

that they'll

I don't think they'd ever have hurt her not really I don't think they

But you clearly think that they . . .

My husband isn't a bad man. The Company isn't bad. It's still run by people. People are good. People are good. They're all good people. My husband is . . .

Then she arrived, and I had to look after this . . . vicious child . . . so that her father would see, and understand, and realise that he needed to surrender. Your daughter is vile. She is . . . rude and disrespectful and stubborn and angry, I've never met a child so angry she is

I never had a child I once there was . . .

And I always imagined that it would be and I thought it was me but actually it's him. It's him, though he still says that it's just something to do with my uterus. Those are his words – 'Your uterus, darling, you have this very special uterus' – and I thought fuck you, nearly had a fucking affair just to get myself knocked up and prove a point but then he . . .

Lucy is fine.

She doesn't really understand what's happened to her. She was in prison, and now she's with us. Simon wants to sell her. Get the paperwork sorted and put her on a plane out to somewhere where he can get a good price for . . .

A good price for her.

The day you came to my house, after they took you away I sat with her and just

just sat with her for a while and

I thought perhaps I could mould her. Make her better. That's something I can do, I mean, with children. They have such problems, and if they just understood that they were being ridiculous! I wanted to tell her that just because she felt trapped, she was just stuck inside her own mind – there are breathing exercises which can help with that kind of thing.

Breathing exercises!

I thought I could give her some breathing exercises and I was thinking that and then I thought

breathing exercises, to help her deal with the fact that my husband ordered her mother killed

her father taken away

is going to sell her to . . .

Breathing exercises!

Maybe some serum to massage into her temples too. A nice Chinese mint smell.

And I suddenly thought

I just don't know anything about people, do I? I started laughing and she looked at me like I was insane and of course I was and I told her

I told her that I thought her troubles could be fixed with breathing exercises

and she looked very angry for a moment but then she saw that it was

and for a little while she was laughing too.

She was

she's just a child.

I don't pretend there's a connection there I don't pretend that we'll ever have but

The vast majority of parenting appears to be ghastly. Poo and crying and refusing to eat things and breaking things and yet you ask a mother what the most important, wonderful thing in her life is and she always says 'my child' and you look at the wriggly little wretch in its smelly little buggy, dribble falling out of its mouth and snot out of its nose and you think, seriously, darling, because if that's your joy and that's your wonder then . . .

Well.

Maybe it would be easier to have a puppy. Or a cat. Lovely self-cleaning things, cats are.

I wanted to talk to you, Mr Miller.

I thought that perhaps

in its way

I owed it to you. Or maybe no, not to you you aren't

but to Lucy.

I owe it to Lucy, to this child who is

she's only a child she's

I owe her, monstrous though she is. To tell you, to tell her father – she's going to be all right. I'm going to, and I don't care what Simon says I'm going to

she's going to be all right. I'll make sure of it I'll make sure she's . . ."

Theo's heads fell into his hands, and from his mouth came a sound, an animal groaning, a grunt of physical pain a roaring a loss of everything a howling a

"Oh my is that um . . ." blurted Heidi, jumping to her feet. "Well yes I suppose it must be . . ."

staggering away
leaving the father behind.

And then
"Up! Move!"
He couldn't be buggered, and let the men carry him down
the hall.
New grey tracksuit.
Wash face.
Wash hands.
Have a piss.
Eat cereal. His stomach couldn't handle it, he had to go straight
back to the toilet, blurgh, just
down to a cluster of three cars, engines running.
The middle black car, tinted windows, heavy doors, into the
back into the middle seat seat belt on!
They drove away.

Chapter 80

Theo Miller sits at the centre of the universe, on the way to his execution, and knows that time has no meaning.

A convoy of three black cars, no number plates, no police interested in asking questions, rushes through a city still spewing smoke into the sky. The hospitals are running emergency services only, the supermarkets are guarded by a ragtag remnant of armed police who aren't sure where their next pay packet will come from but sort of assume that if they do what they did before, maybe it'll be okay eventually.

And as the convoy passes, Neila is in a mooring basin just off the River Thames, she sailed from Maidenhead three days ago. She's been coming to this moment her whole life, and didn't know it, and didn't have the right questions to ask the cards. Checks her fuel line, checks the water. Her breath freezes in the air her hands are strong her back is straight, she is fine. She is fine. She is always fine, when she is by herself.

She lays out the cards

three of wands, the Magician, the Hermit, the Empress, two of cups, six of cups, the queen of wands, the knave of swords, the Hanged Man (inverted) and if only she knew the questions to ask of the future

if only her questions weren't tied up with

– happiness, hope, love, loneliness, dreams –

if only her questions weren't in some way seeking to undo the present, to deny the present, to pretend that maybe the present will make something better of itself even though in her heart she knows that the present just keeps on rolling it keeps on keeps on keeps on

maybe she would see the truth in the cards and on the water as she sails towards the bridge and the north.

and time is

Corn has found the place where the bodies were buried. He hid and now he has left his hiding place there is a hand reaching up through the soil it could be anyone's hand but of course it's hers it's

Theo walks through a winter forest, a gun in his hand, and in his memory his father lives and his daughter grows up beside him and Dani Cumali isn't dead in the bed and Seph Atkins does not pull the trigger and all of this all at once is real and now in his mind and he knows no sense of the past and no sense of the future, lives it all now in this instant all of it lives in him and time is

The truck rammed the first car in the convoy, spinning it a hundred and eighty degrees so its bonnet slammed into the front of the car behind. In this second car Theo's teeth crunched into the top of his skull, before his whole body slammed down and forward, neck and chest bouncing hard against the seat belt, cutting bone-deep before the car bounced back on its suspension, momentum knocked from its wheels. An instant later, the third and final car scraped across its boot as the driver turned hard to avoid a collision, and outside someone opened fire. Hands pushed Theo's head down, holding him by the back of the neck. The driver opened the door, ducking behind its shelter to shoot at the lorry in front, while behind, another scream of brakes announced the arrival of a van adorned with images of swirling flowers and summer leaves, stolen from a florist's. Something was thrown that burst open with a smoke-roaring bang, filling the inside of the car with an acrid stench, clawing at the back of Theo's throat, then the back doors of the florist's van opened and three men in balaclavas scrambled out into the street, one with a rifle, two with handguns, firing fast and wild at the convoy.

The driver of Theo's car fell hard, without a sound, didn't seem to understand that he'd been hit or why he couldn't move. The rear windscreen popped and cracked, buckled at another scattering of shots across the reinforced glass. The car in front tried to reverse, rolled a few inches into the wall of the lorry skewed across its way, bumped back, tried again, couldn't get momentum, bumped again before another man, face hidden behind motorbike helmet and mask, leaned out of the passenger window of the lorry and shot out the back wheels of the car in a pop-bang of rubber and gas.

Somewhere against the din Theo heard swearing, cursing, frightened men who'd trained for this but actually the training was only four hours long, cost-saving they called it cost-fucking-saving and now there are these fuckers with actual fucking guns and

A man screamed and fell, and kept on screaming, clutching at his stomach, he'd probably never screamed like that in his entire life, he thought maybe he could keep the sound in and he couldn't, being silent was so much worse and this wasn't even a choice thing, it wasn't choice it was just

Then someone in the car, someone who intended to survive, put a gun against the back of Theo's head and roared, "I'll fucking kill him! You want him, I'll kill him!"

Slowly, popper-pop-pop, the gunfire went out.

Sense returned, slow, spinning through the boil of blood and adrenaline that blurred Theo's sight. He became aware that someone was trying to push him out of the car, and it was awkward. He had to do a sideways shuffle, realised he was still wearing his seat belt, struggled to find the buckle even as the man hissed, "Move, move!" seemingly oblivious to the strap that held him in place. He didn't seem able to press the button hard enough, earning a knock across the back of the head that bounced his eyes in his skull. When he managed to unclasp the belt, he found the driver's seat pushed back so far he couldn't really get his knees into the space, had to twist and wriggle to swing his legs out of the open door, feet slipping on blood as he touched tarmac. At his back, the man with the gun, a security guard, petrified, full of bravado, on the verge of crying, also struggled to move, tried to manoeuvre his body out of the car while keeping the gun pressed into the base of Theo's neck. It was, Theo decided, a very inelegant way of doing business, a terrible way to die, half in and out of a car, too dumb for a dignified exit.

A shove in the small of the spine propelled him forward, catching on the half-open door for balance, pulling himself up in a sudden stiff uncoiling. The man at his back unwound fast, pressing the gun into Theo's spine, pulling him back and close with his other arm across his throat and bottom of his face, arching his back. It occurred to Theo that if he pulled the trigger, the bullet would probably pass straight through the back of his throat and out the other side, shooting the man who held him in the arm. The thought was almost funny.

"I'll kill him!" the man gabbled, trying to achieve something like a defiant roar and failing at the last. "It's him you want!"

This idea struck Theo as absurd; even more stupid to be shot by a man who thought he mattered. And yet the gunfire had stopped, and now there was just silence and blood on the tarmac.

Men in balaclavas hovered around the sides of the lorry in front. More figures moved around the floral van behind. Of those who'd been in the cars, the survivors hid behind doors and peered out from bullet-pocked chassis, not sure where to point their guns or who was in charge. A single car alarm wailed behind the lorry, set off by the rattle and roar. Somewhere far away, a helicopter chuggered, and a curtain twitched in a window, a light turned on and then quickly turned off again.

They were on a bridge. It hadn't struck Theo until that moment. The lorry sealed off one end, the floral van the other. The bridge was short, with a red-brick wall on either side, and not wide enough for two-lane traffic. Below was a canal, black water turned stiff and matt with a thin sheet of ice. Low houses all around, yellow brick and dark windows, the street lights sparse off-pink lining the cracked towpath. He tried to work out where he was, and guessed somewhere in north-west London. He felt the gun against his skull and wondered if Dani had died with Lucy's name on her lips and if he should try to go for the same effect, and what good that would do.

And on the bridge no one moved, waiting for time to resume its stately course.

Then a man stepped forward from behind the lorry, face hidden behind a dust mask and a baseball cap, and said, "Just give us Miller. No one else has to die."

His face was hidden, but his voice was familiar, and now Theo laughed.

He laughed, a choking halfway sound that couldn't work out what it wanted to be, and his head rolled back and his shoulders bunched up, and he gasped and chuckled with a gun at his head, and only Markse seemed to be undisturbed by this behaviour.

For a moment all things hung in balance at the centre of the universe.

And at the centre of the universe Corn walks towards Nottingham, the shame burning in his heart. He ran from Newton Bridge when the bulldozers came and called out for Bea, Bea, Bea my love my life I love you I never told you I love you I love you you know it I know you know it I'll revenge you I'll find you Bea I'll find you alive not dead and

And at the centre of the universe
    the ones who picked up a gun because it was a job to do to keep their family happy and safe

*

430

the ones who pulled the trigger because there was no way out except this

the ones sleeping, now roused, who in the light of day will say "this thing I saw" and

at the centre of the universe Neila turns over uneasily in her bunk, the *Hector* moored a half-mile or so from a bridge where now blood runs into the water and

at the centre of the universe Heidi takes Lucy's hand and whispers, "I'll make sure you're all right," but Lucy pulls away because she doesn't understand and anyway, all people are good for are lies and

at the centre of the universe a man who's only been in the job for a few days, who was told to ride with a convoy and didn't ask any questions, and who now realises that he's going to die on a bridge above a canal, reaches slowly under the seat of the car he's been riding in, and finds the half-open box where they keep extra ammo and a few other things besides, and his fingers, in fumbling, close around the shape of a grenade.

He isn't sure what he's going to do with it.

He doesn't know why he's here.

He didn't realise his job would wind up like this. It wasn't something he ever really planned on.

He pulls the pin, and as he adjusts his position to throw, someone sees the motion and shouts, "Grenade!" and all hell lets loose.

The first shot kills the man with the grenade, knocking his body backwards, forehead first.

Theo loses counts of who fires what immediately after as the bridge bursts to life again with running, firing, falling, screaming. A thin sense of self-preservation makes him duck, turning as he drops, which is why the bullet that would have taken out his head rushes by his ear, a deafening rupture, a physical force he feels slamming into his eardrum which makes it sing a nightingale shriek. As the gun moved round to fire again, he drove

431

his full body weight into the man behind him, and another shot smacked wide past his shoulder. Then they were on the ground, and Theo caught the man by the wrist, astonished at how much he wanted to live, how much he wanted to hurt the man who would have hurt him. He held on with both hands, and the man seeing this pulled one hand free and clawed at Theo's face. His fingers missed Theo's eyes as he jerked away, but tugged and hooked into the soft flesh below, pulling at his cheeks, sliding towards his throat, driving his chin up and away. Theo felt his arms stretch and buckle, felt the gun turn towards his chest.

On the other side of the car, the grenade, fallen from a dead man's grasp, exploded.

The blast punched Theo in the face, in the ears, lashed his head back and sent him sideways, slamming into the wall of the bridge. The car jumped a foot in the air, smashed back down with a shattering of pipe and suspension and rupture of tyre.

For a moment the gunfire paused, smoke and dust filling the air, soft falling patter of melted tar and shattered safety glass. Then it resumed, a few snapping shots from those furthest from the blast, then a few more as others joined in the fun, heard in Theo's mind through an ocean, the sea sloshing in his ears, a faded-down, tuned-out whomph-whomph of bullets flying, of men screaming, of bones breaking of fire crackling

he rolled onto his front

knows that in some way he's injured, but isn't sure where, or by what

crawled onto his hands and knees

falls

up again, crawled, knew he would die in this place, knew he wouldn't, that it was unacceptable, staggered a few paces forward, fell, cursed his body, the universe, Dani and Lucy and the world, crawled once more, blinking through the smoke and blood, sees a man running towards him, before a stray bullet, maybe from the front, maybe from behind, knocked into the man's chest and he falls, surprised, one hand pressing against the wound and coming away red, who'd have thought it? Who'd have thought that today he died, in this place, who'd have imagined that?

Theo tried to call out, someone's name, wasn't sure whose, maybe Lucy's, couldn't see through the smoke and the blood running down his face, can't make a sound, tried again, noise catching at the back of his mouth

tries to run and can't

falls

feels the ground pop next to his ear as a bullet slams down beside him

sees a dead man staring at him from a few feet away, tongue lodged oddly between his lips like he was about to blow a raspberry, or as if his face had grown a third lip

Heard a helicopter high ahead, and more alarms, sirens now, sirens coming closer, a roar of emergency in the night

Then a hand grabbed him by the scruff of the neck, pulled him to one side, dragged him still clawing at the air, backwards, off the bridge.

Down they roll, messy and down, Theo kicking out, snarling, biting, writhing against the hands that hold him, he manages to strike something squishy and hears a man grunt, they roll down a sloping pavement, bump against a bin, the gunfire is growing less now but the smoke the fire everything moving in shadows against the light, the shadows now long, now short the helicopter's searchlight splashing white across the world and then vanishing Theo kicks again

they roll

a tumbling mess of limbs

tumble off a raised ramp onto the towpath below, slamming down hard enough onto flagstone to knock the breath from both bodies, and for a while they lie there, limp and bleeding by the waters of the canal, while overhead battle rages.

The other man stirred first.

Crawled to hands and knees.

And time is

*

Neila turns and turns and turns again, spinning at the end of the canal, and

the cards fall on the table the Fool the Magician the High Priestess the Empress the Emperor the Hierophant the Lovers the Chariot Justice the Hermit the Wheel of Fortune Strength the

"Theo!"

Theo grappled, clawed at the face of the man who held him, everything in pain, fumbling without direction. His hands were swatted down, fingers curled around his wrists. *"Theo!"*

He blinked blood from his eyes, shook his head at something familiar, then flinched to the side as overhead the helicopter swept in low and bright, white light and sudden gunfire, louder, clearer, cleaner than anything that had been on the bridge, smacking into metal and flesh.

"Theo!" A man in a balaclava, a man with a familiar voice. He pulled his mask away, dragged Theo a little higher, shaking him, pressing him back against the wall that ran beneath the bridge. "Theo! Lucy is alive!"

Theo looked up into Markse's face and didn't understand anything much any more, except the words that had his daughter's name in them.

"Are you with me? Are you here?" Markse shook him again, hissed, dragging off his coat, pressing it into the blood at Theo's side it's a dark wool thing far too big for Theo he wonders what it's doing in his hands. "They'll kill you they'll kill her they'll burn it all *run!*"

He pushed Theo for good measure. He staggered, caught himself against the wall, did not fall, did not raise his head, put one foot in front of the other, tested his weight, stepped, stepped again, did not fall

did not fall

and time is

"You should do it," said Dani. "I think it sounds great."

*

434

"Don't be boring," chided Queen Bess, lady of the patties

blessed is her name blessed are her hands upon the water she washes away the blood of our sins she washes away the shadows her fingers are balm of the eucalyptus tree her eyes are the

And in Leicester two men met, did meet, will meet are meeting and Markse said, "There you are. Shall we?"

And together they walked along the canal, Theo and the spy, and the latter mused as the sun dragged high and the day grew a little less sharp, "The problem is you want everything now. You want change now. But not just change. You want a change that is ... compassionate. You want the world to see that it is cruel, and bleak, and that the powerful have mastery and the weak have nothing. You want the masses to rise, to build a world where the children are safe, the elderly are protected and all men treat each other as equals, and brothers, yes? A new, beautiful world where somehow it all works out for the best. But Mr Miller, all you do, all this that you have done – it just makes the fear worse. The screamers, the faders, the ragers, the silent ones who watch from windows; did you really think that when the world shook on its axis, they would run to their neighbour's aid? Did you really think that this was the way? Did you think that kindness is born of terror?"

And they walked.

And after a while Theo said, "She's alive. The rest is detail."

And Markse sighed, and handed over a piece of paper with an address written on it, and said, "You'd better hurry. They're going to Monaco as soon as the sale goes through. They'll take Lucy and that will be ... " And stopped himself at the look on Theo's face. "These things should never be personal," he muttered, to himself more than the company. "But once they are, you may as well make some sort of choice with your life. They haven't found out it was me, but they're going to work it out tomorrow. That's when they'll catch my driver, and after that all the pieces will fall into place, so I'm heading for the border now. I've got some papers saved up, money, there's a little place

I've had my eye on for a while. That's all, I think, that's all that is . . . "

Through the smoke and the flame and the blood dripping now into the water, Markse watched from the cover of the path beneath the bridge as
 one step at a time
 Theo ran.

Chapter 81

Time is

"Oh my oh yes now of course yes bleeding by the canal do you have an address for that . . . I'm not seeing you on my map do you have premium or standard service support for an extra £4.99 a month you can upgrade . . . "

And time is

"Mike's boy, right?"

"No."

"I've got no time for your boy-shit, boy."

And time, which also seems to spin around the centre of the universe, another product of mass and motion

time is

"Is that . . . cornflower blue?"

"Well, you know it's just what you have to hand . . . "

Theo walks along the canal and sometimes he is in a boat and sometimes there is candlelight and ice and macaroni cheese and

Cormorants can count to seven, very clever birds really, and herons stand fishing on one leg even though the fish are probably dead below the water and

In Nottingham, Theo and Corn walk together along the canal.

"Fucking should have killed you," muttered Corn. "Should

have killed you for what you did. Said we should run, she should run, but Bess said no. Said they'd never come for us, not now. We'd won, the Company was broken, there weren't no point coming for Newton Bridge now. I said that isn't it. You don't come cos you've won. You come cos you lost, and you wanna hurt. All we'd built, you couldn't just let something like that die. It was the principle of the thing the fucking principle Bea is ..."

For a while they stand and watch the water.

Then: "Why'd you tell them? Why'd you let them kill us?"

"Because they had my daughter. They didn't hurt her in front of me. They didn't need to. It was very clear that if I didn't tell them what they wanted to know, they'd hurt her. That was all. That was the only thing that mattered. Everything else seemed very small."

In Leicester Markse says, "I know it's hard for you to believe, but you have to trust Heidi Fardell. She knows you're coming. Simon's never had much respect for his wife. She's turned off the burglar alarms, cut the connection to the security hut. You can get in and they won't come running, she promises that ...

it's nearly over now.

It's nearly over.

I thought I served a thing which was

You arrogant son of a bitch you ignorant stupid fucked-up

I suppose that's ... "

The water flows towards the sea, and they stand in silence a while.

Corn with hands buried in his pockets, watching his own reflection.

"We defended it all right, for about five minutes. That's how long it took them to kill us. They sold the land to some sort of sheikh or something. They're going to redevelop Newton Bridge for a yoga retreat. Or like a place to write poetry, we're eyesores we are the

are you going to kill them?

Are you going to kill them?

I'll give you a gun. Just promise me you'll kill them all."

Theo stands on the top of the hill and looks down towards the house.

The low morning mist rising from frost-cracked grass the sun above burning it clear the moisture in the air blurs the light makes it a swimming-pool sky of reflected gold makes the light across his fingers pale silver makes

There is a gun in his pocket, and he knows who's home.

He looks up at the sky and down at the earth, tastes rain on his lips and feels the heat of blood inside his bones.

He begins to walk, towards the end.

Chapter 82

In the north there was a house where coal and wood burns in the fires.

It was a homey house, the kind of place where there was always a spare soft blanket, and no mould in the bathroom.

It sat behind red-brick walls topped with white stone.

There is fresh gravel on the drive, two cars parked out front. At Christmas they put a wreath on the door, red berries gleaming fat, a silver card reading HOME suspended from silver thread woven into the bows. The windows have eight panes of glass between lines of stiff white wood, and slide up and down to let in the summer breeze. Repointing the chimney cost a small fortune, but not as much as trying to central-heat the place. There's a pantry at the back where they keep eggs collected fresh from the hutches at the end of the garden. When Simon and his siblings were young, they loved to gather eggs, it was the best thing ever, sometimes they'd go out two or three times a day just to see if another hen had laid, but when they got older they lost interest in such things, and Heidi never had children.

A cook and a cleaner sleep upstairs, in the slant-roof rooms at the top of the house, beneath electric blankets. They aren't called a cook and a cleaner; she is executive caterer, he is house manager, and as they sleep, they dream, and the world across the darkness of their minds is full of stars, spinning around a core of darkness.

Theo climbs over the wall by a twisted oak tree.

Walks through mushy leaves.

Stops outside the house, in the dark, waits a while for the lights inside to go out.

Just one lantern burns above the front door.

He goes around the back.

The kitchen door is locked.

The window isn't.

Climbs in, head first, crawling over a table where fresh-cut blue flowers shine in a white porcelain vase. The burglar alarm does not go off. The lines to the security guards, slumbering in the old stables outside, were cut days ago, and no one bothered to check because Heidi says it's fine.

Theo walks barefoot across a floor of cold black stone, leaving his shoes by the still-hot stove, socks dirty and wet.

Runs his fingers over the wall as he walks.

Feels paper, picture frames, portraits and family snaps.

Stops a little while in the living room, pine needles on the floor where the cleaner missed the last remnants of the Christmas tree, embers orange in the fireplace, the TV on standby, a canvas of splashed ochre and red across one wall, longer than a sleeping man's body, colour to the edge of the world, dragging in the eye, spinning the universe.

Climbs the stairs.

Passes the master bedroom, hears snoring, sees the faint movement of shadows against low light under the door as a woman crawls into bed beside her already unconscious husband.

Moves on to the study.

Sits a little while behind Simon Fardell's desk.

Opens it.

Rifles through.

Finds the gun in the second drawer from the top on the right-hand side. It's one of a pair kept in an old wooden box with padded purple lining.

It is a familiar gun. He feels its weight a while, then sights down it. He isn't sure if this is the gun that the real Theo Miller sighted down the day Philip Arnslade killed him. Maybe it's Philip's gun. The thought makes him feel unclean, and he puts the gun back in the box, the box on the table. Pulls out his own gun, thinks about things for a while, then puts it away.

Finds pen and paper in the desk.

Starts to write.

It takes eight pages to say what he wants to say.

When he's done, he folds it, puts it in an envelope, writes his daughter's name. The room is growing cold. There's a fireplace against the eastern wall. He throws on some logs, pressing them down into the char with a black iron poker, sits back down at the desk, turns the TV on. The TV automatically goes to a financial news channel. There is a camera in the top of the screen for conference calls and so many buttons on the remote he struggles to find "Mute". As he looks for it, voices blare out, announcing the latest turbulence, falls in stock prices, speculation, speculation, speculation you have to believe in the future, if you don't then everything falls apart and right now the future is . . .

The noise disturbs someone in the house.

A light comes on.

Footsteps move.

Theo manages to coax the TV into obedience, and sits behind the desk, feet up, waiting.

The door opens.

Simon Fardell stands in the frame.

He looks at Theo, and is instantly afraid, and manages to hide it a moment later.

Looks round the room, and is confused.

Sees the open box on the desk, two guns in velvet, and does not move.

Theo said, "I'm here for my daughter."

Simon licked his lips. To the wiser, richer man it seems for an instant that this moment in time has been coming his whole life, that there is mist rising by the River Thames that Theo Miller – the real Theo Miller – is dying at his feet that soon there shall be mist again and the sound of the fire in the hearth and that for just a moment there is something about time and this second which

442

But then the feeling passes because he's got shit he needs to get on with, and people who depend on him, and no time for this kind of crap.

Simon stepped into the room, closed the door behind him so as not to disturb the house. Glanced towards the muted TV, looked back towards Theo, the box, the guns.

"I remember you," he said at last. "I've been thinking about it. I remember you."

Took a step towards Theo, stopped, testing the motion, discovered that moving didn't cause offence, took another step, stopped again, a little over a metre from the desk.

"There are alarms," he added. "Security are coming."

"No, they're not," sighed Theo. "Markse has betrayed you. He attacked the convoy. Your wife has cut the alarms. She doesn't like the fact you're going to sell my daughter into a life of slavery. She doesn't like my daughter either, but I think ..." A smile crackled at the edge of his lips. "I think it might be the principle of the thing. No one is coming. The Company is dead, and all that's left is tonight."

Simon's head turned a little to the side, lips thin and eyes narrow. He wore striped flannel pyjamas, done up to the topmost button, pushing against the pale skin of his throat, cuffs clinging to his wrists, as if flesh were toxic to the touch. He took another step towards the desk, and when Theo didn't move, sat down in front of him.

For a while they watched as the TV danced with light behind them, silent. Then: "The Company is fine. A lot of jobs have been lost, a lot of investment gone to waste, but we'll recoup. This is a global age. This is an innovative time. *I remember you.* The little coward, Theo Miller's second. You were useless, I remember thinking, do I have to waste my time with this boy-child? but of course, I did. You have to put up with such things, for a little while."

Theo smiled again, nodded slow agreement. "That was me. I suggested we put blanks into the guns. I thought you agreed that this was a good idea. I was wrong. If I hadn't been so afraid, I

443

probably would have been smart enough to know I was wrong. Amazing the capacity of the mind to convince itself of certain things, under pressure."

"And now you're here to kill me?" No fear; polite enquiry.

"I'm here for my daughter."

"Your daughter is sleeping upstairs. I've already sold her to a company in Marseilles that specialises in girls like her. I thought maybe I could get a high-end deal, but actually she's not worth it. She's barely worth the cost of the flight." Watching, face framed in firelight on one side, digital glow from the other, hot and cold mixing to strange shadows beneath his eyes, around his lips. "Do you think you're going to stop it? I don't think you can. The boy I remember from Oxford couldn't do anything worth a damn."

"Which one?" asked Theo. "The boy who lived, or the boy who died?"

Silence a while. Simon's eyes ran over the guns on the table between them, box open, metal eating in the light.

Theo flicked the envelope around between his fingers, then laid it on the desk. Simon's eyes darted to it, then away. Theo planted his feet, sat up straighter, lacing his fingers together on the desk in front of him, chin down, eyes up.

Then Theo said, "You shouldn't let these things get personal."

Simon raised an eyebrow, waited.

"Killing Philip ... destroying Newton Bridge ... you strike me as a deeply infantile man, if I may say so, so some of this probably won't make sense. The patties whisper prayers to their goddess, a goddess without a name; a higher power – blessed is the water blessed is the moonlight between the bars blessed are they who cry out to the dark and hear no answer blessed is ...

At the heart of it we find beauty in the darkness and the moonlight, and meaning in shadows because without that we really are just slaves to other people's fortunes, crawling our way from the cradle to the grave and so ...

Am I here to kill you?

I suppose in a way I am. Lucy might not even be my daughter, but I suppose ... and I'm ashamed to admit it ... that I can't see any other way to ... "

Simon lunged forward, grabbed the nearest gun from the box, sweeping it up off the desk, levelled it at Theo, fired.

He fired four times.

Theo flinched, frozen still, and waited.

Simon lowered the gun.

Lifted it again.

Lowered it again.

"Blanks, of course," Theo mused. "Just so we're clear, it was always going to be – that's how these things ... "

Simon looked down again, raised the gun, fired the last three shots at Theo's head, clicked on empty, nodded once, put the weapon back down on the desk.

Theo pulled his gun from his pocket. Rested it on the edge of the desk, one hand on top of the metal.

Simon licked his lips. Murmured, "Killing me is ... I have money, we can still settle this there are ... "

Theo shook his head. "You shouldn't have taken my daughter."

"Your daughter!" A guffaw, half-hysterical, swallowed down into indignation. "You just said she's probably not even your daughter you think this, for her, all of this for her it's the most stupid thing I've ever heard it's the most pig-headed selfish bloody thing and if killing her would save this country from someone like you then ... "

Theo's eyes flickered to the door, and Simon stopped speaking. Listened. Fire and steam, the hum of the TV, two people breathing, and two more by the door.

Simon turned in his chair.

Lucy, wearing pink pyjamas with teddy bears on, juvenile and absurd, she hated them, but Heidi hadn't known what else to buy, didn't know what teenage girls liked. Behind her, hands resting on the girl's shoulders, protective, Heidi, leaning against the frame of the door, pale green nightgown stitched with thin yellow daisies, squinting a little without her contact lenses.

*

Time is

who knows what time is this moment is the
moment when the universe turns and it is

tick tick tick

the counting down of infinity

tick tick tick

and it strikes Theo as briefly strange, and then briefly laugh-
able, and then finally as correct, that the adults in the room are
paralysed as a child stands in judgement, and looks down upon
them all, and has in her power the final say of truth and

the universe spins

and the child judges

and her face condemns them all.

Until at last there is a flicker in her eyes, and she chooses a path,
and Theo sees a choice.

"You got any cash?" she asked Theo, voice clear and capable.

He shook his head.

She nodded and vanished back into the darkness of the hall.
Heidi put her head on one side, then followed her without
a sound.

A while the two men sat, waiting, as the universe spun
towards destruction.

When Lucy returned, she was wearing jeans, a large fleece
jumper, a coat, scarf and gloves. She had a rucksack on her back,
and carried an orange plastic bag in her right hand. "It's his
mum's jewellery," she explained at Theo's raised eyebrow. "Also
he keeps, like, a grand in cash hidden in this box in the garage."

Theo contemplated this, then nodded, and rose.

He walked to the door, glanced back at Simon.

"Things don't change," blurted Simon. "That's just how the
world is. This is how the world is. The Company is full of people.
They won't change. Change will hurt them. That's what makes
them right. That's what makes—"

Theo turned away, walking down the stairs.

After a moment his daughter followed.

*

446

The gate to the outside world was locked.

There were sirens in the distance.

High walls and no easy climb, the oak tree was on the other side. Theo glanced at Lucy, who shrugged, unimpressed.

Then a crunching of footsteps on hard gravel. Heidi Fardell behind them, a coat and boots pulled on over her nightdress, a handbag slung across that, and a plastic bag containing water and the remnants of yesterday's curry in a Tupperware box, waves the key as she pants breathless up behind them, and blurts:

"Room for a little one?"

Chapter 83

A while they walk, three travellers through the new year's snow.

They do not talk.

A while they rest on a bench in a village without a name.

Then walk again until they come to a railway station.

Heidi rifles through her wallet, finds some money, buys a couple of tickets. Lucy chooses the destination, going further north towards a place she thinks sounds not shit.

They sit a while on a bench waiting for the train. Lucy sits in the middle. Theo and Heidi do not look at each other.

The service is delayed. There is the wrong kind of ice on the line.

Lucy uses her stolen money, buys coffee for Theo, tea for Heidi, hot chocolate for herself.

They drink from cardboard cups, and afterwards he takes the cups to the bin, and they sit a little while longer.

When the train comes, it is packed, sticky and wet, breath condensing on the windows, they lunge for handholds, find a little space at the back, the door connecting the train carriages won't stay shut it goes bang flop bang flop bang flop until Theo puts his knee in front of it. Lucy watches the land. Lucy wasn't tall enough to grab the bar on the ceiling, so clung on to a strap by the window, even though it means she's pressed next to a man reading a magazine about pony trotting in the Welsh valleys. Heidi and Theo press next to each other, awkward and silent as the train goes clacker-clack. Heidi opens her bag, pulls out a thin tube of something pink. Daubs a little something on her fingers, smells her skin once, twice, three times in a slow ritual, rubs her fingertips round and round her temples, lets out a sigh, moves to return the tube to her bag, hesitates. Offers it to Theo. He shakes his head. She shrugs and returns the tube to her bag.

And after a while Lucy reads the letter her father wrote.

When she's done, she folds it and puts it back in her pocket.

They travel north, until they get to Penrith, where she says, "Just so we're clear. It's my money."

Theo nodded, Heidi looked like she might object and stopped herself.

"I didn't come with either of you. I just left *there*."

Theo nodded again.

"Did you really do all that that shit they said you did, the stuff in the letter?"

"Yes."

"You're a nut-job."

Theo shrugged.

"What was . . ." She stopped herself, glanced towards Heidi, then looked away. "I don't want you to tell me what my mum was like. Not yet. But when I want you to, you tell me, okay?"

"Okay."

"I don't know if you're my dad."

"I don't either."

"And you're *not* my mum."

Heidi nodded once and stared at her boots.

"I don't care neither. It doesn't fucking mean anything. You've both never been there for me my whole fucking life, so fuck you if you think you get to just turn up now and be all . . . "

They rocked in silence a little while longer, as the Scottish border patrol shuffled onto the train. Outside, a woman stood on the platform, selling carrot soup from a vat. The locomotive gently rumbled, a slow spinning of disconnected fans.

"You got a plan? Cos I haven't got a fucking clue what the fuck I'm doing here."

Theo thought about it, then smiled.

"I'm sure we'll work something out."

"That don't mean nothing that's just something people say when ... "

"Hey, luv, you okay?"

Neila sits on the side of the canal, and can't remember where north is, or which way the *Hector* is pointing, or where she's meant to go now.

The woman who sits next to her wears a jumper adorned with waddling ducks and a black cap that would look bad on anybody.

"Luv? You all right? You okay?"

Neila is not okay.

She realises that she is not okay, and it is a blessing of majesty, it is the revelation of the divine, it is the most wonderful thing she has ever known, a truth that shines upon her soul. She is not okay, she is not fine, and it is beautiful.

"Come inside," says the stranger. "Have a cuppa tea."

Markse stands at the queue for airport security, a false passport in his pocket, a ticket to somewhere hot in his hand, and wonders what the hell he's going to do now that he's got principles and no pension plan, and concludes that it's probably all a disaster anyway.

Corn watches the water run through Nottingham and says to the man who stands beside him, "Next time I'll open my mouth whenever I please and give people a piece of my ... "

Crows pick at a hand rising from a half-buried ditch in a field, and soon there's only bone and a bit of pink left clawing at the sky.

As the police leave his empty, cold house, Simon Fardell turns off the TV in the study.

It doesn't go immediately to black.

The TV has a camera in it.

The image shows the side of his face, as he listens to a man sitting at his desk.

"You shouldn't let these things get personal."

He watches in silence as he raises the gun, fires four times. Then raises it again, and fires another three. He isn't sure now why he fired those last shots, and looking at his own face on the screen it seems a lot like the man who pulled the trigger isn't entirely convinced about this course of action either.

The footage has been streamed around the world, of course.

That's just what technology does these days. He'll be fine, of course. He's on a plane to Monaco tomorrow and has more than enough assets to recoup any losses. It's just a question of how the Company views these things, the board as a whole. When Philip became a liability they had to get rid of Philip and now Simon is . . .

He's fine.

He'll be fine.

He's fine.

His secretary phones, and asks if he wants to take the helicopter to the airport. He instinctively opens his mouth to say yes, then changes his mind and says he might drive instead.

They claim asylum at the Scottish border, and are put into a transit house just north of Kirtlebridge.

They sign the paperwork as father, mother and daughter, only because it'll make it easier for the officials to . . .

only because of that.

Lucy rereads Theo's letter a couple of times when she thinks he isn't looking.

They have bread and jam for supper, and he sleeps in the men's wing, and Heidi asks if she can pay for a hotel, and Lucy's given her own private room for kids, which has pictures of steam trains and dinosaurs on the wall, which she finds patronising but gets over quickly enough because actually it's sorta . . .

Three days later, as they sit on the coach to Glasgow, she says:

"If I wanted to do a DNA thing, like, to test for – could I do that?"

"Yes."

"And if you weren't then . . . "

"I'll help you find your dad, whoever he is. There's a man in Shawford, he's — but it's your call, I mean, whenever you're . . . "

"Cool. Good. And it's not weird I mean it's not like . . . "

"This is your world. There's a whole time, there was this time before and there is this time now and the future sometimes it seems that these things only exist now, as we remember and imagine, it is only now that we experience all of these things not then and not the yet to come, but the future — it's yours, the future is yours to choose and make and build and it shall be a future of your living and it is . . . "

At the beginning and ending of all things.

Later, it started to snow.

About the author

Claire North is a pseudonym for British author Catherine Webb. *The First Fifteen Lives of Harry August* was her first novel published under the Claire North name, and was one of the fastest-selling new SFF titles of the last ten years. It was selected for the Richard and Judy Book Club, the Radio 2 Book Club and the Waterstones Book Club promotions. Her next novel *Touch* was published in 2015 to widespread critical acclaim and was described by the *Independent* as 'little short of a masterpiece'. Catherine currently works as a theatre lighting designer and is a fan of big cities, urban magic, Thai food and graffiti-spotting. She lives in London. Find her on Twitter as @ClaireNorth42.

Find out more about Claire North and other Orbit authors by registering for the free monthly newsletter at www.orbitbooks.net.